LAST SEEN IN LAPAZ

Books by the author

The Inspector Darko Dawson Mysteries
Wife of the Gods
Children of the Street
Murder at Cape Three Points
Gold of Our Fathers
Death by His Grace

The Emma Djan Mysteries
The Missing American
Sleep Well, My Lady
Last Seen in Lapaz

Other Books
Death at the Voyager Hotel
Kamila

LAST SEEN IN LAPAZ

KWEI QUARTEY

Published by
Soho Press, Inc.
227 W 17th Street
New York, NY 10011

Library of Congress Cataloging-in-Publication Data

Names: Quartey, Kwei, author.
Title: Last seen in Lapaz / Kwei Quartey.
Description: New York, NY : Soho Crime, [2023] | Series: The Emma Djan
investigations ; 3 | Identifiers: LCCN 2022028296

ISBN 978-1-64129-531-4
eISBN 978-1-64129-340-2

Subjects: LCGFT: Detective and mystery fiction. | Novels.
Classification: LCC PS3617.U37 L37 2023
DDC 813'.6—dc23/eng/20220616
LC record available at https://lccn.loc.gov/2022028296

Interior design by Janine Agro, Soho Press, Inc.
Interior Map © Peter Hermes Furian/Shutterstock

Printed in the United States of America

10 9 8 7 6 5 4 3 2 1

To all migrants, dead or alive, who have been through this hell

West African Migratory Routes to
Europe via Niger and Libya

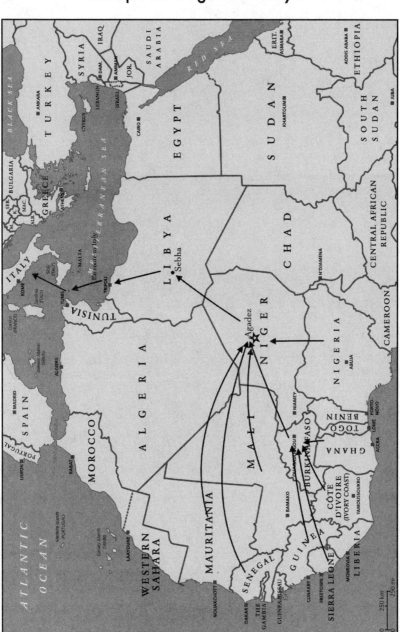

LAST SEEN IN LAPAZ

AUTHOR'S NOTE

THE SUBJECT MATTER IN this novel is a serious one, and some scenes were tough to write and are tough to read. Although fictional, they are based on accounts of West African sex workers and migrant returnees I interviewed at length in the countries of Nigeria, Niger, and Ghana, all settings in the story. Thus, no depictions of violence in the book are baseless, and some have been corroborated independently by different sources. No demonization of any particular group of people is implied by the events in the novel. Rather, the message is that the world must continue to combat human trafficking in all forms.

CAST OF CHARACTERS

Agnes: realtor

Akosua Djan: Emma's mother

Awuni: owner of the White House Hotel and Janet Glover's partner

Ayodele: Femi's work partner, one of Femi's fellow prisoners while incarcerated

Ben-Kwame: Janet Glover's son

Beverly: Yemo Sowah's administrative assistant at Sowah Agency

Bisola: a client of Cliffy's, Kehinde's girlfriend

Boateng, Detective Inspector: CID homicide detective, aka "Diboat"

Bridget: a sex worker at the Alligator Hotel

Cliffy: Femi's partner in crime

Courage: Emma's boyfriend

Diamond: rookie sex worker at the Alligator Hotel; recently from Nigeria

Effia: sex worker and university student

Emma Djan: main character, private investigator at Sowah Agency

Femi Adebanjo: Ngozi's boyfriend

Gambi: Kehinde's friend at the detention center

Gideon: one of Emma's PI colleagues, IT expert

Hasan: Kehinde and Bisola's smuggler into Niger

Ijeoma Ojukwu: Ngozi's mother, Nnamdi's wife

Janet Glover: Awuni's partner

Jojo: one of Emma's PI colleagues and main partner in this case

Kayode, Father: one of Femi's fellow prisoners, later a priest

Kehinde: client of Cliffy's, Bisola's boyfriend

Kojo Agyekum: Femi Adebanjo's grandfather

Lacey: a sex worker at the Alligator Hotel

Maduenu: Nnamdi's chauffeur

Ngozi Ojukwu: Nnamdi's daughter

Nnamdi Ojukwu: Yemo Sowah's friend and Ngozi's father

Ohene, Commissioner: Director-General of the Criminal Investigation Department (CID)

Osarodion Obakozuwa: man who spotted Ngozi in Lapaz

Peju: Kehinde's father

Proph Coleman: university professor acting as Effia and Sade's "pimp"

Ruby: Emma's undercover identity

Sade: sex worker and university student from Nigeria

Salifu: guard and handyman at the White House Hotel

Simi: Kojo Agyekum's wife

Victoria: a sex worker at the Alligator Hotel

Walter Manu: one of Emma's PI colleagues at Sowah Agency

Yemo Sowah: founder and owner of the Sowah Agency

PART ONE

CHAPTER ONE

Week One

AWAKE NOW, EMMA LISTENED to Courage's slow, rhythmic breathing beside her. It was five in the morning, her normal waking time, but she stayed in his bed awhile smiling as she thought about last night and how much fun she had had with Courage. It had been quite unlike her proverbial "first time" many months ago when Courage had repeatedly asked her before, during, and after the act if she was okay. Emma had said yes, which was true, but she had wished it could have been more than just okay. Now that she had gotten to that point, she was happy with it.

Was she the new Emma? Well, in this regard, yes. She had long carried something of an obsession with remaining a virgin until marriage, but lately, things had changed. Emma and Courage had grown much closer to each other on an emotional level during the coronavirus pandemic. Thereafter, Emma had become more comfortable with Courage physically.

Then, one Sunday morning in church as she listened to a priest's sermon declaring what was godly and what was sinful, a lightbulb went off in her brain, and she realized something: first, she had been unconsciously absorbing this virginity rule without ever questioning it. And second, as the priest continued in his mellifluous baritone, it struck her that virginity was a male fetish wrapped tightly around another male fetish called "purity." Emma was certain that whoever originated the concept of virginity was a man.

Now she was looking for a new, more modern and open-minded church she could join. That would represent another change for her as she drifted away from the Catholic church. Its luster had faded for her, dovetailing with a slowly evolving view of sex and the freedom to have it.

She rose to shower. When she emerged from the bathroom,

Courage was awake but still in bed scrolling through his phone. He looked at her and smiled. "You okay?"

She nodded. "Yes, I'm good, and you?"

"Yeah. Slept very well."

"I wonder why," Emma commented.

Courage laughed, got out of bed, and began dressing for work. "They want me in at eight this morning."

"Okay," Emma said, digging in her overnight bag to find her favorite blouse with blue and white geometric patterns. She wriggled into a matching blue skirt.

Courage made a face. "Don't you want me to iron your clothes? They're a bit wrinkled."

Emma looked down, assessing the degree of wrinkledness for barely a second. "It's not that bad," she declared.

He grunted. "You know what our new chief would do if I showed up to work like that?"

"I don't know—court-martial you?"

"Close enough," Courage said wryly.

He worked in the Panther SWAT division of the Ghana Police Service, and like most police or military organizations, they demanded spotless, wrinkle-free uniforms with sharp creases in all the right places.

Courage didn't have his car, which had been in the repair shop for a while, so he couldn't give Emma a ride. At the *tro-tro* park, they said goodbye before going their separate ways. Courage was set to go out of town on an assignment, so he wouldn't see Emma for a couple of days or more. His schedule was always subject to change, sometimes with little or no notice.

EMMA ARRIVED AT the Sowah Private Investigators Agency at seven-forty, twenty minutes before morning briefing. Predictably, she was the first one in. Next would be Beverly, the administrative assistant. The most senior investigator, Walter Manu, would be last because he was always between three and ten minutes late, and the remaining two detectives, Jojo and Gideon, landed somewhere in between Beverly and Manu.

Emma switched on the lights. The air conditioner would come on by ten, when the heat of the day would begin to seep into the pores of the building and turn it into a kiln. The meeting room doubled as the working space with their desks in roughly an open-sided square arrangement. Over the last year, the boss, Yemo Sowah, had renovated and streamlined the space, brightening it with new, efficient LED bulbs and a redesigned window that admitted more natural light. They had more electrical outlets to accommodate their laptops (the old desktops were all gone except one) and phone chargers. Sowah had also had a wall knocked out so Beverly could spread out a little more in the vestibule waiting area.

Emma and her colleagues appreciated that their boss had invested practically all the allotted funds into his employees' amenities while spending almost nothing on his own office down the hall. Most bosses, especially in Ghana's top-down society, would have done the opposite, attending to themselves before anyone else. Emma never forgot that Sowah was the rare species of Ghanaian who wasn't out just for himself, and she would always be grateful for that.

She used the few minutes she had before the meeting to call her mother at home. Akosua was already up and about, cleaning Emma's place.

"What would you like for dinner tonight?" Akosua asked.

"Anything you make is good, Mama," Emma said.

"Thank you, dear. How is Courage this morning?"

Could she be thawing out toward him, or was that a pointed question about what he and her daughter had been up to the night before?

"He's fine," Emma said. "He'll be on a job out of town for a couple of days."

"Oh, great! So, I'll get to see you a little bit, then."

She acted as if Emma had been staying at Courage's house for weeks.

"I hope you're not thinking about some kind of cohabitation with him," Akosua said.

Cohabitation? "No, Mama. Nothing of the kind." She was going to ask what was so bad about cohabitation, but now was no time to have an argument. "I have to get going because we'll be starting our meeting soon."

Beverly had just walked in. She was slim and impeccably turned out—hair, skin, nails, everything. Emma always marveled at the magnificent clothes Beverly wore. She wasn't rich by any means; she just looked it. Somehow, she never repeated an outfit.

"Morning!" Beverly called out, walking up in heels Emma would never have been able to survive. "How was your weekend?"

"Very nice, thanks," Emma said.

Gideon arrived a few minutes later. He was stout and solid; bearded one week, clean-shaven the next, he could seem like more than one person, an asset in the private investigator world. Jojo followed shortly after. Unlike Gideon, his "brother from another mother," he was slight in stature and boyish. At thirty-two, he could pass for a twenty-year-old.

At eight o'clock sharp, Sowah came out of his office for the morning briefing. He was a compact man who kept in shape by playing tennis at the Ghana Police Sports Complex off Ring Road. Up till now, he had managed to avoid the belly bulge that plagued men of his age.

"Morning, all," he said. "I hope you had a good weekend and you're ready for the work week."

"More than ready, boss," Jojo said with confidence and a sparkle in his voice. Emma smiled at him. Always jaunty, he was the kind of person who could pull you out of the worst mood with a well-placed joke.

In turn, starting with Manu, each of the four investigators rendered their updates. Emma's two jobs were a background check on a potential Ecobank employee and an infidelity case that was straightforward and about to conclude. Jojo had three similarly easy assignments.

But while Emma and Jojo had unexacting workloads, Manu and Gideon were bearing the weight of several complex cases that were moving at the speed of a tortoise. Therefore, with little or nothing new to report, they quickly rehashed what was already present knowledge. As far as briefings went, this one was quite succinct and Emma and the other three investigators got to work as Sowah returned to his office.

AFTER LUNCH, A tall man with a slight stoop, a thin face, and a trimmed salt-and-pepper beard entered the anteroom where

Beverly sat. Emma had a good view of the lobby and was usually within earshot of anything said there. The man announced his name, but Emma didn't quite catch it.

"Please, do you have an appointment?" Beverly asked him.

"Not at all. I'm an old friend."

"No problem, sir," Beverly said, reaching for her phone.

"Oh, wait," the man said, quickly. "Could you not tell him I'm here? I wanted to surprise him."

Beverly, not one to break protocol, hesitated, and Emma took that as her cue to jump in. She rose and went to Beverly's aid.

"Good morning, sir," she said. "I'm Emma Djan, one of the investigators here. How can we help?"

He looked down at Emma, who was quite tall herself but nowhere near his height. Dressed in an expensive-looking dark gray suit, the man was in his early sixties and had the air of one accustomed to giving orders, not carrying them out.

"Nnamdi Ojukwu," he said to Emma, his voice a rich bass. "I'm a good friend of Mr. Sowah's from a long time back. We haven't seen each other for several years and he's not expecting me. I want to surprise him."

Ojukwu's name was recognizably Nigerian, and even his refined intonation couldn't conceal the accent from a trained ear.

"Yes, of course, Mr. Ojukwu. Please come with me."

Sowah wasn't with a client right now and Emma saw no reason not to take Mr. Ojukwu straight back without a "pre-clearance." She led him down the short hallway to the boss's open office door. Yemo Sowah, buried in work at his desk, looked up over the rim of his glasses as Emma appeared in the doorway. Ojukwu stayed behind her deliberately out of sight until his signal came.

"Someone here to see you, sir," Emma said. "A big surprise."

"Who is it?"

Emma stepped to the side, and her lean—some would say skinny—body gave way to Mr. Ojukwu's.

Sowah's expression morphed from momentary puzzlement to astonishment. "Nnamdi!" he exclaimed, leaping up and coming around his desk. "What are you doing here?"

Mr. Ojukwu's exuberant laugh echoed around the room. With Sowah's head barely reaching Nnamdi's shoulder, the men embraced awkwardly. Since the advent of Covid, handshakes and embraces were all awkward and no one knew quite what to do.

"Good to see you, Yemo," the man said, clapping him on the back.

"And you as well." Sowah turned to Emma. "This is my dear friend and former college mate, Nnamdi Ojukwu."

"Welcome, sir," Emma said, smiling. "Can I get you anything? Some water?"

"I'm good, thank you."

"Come in, Nnamdi," Sowah said. "Thank you, Emma."

He shut the door and Emma returned to her desk wondering about the arrival of this longtime friend of Sowah's. Was Ojukwu bringing a case to the agency, or was this just a social call? If it were the latter, wouldn't he have called on Sowah at home? Or perhaps it was a combination of personal and business. One way or the other, Emma and her colleagues would soon know. She realized how eager she was for a new case. Frankly, she was bored.

CHAPTER TWO

NNAMDI SAT DOWN HEAVILY on the scarlet sofa, which protested with a tiny squeak.

"My goodness," Sowah said as he pulled up a chair to sit near his friend. "This is wonderful. Let's see—is it about two years since you left Ghana to go back home?"

"A little over three, now. Hard to believe, right? After I returned to Lagos, I decided to retire early from the diplomatic corps and now I'm a consultant for a think tank."

"Congrats," Sowah said with admiration. "How are Ijeoma and your daughter, Ngozi? She must be what, sixteen, seventeen?"

"Ijeoma's doing well—she seems to work on a thousand different projects at a time. And Ngozi has just turned eighteen."

Sowah gave a short groan. "What has happened to time?"

"It seems to have gotten away from us," Nnamdi said wryly.

He and Sowah had attended the University of Ghana together. They had parted once Nnamdi returned to Nigeria, but decades later, having joined the diplomatic service, he had returned to Ghana with his wife, Ijeoma, and only daughter, Ngozi, to fill the post of Nigerian high commissioner.

"So, what brings you back to our neck of the woods?" Sowah asked. "Everything okay?"

"I wish I could say so, but things are not good at all."

"Oh," Sowah said. Nnamdi's tone and demeanor were laden with disquiet—very unlike him. "What's going on?"

"It's Ngozi."

Sowah held his breath, preparing for the worst.

"She's run away from home," Nnamdi said, "and she could be here in Accra."

Then, maybe this isn't too bad, after all, Sowah thought hopefully. "Tell me more."

Nnamdi continued. "February or March this year—we're not sure the exact month, Ngozi got involved with a Ghanaian-Nigerian called Femi Adebanjo. We only met him once because Ngozi shielded a lot from us, but the little we knew about him started to raise red flags. He was a high school dropout, cocky, had bad manners—the sort of man we would never want our daughter to get involved with. I mean, he was on his best behavior when he met Ijeoma and me, but I can tell these types from a mile away."

"Of course. The question is what Ngozi saw in him."

"I'm not sure," Nnamdi said, his exasperation clear. "Ijeoma thinks it was the 'bad boy' allure—you know, the appeal of the forbidden. At any rate, this introduced conflict and tension at home. In June, when we were just about to return to Lagos at the conclusion of my post, Ngozi didn't want to leave Ghana, nor did she want to go to university. From the time we arrived in Nigeria, Ngozi clammed up, except with her friends, of course. We had no warning of what was to come. The morning of the thirty-first of August, Ngozi was gone. Her bedroom was empty with the bed still made up, the window was open, and the mosquito screen had been slashed. There was a kitchen knife on the floor and bloodstains on the bed and windowsill. We thought the worst had happened: that someone had gotten into the house and into Ngozi's bedroom, attacked her with a knife, and kidnapped her.

"We called our friends and the few contacts of Ngozi's we knew, but no one had any useful information for us. Some of Ngozi's girlfriends said they had seen her a day or two before but had no idea what she had been up to since. We didn't understand how that was possible. Were they hiding something from us?

"But then, we realized that the person most likely to have something to do with Ngozi's disappearance was this guy, Femi. We knew she was in close phone contact with him after we got back to Nigeria. We tried tracking him down through Ngozi's friends, but the numbers they had were outdated.

"Six weeks passed, and we never received a ransom demand. Then, unexpectedly, I got a call from an old Nigerian friend who was in Accra and who knew Ngozi when she was growing up. He told me he had spotted Ngozi in a supermarket in Lapaz."

"How certain was he that it was Ngozi?" Sowah asked.

"Very certain, and I believe him. And it made sense that if Ngozi had fled Nigeria, the most logical place to go would be Ghana, especially if she had eloped with Femi.

"So, I got the earliest flight possible to Accra and arrived yesterday afternoon. I filed a report at CID headquarters, but I felt like I was whistling into the wind. They were skeptical that Ngozi was in Accra and seemed to be merely humoring me. I knew my immediate next stop would be you, and so, here I am."

"I'm glad you came." Sowah nodded soberly. "I presume you want us to find Ngozi."

"That's exactly what I want."

CHAPTER THREE

CLOSE TO SEVEN THAT Monday evening, Emma arrived from work to her home in Madina, the once-tiny suburb of Accra that had burgeoned into a large town. Emma's home was one of four around a common compound. A delicious, peppery aroma cloaked Emma as she came through the door, as it had done every evening for the past two months while her mother, an accomplished cook, had been staying with her.

Emma pulled the screen door shut but left the main door open to allow some of the warmth and fumes to escape. Akosua didn't mind it hot and stuffy, but Emma needed fresh air all the time. She put her head around the kitchen entry, where Akosua was at work at the stove. "Hello, Mama!"

Akosua looked up and smiled. "Hi, dear. Welcome!" She was thin, like her daughter, but not as tall as Emma. "How are you?"

"I'm okay—long day."

"Like every day, no?" Akosua commented, stirring soup in a large pot. "Dinner will be ready in about thirty minutes, so you can take your bath now."

"I will," Emma said, smiling slightly at the directive. *Mothers will always be mothers.* She went to her bedroom to put down her belongings, which nowadays included a vital laptop, a used model she had found in town for a reasonable price. No matter what people said about not bringing one's work home, sometimes it was unavoidable.

Emma sat at the edge of her bed for a moment, taking off her shoes and rubbing her feet. She was dead tired, and yes, it was nice to have Mama cook for her every day and save Emma from the chore after returning home. But sometimes she longed for the good old days when she could arrive home from work to a quiet house where she could unwind and think her own thoughts without distraction. She was something of a loner.

What she felt most uncomfortable about was that Courage tended to stay away while Akosua was living with Emma. No defined animosity existed between Courage and Akosua, but he felt awkward in her presence.

As Emma showered, she decided it was time to tackle the subject.

Mother and daughter were alike in one respect: they had identical tastes in food. Both relished seriously hot peppers like Scotch bonnet and habanero; they were both *fufu* people and not at all fond of *banku*.

Akosua's tomato-based soup was known as "light soup," but with goat meat, onions, ginger, garlic, and garden eggs, there was nothing light about it.

"It's wonderful, Mama," Emma said, after her first taste, and it was, even for someone like Emma who ate little. Not that she disliked food; she simply forgot to consume it sometimes.

Her mother smiled warmly. She wore compliments quite well.

"Mama?" Emma didn't want to put this off.

"Yes, dear."

Emma leaned back for a moment. "Do you like Courage?"

Akosua appeared startled. "Do I like Courage? But of course, I do! What makes you ask that?"

"I think he feels like you disapprove of him."

Akosua touched her fingertips to her sternum. "*Me?* But why? Did he tell you that?"

"He didn't need to," Emma said. "I know him. He may be on the SWAT Panther team, but when he's in the presence of elders, he turns into a little boy almost."

"I think he's just fine," Akosua reassured Emma. She went on brightly, "So? What are your plans with him?"

Emma had been going for another ladle of soup but stopped. "Plans?"

"Well, you're both at the age you should be thinking about the future."

"If you're talking about marriage, Mama . . ."

"You're on the other side of twenty-five now, and in prime

childrearing age. You must think about those kinds of things. Okay? Just . . . just think about it. I want you to be happy—to have the right man."

To Emma, Mama seemed to be juxtaposing the two entities as if they were codependent: happiness, and having the "right" man. Still, she was willing to give her mother the benefit of the doubt, that she *did* want her daughter to be happy. So, Emma nodded. "Okay, Mama. I'll think about it."

After a moment's silence, Akosua said, "Anyway, how are things at work? Do you have a new case?"

"Maybe," Emma replied. "One of Mr. Sowah's old friends came in to see him. I'm hoping he brought an assignment for us."

"I pray it's something nice and calm," Akosua said. "I think you've had enough of murders and the like."

Emma chuckled. "We sometimes need an injection of Vitamin M—murder—to keep our wits sharp."

"You could do a good jigsaw puzzle and get the same outcome," Akosua said primly. For no reason that Emma completely understood, her mother had a love for difficult jigsaws.

"Maybe so," Emma said, "but there's no excitement in a jigsaw puzzle."

Feigning shock, Akosua gasped, and the two women giggled, sounding very much like each other.

"Don't be annoyed when I say this, Emma, honey," Akosua said, changing the subject, "but how about a brand-new hairstyle in the next couple of months for the coming new year? Aren't you a bit tired of this one? I think it's too plain. What about some extensions, some nice long braids? You would look so pretty."

"Extensions just ruin your natural hair," Emma said flatly.

"That's not true," Akosua challenged. "You could wear them for a few months and then change to another style."

"It's exhausting," Emma said. "A couple of my girlfriends tell me they sit up to four hours getting the extensions. I don't think so."

"It's worth the trouble to be more, you know, feminine."

At a loss for words, Emma stared blankly at her mother for a moment and then laughed.

"What amuses you so?" Akosua asked, her face confused over whether to smile or frown.

"It just sounded so funny when you said I should be more feminine, but now I understand why you said it."

"How do you mean, 'Why I said it'?"

Emma shook her head. "We'll talk about it one day. This isn't the right time."

After shooting her daughter a quizzical look, Akosua said, "Have some more soup."

CHAPTER FOUR

"WE HAVE A NEW assignment today," Sowah said to the group at the Tuesday morning briefing.

He paused as Manu rushed in looking apologetic. "Morning, boss. Sorry I'm late."

"Morning," Sowah replied. "We were just getting started. My old friend Nnamdi Ojukwu brought us the new case. Some of you might have seen him yesterday when he arrived. I know Emma did."

"When had you last seen him, boss?" she asked.

"A little over three years ago, when he arrived in Ghana to be the Nigerian high commissioner, but we *first* met decades ago at the University of Ghana, where he and I studied. After university, when he returned to Nigeria, we kept in touch off and on, but I had no inkling he would one day return to Ghana as a top diplomat.

"So, with that, here's the story: At the end of August, Nnamdi and his wife, Ijeoma, discovered their only child, Ngozi, who is eighteen, had disappeared overnight from her bedroom. It looked like she left through the window, using a ladder to climb down into the back garden, and then over the security wall around the house. The question is whether she left voluntarily or by coercion, but over the next few days, it didn't appear to be an abduction, because no ransom demand came through. Nnamdi and his wife thought it was most likely she had eloped with a plus or minus thirty-year-old man called Femi Adebanjo, with whom Ngozi was romantically involved. I must emphasize we don't know that *yet*."

"Sorry, boss," Jojo piped up, "what's the spelling of Femi's last name?"

Sowah spelled it out and continued. "A week ago—Nnamdi

said he remembered the date was the thirteenth—a Nigerian friend of his living in Ghana called him to say he had spotted Ngozi shopping at the Lapaz MaxMart. This friend was positive it was her. Nnamdi called the head of Ghana's CID, who advised him to go to CID headquarters in person to submit a statement, which he has done. Nnamdi doesn't trust the police, though. Our assignment is simple: find Ngozi." He paused. "I know why you're all smiling—simple assignments are often not simple."

Manu said, "You described how Ngozi might have been infatuated with Femi, sir, and I guess she was impressionable, especially at her age, but how were things at home? I imagine her life as a high commissioner's daughter wasn't bad at all. Why would she run away?"

"Good question," Sowah said. "Due to Femi's presumed influence on her, Ngozi was in conflict with her parents to the extent that she and Ijeoma were having shouting matches."

"Boss," Emma said, "did anyone show pictures of Ngozi to the MaxMart staff to see if some of the workers there recognized her? That would back up the man's claim that he recognized Ngozi in the store."

"I don't believe that was done, no," Sowah said.

"Do we have the guy's contact information?" Gideon asked, his four different mobile phones lined up in front of him on the table. He was a gadget freak and an IT genius. "I mean the guy who says he recognized Ngozi in the store."

"I don't have it," Sowah replied, "but Nnamdi does."

"Is Mr. Ojukwu still in Ghana, or did he return to Nigeria?" Jojo asked.

"He's still here," Sowah replied, "and he'll stay as long as he has to. Any other questions?"

Emma and the other investigators shook their heads.

"Now, Manu," Sowah continued, "I know you have quite a few pending cases on your roster."

"Five," Manu said, pulling a face. "Having trouble getting information and contacts."

"Gideon?" Sowah asked.

"Four open—I hope I can close one by the end of this week. No, let's say end of next week to be on the safe side."

"Which means Emma and Jojo get the assignment," Sowah said, "because you both have what, four or five cases between you?"

Emma nodded. "Something like that."

Jojo murmured his confirmation and exchanged a smile with Emma. They liked working together. It was Emma's relationship with Manu that was up and down. Sometimes he seemed wise and intuitive, but on other occasions, Emma had to steer him back to the twenty-first century.

"So, Gideon," Sowah continued, "please set up a Zoom call early tomorrow with Nnamdi so I can formally introduce Emma and Jojo to him as the investigators, as well as ask him for the information we need—photos, contact information, and so on."

"Okay, boss," Gideon said. "I'll get on that right away."

"Sir, I was wondering about something," Emma said. "If we need to ask questions along the way, is Mr. Ojukwu—how should I say it—is he sensitive about the family *wahala* involving him and his wife and Ngozi?"

Sowah was thoughtful. "Well, I think he will be very forthcoming and transparent. On the other hand, if there's a question you feel awkward about asking, let me know and I will pose it to him, okay?"

"Thank you, sir."

At the end of the day, Emma took a Bolt—Uber's cheaper competitor—home, not that she was flush with cash, but sometimes she simply didn't feel like enduring the rickety, bouncing, bone-shaking rattle of a *tro-tro*. Trapped in traffic, Emma took the time to call Courage.

"Where did they end up sending you?" she asked.

"We're in Sekondi-Takoradi for the climate change conference and the president will be in attendance, so there's extra security for her protection."

Emma reminded herself that, yes, for the first time ever, the country had a female president.

"I have bad news, though," Courage said. "Day after tomorrow, we go to the Upper East Region until at least Sunday."

"Oh," Emma said, with some anxiety. Sporadic clashes over

chieftaincy rights had been breaking out in the northern regions of the country. "Please be careful up there."

"Always," Courage reassured her. "How's work?"

"Jojo and I have a new assignment. A Nigerian man—Sowah's former college mate—came in to report his daughter missing after she apparently ran off with some guy. The investigation starts in earnest tomorrow. And I'm ready to go."

CHAPTER FIVE

DURING THE ZOOM MEETING on Wednesday morning with Nnamdi Ojukwu, Emma saw a man who was aging well with the perfect proportions of gray and black in his hair and beard, and a residual hint of his youth when he smiled. But as they discussed his daughter's disappearance, he didn't have many smiles to offer. Instead, his brow creased with worry.

"We're starting the investigation today," Sowah told him. "I'll give Emma and Jojo your contact number, and they'll text you in a little while so you have theirs. We need a couple of things from you, Nnamdi: first, the phone number of your friend who says he spotted Ngozi in Lapaz, and second, a few pics of your daughter for when we begin asking around if anyone has seen her."

"Mr. Ojukwu, as you informed us, you carried out your own social media search for this Femi Adebanjo without success," Emma said, "and we'll do the same, hopefully with better results. I anticipate we'll find several Femi Adebanjos, so we'll send you photos of different Femis to see if you recognize any of them."

"Yes, of course," Ojukwu said. "Listen, I said I tried looking on social media, but I'm not proficient at this stuff. It wouldn't surprise me if I missed him."

The Zoom session over, Emma and Jojo stayed with the boss for a little longer to discuss and plan. Sowah's phone buzzed and he squinted at it, shook his head, and cast around for his glasses. "My eyes are so bad these days," he muttered. "Don't get old, you two. Okay, Nnamdi has just sent me the contact info for his friend, and he says the pics are coming shortly, so I'll send you those, as well as Nnamdi's number. Meanwhile, you can get started. Jojo, get in touch with the friend, and if possible, meet with him in person—that's preferable. Emma, you're going to Lapaz MaxMart, but I want you to ask around not only in the store itself, but all the shops in the vicinity as well. Talk to the security guards and so on."

"We got you, boss," Jojo said, as he stood up. "Come on, Emma, let's go."

BESIDES THE MAXMART, the Lapaz strip mall of the same name had a Goil fuel station, a Burger King, a Stanbic Bank branch, a home décor outlet, and a woman selling roasted plantains and groundnuts under a flimsily constructed shade canopy.

MaxMart's interior resembled any other supermarket like Shop-Rite and Game, except it tended to build its square footage vertically instead of as one vast horizontal space. The shelves overflowed with merchandise, most of which originated in South Africa, the Middle East, and of course, China. A very small proportion came from Ghana. Emma walked in and strolled through a couple of aisles until she found a young shop associate restocking laundry detergent.

"Good morning," Emma greeted him. "I need some help."

"Yes?"

"I'm searching for my sister who has gone missing," Emma explained. "Someone told me he saw her in this shop very recently, so I want to show you a picture of her to see if you remember seeing her here."

He nodded. "No problem."

Emma brought up Ngozi's picture on her phone and the stocker studied it a minute. He shook his head. "No, sorry. I don't remember anyone like that, but I've been working here for only a few days, so, please ask the cashiers also."

"I will. Thank you, eh? By the way, how much is that big box of Omo?"

When Emma heard the price, she pulled a face and said, "Well, maybe next time."

With something of a lull in customers, two of the checkout women were free, and Emma approached the first one. She examined Ngozi's picture with care, but eventually shook her head. "No, sorry. Check with Nancy." She gestured to her neighboring cashier.

Nancy's response was the same, and Emma had no success with the other two cashiers either. Nancy suggested Emma talk to the receipt inspector at the exit of the store. This man was completely uninterested in Emma's inquiry and dismissed her with barely a glance at Ngozi's image. He had more important work to do, Emma supposed.

Outside the store again in the growing heat, Emma headed to the Stanbic where she asked the security man in the car park and then the doorman. No success there either, and the same story at the other businesses including the Goil station. The only entity left was the plantain seller, who was expertly rotating the plantains on the charcoal grill for a nice, even golden-brown roast. She was a middle-aged woman who, Emma guessed, had been doing this for decades.

"*Maakye*," Emma saluted her in Twi.

She replied in kind. Emma decided to buy a serving of plantains and groundnuts to engage the seller, who chose two of the most well-done pieces and gave them to Emma in a black plastic bag. Emma thanked her with a smile and made as if to walk away, turning back to make it seem like a thought had just struck her.

"Auntie, can you help me?" Emma asked her, attaching the courteous term of endearment deliberately.

"Yes?" She appeared willing.

Emma showed her Ngozi's pics and she studied them, looking up at Emma after a moment. "Nigerian, girl, right?"

Emma almost jumped for joy. "Yes! That's my friend, Ngozi. Have you seen her?"

"Of course!" the woman said. "She bought something from me on two different occasions. Oh, what a very nice girl! I ax her if she's Nigerian because of how she talked. Has something happened to her?"

"She's disappeared, but someone reported seeing her at this MaxMart. Please, madam, do you remember when you saw her?"

"About one week, now."

"Was she alone?"

"Yes, only her. She was driving one of those big cars, like . . ." She looked around. "Something like that one," she said, pointing across the square at a clunky red Toyota SUV with massive tires.

"Okay," Emma said. "And did you see which way she passed when she left?"

"No, sorry, o," the seller said. "I didn't see."

"Auntie, thank you so much," Emma said.

"Thank you too. I hope you find your Ngozi. Good luck."

I should have gone to her first, Emma thought.

INITIALLY, JOJO DIDN'T make as much progress as Emma. Osarodion Obakozuwa, the man who claimed to have spotted Ngozi at the MaxMart, didn't answer any calls or texts the entire day. In the time being, Jojo looked for an Adebanjo-Ngozi connection on social media. He found three Femi Adebanjos: one born and raised in New York with no evidence he'd ever traveled to West Africa, let alone Ghana; a flashy guy in sunglasses and a colorful traditional Nigerian outfit; and a third was a pastor from Abeokuta, Nigeria, who had posted photos only a couple of days before. So, of the three, only "flashy guy" might have matched the profile of the Femi they wanted, but his timeline showed no connection to Ngozi. After some more searching, Jojo ended his day and went home.

IN THE MORNING, he and Emma brought the boss up to date.

"It seems likely it really was Ngozi in the MaxMart," Emma told Sowah, going on to recount her experience with the astute plantain seller.

"Good," Sowah said. "So, you've made some headway. And Jojo?"

"Yesterday, I tried several times to get Mr. Osarodion," Jojo said, stumbling over the Nigerian name, "but he hasn't gotten back to me. It's always possible he's changed his phone or SIM card. If so, we might never get hold of him. Meanwhile, I've found several Femi Adebanjos on Instagram, but it will take me a while to message them all. With Ngozi, it's more promising. I found her on Instagram."

"Really?" Sowah said, perking up.

"Yeah, she has about eight hundred followers." Jojo pulled it up on his phone to show it to Sowah. "The posts go back three years."

Sowah scrolled through the photos, which showed off Ngozi's sophisticated sartorial tastes.

"But her posts stop abruptly toward the end of August," Jojo continued, "just before she disappeared from home."

"Can you make use of these, em, followers, as you call them?" Sowah asked.

"Obviously I can't contact eight hundred people or I'll be here until the Second Coming," Jojo said, "but what I plan is first to go through her posts and stories to see if she's tagged any Femi Adebanjos, and second, I will follow her, like her posts, and then ask if anyone has information about her whereabouts."

"Okay," Sowah said, making a face, "I have no idea what any of that means, but I'm glad you do."

Emma and Jojo couldn't stop themselves from bursting into laughter.

"I can help you with the Instagram stuff," Emma said to Jojo.

IT-savvy Gideon had used Facebook, Instagram, and LinkedIn to the agency's benefit by attracting more clients, including foreign accounts paying in precious dollars and euros.

Jojo's phone rang. "It's Osarodion," he said eagerly, putting the call on speaker. The voice on the other side was curt. "You called me. Who is this, please?"

"Good afternoon, sir. My name is Jojo, with Sowah Private Investigators, and I'm here with my boss and detective partner. We're contracted to find Ngozi Ojukwu."

"Eh-heh, good, good!" Osarodion said, his voice relaxing. "I know her family well, and even though I hadn't seen Ngozi for some time, when I saw the lady in the shop, I was positive it was her. She denied it and walked away, so I thought I had made a mistake. You know, they say everyone has a double somewhere. I was still curious, so I called Nnamdi and he confirmed, yes, Ngozi had disappeared. So, I took that as proof."

"I see," Jojo said. "Thank you, sir. We'd like to text you a recent photo of Ngozi so you can let us know whether that was the woman you saw."

"Of course. No problem."

Jojo sent it, waiting a couple of minutes, after which Osarodion returned to the line and said, "Yes, that's her. No doubt. So far, do you have any idea where she is?"

"No, we don't, but we're working on it. Thank you for your help, sir."

Jojo hung up and triumphantly pumped his fist.

"This is good," Sowah said, slapping his desk. "Nice work, but there's more to do, so let's keep up the pace."

CHAPTER SIX

Week Two

AFTER FOUR DAYS IN the scorching, dry heat of Northern Ghana, Courage returned dead tired late Sunday night. He squeezed in a few hours of sleep before he rose early in the morning to drag himself to the biweekly interdepartmental meeting they called the BIM. Commissioner Ohene, the new Director-General of the Criminal Investigations Department, was strict about this gathering as part of his "CID reform initiative." Unable to attend that morning's meeting, the director of Courage's unit had chosen to send Courage instead.

In a rush, Courage left home a trifle late and arrived at a minute past seven, hoping Ohene was at least two minutes tardy. He was not. He was already there at the head of the table impeccably dressed in a suit, and the meeting had begun. Courage almost melted under Ohene's glare, sheepishly finding a chair behind the main body of attendants at the table.

"Since you are late, Sergeant," Ohene said dryly, "why don't you give us a full report on the SWAT missions to Takoradi and the Upper East Region?"

Courage hadn't expected Ohene to call on him the second he joined the meeting. Aware all eyes were on him, Courage dove into his backpack and fished for his tablet. For one blood-freezing moment, he thought he had left it behind. But it was there.

"Um, please, sir, should I stand?" Courage asked.

"You may hang from the ceiling if you want," Ohene replied. "As long as we can hear you."

People around the table tittered. Choosing to stand, Courage delivered the report nervously, but Ohene appeared satisfied that the SWAT mission had proceeded without a hitch.

"Next, Homicide," he went on. "Last week, a homicide case was referred to us. Do you have more information about it, Inspector Boateng?"

Courage leaned back, relieved the torture was over. Detective Inspector Boateng, who had recently risen to the rank of Sergeant and whom Courage had nicknamed "Diboat," began his report. The murder had taken place nine days before on the night of Saturday, the sixteenth of October in the affluent East Legon suburb of Accra. The local police had begun the investigation but then requested that CID Headquarters take over. HQ was certainly not rolling in money—these days, who was?—but it certainly had more resources than the smaller police departments, so it wasn't uncommon to refer more complex cases up the chain.

"The victim is a Nigerian man, Femi Ade . . . Adebanjo," Boateng began.

Courage recalled Emma talking about her new case involving a Nigerian girl who had run off with some man. Was that man, Femi Adebanjo, the victim?

"He was twenty-eight, according to the voter registration card in his wallet," Boateng continued, "and he was found shot in the head at the East Legon hotel he was managing."

"Witnesses? Suspects?" Ohene asked.

"Sir, the night watchman told us a man in a cap and Covid mask approached the building around eleven-thirty when the security guard was standing outside the gate. After a short conversation and a brief struggle, the man knocked out the guard with a blow to his head and then bound and gagged him. The guard regained consciousness after the shooting had already taken place, so we don't know if a second person was the shooter or if it was the same guy who knocked the guard out."

"It seems like a professional job, don't you think?" Ohene asked.

"Like a contract killing? Yes, sir."

"What about the guard?" Ohene asked. "Could he have done it?"

Boateng cleared his throat. "Well, just judging by his demeanor, sir—he was in such deep distress—and the deep wound on his head, I don't think it's likely, sir. In addition to that, he's an agency guard with a spotless background check."

"Is it he who first discovered Adebanjo's body?"

"The way it happened, sir, when the guard first regained consciousness, he managed to get to his feet and pull his gag off using the latch on the inside of the gate, after which he began screaming for help. The caretaker, who had been sleeping in the boy's quarters, woke up to the shouts. It was only after he had untied the guard that they discovered the body."

Ohene nodded, playing absent-mindedly with his wedding band. "Then you must dig into this Nigerian fellow's past," he said. "Since he was managing this hotel, I would look for anything like financial disputes with other people in the hospitality business, or a direct competitor, or someone he swindled. Things along those lines. We're looking for motive. Also, get in touch with Nigeria's CID in case the victim had a criminal record."

"Yes, sir."

Courage, making sure he was out of Ohene's line of sight, surreptitiously texted Emma.

What was the name of the Nigerian guy you told me about?

Femi Adebanjo, she replied.

I think we might have found him. A guy of the same name was shot dead at an East Legon hotel two Saturdays ago. Diboat has the case

Do you have a photo?

Diboat found an ID on the guy, I'll ask him to send you a pic, but I'll need to tell him about the possible Ngozi connection.

Np, we share info

Ok, I'll get back to you

As soon as Emma had finished the call with Courage, she swung around to Jojo. "They've found a Femi Adebanjo shot dead at an East Legon hotel."

In turn, Jojo swiveled in his seat. "Really?" he said, his voice betraying the excitement of discovering a potential lead. "Any signs of Ngozi?"

Emma shook her head. "No, but it's early—we have so few details right now, but Courage is following up with Diboat about it."

Hoping for rapid success, they were intent and silent as they carried out their respective tasks. Jojo returned to his Instagram research. Ngozi had multiple posts and stories, including those from the agonizing Covid lockdown. In particular, he searched for selfies with others she might have tagged.

A few people had responded in the negative to Jojo's query: We're looking for Ngozi Ojukwu, who has disappeared. Any info on her or a man called Femi Adebanjo, believed to have a connection with Ngozi, please DM @sowahprivateinvestigators.

For Emma's part, she had been messaging friends tagged in Ngozi's posts. Of those who answered, none knew her present whereabouts, although a couple of them had been with Ngozi up to three weeks before she disappeared. One reply in particular captured Emma's attention.

I've been wondering where she is too. Last time I saw her was three months ago in July when I visited her in the hospital

Emma wrote back, Was she sick?

All I know she slipped or fainted in the bathroom and got a wound on her head. She had a contusion or a concussion one of those two I don't know the correct name.

Without knowing how significant this was, Emma made a note to ask Nnamdi about it.

Her phone buzzed. "DI Boateng, big boss! How are you?"

"I'm well, and you?"

"We're all good here. Please, my work partner Jojo is here with me at the office, so can I put you on speaker?"

"Sure, no problem. So, what is going on?"

Emma explained the new assignment from Nnamdi Ojukwu the week before, and the possible link between Ngozi and Femi Adebanjo. Since then, Emma and Jojo had been trying, without success, to establish the connection, if it existed, that is.

"Yes, Courage just told me about your new case," Boateng said, sounding less than happy, "but I let him know he should not have divulged details of our briefing this morning without first letting me know. These proceedings are supposed to be confidential."

"Yes, you're right," Emma conceded. "Sorry about that." Not that she had committed the blunder, but she agreed Courage had taken something of a liberty and it didn't cost her anything to apologize on his behalf.

"It's okay," Boateng said, his voice softening.

"Can you help us, DI?" Emma asked. "We need a photo of the Femi who was shot."

"Yes, I do have the victim's voter registration card. I'll text you a copy."

"Oh, thank you, thank you!" Emma said, winking at Jojo. "That's why we love you so much here at the agency."

"Oh, is that so?" Boateng said with a snort.

"Yes, boss," Jojo chimed in. "We do love you."

"Okay, then. Thank you."

Emma and Jojo grinned at each other. Even accepting a compliment, DI Boateng could sound grumpy.

"I'm sending it now," he said. "But in return, please apprise me of any new information that may be helpful for *my* investigation."

"Of course, Inspector," Emma said. "My hope is that we're looking into two aspects of the same thing."

Boateng grunted and ended the call. A few minutes later, his text arrived.

Jojo leaned over to examine the image with Emma. The Federal Republic of Nigeria voter's card had a greenish tint, the national crest at top left; Femi's picture center left; and name, date of birth, and other data on the right. He had lived for only twenty-eight years.

"Wait, wait," Jojo said, eagerly returning to his own phone to search through Ngozi's Instagram photos again. After a few moments, he exclaimed, "*Got him!*"

"No!" Emma said, jumping up to look over Jojo's shoulder. "Seriously? Where?"

"There he is with Ngozi."

"That *is* him!" Emma said with excitement. "Well done, bro!" They high-fived.

"I missed him because I hadn't yet checked out her story highlights," Jojo explained.

"Did she tag Femi?"

"Let's see. Yes, she did. His profile name is 'Naijolufemi.' No wonder I couldn't find him."

"I get the 'Naija'—the popular name for Nigeria or Nigerians," Emma said, "but what's the 'Olu' about?"

"One second, and I'll tell you," Jojo said, googling "olu femi." "See what it says: Olufemi means 'God loves me' in the Yoruba language, and Femi is short for Olufemi. So . . . here's his profile. And he has a lot of pics with Ngozi, as well."

"He looks a like a Yahoo boy, doesn't he?" Emma commented.

Jojo agreed. Yahoo boys were young internet swindlers who dressed fashionably and had a taste for twist hairstyles and expensive cars. "Let's see if we can make a timeline on him," he said. "Femi's posts go back a couple of years, but in March this year, after Nigeria reopened its borders post-Covid, he was here in Accra."

"Look," Emma said. "He has family here. 'Me and the greatest man in all my life, Grandpa Kojo.'"

"Oh," Jojo said in some surprise. "Then maybe he's part Ghanaian."

"Possible," Emma said, taking her seat again to open her Instagram app. "A lot of Ghanaians went off to Nigeria during the oil rush."

"No pics of his parents," Jojo said, "or with any girls besides Ngozi."

"That doesn't necessarily mean anything," Emma said dryly, concentrating on her screen. "He probably deleted all his incriminating pics when he met Ngozi. When *did* he meet her?"

"The lovey-dovey selfies of the two of them start in April, a month after he got to Accra," Jojo said, "and they continue through, May . . . June . . . July, and part of August."

"And then they stop by the end of August," Emma said, following along, "which is when Ngozi disappears, but then Femi shows up in a pic by himself—no Ngozi in sight—in September in front of the hotel he was managing—what is it called?—the White House."

"Maybe he didn't want to risk giving Ngozi's location away," Jojo suggested.

"Or maybe he didn't want to give *himself* away," Emma said. "What if Femi forcibly removed Ngozi from her home in Lagos? Remember? Blood on the windowsill in her bedroom?"

"Yes," Jojo said. "Hmm." He shook his head. "I'm confused. Did Ngozi really run away with Femi, and if so, does she have anything to do with his murder?"

"And where is she now?" Emma added. "What if she's dead too?"

"Let's hope not," Jojo said, wrinkling his nose. "We want this to be a missing-person case, not a dead-person."

"Yes, we should remain optimistic," Emma said, attempting to sound bright. She was trying to be a positive thinker these days.

"Look at this, Jojo. In that September pic, Adebanjo tagged the White House. Let's see that profile. 'Luxury hotel catering to your every need,' it says. Which could mean a lot of different things."

"I was about to say the same," Jojo said. "It wouldn't surprise me if it catered to prostitutes and their clients."

"I think they're called sex workers now," Emma commented.

Jojo looked up. "Is 'prostitutes' a bad word these days?"

"Well, it's kind of ugly, don't you think? A lot of stigma attached to it." She clicked through several photographs of the hotel: the imposing front gate and beyond that, parking spaces in a driveway shaded with a mango, avocado, and jacaranda tree. "Looks nice," she murmured.

The images continued with the interior of the hotel—the downstairs lobby, the stairway, the second floor, and the rooms.

"Wow," Jojo muttered. "You see these suites?"

Emma leaned over to look at his screen as he scrolled through pictures of the clearly luxurious accommodations—at least if the photos were accurate.

"Stop, wait," Emma said suddenly. "Go back. Not that one—the one before."

The photograph that had caught her attention was in landscape orientation taken from the suite's doorway. To the left was a king-size bed with matching bedside lamps, but that wasn't the object drawing her curiosity. Rather, it was a floor-standing mirror on the right.

"See?" Emma said. "The picture taker—maybe Femi—is reflected in the mirror, but look *behind* him."

Jojo peered closer. "Ohh, you're right—there's someone standing behind him, but the lighting is poor. I'll try some filters."

He worked on brightening and sharpening the image. "I'd say it's a woman for sure, but the features still aren't that clear. Let's ask Gideon if he can do any better."

"Okay, and the date of the pic is the ninth of October, a week before Adebanjo was killed," Emma observed, "So, if that's her reflection in the mirror, we can say he and Ngozi were together at least until then, and that during that one-week interval, something crucial happened to lead to his death and her disappearance. You know what I'm thinking?"

"That it's almost time for lunch?"

Emma snorted. "Do you have a pet tapeworm in your guts? No, I'm thinking there must be more clues—photos, yes, but even more than that—on Femi's phone. Just think of how many pics you take that don't end up on Instagram."

"Did they find a phone?"

"I don't know," Emma replied, "but I'm going to call Diboat now to find out. Can you reach the boss, Jojo? He's not in the office and we need to give him an update."

"Sure, I will."

Sowah didn't pick up Jojo's call, but DI Boateng answered Emma's. "No phone," he said, in response to her query, "neither at the spot he was killed nor anywhere inside, including the victim's office, but Mr. Salifu, the caretaker who showed us around, told us Adebanjo certainly had a phone, so someone must have it."

"The murderer," Emma suggested. "There might be incriminating phone evidence if the killer knew Adebanjo."

"My thinking too."

"Any trace evidence, DI? Or DNA samples?"

"By the time the police arrived on the scene, onlookers and busybodies from the neighborhood had crowded around the body, trampling in the blood, and so on. It could be Adebanjo's phone had been lying on the ground at the scene and in all the confusion, someone stole it or grabbed it for some reason. Now, all the witnesses have scattered and no one wants to come forward. You know our people—scared the police will arrest them just for bearing witness."

Boateng, a university graduate in biochemistry who had had formal investigative and forensic training, was unlikely to operate in that fashion, but among garden-variety Ghanaian police officers without training, scapegoating the most convenient witness or bystander was common. Countless people languished in prison for crimes they didn't commit.

"But we'll keep looking," Boateng added.

"Thank you, DI. I appreciate it. Now, we have a new development to report, sir. Through social media, we've confirmed the connection between Ngozi Ojukwu and the Femi Adebanjo killed over the weekend."

"Really! You've seen pictures of them together, or what?"

"Yes, I'll send them to you."

"Boyfriend and girlfriend?"

"It appears so—no evidence I saw that they were married. Bottom line is Adebanjo's murder and Ngozi's disappearance could be related."

"Thank you for establishing the link," Boateng said. "It makes a difference. You remember I mentioned Salifu, the hotel caretaker?"

"Yes."

"He didn't reference Ngozi when I questioned him about Adebanjo. Why not? Because he'd never met her before? I need to go back to him."

"Can I ask you a favor?"

"What's that?"

"May I accompany you?" Emma said. "I would like to see the place for myself, as well as meet this Salifu."

"Sure, no problem. I owe you for doing the social media legwork."

"Of course. When and where should we meet?"

"My turn to pick up the kids from school this afternoon, so let's meet at the hotel tomorrow morning to start afresh. I'll send you the location."

"Thank you, DI."

As Emma finished with Boateng, Sowah returned Jojo's call.

"Boss, we've been in touch with DI Boateng," Jojo told him. "A Femi Adebanjo was shot to death late Saturday night—two weekends ago; we've established it's *our* Femi and that he was connected to Ngozi Ojukwu."

EAGER FOR NEWS, Nnamdi Ojukwu returned to Sowah's office that same afternoon.

"I can confirm that your friend was right," Sowah told him. "It was Ngozi he saw at the Lapaz MaxMart."

Nnamdi's face lit up momentarily before falling again. "Still, it's been a while now," he said. "I wish there were a more recent sighting."

"It would certainly help," Sowah said. "There's something else I need to inform you about."

"Yes?"

Sowah related the recent discovery about Adebanjo—that he had had a connection to Ngozi as they had suspected, and that now he was dead.

Nnamdi slumped in his seat and rested his forehead in his palm. "Oh, no," he moaned. "This is not good."

Sowah grasped his shoulder and gave it a gentle shake. "I know it's not easy."

"You don't need to humor me, Yemo," Nnamdi said hopelessly. "It's simply not possible that the Adebanjo murder would have nothing to do with Ngozi's disappearance. The events can't be unrelated. The same people who killed him probably abducted her."

"We don't know enough to make that statement. You're imagining the worst possible scenario. Keep your spirits up."

Nnamdi let out a heavy sigh. "I'll try. Should I tell Ijeoma? I think it's going to worry her sick."

"In the long run, I don't see how you can avoid it," Sowah said, "but maybe for now you can hold off until we have more information? It's really up to what you feel is best."

The two men rose together.

"Thank you for coming by," Sowah said. "So good to see you. One of these days, God willing, it will be purely a social visit."

"Amen," Nnamdi said.

Sowah walked Nnamdi to the front door, where the two men, big and small, parted. Nnamdi got into the rear of a black SUV and his driver pulled into traffic. Sowah waved and turned back to the office admitting to himself that he felt deeply uneasy.

CHAPTER SEVEN

A LARGE SIGN WITH the name WHITE HOUSE stood outside the gate entrance at 31 Senchi Street in East Legon. When Emma arrived, she wondered if Boateng had beaten her to it. She pressed the bell button on the right-hand pillar and waited a moment before trying again. The pedestrian entry to one side opened and a Goliath of a man stepped out. He didn't seem particularly friendly. "Yes?"

"Good afternoon. Are you Salifu?"

"Yes?"

Like many from northern Ghana, he had jet-black skin that was exquisitely fine in texture and sheen.

"Glad to meet you. My name is Emma Djan. I'm Inspector Boateng's assistant. Please, has he arrived?"

"No. He texted me just now that he's on the way coming."

"Detective Inspector Boateng tells me you're the caretaker here. Very sorry for the death of your boss."

He stared at her blankly. "Okay."

Must be a man of few words, she thought. "Well, do you mind if I wait for Inspector Boateng inside?"

Salifu shot her a wary look but moved aside to give her access. Entering the courtyard felt like stepping into a Shangri-la of rich surroundings—just like in the photos, only better. The jacaranda, mango, and sprawling avocado trees offered a merciful rim of shade around the perimeter of the yard. From there, Emma's gaze went to the two-story building with the name WHITE HOUSE emblazoned along the top in elegant typeface. Closer to cream than white, it was striking and luminous in the morning sun.

"You can have a seat," Salifu said, pointing at a pair of blue plastic chairs under the avocado tree.

"Thank you." Emma was itching to ask him questions, but she didn't want to steal Boateng's thunder, so she waited patiently while continuing her task of trying to contact the people Ngozi had tagged on Instagram.

Boateng arrived twenty minutes later holding a dog-eared folder of papers under his arm and wearing a rumpled light-blue shirt with unguinous stains.

"Good afternoon, sir," Salifu said as he let Boateng inside the yard.

Emma watched the two men chatting, noticing how deferential the giant was toward the DI, calling him "sir" and using his pleases and thank-yous liberally. Emma conceded, in his defense, that the two men had met before when Boateng had first arrived at the crime scene, whereas Emma was a stranger. She shrugged mentally. It made no difference to her.

Boateng gestured toward Emma and Salifu followed him.

"I think you've met?" Boateng said.

"Yes, we have," Emma said. "I told Mr. Salifu I'm your assistant."

"Ah, right," Boateng said vaguely.

"Please, I'm coming," Salifu said, trotting off along the side of the house. He returned with another chair so that he could sit with the other two.

"So, yes, Mr. Salifu," Boateng began, "as I told you last time, I'm working on this case—with the help of Miss Djan here—to find out who killed your boss. We now know that Mr. Adebanjo arrived at the hotel one day with a young woman called Ngozi Ojukwu. Is that correct?"

"Yes please," he said, his face betraying nothing—no panic, no surprise, no distress.

"But my brother," Boateng said, flipping his right palm up, "why didn't you tell me that before?"

"Yes please, it's true," Salifu said. "Sorry, sir. I forgot to tell you that. In fact, I was going to call you about it just today."

Nicely done, Emma thought. He had defanged the inspector.

"Anyway," Boateng said, waving the matter away, "no problem. Just for the future, you tell me everything and anything you know or have seen. You get me?"

"Yes please."

"This Ngozi girl," Boateng said, "around eighteen, very nice looking? That's the one?"

"Yes please. She came with Mr. Femi from Naija."

"When was that?"

"Em . . ." Salifu stared at the ground as he cast his mind back. "End of August, like thirtieth or thirty-first, around there."

"Is that the first time you had met them?"

"The girl, yes. But Mr. Femi, I met him last . . . April or May, when he came here with Mr. Awuni and Madam Janet."

Emma's ears pricked up. Those names were new to her.

Apparently to Boateng as well. "Who are they?" he asked.

"The ones who own the hotel."

Emma exchanged a glance with Boateng. "So, Mr. Femi didn't buy the hotel?" she asked Salifu.

"No please," Salifu replied. "He was just the manager."

"Do you have contact numbers for those people?" Boateng asked. "You said, Mr. Awuni and who?"

"Madam Janet. Yes, I have the contact, please."

"Are they married? Tell me more about them."

"No please, not married. Mr. Awuni owns some other hotels, one of them is in Lapaz and the other one is in Kasoa. Madam Janet is the manager at Lapaz; the place is called Alligator."

What an unlikely name, Emma thought, but then again, Ghanaians were champions of imaginative appellations.

"First, I was working for Madam Janet at Alligator for two years," Salifu continued, "but I came here to the White House in April of this year."

"Then, how did Femi and Ngozi come into the picture?" Emma asked.

Salifu shrugged. "Just one day, Mr. Awuni and Madam Janet came here with Mr. Femi and showed him the place. After that, Mr. Awuni told me that Mr. Femi was coming to be the manager here."

Something about Salifu's tone indicated to Emma that Awuni's move had been an unpleasant surprise.

"You were thinking you were going to be the manager, rather?" she asked.

Salifu gave a small one-sided smile but otherwise didn't respond, which, by itself, all but confirmed Emma's suspicions.

"Did Mr. Femi get along well with Awuni and Janet?" Boateng asked Salifu.

"Yes please." Again, he assumed that blank look.

"No problems or disagreements?"

"Yes please—no problems at all."

If Salifu was being untruthful, it would come as no surprise to Emma. He didn't want to cast aspersions on his boss. She picked up, "Mr. Salifu, what about between Mr. Femi and Madam Ngozi? Did they have some disagreements or quarrels that you saw?"

"Hmm," Salifu said heavily, as if contemplating a dire predicament. "I can say that by the time Mr. Femi was killed, things were not so good between him and Madam Ngozi."

"Is that so?" Boateng said. "Why, what happened?"

"I don't know," Salifu said. "You see, on Wednesday night, three days before Mr. Femi was shot, he started to sleep in the office instead of the house. When I came in Thursday morning, he had been here overnight, and until the day they shot him, he never went back home to her. So, I knew it was *wahala* or something like that."

"Did you ask Mr. Femi about it?"

"Yes, sir, but he didn't answer me."

Boateng looked at Emma. "Any other questions?"

She recalled her discussion with Jojo about sex workers. "I'm sure many beautiful ladies came here, Salifu?" she asked suggestively. "For the men? Maybe Ngozi caught her husband with one of them and so she became jealous. What do you think?"

"I don't know, please."

Emma wouldn't let him off that easily. "But it's possible?"

With brilliant timing, Boateng stepped in and this time his voice was as sharp as a butcher's knife. "Salifu, this is the last time I warn you. If you continue to keep information from us, I will arrest you. I'm not playing, eh? Do you want to go to jail?"

"No please," he said quickly.

"Then answer Madam Djan's question and stop wasting our time. Was Mr. Femi having sexual relations with one of the prostitutes?"

This was one situation where Boateng had a clear advantage over Emma: he could make a threat with real teeth in it, even if he was bluffing.

Salifu became willing very quickly. "Okay, there was one girl—Diamond."

"Go on," Boateng pushed.

"Well, Diamond worked at Madam Janet's guesthouse in Lapaz. On that same Wednesday night, Madam Ngozi took Diamond from that place to their house."

"Whose house?" Emma asked, bemused.

"Femi and Madam Ngozi's."

"Why did they take Diamond away?"

"I don't know the whole story," Salifu said. "All I know is that on Thursday morning, Mr. Awuni and Madam Janet came to ask Femi, 'Where is Diamond? We know you and the girlfriend kidnapped her, so where is she?' Femi told them he didn't know anything about it. They were *angry*, shouting very loud. Then they left."

Significant, Emma thought. Salifu was describing friction between Adebanjo and the Awuni-Janet couple. Emma wondered how Diamond's kidnapping had transpired. "Do you know where Diamond is now?" she asked.

"No—unless you check with Mr. Awuni to find out," Salifu answered.

Boateng looked at Emma with eyebrows raised, as in, *anything else?* She shook her head.

"Thank you," Boateng said to Salifu. "Please show us the place where Mr. Adebanjo was killed."

Emma and Boateng walked alongside Salifu past the main entrance to the White House.

"Salifu," Boateng took up, "where were you at the time Mr. Adebanjo was killed?"

"I was sleeping in the boy's quarters at the back," Salifu said, referring to the domestic workers' accommodations, "but I woke up to hear someone shouting for help. I ran to the gate to find the guard with his hands and feet tied. I asked him what happened, and he told me a man had attacked him. I untied him and went to check the place. The front entrance, there was no problem, but when I went to the side of the building, I found Mr. Femi."

The trio walked along the concrete pavement around the east side of the building to a locked door.

"This is an emergency exit," Salifu explained, as he unlocked it.

"Where does that lead to?" Boateng asked, pointing to a second door beyond.

"To the hotel lounge."

"Is that also locked?"

"Yes please."

"Okay, fine. So, this is the place you found Mr. Femi, right? Can you show us how he was?"

Salifu went to his knees and then lay well inside the doorway crumpled halfway between the recumbent position and his left side.

"A lot of blood?" Emma asked.

"*Wallahi!*" Salifu said, shaking his head. "I never saw so much blood."

Emma had a question she considered essential. "Did you see a phone on the ground or on the floor inside?"

"No please."

"But you had seen Mr. Femi use a phone often, right?"

"Yes, he was having a Samsung."

Emma glanced at Boateng, wondering what he was thinking.

A car horn honked from behind the gate.

"I think that's Madam Janet and Mr. Awuni," Salifu said. "I'm coming, eh?"

"Couldn't be more convenient," Boateng said. "Let's meet them."

"You go, Inspector," Emma said. "Me, I'll make myself scarce for a while."

"Why, what's wrong?" Boateng asked, puzzled.

"I'll tell you later," Emma said over her shoulder as she trotted toward the rear side of the building in search of a secure hiding place. "Text me once they've left."

CHAPTER EIGHT

MADAM JANET AND MR. Awuni alighted from a silver Escalade and walked up to Boateng.

Dressed in black slacks and an African-print halter top, she was well built and taller than the man, who was dumpy and bespectacled.

"Good afternoon," Awuni said, regarding Boateng with curiosity. "Who are you, please?"

"Detective Inspector Boateng. I'm investigating the death of Femi Adebanjo. You are Mr. Awuni, the owner of the hotel?"

"Yes, I am. This is Janet Glover, my associate."

"Hello," she said, smoothing back her long black braids with an air of importance.

"Nice to meet you both. May I ask you a few questions inside?"

"By all means," Awuni said, after a brief hesitation. He took the lead to the front entrance and unlocked the door.

"I understand Mr. Adebanjo was managing your facility here," Boateng said.

"That's correct," Awuni said. "Inspector, please, come this way to the office."

Awuni courteously gestured to Janet. "After you, madam."

She smiled and murmured, "Thank you."

Boateng looked around the room quickly. The furnishings were of superior quality, no doubt. No good at finances, he wondered how long it would take to break even with expenses as high as these.

"Please, make yourself comfortable," Awuni said, clicking on the air with the remote.

He and Janet sat on the cream sofa and Boateng took the matching seat directly opposite.

"So," Boateng said, "this is where Mr. Adebanjo worked?"

"Correct," Awuni said. "Inspector, we are very shocked about this murder, not so, Janet?"

"Terrible," she said.

Their disingenuousness was plain to Boateng.

"When did you last see him?" he asked.

"Only two days before his death," Awuni responded. "It's hard to believe he's gone so suddenly."

Janet murmured agreement and shook her head in a show of sorrow.

"You know," Awuni continued. "I built this hotel, and Femi had done a very good job setting everything up. I expected him to do well as a manager for years to come."

"Of course," Boateng said. "I want to know a little bit about your business, or should I say businesses? You both own a couple of hotels or guesthouses, correct?"

"Yes," Awuni said. "Three, including this one."

"I must say, this is a beautiful environment," Boateng said admiringly, looking around.

"Thank you," Awuni said.

"No disagreements between Mr. Adebanjo and either you or Madam Janet?"

They looked at each other and this time Janet answered. "Not in the least bit, Inspector," she said. "I can assure you of that. We would have no reason to do any harm to Femi, if that's what you're wondering."

"Do you know of anyone who might have? Wanted to harm or kill Femi?"

"No one we know personally," Awuni said. "But as to his life in Nigeria and Ghana prior to now, there's little we can say. If there was some bad blood back home in Nigeria, there might have been a contract on him. You know these Nigerians—don't mess around with them. They're serious. Femi was a business-man there and I'm sure he must have developed enemies."

"Perhaps," Boateng said. "By the way, what business was he in? Do you know?"

"He told us he ran a small shop in Lagos."

"Did you ever run a background check?"

"Yes, but we didn't find anything."

Depends on how thorough your check was, Boateng thought. "What about Femi's relationship with Salifu?"

"It was brought to my attention that Femi's girlfriend, Ngozi, did not like Salifu and asked Femi to stop him from working inside the hotel," Janet said. "Salifu is a jack-of-all-trades. He knows electrical stuff, carpentry, and just generally how to repair things. It was a shame to restrict him to only doing things outside, and that was one area of disagreement that I certainly had with Femi."

"Was Salifu very upset, angry?" Boateng asked.

"Wouldn't you have been, Inspector?" Janet said.

"Definitely. Whether enough to kill someone, I'm not sure. What was the situation concerning Diamond?"

Janet froze, but Awuni sat up straight and tilted up his chin slightly. "What do you know about Diamond?"

Ah, now their serenity bubble had popped. "Not enough," Boateng said. "That's why I'm asking."

Unexpectedly, Janet leaned forward and cried, "Femi and that girl, Ngozi, kidnapped Diamond from the Alligator to make her work at the White House instead. My son, Ben, tried to rescue Diamond, there was a fight, and they cut off his finger."

"Oh, I'm sorry," Boateng said, in sympathy, well aware that this was only *Janet's* side of the story, and a murky one at that. "But why should they try to kidnap Diamond?"

"Because they fancied her for their perverted sexual practices," Awuni said, as if it should have been obvious to Boateng.

"What was Diamond's role at the Alligator in the first place?"

"She's one of our domestic staff," Janet said quickly.

"So, where is Diamond at the moment?"

"She is back with us," Janet said. "She saw the folly of her ways."

"Okay." Boateng had exhausted the Diamond discussion. He tried something else. "We're looking for Mr. Adebanjo's mobile phone. He must have had one on him, or in this or another room. The question is, where is it? It must be somewhere. Do you know anything about it?"

"Not at all," Awuni said, "but you are welcome to look through the desk and the cabinets. Perhaps he left it there."

"Thank you for the permission to do that," Boateng said, standing up and going over to the brilliantly polished desk. None of its four drawers on either side contained anything of any importance, and certainly no phone. Boateng stood where he was with arms akimbo. "No desktop either," he murmured, turning to Janet and Awuni. "To your knowledge, did Femi have a laptop?"

"I don't know," Awuni said at once, looking stiff, while Janet stared at Boateng without blinking.

Liar, Boateng thought cynically. *They've pilfered the laptop.*

Adebanjo must have had a computer of some kind. How could he manage a hotel without it?

Boateng moved across the room to the two file cabinets. One of them contained invoices and receipts for building materials, furniture, and the like. Boateng eyeballed them all, but there seemed to be nothing of value—at least, not for his investigation.

"Okay," he said, with something of a sigh. "Thank you very much for all your assistance, Mr. Awuni and Madam Janet."

"You're most welcome," she said with a beamish smile, which Boateng thought might be, at least in part, relief that he was leaving, but his instincts told him that he was not in the least done with them.

As Boateng left the White House, he noticed something. He crossed the street to stare at the mansion diametrically opposite to the hotel. Painted a pale yellow, the house was mostly concealed behind a high-security wall and only the upper part of the building was visible.

He texted Emma to discover she was waiting for him around the corner.

"Why did you hide, Djan?" Boateng asked her as they reunited.

"Something tells me not to expose my identity to Janet and Awuni this early," Emma said, adding, "in case I need to go undercover."

Boateng grunted. Emma knew his feelings about PI under-cover work vacillated between disapproval and cautious approbation, depending on the circumstances.

"Are you suspecting either or both of foul play?" she asked him.

"Early to say, but there was definitely *wahala* between Adebanjo on one side, and Awuni and Madam Janet on the other. They claim that Ben-Kwame tried to prevent the alleged Diamond kidnapping, and during the altercation, Adebanjo cut off her son Ben-Kwame's finger. The point is that Awuni, Janet, now Ben-Kwame, and maybe even Ngozi could all have had motives to kill Adebanjo."

"Then, let's sort them out, starting with Madam Janet," Emma said. "First she is irate about the so-called Diamond kidnapping and what happened to Ben. Mr. Awuni's feelings echo Janet's because they're in business together. Diamond is a source of income, so if Femi really brought Diamond over to the White House without their consent, it's basically stealing their money."

"And with regard to Salifu," Boateng said, "Femi sacked him from the house and limited him to working only outside."

Emma raised her eyebrows at this revelation. "Oh, is that so? That must have upset Salifu. I believe he had had ambitions of becoming the manager of the White House, but then, here comes this cocky young guy with his even younger girlfriend to uproot his plans."

"Is that enough for Salifu to violently hate Femi? I'm not sure."

"I think so, but wait a moment." Emma closed her eyes and paused to reflect. "What about another way? If Janet and Awuni approach Salifu and tell him they want to get rid of Femi for good, Salifu is willing to do the job because he resents Femi in any case. Different motives, but the streams run into the same river."

Boateng smiled in apparent appreciation of the metaphor. "And as for Ngozi," he said, "all I can think of is if Femi was having an affair with Diamond, Ngozi might have become furi-ous enough to kill Femi, although I quite doubt it. But, anyway, we haven't established any such relationship between Femi and Diamond."

Emma was nodding in agreement. "And that's why we need to get to Diamond. She's a link to them all—Ngozi, Janet, Awuni, Ben-Kwame, and Femi. She may have information that might put the jigsaw together."

"How to get to her is the question," Boateng said. "Right now, I'm sure she's under very close watch. She's not going to volunteer such info."

THERE MIGHT BE a way, Emma thought, but she didn't share it with Boateng—not yet, at least.

"We need more information or clues," Emma murmured. "I should have asked before, but have you already searched Femi and Ngozi's house?"

"Of course," Boateng said. "The day I went, I was lucky enough to find the realtor there, so she granted me entry. I didn't discover anything of interest at the time, but now that I have more background on Femi and the people in his life, I'll need another look."

"May I please come with you?" Emma asked, and then, perceiving the inspector's hesitation, quickly added, "I'll ask my mother to make you the best *okro* stew in the world."

Boateng's face lit up. "It's a deal. You may accompany me."

Food. It always did the trick.

"Come with me," Boateng said.

"Where are we going?" Emma asked, following him across the street.

Boateng pointed at the yellow house. "What do you see?"

"Nothing much," Emma said.

"Look harder," Boateng encouraged her, as they approached.

Emma frowned, wondering what he was driving at. Then, "Oh!" she exclaimed, as she saw it. High up on a corner of the building was a small CCTV camera. "You're a genius, DI Boateng."

"Ha!" he said, as they arrived at the front gate. He pressed the call button on the wall and waited.

A security guard opened the side entrance and looked out.

"Good afternoon, sah," Boateng greeted him.

"Afternoon. Can I help you?"

"I'm Inspector Boateng from CID. Is the homeowner available?"

The guard shook his head. "He has traveled."

"Do you know when he'll return?"

"No please."

"Okay," Boateng said. He pointed up. "Does that camera work?"

The guard followed his gaze. "Yes please."

"We are seeking information about the murder of one Femi Adebanjo on the sixteenth of this month. He was killed at the hotel."

The guard nodded. "Yes please. I heard of it."

"Were you at your post that night?" Boateng asked.

"No please."

"But at that time, the CCTV camera was working, I'm sure?"

The guard nodded.

"Good," Boateng said. "Your name, please?"

"Joshua."

"Okay, thank you, Joshua. Can you call me when the homeowner returns?"

The two men exchanged numbers and the guard went back inside.

"That would be great if the camera picked up something that night," Emma said to Boateng, as they walked off.

"It would," he agreed. "Provided the video quality is good. This one is a little bit far back from the street, and some of these cams aren't so great. But, we'll see." Boateng looked at his watch. "Let's get to Adebanjo's house now. I hope the realtor is around."

Boateng tried to reach her, succeeding only after multiple failed calls.

"Please, can you meet us at the residence?" Boateng asked her when she finally picked up.

From what Emma could overhear from the other end of the inspector's line, the realtor was presenting a labyrinth of excuses, acquiescing only under Boateng's persistent application of pressure. She said she could be there in an hour.

Emma got a Bolt and they headed to Ngozi and Femi's home, also in East Legon, to wait outside the gated building.

The realtor's promised one hour became ninety minutes. The inspector was in a foul mood now. "If we were looking to buy the place," he said, cheupsing in annoyance, "she would have been here in twenty minutes."

He was on the verge of calling the errant realtor again when she pulled up to the gate in a silver Mercedes.

CHAPTER NINE

THE REALTOR'S NAME WAS Agnes. A small woman with the quick movements of a sparrow, she apologized to Boateng and Emma for her tardiness and led them to the house's front gate. She unlocked it and slid it aside to reveal a two-story building painted maroon with white trim. The darkened, reflective windows added to the chic appearance. A glass-rimmed balcony on the second floor overlooked the driveway.

Agnes unlocked and opened the front door to reveal a high-ceilinged foyer with a polished red-marble floor. Emma looked up at the skylight and it twinkled back at her. The foyer merged with the sitting room, it with the dining area, and it, in turn, with the kitchen, all connected with cream-gold porcelain tile as flat and shimmering as a perfectly calm lake reflecting light. Everything glistened or shone—the chairs, dining table, the kitchen counters, and stovetop. *My God.* Emma had never seen anything quite so dazzling.

Agnes's phone rang. Pausing briefly before answering, she said to her guests, "Please, I'm coming. Feel free to look around."

The first floor was spotless, and from Emma's initial perspective, rather empty. Another way to put it was the room wasn't empty of objects; it was simply full of space.

She went up the half-turn spiral staircase with Boateng to find four bedrooms, but only one furnished and in use. In contrast to the starkness of the first floor, this room felt far warmer to Emma—more welcoming. The floor was bamboo veneer set in a geometric pattern. Sitting squarely in the middle was a low-profile platform bed with a tall headboard and matching nightstands. Makeup brushes, cosmetics, and perfumes sat neatly on a long vanity with a mirror and several drawers. The nightstand had nothing more than a few scraps of paper, but no notes or written messages.

Emma and Boateng looked inside the two walk-in closets—his and hers—and found clothes—a lot of them—hung or neatly folded, a good habit Emma was yet to master. She marveled at the number of shoes in Ngozi's closet, all stacked neatly on a tall rack with heels facing out. *Fabulous*, Emma thought, trying to recall if she had five pairs of shoes to her name.

Boateng, looking around, frowned. "I notice this room has no pens." For the time being, he had told Agnes that everything should be left in place until the investigation was over.

"Pens?" Emma shrugged. "No one writes anymore, Inspector. Straight to phone."

Boateng grunted. "You seem to be studying this room closely, Djan. What do you see?"

"No disorder, no chaos. It has a controlled feeling. Someone who has been in this room was trying to gain control over the other, but couldn't quite do it."

"Or they had a good housekeeper," Boateng said, languidly.

Emma chortled. "I take your point. Nevertheless."

The bathroom, too, showed order and precision. Boateng shrugged. "Nothing. The house is clean."

They went back downstairs, where Agnes was having a furious discussion on the phone—something about the transfer of funds via a courier service.

As Emma and Boateng waited for Agnes to finish, he said in a low voice, "Just look at this place. Only in my dreams."

Emma made a face. "And mine."

"Not a single clue," Boateng muttered.

"The entire house is a clue," Emma said.

"What do you mean?"

"Sorry about that," Agnes said, putting her phone away. "I hope you found everything you need? I must confess, I'm running late for a meeting and would appreciate it if we could wrap it up as soon as possible."

"We're done, yes," Boateng said. "Thank you—"

"Oh, wait," Emma said to him. "I forgot to ask, were any vehicles on the property?"

"Miss Ojukwu had a Range Rover, which she had parked in the garage," Boateng replied. "Adebanjo's Benz was at the hotel. We've confiscated both to CID for safekeeping."

"Do you mind if we look in the garage again, please?" Emma persisted, looking at Agnes.

"Okay, well," Agnes said, with a hurried glance at her watch. "I can lock up here and then show you."

She led them to their right where they found the open garage, which, apart from a car battery, some tools, a few boxes, and two cans of paint on a shelf, was uncluttered.

"The car was unlocked when I was first here," Boateng said, making a horizontal gesture to indicate where the vehicle had been parked.

They stood looking around rather fruitlessly. In Emma's peripheral vision, Agnes was becoming more and more fidgety.

"Well," Emma said, arms akimbo, "not much here to see."

"I don't know what you were expecting," Boateng grumbled.

She was staring at the ground. "What is that dark line?"

"What dark line?" Boateng asked.

"Over here on the ground," Emma replied. "Like a long scuff mark starting here, where the left passenger door would be, and continuing . . ." Emma followed the trail to an imaginary left rear bumper, where the line changed direction and continued to the outer edge of the garage floor before disappearing.

"I have no idea what it is," Boateng said with something of a shrug. "It could be anything."

Emma walked out of the garage space onto the asphalt, scrutinizing its surface as she paced in slow, tight circles.

"Aha!" She stopped to pick up a small, black plastic object that resembled a thimble.

Boateng joined her as she examined the item. "What do you have there?"

"I'm not quite sure, yet," Emma said, "but you see how the base, the closed end, is worn down on one side?"

"I do see that, yes," Boateng responded. "What's the importance of that, if any, Djan? You latch on to the strangest things."

Emma returned to where she imagined the side of the SUV would be and went down on one knee to scrape the base of the thimble hard against the concrete floor. "Look," she said, with a slight smile. "It marks the ground the same way as that dark line."

"What of it?" Boateng asked.

Emma stood up. "Ngozi was kidnapped here."

Boateng frowned. "Why do you say that? How do you know?"

"Did you notice Ngozi's shoes in her bedroom?" Emma said. "The heels are all capped with one of these." She held up the thimble. "When high heels wear down, they expose a nail, which makes the heels click, and that's a signal you need to put on a new cap. In this case, one of the heels of Ngozi's shoes scraped along the ground from here to the edge of the concrete and then the cap snapped off with the friction on the asphalt."

"Ohh," Boateng said, the light dawning. "I get you now. You're saying the kidnapper dragged her by her shoulders out of the garage so that her shoes were scraping along until the heel cap came off."

"Exactly, Inspector. He may have overpowered her first. Perhaps partially knocked her out."

"Very good theory, Djan. Unfortunately, even if your deduction is correct, none of this tells us whether she was alive at the time or not."

"I think she was," Emma murmured, following the scuff mark again. "See? The trail stops here, then there's an isolated, sharp mark the shape of a teardrop, and then the trail resumes and the pattern repeats. I think that's where she was struggling—kicking her feet out and trying to regain her footing so the heel cap was stabbing the ground at intervals."

Boateng nodded. "That gives us a little hope. Let's pray you're right, and that the young lady is still alive. Oh, I forgot to tell you something. Nigerian Police were surprisingly quick with my info request. Eleven years ago, our Femi Adebanjo went to prison for robbery. So, no, this gentleman was no saint. Question is what an upper-class girl was doing with a man like him."

"You wouldn't understand, Inspector," Emma said, grinning.

"Whatever," he said dismissively. "By the way, why did you say, 'the whole house is the clue?'" Boateng asked her.

"It has an unfinished feeling," Emma said. "The two empty bedrooms, unfilled spaces."

"And so?"

"You know how in Accra you see buildings in an uncompleted state because the owner ran out of money? I felt the house was like that, only inside."

"Meaning?"

"Maybe Femi and Ngozi were living beyond their means. What if he had swindled someone in Nigeria? So, he and his girl-friend flee to Ghana to escape retribution and start renting this apartment with the stolen money. Some of it goes to the six- or twelve-months' rent in advance, and the rest for the two vehicles. But funds are running low now, so they postpone furnishing the two smaller bedrooms. Meanwhile, his enemies in Nigeria track him down and kill him."

Boateng turned out his bottom lip as he considered Emma's hypothesis. "Could be so, but I'll bet you Femi's murderer is local. He was living in Accra then, and is living here now."

PART TWO

CHAPTER TEN

FEMI ADEBANJO WAS ONE-QUARTER Ghanaian. The rest was Nigerian. Among the Ghanaians who flocked to Nigeria looking for work in the oil industry was a young Kojo Agyekum, who married a Yoruba woman, Simi. Kojo was content for the moment to remain in Nigeria. Kojo and Simi's daughter, Modupe, wedded a Nigerian called Tunde Adebanjo. Together, they had Femi and his baby sister, Charlotte. Tunde, cursed with sickle cell disease, had suffered sickle crises all his life. They were excruciating, and one killed him when he was only forty-two. Femi was eight at the time. Without Tunde to help raise the kids, Modupe sent Femi to Grandpa Kojo and Grandma Simi to discipline, describing Femi as a bad child she simply couldn't handle.

He was sixteen when he first fell into serious trouble. He tried to pickpocket an old man in Benin City's Ugbighoko Market on Ekenwa Road, and got caught. In Nigeria, or Ghana, for that matter, no one grabs you by the ear to march you off to the police station. Vigilante justice is much faster and more effective. In any case, the police would take the same action and beat you senseless.

Femi survived with a busted lip and a face so bruised and swollen that his eyes were like slits. It took him three weeks to return to normal. His friend Cliffy, older than Femi by two years, laughed at the story and called Femi an idiot. "That's not how you pickpocket. I need to teach you. Anyway, it's much better to work in pairs."

Cliffy schooled him in some techniques, and they began to work together picking pockets in the city's markets, and they did well until they tried to take a wallet from a guy who turned out to be an off-duty policeman. Cliffy escaped and disappeared as if into the ether, but the policeman had Femi, who suffered the second severe thrashing of his young life.

This time, he was thrown into a jail full of grown men, including a madman who conversed incessantly to himself. Femi was the only boy there. The police never officially charged him, but they detained him for seven days and gave him a daily whipping to teach him a lesson.

But far from this experience reforming Femi, it hardened him instead, and he withdrew into a tough, protective shell. His father had been dead for years and Femi's mother had given him up practically for good. Femi was out of the house all day and most of the night. He graduated from pickpocketing to purse-snatching, robbery, and burglary.

For a second time, the police caught and arrested him, and at the young age of seventeen, Femi went to jail for eight years at the overcrowded and bedbug-infested Kirikiri medium-security prison. The three meals a day, if you could even call them that, were awful. The best part of the day was in the afternoon when inmates could exercise and play soccer in a large, dusty yard. But at the dreaded hour, they had to return to the cells for the evening count, stuffed into a hot, sweaty space designed for half the number of the extant population.

From the choices of vocational training offered, Femi chose painting and joined a "Beautify Your Prison" initiative that spruced up the place with new colors. The third week of his training, Femi noticed a new inmate who was painting a spot on the wall of one of the cell blocks. He was so small; his physique was more like a boy's. The supervising prison officer was yelling at him for his lousy technique. In Femi's assessment, though, it wasn't that the newcomer couldn't do the job if he had wanted to, he just wasn't interested.

During a short break from painting, Femi went over to the small, quiet man who was sitting alone in a corner of the yard reading a tattered Bible.

"You don't like to paint," Femi said to him.

The man looked up. "No."

Introducing himself, Femi sat down next to him. "What's your name?"

"Kayode."

"What are you reading?"

"The Epistle of Paul to the Galatians."

That meant nothing to Femi, but he grunted and nodded. "You read the Bible every day?"

"Yes."

"Why?"

Kayode looked off into the distance. "For inspiration and peace in the Lord. And I'm also studying for the ministry because I will become a Catholic priest when I leave this place."

Femi squinted at him. "When will that be? How long is your sentence?"

"Six years," Kayode said, "but I'll be out long before then."

"Like how?"

"Because I didn't do the crime they claim I did. My uncle is a lawyer and he's working on my case to get me out of here."

Femi didn't comment, but Kayode's assertions didn't impress him. Most inmates denied their alleged crimes and the fantasy of "getting out early" practically never happened. "Can you become a priest if you've been in prison?"

"Yes."

"Are you sure?" Femi said askance.

"I'm positive."

"Okay." Femi stared at him for a moment. "What is your favorite part of the Bible?"

"The Gospel of John says, 'Beloved, let us love one another, because love is of God; everyone who loves is begotten by God and knows God. Whoever is without love does not know God, for God is love.'"

"So, do you love everyone here?"

"No, but I try to. The Lord does not cast you away if you fail, only if you stop trying."

"Okay," Femi said, getting up. "I take your word for it."

AFTER A LUNCH of overcooked spaghetti, Femi joined a soccer team for a match. He noticed Kayode at the side of the yard ostensibly reading his Bible, but he appeared distracted by the game. More specifically, he was clearly paying almost exclusive attention to Femi.

His team scored a goal, and while they jubilated and teased the opposing side, Femi caught something in his peripheral vision and turned his full attention to it.

Two inmates had approached Kayode, apparently to start up a conversation. Femi knew one of them—they called him Rufus—but not the other. Rufus smacked the back of Kayode's head. As he tried to duck away, the other inmate slapped him from the opposite side and snatched Kayode's Bible away. Then Rufus and his fellow bully began to taunt Kayode with the come-and-get-it game. Each time the little man reached for his Bible at their urging, they pulled it away or tossed it to each other, all this with a mocking cackle of laughter.

"Wait, I'm coming," Femi said to his teammates.

He walked over to Kayode and tapped Rufus on the shoulder. He turned, startled to find Femi standing chest-to-chest with him.

"*Wetin* you dey do?" Femi asked, so close that Rufus took a half-step back.

"Oh, no *wahala*, boss," Rufus said lightly but nervously. "Just playing."

Femi closed his left hand around Rufus's neck and forced him to back up. "*Na so?* Did he ask you to play with him?"

Rufus, trying to escape Femi's grasp, didn't respond.

"Try harder," Femi said. "Aren't you a man? *Fight!*"

Rufus swung his fists, but they didn't reach the target.

Femi socked him in the middle of his face, smashing his nose. "I'm just playing with you, okay?"

He hit him again and Rufus let out a shriek, kicking and struggling as Femi battered his face with more punches. Very quickly, spectators gathered, for who didn't like a good fight?

Two prison guards showed up, yelling furiously. "*Hey!* Stop!"

They pulled Rufus and Femi apart. Rufus's nose and upper lip were pouring with blood.

"What is going on?" one of the wardens thundered.

"He and his friend were attacking Kayode," Femi said.

"Fuck you!" Rufus said, from the safety of his position next to the guard. "It's a lie!"

The guards told the two men to shut up and ordered them to

opposite ends of the yard. If they ever fought again, strong disciplinary action would follow.

Since the soccer match had dissolved, Femi found some shade where he could relax. He had dozed off when Kayode appeared at his side. Femi squinted up at him.

"Thank you for what you did," Kayode said. "You saved me."

"Don't mention it," Femi replied. "Let me know if anyone worries you. I'll take care of it."

FEMI HAD SCOFFED at Kayode's prediction of early release, but one day, it really happened. Two years into Femi's sentence, Kayode's accuser retracted his story and confessed that he had lied. This almost never occurred. Kayode was now a free man. He was lucky that the slow, squeaky wheels of Nigerian justice had turned in his favor, because even this withdrawal of the accusation might have made no difference.

But Kayode and Femi never said goodbye to each other. Something upsetting had occurred one night, and in the morning, four fellow prisoners set upon Kayode and beat him almost to death. Thereafter, they moved him permanently to another section. The day they released the would-be priest, everyone was talking about it. To most inmates, Kayode's stroke of providence was but a dream.

Several times during the remainder of Femi's sentence, he wished for the same divine intervention Kayode had had, but nothing ever materialized. Femi supposed he wasn't enough of a believer for God to favor him.

FEMI'S DISCHARGE AFTER eight years fell on a Friday in November. As he emerged from Kirikiri with few possessions besides the clothes he was wearing, he didn't feel the joy he had been expecting, nor the desire to kiss the ground. With other just-released inmates, Femi joined a line to receive the paltry sum of money given to freed prisoners—enough to get them at least partway home. Femi hoped home would be Grandpa Kojo's apartment in Ikeja, the capital of Lagos State. He prayed his grandfather lived at the same place.

Femi, having had sufficient prison time to contemplate the folly of his past young life, now understood how appalling a miscreant he had been, and he was very sorry about it. Femi intended to ask Grandpa Kojo to forgive him. His grandfather had done his best to take care of Femi, who had rewarded him only with tribulation.

Ayodele, a bricklayer by trade and Femi's acquaintance while in prison, was interested in teaming up to find work, even if it consisted of transient day jobs for them. Ayodele planned to live temporarily with his sister, Sarah, and her kids in Ikeja, and although there was scarce space in their apartment, Ayodele offered to accommodate Femi overnight, because the hour was late. In the morning, Femi would go to his grandfather to live there.

SATURDAY MORNING, FEMI alighted from a *danfo* on Unity Road in Ikeja. The street was quiet by Lagos standards, the calm pierced by the guttural roar of a passing motorbike or the drone of an electricity generator. Femi took notice of some changes—more pharmacies and air-conditioned clothing stores and barbershops, and more satellite dishes on apartment balconies—there were almost no single-family homes—but the neighborhood had not transformed so much in his eight-year absence that he didn't still know his way around by heart. Some landmarks were as he remembered them, like the Celestial Church of Christ, whose congregants filled the air every Sunday morning with hymns.

After Muslim Avenue, the rusty gate at the entrance to Kojo's block of flats came up on Femi's left, as did the gutter clogged with trash and semi-solid muck. The gate, never locked, groaned loudly as Femi pushed it open. Inside the courtyard, a happy group of kids played soccer with an under-pumped ball. As Femi walked directly to ground floor apartment number three and knocked on the door he remembered so well, he felt both eager and nervous. After a few minutes and a second knock, a young woman holding a child on her hip opened the door. "Yes?"

"Good morning," Femi said. "Please, is Mr. Agyekum in?"

The woman frowned. "No one dey here by that name."

Femi, momentarily disoriented, glanced at the door of the neighboring apartment. Had he gotten the wrong one?

Sweeping the other side of the courtyard was a middle-aged woman with a traditional cloth wrapped around her plump body and folded above her breasts, leaving her shoulders exposed. She stopped and looked up. "Is that you, Femi?"

He turned, searching his memory. "Ei, Auntie Mary! How far na?"

She smiled. "I dey, o! E don tey."

"Yes, Auntie," Femi said, approaching her. The door to apartment number three slammed shut behind him. "Grandpa Kojo no dey?"

Mary turned her bottom lip out and shook her head. "E don travel Ghana some six months now."

"*Na so!*" Femi felt shattered. "When e go come back?"

"Oh, sorry," Mary said. "E tell me say he no go come for Nigeria again. But e don give me letter make I give am to you. Wait, please."

She rested her broom against the wall and went into her apartment, emerging two minutes later with a grubby envelope, which she handed to Femi.

"Thank you." Femi hurriedly opened the envelope to find Kojo's short letter.

Dear Olufemi,

Since you are reading this letter, it means you are out of prison, thanks be to God. I wanted to see you before I returned to my homeland, but you know, I'm old now, and time is not on my side. Grandma Simi has died and Charlotte is now abroad with her oyibo husband, and so I feel very alone. My sister, your Auntie Gladys, has been begging me to come home now that Grandma has died, so I am leaving Nigeria to live with her in Accra. Please, try to visit me in Accra, after all, you have Ghanaian blood in your veins. Please call me at Auntie Gladys's number below.

Love,
Grandpa Kojo

The scribbled phone number underneath Kojo's signature was tricky to read. What looked like a five could also have been a six. In any case, Femi didn't have a phone.

"Oh, okay," Femi said, reading the letter one more time as dejection swept over him. He tried to smile cheerfully at Mary. "Thank you very much, Auntie."

On the street once again, he experienced profound sadness. He felt as if Kojo had been snatched away and feared that his grand-father's death was imminent. Femi had no means, financially or otherwise, of getting to Ghana and worried he might never see his grandfather again.

Despondent, Femi returned to Ayodele with his tail between his legs. He was imposing on Sarah, and she wasn't happy about it. Femi felt she resented him for being an ex-convict—maybe even him *and* Ayodele. It was an ugly feeling that kept him awake for a long time as he lay on a thin floor mat and stared into the inky darkness.

CHAPTER ELEVEN

AYODELE AND FEMI STUCK together, grabbing any temporary work they could find no matter how much or little they earned. After two months, they were able to scrape together enough funds to rent a room in a decrepit building, and just in time to forestall an explosive chemical reaction between Femi and Ayodele's sister, who had taken a blatant disliking to him. The feeling was mutual.

Keeping his history of incarceration a tightly guarded secret, Ayodele had been fortunate enough to secure a job with a building contractor. Remaining friends, he and Femi struck out on different employment paths. While Ayodele's work was steady, Femi's was intermittent and less predictable. Even so, as the Christmas season arrived, Femi was thankful for what little he had. He had bought a cheap phone, life's second-most-important prerequisite after accommodation.

At the beginning of the new year, he landed a substantial painting job when a previous client recommended him to a business owner who had just completed an addition to her home. When Femi arrived, he stared in awe at the peach-colored mansion with white, towering columns. He estimated the house contained at least eight bedrooms. The guesthouse he was about to paint inside and out contained two. Sitting in the four-car garage were a Bentley, Range Rover, and Femi's all-time favorite, a Mercedes-Benz.

Approximately one hour after Femi had begun work, the business owner stepped out of her house and into the Bentley as her chauffeur stood to attention and held the door open for her. Femi felt an extraordinary mixture of envy, a powerful desire to be that rich, and ire that he wasn't. The feeling stayed with him throughout the day and until he returned home. Still awake as Ayodele slept, Femi contemplated his condition and how he might rise above it and soar. He found no immediate answer, but he knew he had to seek one.

ON A NIGHT in February, Femi and Ayodele were watching a soccer match on TV at one of the nearby drinking bars when Femi's phone lit up with a WhatsApp notification that someone was inviting him to chat. For a moment, he was incredulous. It was his old *paddi* Cliffy. Femi responded immediately.

> Cliffy? E don tey! I dey get different phone now, so I don lose all my contacts. How far?
> I dey o!
> Where you dey live now?
> I dey Benin City. You just disappear. Wetin happen?
> Remember when you dey go to your town? Around that time, I go rob one guy na so dem catch me and send me to Kirikiri for eight years.
> *Fuck!* Eight years!
> Yeah, na November I comot
> Na so? So wetin you dey do now?
> Na painter work I dey manage.
> How dat one dey go?
> E be okay. And you?
> Travel agent.
> Na waa! Nice one
> You dey Lagos?
> Yeah, bros
> Make you come Benin City, naa?
> Hmm, money no dey, bros
> I go mo-mo you for the journey
> Na so? So you get money now!
> Haha, you too fit get some. When you go come?
> Make I finish one painting job wey I dey do now then I go tell you the time wey I go come

As Femi and Ayodele walked home together, Femi thought his friend was quieter than usual. When Ayodele did speak, he was hesitant and sounded almost apologetic. Sarah had found a larger apartment, but she couldn't afford it on her own. Thus, the plan was for Ayodele, Sarah, and the kids to move to the new place at the beginning of the next month.

"Okay," Femi said. "I'm happy for you."

Ayodele was surprised. He had expected Femi to feel angry and betrayed.

"Me too, I go move by March or April," Femi explained, "I go go Benin City to stay with my *paddi*—the one I told you about."

Ayodele laughed with relief. Their friendship was still intact.

ON APRIL FOOLS' Day, Femi made the trek from Lagos to Benin City not in a rickety *danfo*, but through Cliffy's generosity, in a comfortable, air-conditioned bus. Femi left at seven in the morning and arrived in Benin City just before noon.

Cliffy met him at the lorry station. They embraced, glad to see each other and to have reestablished contact. First, they went to a small place called Feedwell Restaurant on Oghogho Street. Femi, ravenous by now and thankful Cliffy was paying for their meal, ordered goat *egusi* soup with pounded yam, while Cliffy had pepper soup with *swallow*. Cliffy was married now and had a little girl, but he had left her and his wife behind in Lagos. He had a new, spiky hairstyle, and Femi noticed how his friend, albeit still on the thin side, had put on just the right amount of weight and looked good with it. Wearing an olive-and-black track suit, he had a new air of confident sophistication. Never having heard the full story of Femi's arrest, detention, and imprisonment, Cliffy was curious to know what had happened. Then, Femi told him about Kirikiri—the overcrowded conditions, the infernal bedbugs, and perhaps worst of all, the barely edible food.

To the contrary, the meal they were relishing now was beyond sumptuous.

"You dey look good, my *paddi*," Femi said. He couldn't wait any longer. "So, how dat your job dey go—you say travel agent?"

Cliffy slurped up some soup and licked his plump lips. "I be agent, wey I dey help dem who wan' travel go Europe for work. I dey tell dem say dem go go Italy make good money for fashion or work for person shop, or babysit for rich Italian or German."

"So dem dey get Europe job easy like dat, *abi?*"

Cliffy shot Femi a look of amusement with condescension. "*Abeg*, Femi. Dem no go get job like dat at all-at all. When dey reach Europe, dem go go to a madam who dey make dem do *ashawo* work for her to pay back money wey dem dey owe."

"How dey come enter debt like this, *naa?*"

"Because na the madam pay the *kishi* wey dem use come from Libya to Italy."

Femi was still a little confused. "*Wetin* be dat Libya?"

"Bro, from there, di migrant dem go pass di sea, follow di water to Italy."

"*Na so?* So, from Nigeria how dem go go to Libya?"

"From Kano to Agadez, Niger; then to Sabha in Libya; then Tripoli."

"*Na* dangerous, the journey, *abi?*"

"Very dangerous, *oga*. Dem dey die on di way. Armed robber se'f dey worry dem. But no be our *wahala*."

"But when you dey tell dem say the journey dey hard, dem no dey fear?"

"I dey tell dem," Cliffy said, sucking his fingers and shrugging, "but still dem wan' go."

"So how much dem dey pay you?"

Cliffy had annihilated his meal and was rinsing his fingers in clean water in the bowl provided. "For one migrant, I dey take between one thousand and one five. US dollar."

Femi gave a chuckle, but then saw the dead seriousness on Cliffy's face. "You dey make joke, *abi?*"

"I no dey joke, bros."

Femi gasped as he quickly converted it to naira. "And how much client wey you dey get for one month?"

"Like . . . four."

If each client paid twelve hundred dollars, and each month supplied conservatively three clients, that added up to more than forty thousand a year.

"But listen well-well," Cliffy warned. "You must work hard for di money. E no dey easy at all-at all."

"*Na so?*"

"Every day you go dey recruit, recruit, recruit, because you no *sabi,* some of dem go say dem go pay today, but tomorrow dem go yarn different story. Dem dey fall your hand all the time, so you too, you gats to hustle well-well, you get me?"

Femi nodded soberly, but he was still stunned and couldn't get his mind off that staggering sum of money.

"So," Cliffy continued, "e don tey wey I know you, so I dey trust you well-well. Na becos of dat, I say make we work together, maybe each month we go dey get seven or eight migrant."

Incredible. Femi gazed at Cliffy for a long moment and then leaned forward to embrace him. "Thank you, bros. Thank you."

CLIFFY'S APARTMENT, SPACIOUS by Lagos standards, had a cozy kitchen, one bedroom, and an adjoining bathroom. The sitting room was as messy as an infant's bib at feeding time. Discarded plastic bags, empty beer bottles, shoes, clothing, and ashtrays with marijuana remains marred what was otherwise a fine dwelling. A laptop sat open on an all-purpose table by the rear window, which looked out onto the next uninspired apartment block. That Cliffy was paying the rent single-handedly meant to Femi that his friend was doing well. It wasn't just empty boastfulness.

"*Wetin* be dat?" Femi asked, pointing at a bulky object underneath a blue plastic sheet on the floor in the bedroom.

Cliffy flipped up the sheet to reveal a safe with a digital lock. "I dey keep my money here," he said. "You go get one too."

Femi subdued a powerful desire to see just how much cash Cliffy had tucked away in that safe. They sat on the sofa and drank beer. Femi was eager to learn about Cliffy's "travel agency," which he had begun three years into Femi's sentence. At the time, Cliffy had struck up a friendship with a group of Yahoo boys taking advantage of girls who wanted to travel to Ghana for work. The prevailing belief was that jobs were easier to find in Ghana than in Nigeria, and true or not, that gave the Yahoo boys leverage.

Then, a cousin of Cliffy's asked him if he knew a way to get to Europe via North Africa. Cliffy knew nothing about it, so he asked his friends if they could manage it. This was their first experience in getting someone to a destination outside of

West Africa. As they worked on it, Cliffy acted as a go-between for his cousin. In that way, he saw the mechanics of making such complicated arrangements while learning from his friends' mistakes.

Cliffy's cousin did make it eventually to Germany, which Cliffy found exciting. He had helped someone achieve her goal and had made a little money with his finder's fee. Now Cliffy had tasted of the fruit, and it was very good—too good to turn away from.

He asked his cousin to call up her friends to tell them it had been Cliffy who had gotten her to Europe, and he could do the same for anyone else. Cliffy knew testimonials were the most powerful persuaders, and he cannily used that technique to steadily grow his clientele. Now, he had almost too much of a good thing.

"I no fit handle so many customers, Femi," Cliffy said. "So e be good time for make you join me. I know you, you know me, so we go be good partners."

"Yes, yes," Femi agreed.

"Good." Cliffy swept a small pile of clothes off a chair and pulled it up to the table with the laptop. "Have a seat, now. I go show you how I dey do dis business. But first, make I tell you the most important thing wey you should never to forget."

"*Wetin* be dat?"

"Truth never sell; only lies, you *sabi?*"

Femi wasn't sure he did. "Dat mean to say . . ."

"In times past," Cliffy said, "I dey tell people traveling to Europe from Nigeria, dem go have tough time cross the desert from Niger to Libya, and so some of dem dey fear and decide not to go. Then I realize I no get sense! If you go sell your car, for 'zample, you no go tell di buyer the engine no dey work well, *abi?*"

Femi grinned. "You dey talk true."

"Yeah, so now if someone dey ask me about that desert thing, I tell dem say, no be bad at all, the journey."

"Dat desert na dangerous, *abi?*"

"You no *sabi?* People dey die there, *oga!*"

"*Na so?*"

"Yeah," Cliffy said gravely. "No be easy, o! Make I show you everything on my laptop concerning this work. I call my company Cliffy Travels. If you like, we go call am Cliffemi Travels."

Femi laughed and high-fived his friend. "I like it."

His future was looking brighter than it had in a long while.

CHAPTER TWELVE

APART FROM CLIFFY'S APHORISM that in this business, "lies sell; truth doesn't," Femi found he had a lot to learn. It became clear to him that this kind of work wasn't a sitting-around-doing-nothing matter. Like Cliffy, Femi had to search *every day* for potential clients to keep cash flow steady, instead of coming in peaks and valleys. In some cases where the payoff was substantial, other clients could drop in importance. One of Cliffy's clients had paid him five thousand dollars to travel by air illegally from Nigeria to Europe. With that amount of money on the table, Cliffy had put some of his clients on hold to concentrate on the tricky and expensive business of creating a false identity, passport, and visa. That story alone gave Femi a fair idea how much money Cliffy might have in his safe.

For six weeks, Femi shadowed Cliffy, who handed over two ongoing projects from which Femi could gain experience. Each was a case of Nigerian girls who wanted to get to Accra to avail themselves of Ghana's widely touted employment opportunities. Femi learned about one essential step the girls had to fulfill before embarking on their journey: a visit to a traditional priest for an elaborate ritual involving the sacrifice of a goat or chicken, and a warning from the priest that if they strayed in any way from their commitment to pay all required fees, or, if on their arrival in Ghana they didn't like their assigned job and they attempted to abandon it, the gods would smite them with illness or death. The gravitas and eeriness of the ceremony was more than enough to strike fear into the girls.

Femi was thrilled as the cash slowly but steadily began to flow like a rivulet gathering strength and volume, and he became thirsty for more. But then it was time for him to attempt his first independent recruitment job, and one night he took up Cliffy's challenge to land the most lucrative endeavor: setting up a migration to Europe.

Nine the following morning, Femi loitered nonchalantly around Benin City's Ugbighoko Market as he looked out for customers who appeared most approachable. His attempts were amateurish, and the women he attempted to engage all rejected him, looking at him like the hustler he really was.

Recent rains had left the ground sodden and messy and the air oppressive. Feeling deflated, he found some shade and wiped his sweat-drenched face and neck. As he watched the bustle and clamor of the place, he realized he was doing it all wrong. He'd been going up to busy shoppers who had no time to listen to him. They weren't a captive audience; they were an *escaping* one. Instead, he should have been talking to the sellers, since they wouldn't be going anywhere for a while. He had an idea. He walked to the other end of the market, where he found men's clothing. He passed by different kiosks, keeping an eye out without appearing to. As the number of stalls began to fade, he saw a gem of a girl folding shirts alongside an older woman Femi guessed was her mother.

Femi greeted them and smiled, telling them he was looking for a dress shirt.

"Something like this," he said, pointing to one hanging from the top rail of the stall. "Is that the only one?"

"We have more in the back," the girl said.

"Can you show me?"

"Sure, come around."

He skirted the counter and followed her to the rear part of the stall, where they found a greater selection.

"I like this one," Femi said, picking up a golden shirt with traditional embroidery around the neck. "Can I try it?"

"Of course," she said.

"Please, what's your name?"

"I'm Bisola," she said. "And you?"

"Femi. Did you know you're very beautiful?"

She smiled and looked away bashfully. "Thank you."

"How old are you?"

"Twenty."

"Do you have a boyfriend?"

"Yes please."

Femi let out a raspy breath in mock regret. "Then I'm too late? Is that what you're trying to tell me?"

They both laughed and Femi took off his T-shirt, showing off his muscles without any modesty whatsoever. He caught her looking.

"So, is that your mom?" he asked her before pulling on the trial garment.

"Yes," she said.

"Like mother, like daughter. She's also beautiful."

"Aw, thank you so much, Femi. You can use this mirror over here to see yourself."

Femi checked his reflection. "Let me try the blue one, there. I need a large, please."

Bisola looked through the pile until she found the correct size.

"How long have you been working with your mom?" Femi asked. With some nervousness, he was slowly warming up to the topic.

"About two years. I was going to finish high school until she told me I should come and help her."

"Oh, that's good but . . . you've missed your schooling."

She shrugged. "What can you do. Do you like that one?"

"Just hold it for me, then I will decide. Did you want to go to university too? You seem like someone who would do well."

"If I had the chance, of course I would go, but I need to help the family, especially since my father has gone—where, I don't even know."

"And how is business?" Femi asked, looking through more choices of shirts.

Bisola shook her head. "No money is circulating in the country and no one is buying."

Femi nodded his head in sympathy. "E no dey easy at all-at all. So, with all this going on, how do you see yourself in, say, five years?"

Bisola took a deep breath and let it out. "To be honest, I don't know."

"What would you say if I told you there's a way you can have your own hair salon, beauty shop, or clothing shop, make enough money to have your own apartment, and support yourself and your family?"

"I would say you're a liar," she said, laughing.

Femi laughed too, but only briefly. "But what I say is true. For example, I have friends in Italy, Germany, and Holland who have made a lot of money. They make enough to live a very nice life and still have money left over to support Mom and the rest. Some of them are business owners, tourist agents—all kinds of things."

"Really?" she said, her skeptical gaze fixed on him. "But you must have money to go to those places."

"It's not a matter of money, it's whether you really want it or not."

"But . . . how do you go there—to Italy?"

"From Nigeria is no problem. From Kaduna State in northern Nigeria, you go to Agadez, Niger—not too far. After that you will cross the desert to get to Libya, which is only a couple of days, and then you will go across the sea in a boat to Italy."

"What about . . . I mean, you need some documents to pass through, right?"

"Oh, you don't have to worry about documents," Femi said. "That you can always get. Let's look for more shirts. I want a different style."

Bisola held one up. "What about this? Do you like it?"

"It's not bad, but I want one with a collar."

"Okay, let me look," she said. "Who is the one who will help you get the papers to go to Italy?"

"Me and my *paddi* have that business."

"Is that so?" Bisola said with tentative curiosity.

"If you give me your contact, I can start making the arrangements for you."

She laughed nervously. "You act as though I've told you I want to go."

"You haven't told me, but I can see it in your eyes. They are shining."

She giggled. "Liar."

"It's true."

"How much to go there?"

"It's just twelve hundred dollars—around six hundred thousand

Nigerian naira—for the transportation and documents and all that."

"*Na waa!*" she said, aghast. "That's too much money."

Femi locked her eyes into his gaze. "Are you saying you're not worth it?"

"Of course not, but . . ."

"Let me ask you something. Does your family care about you?"

"Yes," she said at once.

"So why wouldn't they make a one-time investment in your future—and *their* future too—so you can leave this focking Nigeria to a good life in Italy or Germany."

"Hmm," she said, looking away in contemplation. "I'm not sure what they will say about this idea."

Femi took out his phone. "Let me get your number and I'll flash you."

She recited it and he buzzed her.

"Okay, I have it now," she said. "But, Mr. Femi, what about if my boyfriend wants to go with me?"

"Sure. In fact, I recommend that, so you can support each other."

"And he will also pay you six hundred thousand? *Ei*, it's too much! Bring down the price small." Bargaining was in every Nigerian's DNA. "I think four hundred thousand is okay."

"What about this?" Femi said, brightening. "For the two of you together, I can make it one million naira, last price," Femi said.

"I see," she said. His 200,000-naira discount had her thinking. "What's your boyfriend's name?"

"Kehinde."

"Nice."

"Then maybe I will call you," Bisola said.

"I would love to hear your sweet voice."

She was pleased at that. "Which shirt do you like?"

"I'll take the gold one after all."

"Fine."

They haggled over the price, and then Bisola folded it nicely and slipped it into a plastic bag.

"Thank you, Bisola. Call me, okay?"

"I will."

In the evening, Kehinde often came by to help Bisola and "Mama"—as he called her—put things away and close for the day. Kehinde, twenty-two, and Bisola were childhood sweethearts and they planned to get married soon, which meant in a year or two. By that time, God willing, Kehinde would have found new employment. He had lost his job at an electronics store, and now he spent his days searching in vain for work. It was discouraging, but Kehinde wasn't about to give up. He desperately wanted to have a full-time job by the time he became Bisola's husband and certainly by the birth of their first child. He would feel mortified if the baby in his arms looked up to see an unemployed father.

They went off together to the Market Square Mall on Sapele Road, holding hands and speaking in Yoruba and Pidgin. It was while they were people-watching in the mall that Bisola told Kehinde about Femi and how he claimed he could get them to Europe.

Kehinde laughed and shook his head. "And you believed him? Oh, sweetie, you're so naive!"

"But it's true people have been going to Europe from Nigeria," Bisola pointed out.

"Yes, but they have the money and passport and visa and all that."

"It won't be flying—it's by road."

Kehinde was momentarily derailed, but he got back on track. "But be careful with these people who tell you this stuff. They can easily trick you. Unless this guy can show me evidence of people who have gone to those places, Italy and Germany, or whatever, I don't think we should even pay attention."

"What if this is a real opportunity, Kehinde?" Bisola asked. "I could finish my schooling and go to fashion school and everything. And you want to be a business executive. There are so many opportunities there for us. I mean, seriously, life in Nigeria is shit. Look at you, unemployed for almost a year. You, who even went to university, can't find work? What kind of nonsense is that?" She cheupsed and shook her head with frustration.

Kehinde was silent a moment. "You have his contact info?"

"Yes, I'll send it to you right now on WhatsApp."

"We'll call him, but if he starts talking shit, we won't mind him again."

FEMI WAS DRINKING beer with Cliffy and had just told him about Bisola when she called. Femi gave a thumbs-up to his friend.

"*Na waa*, Bisola!" Femi exclaimed. "I'm so glad to hear from you. How are you doing?"

"I'm good. But you remember I told you I had a boyfriend?"

"Yes, and remember how sad I was when I found out you were already spoken for?"

She giggled. "You dey joke. But seriously, I was telling him about you and he didn't believe that this is a real thing."

"Most people don't—that is until they arrive in Italy and get their first rent-free apartment."

"Rent-free? Like how?"

"They have a system where, if you are an immigrant, you can live in an apartment for three months without paying rent until you find a job, and everyone finds a job by that time."

Femi glanced up at Cliffy, who nodded his approval.

Bisola paused. "Please, I have Kehinde here. Can you talk to him?"

"Of course. I would love to." He covered the phone's mic and whispered to Cliffy, "The boyfriend wants to speak to me."

"Put it on speaker. Tell him I'm your associate."

"Hello? Yes, Kehinde? How are you?"

"Fine," he said. "Em, Bisola was telling me something about you, so I want to know more. What is this Europe thing all about?"

"Do you mind if I put it on speaker so we can include my business partner?"

"It's cool."

"Kehinde," Femi said, "this is all about achieving what you want in life. Are you satisfied with your life?"

Kehinde snickered. "In Nigeria? Not at all."

"And what is stopping you from getting what you want?"

There was a pause. "The system. Everywhere you turn in Nigeria, you go down a road leading to nowhere."

"Eh-heh! Now you're getting it. You will fight all your life and go down hundreds of blind alleys, and one day you'll be an old man looking back on everything and asking yourself why you didn't seize the opportunities when they came to you."

"Yes, that's all well and good, but if you don't have proof to show me of these people you say are so successful in Europe, how do I know you won't just take our money?"

Cliffy chipped in. "Kehinde, my name is Cliffy; I work with Femi. It's nice to talk to you. We like customers like you because you ask good questions and you are very careful. So, yes, it's true: If we don't show you the evidence, then how can you believe us? Well, I can tell you we do have a lot of material to show you, if only you'll be patient and make some time for us."

"Oh. Okay." Kehinde sounded surprised, now on the back foot.

"You're at the mall, right?" Cliffy said. "I can hear the noise. If you like, Femi can meet you there tomorrow evening around six o'clock so he can show you everything."

"Okay, that's fine."

"Thank you, my brother. See you tomorrow."

CHAPTER THIRTEEN

FEMI TREATED BISOLA AND Kehinde to soft drinks, and they sat together at the food court in a booth with Femi facing his guests. This was his first presentation, so albeit a trifle nervous, he felt reassured by the practice he'd had with Cliffy, who would have accompanied him had he not had his own appointment with a potential client.

Femi looked sharp in a tight-fitting shirt and tie.

"So different from when I saw you at the market," Bisola commented.

"It's because I'm coming directly from the office."

"Where is that?" Kehinde asked, maybe a little suspiciously.

"We're on Victoria Island—Cliffemi Travels, from combining my name with that of my partner Cliffy."

"VI, really?" Kehinde said. VI was where rich people lived. "How long in business now?"

"Almost six years."

Kehinde nodded. "So, you have something to show us?"

"Yes," Femi said, "but first, let me explain a little how it works. I am your connection man. I arrange everything including transportation, documents, and so on. Each of you will pay me one thousand dollars. You won't need to pay anybody after that, okay?"

The other two nodded. Femi could feel their uneasiness—and their desperate hope that this was the real deal. He removed Cliffy's laptop from a faux leather satchel and placed it on the table so Bisola and Kehinde could see the screen. Femi brought up the slideshow. "This first picture shows my partner with one of our customers just before he left for Italy three months ago."

"And how is he doing now? The customer, I mean."

"You'll see," Femi said, chuckling. "Kehinde, your mind is

working too fast. The next one is a picture taken from the front of the bus our clients—and other people's clients too—used to travel across Nigeria's border with Niger. So, you can see it's quite comfortable. You don't need a visa between West African countries, but you must have personal identification. The security guys come onto the bus to check everyone, and then from there you will travel to Agadez.

"This is Agadez—you see, typical desert town, but the place is still nice. Well, it's not Lagos, but you can find all the necessities there. At Agadez, you will get down and write your name on the list so that when it's your turn to cross to Libya, they will call you."

"Libya?" Kehinde asked, frowning. "What is going on? First you say Italy, and now it's Libya?"

"Oh, sorry, sorry," Femi said hurriedly. "I should have explained. You get to Italy by crossing the sea from Tripoli in Libya."

"Wow," Kehinde said. "Is it by boat, or ship, or what?"

"Boat."

"A big one?"

Femi nodded. "It can hold about forty people."

"How long does someone stay there at Agadez and Tripoli?"

"It can be a week or so," Femi said. "It depends on how many people are waiting.

"But let's continue. You see here where the guys wait for their turn in a compound. Here's a pic of them having fun playing football. Next: this is one of the pickup trucks that takes the people."

The image they were looking at showed four men seated in the back of a Toyota Hilux pickup with their luggage and water supply.

"I thought the pickups were more crowded than that," Kehinde said. "I saw something on the internet."

"Formerly, yes," Femi said, "but nowadays it's much better, because less people are going to Europe. Some of those internet pics are old. Next is a picture of an oasis, one of the places you will stop along the way. It has fresh water and shelter from the heat.

"Next, you can see this picture of some of the guys in Libya waiting for their turn to cross the sea. It's the same like in Agadez. You just have to be patient."

"How will we eat?" Kehinde asked.

"Well, you should have cash on you at all times for food and drink, just like any place you travel," Femi said. "Now, when you get to Italy, you will tell the authorities there that you are a refugee fleeing persecution in Nigeria, and by law they can't deport you. You will stay at a reception center until they give you a work permit for three months."

Kehinde looked at Femi with incredulity. "Three months? Are you serious?"

Femi laughed. "*Na so!* Wait eh? Here is the best part. This is my friend Doris in Florence, Italy. She's a hairdresser and she owns her shop. She even got a loan from the government to buy it.

"Most of the people are from Nigeria, but this pic is of a Ghanaian guy—his name is Akuffo—who went to Rome, and he's now working at an auto parts store, but he's able to study at the same time and complete his master's degree."

Bisola and Kehinde exchanged smiles.

"Now, Germany is another good place," Femi continued. "They are richer than Italy. They say the roads there are so smooth you feel like you're floating in your car. This woman here is Osato from Edo State. She's a manager at a store where they make cakes and sweets. The Germans really like those places, so the business is always booming. Look at how happy she is in the store."

"Do they like Black people there?" Bisola asked.

Femi grunted. "They treat Black people there better than we treat each other right here in Nigeria. They don't have Boko Haram."

They laughed at the biting joke, which was funny, but not funny.

"The next slides are testimonials from some of our clients," Femi continued. "This guy, Ray M., says, 'Clifford and Femi treated me as if I belonged to their families, answered all my questions. They lived up to their promise.' Well, you can read them all for yourself." He paused to let them get through all the glowing testimonials.

"But don't you get complaints sometimes?" Kehinde probed. "Not everyone is going to like everything one hundred percent of the time, right?"

"One complaint is that the transport from Agadez takes too long," Femi responded, "but once you know to expect that, you'll be okay." He pointed at Bisola's empty glass. "Oh, would you like some more?"

"No, thank you—I'm good," Bisola said with her sweet smile. Femi felt a twinge of guilt with that smile, but then again, there was the prospect of two thousand dollars.

"But which one is better? Germany or Italy?" Kehinde asked.

"You know, Italy is the easiest to reach by sea, but once you're there, you can move to different European countries, and they won't ask you for any papers. So, some of our clients choose to go to Germany or Holland after Italy."

"What about the language?" Kehinde said, always with some searching question. "German, Italian, and what do they speak in Holland? Hollandish, or what?"

Femi grinned. "Dutch. Don't worry. All the European countries, especially Germany, give language lessons to immigrants so that you can pick it up in three months or less."

"Really?" Kehinde said, his amazement tinged with skepticism.

"Yeah," Femi said. "My *paddi*, things are still good right now, but they are tightening up the restrictions, so now is the time to go."

Bisola and Kehinde exchanged a good, long look. Then, Kehinde put his head back and heaved a long sigh. "I don't know," he muttered. "Two thousand dollars is a lot of money."

"What about you, Bisola?" Femi said. "How do you feel?"

"I want to go," she said forcefully and without hesitation. She turned to Kehinde and lowered her voice. "Baby, both of our families have been putting aside money for the wedding. We can use that."

Kehinde looked appalled. "You dey craze, Bisola?"

"No, wait," she persisted. "You se'f, you said you're not ready for marriage yet, so what is that money sitting there for, then? It doesn't make sense."

Kehinde, with no comeback to that, rested his head in his hands, torn by indecision.

Femi said to him, "Are you working right now?"

Kehinde shook his head miserably.

"You see?" Femi said. "You can't find a job in Benin City, and so what are you going to do now? Go to Ibadan? And then where after that? You can search the whole Naija and not find any work."

Kehinde clicked his tongue and looked away in frustration.

"You know, it's not many agents who will allow a couple to go together," Femi said.

"Really?" Bisola said. She looked back at Kehinde. "Babe, come on. We may never get a chance again."

Kehinde twirled his empty glass back and forth, his jaw working as he pondered the conundrum. "Okay," he said finally. "I'll discuss with my father about it and Bisola you can talk to Mom. Let's see what they say."

CHAPTER FOURTEEN

CLIFFY HAD SWUNG ANOTHER sweet deal in which a Nigerian man traveling to Europe was paying the required fee in American dollars, the best of all possible worlds. Femi watched Cliffy at the work table tallying his earnings and losses.

"So, now, *wetin* dey happen with Bisola and Kehinde?" Cliffy asked as he rose to take his cash to the safe.

Femi followed him to the doorway of the bedroom, where he was punching in his code on the safe's digital dial.

"I think say dem go pay me today," Femi said hopefully. Although he had pocketed some money from one of Cliffy's legacy cases, the transaction with Bisola and Kehinde promised a far greater chunk of cash. Five weeks had passed since Femi had first met the couple in July. During that time, Femi had kept in constant touch with them, an important component of the job, empathizing with them as they related how difficult it was proving to persuade their respective families to come up with the cash. Femi had continued to encourage Bisola and Kehinde to think about the *future*, not the now. The last to come around had been Kehinde's father, a civil servant who had worked at the same job for two decades. Now persuaded, he was financing a large portion of Femi's fee, promising to pay half of the total as soon as he was able, and then the rest later. Femi was anxious for that step to finalize, because it would lock Kehinde and Bisola into the agreement and make it difficult to back out.

Cliffy's phone rang from the sitting room. He hurried to answer it, leaving the safe door slightly open. Until this point, Femi hadn't had a glimpse inside that safe, and now he saw his chance.

But before he could make his move, Femi's phone, too, alerted. He smiled when he saw who was calling. "Grandpa!"

"How you dey, Olufemi?" Kojo's voice was as rough and grainy as coarse sand.

"I dey, o, Grandpa."

"Eh?" Kojo's hearing had deteriorated.

"I dey, Grandpa."

"When you go come see me?" Kojo said. "You go wait my funeral, *abi*?"

"Oh, no, Grandpa!" Femi exclaimed, both amused and horrified. "I go come, like dis year end, Christmastime."

"Oh, Olufemi," Kojo said, his voice betraying his profound disappointment. "You no go fit come before?"

Femi bit his bottom lip. "I no fit right now, Grandpa, but I go try."

"Okay, I dey wait you. Bye."

Grandpa Kojo never said very much on the phone. The main purpose of his calls was to find out when his grandson would be arriving in Ghana. Each succeeding day, Femi felt progressively more guilt-ridden that he hadn't seen his grandfather in so long, but right now, such a trip to Ghana wasn't possible. Not only was Femi still waiting for his ECOWAS passport application to go through, he wasn't financially steady yet.

Obviously chatting with family, Cliffy had flopped onto the sitting room sofa and was lying stretched out all the way. For the moment, he couldn't see Femi, who took the opportunity to quickly look inside the safe. Finding it stacked with naira, dollar, and euro bills, Femi suppressed a gasp. He wasn't sure what he had been expecting, but certainly not this astonishing amount of money.

Mentally reeling, he left the bedroom and sat down opposite Cliffy, who looked annoyed as he hung up his phone, shaking his head. He cheupsed and muttered, "Dis my family dey make *wahala* for me."

Femi murmured in commiseration, "E no dey easy at all-at all."

Cliffy sat up straight. "How your grandpa dey?"

"'Im dey o, but 'im talk say make I visit him soon before am die. I tell am say I no fit come now—maybe this year ending."

Clifford agreed. "*Na so.* Little by little."

That was a good cue for Femi. "Yeah, like one day we go fit buy six-bedroom house, *abi wetin* dey more on top your mind?"

"Benz," Cliffy said immediately. "Even two."

"Na Benz you dey save your money for?"

"Yeah, and soon I go fit buy brand-new one."

Now Femi understood the purpose of all that money in the safe. "Why you no go invest some money in another business?" he suggested.

Clifford raised his eyebrows. "Like *wetin*?"

"Like, for 'zample, *ashawo* hotel. Dis migration thing to Europe, di money dey good, but it takes long. Look at me se'f, see how I dey wait for Bisola and Kehinde. *Ashawo* house, di money dey flow day and night."

Clifford nodded. "I 'gree. Maybe one day."

Femi was coming to understand a fundamental difference between him and Cliffy: Femi had far more drive than his friend.

"But for the prostitution," Clifford added, "Ghana make betta than Naija, o."

"*Na so?*"

"Yeah. Ghanaian prostitutes fit charge two times more than Nigerian."

"Interesting. How you know dat kain info?"

"I dey talk to one madam in Accra last year," Cliffy said. "Wait, I dey come."

He grabbed his phone began a search through his phone book. "She get plenty girls wey dem work for her, so maybe we go fit talk to her about doing business with her." He scrolled through his contacts list. "Aha, here. Her name is Madam Janet Glover. I dey send the number now-now."

The contact information arrived on Femi's phone. *Janet Glover.* Who was this woman? Femi intended to find out.

PART THREE

CHAPTER FIFTEEN

WHEN JANET GLOVER WAS fifteen and about to enter senior high school, a boy raped and impregnated her behind a shed at the Accra Arts Center. Teenage pregnancy, the commonest reason for girls to drop out of school, obliterated Janet's chances of continuing her education.

Her father, who had borne tremendous pride over his girl doing so well in school, was at first horrified by the news, and then livid. "How could you be so *stupid?*" he shouted at her as she wept.

During Janet's pregnancy, her extreme and protracted nausea and vomiting rendered her sick and weak. What people had claimed about "morning sickness" lasting only three months was all a lie, as far as she was concerned. Neither doctor-prescribed nor traditional medicines alleviated her misery, leading Janet's father to accuse her of faking her symptoms just to get attention.

At the end of a tortuous nine months, Janet gave birth to a boy she christened Ben-Kwame. Janet got back into school at her parents' urging, but her will had evaporated. She didn't appear to apply herself even in the least bit and failed every subject. The school expelled her.

Janet's mother sold fruits and vegetables at a kiosk near a gas station on Liberation Road. She asked Janet to help with the vending, because Janet's father had begun to complain that she was contributing no money to the household. He threatened to kick her out if she didn't get a job soon.

But what job? Easier said than done. Janet tried to establish herself as an itinerant vendor selling food and merchandise to would-be customers trapped in Accra's immoveable traffic, but the profit margins were tiny and Janet suffered excruciating headaches at the end of each day from carrying hefty loads of merchandise on her head. After a couple of months, she gave up. Just before her eighteenth birthday, her father told her to pack her belongings, get out, and take her baby with her. Thinking he was joking, Janet expected her father to break out with an impish grin. When she realized he was dead serious, she began to weep. Janet's mother cried too, but she was powerless against her husband's decision. The best she could do was to plead with her mother, Thelma, to take Janet in.

Grandma Thelma said she would, but made it clear that Janet should provide for herself and her baby. The household had enough family to babysit Benjamin-Kwame while Janet went out in search of work. She hung around chop bars, motels, and guesthouses in the hope of picking up odd jobs. But she was no luckier than any other unemployed Ghanaian. No one hired in the absence of some personal connection to the employer. Most people Janet approached dismissed her before she had even finished her sentence. Finally, one would-be employer gave Janet a lead—someone called Queenie, who was recruiting for "night work."

Janet met Queenie off the busy Nsawam Road by the Vodafone office. The aroma of food from several restaurants on the opposite side of the street wafted over and doubled Janet's hunger pangs. She hadn't had a good meal in days.

Queenie was a small woman with a face deeply scarred by pockmarks her heavy makeup barely obscured.

"Have you done this kind of work before?" Queenie asked Janet. The way she pronounced "work" like "walk" gave away that she was Nigerian.

"Please, what kind of work?" Janet said.

Queenie frowned and beckoned to Janet to follow her to a quieter area next to a huge sinkhole where a parking space had once been.

Queenie folded her arms. "You can make fifty *cedis* for every customer. So, in one night if you have five customers, already you get two hundred and fifty."

Janet didn't understand. "Please, which customers is that?"

Queenie was showing her irritation now. "Do you even know why you're here or who I am?"

"They said you have night work."

"Yes, but what do you think that means? You're going to be engaging with men who pay you for your services."

Janet went blank for a second. Then she understood. "Oh. *Ashawo.*"

"Whatever you want to call it," Queenie said impatiently. "So, if you're interested, tell me, else I go my way, you go yours."

"Sorry," Janet stammered, taking a small, hesitant step back. "Sorry, please. I made a mistake."

Ashawo? Me? Mortified, she walked away quickly.

She returned home to find Ben sick with vomiting, diarrhea, and a fever. She decided to wait till morning, and if the boy was no better, she would take him to the doctor. Grandma Thelma was trying to get Ben to swallow a spoonful of a traditional antidiarrheal medicine called *boreadaso,* but he wasn't having it. He wouldn't take any fluids either.

Overnight, he didn't improve much, and in the morning, Janet got him ready to go to the clinic. She would have to pay to see the doctor and then purchase whatever medication they prescribed. There was one problem: she didn't have any money. Feeling humiliated, Janet asked Grandma for some funds.

Thelma grunted and pressed her lips together in disapproval. "You're lucky it's for your child."

"Thank you, Grandma," Janet said. "God bless you."

On the way to the clinic, she thought about her circumstances and felt anguish, helplessness, and desperation. She couldn't go on like this. She had to do something to be self-sufficient. Tears pricked her eyes like tiny needles. If she didn't get a job—and soon—she could see Grandma kicking her out of the house the same way her father had done.

Janet thought about Queenie. She was offering a job, and Janet would be a fool not to take it.

THE NEXT EVENING, completely uninitiated, she began sex work under Queenie's watchful and merciless eye. She ruled over fourteen girls, all Nigerians brought to Accra on the pretext that they could find jobs as restaurant servers or hairstylists. Should any of them fail to pay their dues, which was 80 percent of whatever they earned, Queenie informed them that they were all replaceable within minutes if she were to kick them out. Short of that, she used a bamboo cane to whip them for any infraction. Janet was never able to confirm a rumor that Queenie had stabbed one of her sex workers for not paying up, but it was credible.

The difference between Janet and the other sex workers was that she had family in Accra, where she could live; the Nigerian girls did not. Thus, Janet had lower living expenses. She was one of the most productive and industrious sex workers at the Alligator Hotel, and she was smart. Queenie rewarded her by giving her a post as assistant manager. Janet was so good at her job that she had risen to manager by the time she was thirty.

As Janet turned thirty-eight, the idea of owning the Alligator and taking over Queenie's position took hold in her mind and wouldn't go away.

And then, as if she had willed it, two unexpected developments took place: first, Queenie died from complications of the diabetes she had ignored for years; and second, Janet met a man called Mr. Awuni.

CHAPTER SIXTEEN

AWUNI PRINCE AWUNI HAD been a primary school teacher, an assistant in the Office of the President, a warehouse supervisor, a customs inspector, a manager at the Electricity Corporation of Ghana, and a clerk at the State Housing Company—the most chaotic and inefficient of them all. He had performed well enough in all of his positions but had found them uninspiring almost without exception.

Awuni got married when he was thirty-two and had two children. Beset with conflict, the marriage deteriorated and Awuni and his wife became estranged from each other. At fifty-four, Awuni decided to run for mayor of Accra.

ONE AFTERNOON, AS Awuni was campaigning in Jamestown, one of Accra's oldest neighborhoods, he spotted a woman who had just joined the sparse audience. Dressed in a white silk blouse and long, flowing maroon pants, she was tall, solidly built, and in her late thirties. The defined bony structure of her face gave her a look of determination, but her eyes softened that effect and held Awuni's attention. Distracted, Awuni accidentally dropped the piece of paper on which he had jotted down his talking points.

At the end of the campaign stop, he shook hands with a couple of Accra Metropolitan Association members and chatted briefly with some of his supporters. As he headed to his waiting car, he glanced around, looking for the woman he had seen in the crowd, but she had disappeared. He felt as if he had missed out on something—or someone—promising.

Joe, Awuni's driver, hastened to open the rear door of the

SUV for his boss, who climbed in and mopped his sweaty brow. The heat out there was brutal. The driver started up the Toyota, switched the air conditioner on full blast, and pulled away to return to campaign headquarters. As they passed Ussher Fort on their right, he saw the woman standing on the opposite side of the street, evidently looking to hail a taxi.

Awuni's heart leapt. "Stop the car. Stop, stop."

Joe pulled over.

"You see that woman?" Awuni said, pointing. "The one with the white blouse and somehow-red pants? Call her for me."

"Yes, sir." The driver hopped out and trotted over to where the woman was standing. Awuni watched as he spoke to her. She appeared uncertain for a moment, and then followed the driver back to the SUV. As Awuni's driver opened the rear door for the woman to get in, a blast of heat from outside fought briefly with the air conditioning.

She slid in beside Awuni and gave him a shy smile. "Good afternoon, Mayor Awuni."

"Good afternoon. I'm not quite there yet, but thank you."

"You will be, sir. I have confidence in you."

"I appreciate that." He studied her as Joe pulled into traffic again. "What's your name, my lovely one?"

"Janet."

"I've been waiting for you all my life."

"Oh, really." She smiled. "Why is that?"

"Everyone needs a soulmate. Am I right, Janet?"

"So they say."

"Have you found yours?"

"I'm not quite there yet," she echoed him.

They laughed and Awuni knew with certainty that he liked her.

"I'm returning to my campaign headquarters," he said, "but we can drop you wherever you like."

"I live in Lapaz."

"No problem. Joe, to Lapaz."

"Yes, sir."

"But what brings you to this part of town?" Awuni asked Janet.

"I came to visit a friend. I was on my way back from her place when I saw the rally going on, so I stopped to watch."

"I'm glad you did. Did you like my speech?"

"Yes, of course. I much prefer you to the other candidate."

"Nice," Awuni said. "Where do you work, or what do you do?"

"I'm the manager of a guesthouse in Lapaz."

"Interesting. What's the name of the place?"

"The Alligator."

Awuni nodded. "Is that the one owned by some old Nigerian guy?"

"Yes, although he bought it for his daughter, Queenie, but she's dead now."

"So then, what happened after Queenie died? Who's in charge now?"

"For the time being, I am. Queenie's father knew me well and he made me the acting boss."

Awuni gave a half-smile. "Good for you. How's business now?"

"Well, so-so," she said with some hesitation.

Awuni was quiet a moment. "I've passed the Alligator a few times. I'm sorry to say, it doesn't appear as inviting as I think it could be—or should be."

"I agree," Janet said, shifting her position so that she was facing him more directly. "But Queenie's father doesn't care. I mean, I'm sending him the hotel remittances, but he's looking to greater things. I heard he's doing business with some people in Dubai, now, so that's where he's putting all his energy. I think he wants to sell the Alligator."

Awuni was rubbing his chin in thought. "I'd like to talk to him, then."

"Are you looking to buy some property?"

"Yes," Awuni said, with an air of importance. "You know, I own one hotel in town, and I'm building another."

"Really!" Janet said, with admiration. "You own hotel property and you're running for mayor of Accra?"

Awuni chortled. "I've always done several things at once. Listen, do you have the contact info for the Alligator's owner?"

"Yes, I do. I can send it to you if you give me your number."

"I will do that, because I'd like to see you again under better circumstances."

She raised her eyebrows. "How do you know I'm not married?"

"Are you?"

"Widowed. Four years ago."

"Sorry."

"Thank you. I have a son, though—he's twenty-four."

"How is that possible? That would mean you had him when you were about eight years old."

She threw back her head and laughed. "You are very kind. Not quite that young, but it's true I was a teenager when I had Ben-Kwame."

"He lives in Accra?"

"Yes, he stays with me. He also helps me at the guesthouse and stays there sometimes."

"That's a good boy, then."

Five o'clock traffic had them crawling along Kojo Thompson Road through the cacophonous, choked lorry park from Nkrumah Circle to Nsawam Road. And then on to tackle the George W Bush Highway before they were even remotely within reach of Lapaz.

"Come and meet my son," Janet said to Awuni as they at last pulled to a stop outside her home.

Awuni followed her along the pavement to the front door of the small olive-colored house. Inside, it was very warm and Janet switched on the air with a remote.

In admiration, Awuni looked around the living room space. "Very nice. Such a cute place."

"Thank you. Quite honestly, when it comes to homes, I prefer big over cute. Please have a seat, Mayor."

They sat opposite each other.

"Truthfully, Ben is not home," Janet said. "He has my car today. I only said that to give you a plausible reason to come inside."

"Is that so?" Awuni wasn't sure what exactly she had in mind.

"I wanted to talk more in private—away from your driver's ears. I told you I manage the Alligator, which is true, except it's past tense. I *was* a manager, but now I'm a madam."

"Aha," Awuni said. This interested him. "How many women do you manage?"

"Right now, fourteen."

"You could have more—many more. If I buy the place, I will put money into it and at least double the number of girls and your clientele."

"Nice, but I have another idea. I'd like to add my money to

the pot so I can be part owner. You will, of course, have the majority share."

"I think that would be great. Owning the place and being the madam—that's real power. How about your son's role? I'm not clear what he does."

"He's security. Makes sure customers don't misbehave."

"He's your macho man," Awuni said. "What kinds of trouble do you see?"

"Guys who refuse to pay the stated fee, or try to harm the girls or demand more sex than they've paid for."

"What happens in such a situation?"

Janet shifted in her seat, demurely crossing her ankles. "We take care of it. We have other macho men besides Ben. Woe betide any clients who abuse my girls in any way."

"I see. So . . ." Awuni paused. "Maybe this question will be too much, but were you a sex worker in the past?"

"Yes, I was." Awuni thought he saw a trace of anguish move quickly over her face. "How do you feel about that, Mayor?"

"I admire you for it," Awuni affirmed. "It's not easy going out there and opening yourself up to the world, so to speak. And the abuse from both ends: the madam and the customers."

Janet murmured her agreement and a mutual silence ensued.

"When we were on our periods," Janet resumed suddenly, "Queenie gave us a sponge to block the blood and hide it from the men. Some of them refused to wear a condom, saying they can't feel anything. I got pregnant twice and both times Queenie made me get an abortion, and she added the cost to what I was paying her. The second abortion went badly. I was in pain, but still, she made me work. I contracted a pelvic infection, which scarred my insides and left me barren. No man likes a barren woman." Janet shook her head, almost to herself.

"Sorry," Awuni said.

Janet shrugged, but her eyes appeared saturated with pain.

"I'm surprised you've told me all this," Awuni said.

"Me too," she said. "I've never spoken about it to anyone."

"And here I am—a stranger."

Janet smiled weakly. "Maybe a stranger who listens is the best audience. People close to you are judgmental."

"That's true," Awuni said. "I've never heard anyone say it quite that way."

Janet pulled herself together. "That's enough about me. Now, let's talk about you."

CHAPTER SEVENTEEN

FEMI DIDN'T MAKE IT to Ghana by Christmastime as he had hoped. The new year began with Femi planning to visit Grandpa Kojo in March, but that was the same month the global pandemic hit, forcing Nigeria to close its borders to all traffic. Femi wouldn't be able to travel anytime soon. It was yet another crushing disappointment for Kojo especially.

"I dey fear dis Covid shit go kill my grandpa," Femi confided to Cliffy on a sweltering June evening.

"Yeah, you talk true," he said with empathy. "Make we pray hard 'im no go get am."

"What bring dis Covid *wahala?*" Femi said in frustration. "People dey die, no money, no business."

Femi conceded that the Covid delay was giving him time to earn some money before the journey to Ghana. After successfully closing Bisola and Kehinde's case, Femi picked up another just as he was finishing up with one of Cliffy's legacy projects. But it was a mixed picture. The pandemic had slowed migration by 50 percent or more, and although the illegal border crossings into Niger and Libya were still ongoing, the imposition of travel restrictions made the journeys even more hazardous.

By the end of that year, he and Grandpa Kojo, who sounded progressively weaker on the phone, were both waiting anxiously for the Nigeria, Benin, and Togo borders to open, which came to pass, at last, in March of the following year. Femi wasted no time and grabbed a bus to Ghana along with other Covid-masked passengers.

IN ACCRA, FEMI felt as if he were home again, but the city held some surprises for him—new hotels, restaurants, and gyms seemed to be everywhere. The city was at once familiar and strange.

He directed his taxi driver to Accra New Town, where Grandpa lived, and which, funnily enough, people called Lagos Town because of a large Nigerian settlement there. What Femi liked about *Zongos* like Accra New Town and Nima—neighborhoods with large Muslim populations—was the live-and-let-live atmosphere. Mosques and churches stood next to each other, mixed in with offices, banks, and small stores selling everything from clothes to hardware. People minded their own business, walking on both the sidewalks and in the street, navigating the toxic gutters on either side. Music stores blared distorted hiplife from their shopfront speakers.

It had begun to drizzle as Femi alighted in front of the Seventh-Day Adventist Church. He went off the main road into the interior where shacks hugged a zigzagging pathway. Even if the ground hadn't been wet, the spinners on Femi's fancy new crimson-and-black suitcase wouldn't have been able to negotiate the terrain, so he collapsed the handle and carried it instead. Without even thinking about it, he stepped over the ditches and channels choked with garbage and dark, trickling liquids of obscure origin. A couple of shirtless kids ran past him laughing as one chased the other. A goat in Femi's path gave him a side-eye and scuttled away with a nervous bleat.

As Femi made another turn to arrive at Grandpa Kojo's compound, he caught the delicious aroma of pepper soup. Sure enough, right in the center of the compound was Gladys, his great-aunt, fanning the wood stove under a large, steaming pot. She looked up, saw Femi, and broke into happy laughter.

"*Ei!* He has come, o!" she shouted. "Femi is here!"

Gladys rose with as much speed as her age allowed and met Femi with arms spread wide before they embraced. She had shrunk in height and her head reached only to his lower chest.

The place magically filled with jubilant people from the households around the compound. Some were Femi's extended relatives, others weren't. Teenagers he hadn't seen in a while seemed to have sprouted a foot or two in height. As was customary when receiving guests, one of the teens immediately relieved Femi of his bag and carried it inside.

Once Femi had duly greeted everyone and shaken hands

deferentially with the elders, Auntie Gladys led him into Grandpa's house.

"Kojo!" she called out. "Look who has come."

In a chair in front of the TV, the old man had obviously been dozing off. He started and squinted up. The room was dim, and initially he couldn't make out who or what he was looking at. "Is that you, Femi?"

"Grandpa." Femi went down on one knee to be at the old man's level of sight. "Yes, it's me."

They hugged and Femi inhaled Grandpa's familiar, slightly musty smell.

"*Ei*," Kojo said, his voice sounding feeble. "I've missed you, o! I'm so glad you are back. You know, the Lord might summon me very soon."

"Ah, Grandpa," Femi said, dismissively sucking his teeth. "You know you're going to live another one hundred years."

Kojo gave a raspy laugh. "But sit down, Femi!"

Femi pulled up a chair.

Kojo looked at his sister. "Tell them to bring us two Club Beer, okay?"

Gladys shuffled to the door and yelled out to one of the youngsters hanging around. Kojo began to fumble for some money.

"It's okay, Grandpa," Femi said. He fished for his own wallet and gave the kid a twenty-*cedi* bill. "Here. Go and come quick, okay?"

The boy ran off down the street somewhere to pick up the drinks.

"Grandpa, how are you?"

"Ah, well," Kojo said, throwing up his craggy hands. "What can you do? I can't see, I can't hear, I can hardly move for the arthritis. But apart from that, I'm fine."

Femi laughed with him, but the old man had clearly lost weight, making his face more skeletal and his eyes more prominent, as if he were staring.

Femi asked him a lot of questions about his health, but Kojo didn't seem that connected. "Grandpa, I want to take you to see an eye doctor, okay?" Femi said, bothered by Kojo's loss of vision. "Maybe there's something we can do, so you can see better."

"You think so?" Kojo was hopeful and skeptical at the same time.

"We should try," Femi said. "I want to do whatever we can." He took Grandpa's hand. "And I want to help with the house too—any repairs, and we need to get the lights in the house fixed. How can you see anything in this dim light?"

"Thank you." Grandpa squeezed Femi's hand back. "Thank you."

Femi knew people who had never helped their parents out with a single *pesewa* while they had been alive, but shelled out a small fortune for an impressive funeral. Femi didn't want to behave that way.

HE SPENT A marvelous two weeks with Grandpa and the extended family. As he had brought everyone gifts, he was the most popular man within earshot. On Femi's last night before he was to return to Nigeria, he joined the family to eat a hearty meal and listen to Grandpa's tales, which were highly entertaining, and no doubt greatly exaggerated for effect. It was a happy time.

Femi was to be at the airport by 5 A.M. After barely two hours of sleep, he rose to finish packing. Auntie Gladys joined him, and as the hour of his departure grew nearer, she went to wake up her brother for the big farewell. Femi had just begun to check his travel documents when he heard her scream from Grandpa's bedroom. Femi dropped everything and ran in. Gladys was at Kojo's bedside shaking his still body, shouting at him to wake up.

Femi came to his grandfather's side and grasped his arm to give him a firm shake. But the body was already cool to the touch. Grandpa Kojo had died in his sleep.

CHAPTER EIGHTEEN

FEMI WEPT IN ANGUISH that he had been too late to renovate Grandpa Kojo's house or help him regain at least some of his vision. He had wanted to make these grand gestures to show how much his grandfather had meant to him and still did. Femi regretted having imposed the belligerence of his teenage years on Kojo and he had wanted to make up for it.

Femi would bear much of the cost of the funeral, but that wouldn't take place for another month or two. Before that, there were other matters to attend to: determining how much each branch of the family would be contributing toward the event, for example. Kojo's extended family was scattered far and wide. Not only could everyone not be reached quickly; some needed time to pull together the resources to travel to Accra. So, the first step was to rent cold storage at a funeral home or hospital morgue for as long as needed. Beyond that point, it wasn't unheard of for a family to abandon its dead. When corpses went unclaimed beyond several years, they were released for mass burial—a kind of tomb of the unknown.

The activity and stress had Femi exhausted physically and emotionally. He wanted to escape for a quiet evening without funeral agenda items and family bickering. They kept pushing back the funeral date, to Femi's irritation. Now, April had arrived, and the family elders were forecasting June for the funeral.

He took a Bolt to the Labadi Beach Hotel for drinks and grabbed a table at the Viewpoint Bar & Restaurant overlooking the shore. He ordered a scotch neat—his present favorite—and a basket of yam chips with hot sauce.

The patio lights reflected against the fluffy white of the waves as they broke on the shore with a wholesome *whoosh*. Femi's sight blurred as tears moistened his eyes for a moment at the thought of Grandpa Kojo.

Femi turned his head as he heard an angelic female voice. And when he saw her, it was as if she were in a picture frame dead center in his line of vision. She was chatting with two girlfriends as they slipped into a restaurant booth. She was lean, with long legs and a firm, lithe body. She threw her head back when she laughed in a manner Femi had never seen.

He summoned the waiter and beckoned him to get closer as he whispered, "I'll pay for all their drinks, okay?"

The waiter nodded. "Yes, sir."

Femi ordered *chinchinga* and another drink, pacing himself with the three women. Overhearing snatches of their conversation, he could tell from her accent and pronunciation that the object of his desire was Nigerian. The other two were clearly Ghanaian. When it was time for their bill, Femi watched their confusion as they looked from bill to waiter, who discreetly indicated who was responsible for the discrepancy. The drinks had been paid for. All three heads turned toward Femi, but he registered only one of them—the one in the middle with the angelic voice. He beckoned to her. She looked at her friends and then leaned over to one of them to whisper something. The friend got up, came over to Femi's table and said to him, "Hi, I'm Rosemary. Ngozi wants me to ask you your name."

"Oh, wow," he said. "Is she such a princess that she sends you on this errand?"

She giggled. "Something like that."

"Okay, well, tell Princess Ngozi my name is Prince Femi from Lagos."

And that was how Femi and Ngozi met.

DURING THE REMAINING three weeks of April, Ngozi, eighteen, and Femi, twenty-eight, spent as much time as possible getting to know each other. Ngozi's father, Nnamdi Ojukwu, was the Nigerian high commissioner to Ghana. She had an SUV at her disposal, and she often went out with a bunch of her girlfriends. Using his supply of charm, Femi ingratiated himself with them until he was part of the crowd, joining them on their joy rides. He projected a persona of a successful businessman with more money to throw around than he really had.

CLIFFY HAD BEEN calling frequently. "When you go comot from Ghana?" he grumbled.

"I no go fit return to Naija until my grandfather funeral finish. Sorry, brother. Dis my family dey delay too much."

Cliffy sighed. "Okay, no *wahala*. But make you come back soon."

"Sure, my brother. Thank you."

As Femi hung up, he became aware of a profound dissatisfaction with his life's trajectory. When he had left prison and begun working with Cliffy, the future had looked rosy, like first light at dawn. But now, Femi wondered if he was achieving his full potential working with his friend. Femi didn't believe so, and now he was wondering about what opportunities Ghana might offer. It had the best of both worlds: a sophisticated online network of sex workers, along with the old system of streetwalkers, pimps, and madams. He was seeing Accra as the new frontier. With that in mind, he dialed Madam Janet Glover's number. After three tries, she didn't respond, but within the next hour, she called back.

"Who are you?" she asked Femi in a flat, cautious voice.

"Please, my name Femi Adebanjo. You remember Cliffy from Nigeria?"

"Oh, yes, I've worked with him before."

"Okay, well, I'm his business associate. I know he has sent a few ladies to you. I would like to discuss going further and partnering with you."

"Aha," she said mildly, but with obvious interest. "Do you know the restaurant Breakfast to Breakfast in Osu?"

"Yes, it's one of my favorites." That wasn't true, but he knew where the place was.

"Meet me there tomorrow morning, ten o'clock, and we'll talk."

CHAPTER NINETEEN

OFF OXFORD STREET, OSU'S tacky and blighted tourist prom-
enade, Breakfast to Breakfast was a chic spot with adequate space
for both business and social meetings. The customers were fash-
ionable and well-off Ghanaians and foreigners who frequented the
restaurant for its western-style dishes from pancakes to grilled
lemon chicken, and stylish beverages like hibiscus spiked with
ginger.

Femi arrived before Glover and chose a table from which he
could keep an eye on the door as customers went in and out.
After some twenty minutes, a tall woman entered clad in a Ghanaian wax-print of sapphire and white cowry shells on a jade
background. Her blouse, headwrap, and dangling earrings were all
sapphire to match. Something told Femi that this was the woman
he was to meet, and he was correct. After stopping at the front
desk to ask for Femi by name, she saw him, nodded, and waved.
She approached Femi's table with an air of authority about her.
But who was the smallish, bespectacled man with her?

Femi rose to shake hands.

"This is Mr. Awuni," Janet said, introducing him. "We work
together."

"Good morning, sir," Femi said.

"Where from, in Nigeria?" Awuni asked, his voice surprisingly
deep and rich for that little body.

"Originally Lagos, but I live in Benin City now."

They exchanged pleasantries until the server arrived to take
their orders—iced latte for Janet, and pineapple-ginger and lemon
mint for Awuni and Femi respectively.

"So, Mr. Femi," Janet said, setting her Gucci purse to the side,
"what brings us together today?"

"Madam, you are one of the most successful businesswomen in Accra," he said, leaning forward for emphasis. "I know you own one or two guesthouses in Accra. That's why I've come to consult you. As you already know, my partner Cliffy and I are migration agents in Benin City. We hook people up to travel to Libya and Italy, and now I'm looking into growing the business with you as partners. I can guarantee that if we're in business together, I will supply you twice the number of Nigerian girls you have now."

Janet's eyebrows shot up.

"You see," Femi pushed on with confidence, "because I go back and forth between Ghana and Nigeria, I'm on the ground in both countries; I can supervise, I can coordinate."

Awuni was studying Femi without indicating either enthusiasm or a lack thereof. "Do you have guesthouse or hotel experience?"

"Yes, sir," Femi lied, more smoothly than even he had expected. "I've been a manager at the Radisson in Lagos and Benin City."

"Really?" Janet said with a little laugh. "You look rather young."

Aha. Flirting. "Thank you, madam," Femi said, looking suitably bashful. "Good work is good work at any age, young or old. And my work is excellent."

The expression in Janet's eyes had softened like heated wax.

"Please, may I ask of your interest in my hotel experience?" Femi asked the little man.

Awuni was rubbing his chin in contemplation. He leaned forward and lowered his voice.

"Listen, I'm building a new hotel in East Legon," he said to Femi. "It will be the base for the highest quality sex workers."

Femi sat up a little straighter. East Legon was another way of saying *a lot of money.*

"Ten rooms for high-paying customers," Awuni continued, "like top military officers, MPs, and businessmen—especially expatriates, and so on. Appointment only. No street people. We would encourage clients to go there, but if they can't, we can offer them service at their location for a substantial additional cost."

"That sounds interesting," Femi said. "When will the guesthouse be completed?"

"Two to three months, hopefully," Awuni said. "You know Ghana—there's all manner of disappointment every day. I have a man there, Salifu, who is handling the place for now, but when it is fully operational, we will need someone who knows what he's doing. Salifu will not be up to that task, even though he's a very good jack-of-all-trades to have around. If we were to ask you to handle East Legon Hotel, could you do it?"

"Tell me more, sir."

Janet said, "Femi, the point is, I already have enough to do with the Lapaz guesthouse, and Mr. Awuni is busy with his own."

"The hotel will have a manager's suite on the first floor," Awuni said. "The clients' rooms are on the second floor."

"I would like to see the place," Femi said at once.

"What about tomorrow?" Awuni suggested. "Are you free?"

"Absolutely."

"Then let's meet somewhere and you ride with us," Janet said, smiling at Femi.

Dis woman wan me fock am well-well, Femi thought in amusement. Theoretically, he could oblige, but he wasn't planning on it.

In THE MORNING, Femi rode with Awuni and Janet to the new hotel in East Legon, a part of town where two- or three-car homes were common. Palm trees lined good roads, and hotels had names like Olive Gold and The Ivy. Li Beirut was the best Lebanese restaurant for miles around. Houses with innovative designs sold for half a million to a million dollars, or rented for at least $2,000 a month.

Awuni drove, but the vehicle, an Escalade, belonged to Janet, Femi learned. He took a moment to text Ngozi, letting her know how much he cared about her and filling his texts with love emojis and kisses. She responded in kind. They were still at the deeply romantic stage, but it bothered Femi he couldn't see Ngozi more often. In a mere couple of months, she would be returning to Nigeria with her parents to start university.

As Awuni pulled up at a six-foot-high black gate, he pumped the horn, and a man poked his head out of the side access for a second, before disappearing again to open the gate.

The Escalade swept into a shaded yard with parking spaces. The off-white house in front of them had dark, almost black, reflecting windows. Awuni parked off the driveway under the avocado tree and the three alighted. The tall, powerful man who had opened the gate approached them with a long, easy stride.

"Good morning, sir," he addressed Awuni. "Good morning, madam."

"That's Salifu," Awuni said to Femi, "the one I told you about. Salifu, meet Femi."

"Morning, sir."

"How is everything?" Awuni asked Salifu.

"Everything is fine, please."

"Good, good," Awuni said. "Madam Janet and I will be showing Mr. Femi around the house, and then we'll talk."

"Yes please," Salifu said, nodding. His head was square, like a cube, and his neck was as thick as the trunk of a baobab tree.

"Let's go inside now," Awuni said.

Salifu beat them to the house and opened the front door for them. They entered a small foyer beyond which was a large, partially furnished room.

"Guests will be able to relax here if they want," Awuni said. "The furniture will arrive soon."

To their right was a skylighted staircase. Awuni led him to a small, partially concealed chamber beneath it.

"What is this for?" Femi asked, looking around. He thought the room could comfortably accommodate about five or six people.

"The girls can perch here between clients," Awuni said.

"Ah, okay, okay."

When they emerged from the room, Salifu was leaning against the wall. He rested his gaze on Femi for a moment and then redirected it to Awuni. "Please, the pool is now clean."

"Okay, good job."

Salifu nodded and went away.

"We have a pool outside in the back of the building," Awuni explained, turning back to the staircase. "We can go upstairs now."

When they got to the second floor, Awuni said in a low voice, "Don't worry about Salifu. He is intimidating and sometimes awkward to deal with, but he means no harm."

"Oh, sure, no problem," Femi said, not entirely persuaded. Since arriving, he had sensed resentment from Salifu. Maybe he found Femi's arrival threatening.

They were now at one end of a long corridor with several door-ways.

"This is where the girls bring the clients to do their thing," Awuni said. "We have a total of ten rooms."

He opened the door closest to them. The vacant space was on the smaller side of a conventional hotel room.

"All the rooms are the same?" Femi asked.

"Not all," Awuni said. "Let me show you."

They crossed to the other end of the corridor to enter another much larger space.

"We have three suites like this," Awuni explained. "They are for men who want a lady for the whole night, and for regular guests too. Nothing is stopping anyone from booking accommodation like a regular hotel."

"So," Femi said, "where are the clients from?"

"Word of mouth and through our website, Whitehouse.gh.com, or the app, and we can cross-link with other sex sites like Locanto.com and ExoticGhana.com. It will be a tight but expansive circle of high-paying customers who come to us—deep, but not wide. Our minimum charge is six hundred *cedis*. If they're foreigners, we encourage them to pay in dollars to earn a hefty discount."

"What about security?" Femi asked.

"Twenty-four seven," Awuni said. "Security guard at the entrance and we will install exterior CCTV. Salifu will supervise. Now, let's go to your office. That's the only part we've furnished so far."

Downstairs again, he followed Awuni's lead to a door on the western end of the building. Awuni unlocked it, and Femi followed after Janet into a stunning, low-profile space with a gleaming wood floor, two black lacquer desks each with an executive chair, two matching cream sofas and chairs, and recessed LED lighting.

This is beautiful, Femi thought with growing excitement. He wanted this job.

"Would you like some water?" Awuni asked, going to the small fridge under the counter behind the desk.

Both Femi and Janet took a bottle and sat down with Awuni to talk.

"So, what do you think?" Awuni addressed Femi. "You will have full management of this location, in conjunction with any necessary direction from Janet and me, of course, but a chance to be creative."

"I will do wonders with this place," Femi said with an easy, assured smile.

"Great," Janet said, her eyes brightening.

"That is, if your terms are good."

Awuni steepled his fingers. "Okay, what we would like to offer you is thirty percent of the net profit on the house."

"Thirty percent?" Femi stared at them with a frozen half-smile. "I'm busting my ass turning the hotel into your biggest money-maker yet, and you're going to pay me thirty percent? *Thirty!* It should at least be forty-five percent."

"I built this house," Awuni said. "I have to make my money back."

"I understand, but in a fair way."

Awuni hesitated. "Thirty-five is as high as we'll go."

Femi pushed back his chair and stood up. "Nice meeting you both."

Awuni's jaw dropped and his eyes rounded to twice their size.

Janet stared at Femi as he turned away to leave. "Mr. Adebanjo, please come back." Before he got to the door, she rose hastily to catch up, then touched him on the shoulder.

He turned. "Please, madam, hear me well, I will accept nothing less than forty percent, and you may communicate that to your partner."

"Have a seat, Mr. Adebanjo," Awuni called out, gesturing to Femi's chair. "You've made yourself clear. Forty percent is okay."

AFTER FINALIZING NEGOTIATIONS, Awuni put Femi in touch with a real estate office with properties in East Legon, and the following day, Femi met with an agent, who turned out to be a cousin of Awuni's. The initial four houses Femi saw were nice enough, but it was the fifth one that was, in his view, spectacular. Three stories high, the outside was maroon with white trim, and a glass-rimmed balcony on the second floor overlooked the driveway. Inside was an open-design kitchen, a living room with ceramic tiling and a view of the back garden and pool, and an elevator. The largest bedroom on the top floor was beautiful, and Femi could imagine waking up each morning in this magnificent space with a beautiful woman in bed beside him—Ngozi, maybe?

As was common, the agent quoted the rent in dollars—twenty-five hundred a month, negotiable. The agent was open to a good bargaining session, and Femi wore her down to seventeen hundred. The catch was that the property owners required payment in advance for six months. Femi was lucky it wasn't twelve. He had some cash, but he needed more.

"One minute, please," Femi said to the agent. "I need to call someone."

Just when Femi needed Cliffy most, he wasn't answering his phone. Femi waited five minutes and tried again.

This time, Cliffy picked up. "Yeah, brotha, how you dey?" he said.

"Cliffy, I dey short bread."

Silence, at first, so Femi rushed on to explain the situation. He had about one-third of the required amount. He just needed a little push.

Cliffy grunted. "My *paddi*, you go kill me, o."

"*Abeg, abeg.*"

"I no dey get money."

"Oh, *oga*," Femi said in his best beseeching voice. "Look at the money you've been making all the time I was at Kirikiri, and you no dey spend it se'f."

"Who dey tell you dat kain thing?"

"I don see inside your safe, Cliffy. I know. It's full."

Not waiting for Cliffy's response to that, Femi kept going until his friend relented. He could send some cash the following day. Just a little bit more, and Femi would have all he needed. The agent gave him until the end of May.

After finishing up at East Legon, Femi texted Ngozi: Could they get together tonight?

I think so, but let me check, she responded.

After an hour, Ngozi got back to Femi in the affirmative. Her parents had a function, so she would be able to get out. They picked M Plaza Hotel, which was less than two kilometers away from Ngozi's home.

IT WAS THEIR second tryst at M Plaza, and this time, sexual magic took place. Ngozi cried out as her climaxes came wave after wave, rising to the crest, breaking on the shore and then receding as the next swell gathered strength. Femi, who had smoked marijuana prior, peaked twice in a row and then went limp. She allowed him to stay that way for a moment before coaxing him off to the side. They lay panting.

"My God," Ngozi whispered. "What the hell did you do to me?"

Femi chortled weakly. "Magic mouth," he muttered and began to doze off.

She shook him. "Honey, don't fall asleep." She looked at her phone. "I'll have to be leaving soon."

He laid his heavy arm on top of her. "No, don't go," he said.

Ngozi kissed him. "I don't want to, but I must."

Femi put a couple of pillows against the headboard and sat up. "What day do you return to Naija?"

"Fifteenth of June," she said, resting her head on his lap. "What about you?"

"End of June or beginning of July," Femi said. "After Grandpa's funeral."

"Good, so we'll see each other again in Nigeria."

He was quiet for a moment. "Ngo, I'm taking a job as a hotel manager."

She sat up. "Where?"

"Here in Accra. After I get back to Naija, I'll pack up my stuff and finish up some business, then return to Ghana after two or three months."

"Oh," she said, her mind racing through several scenarios and just as many emotions. "Well, that's great. Congrats. But . . . so . . . "

"I'll be back and forth between here and there," he added quickly. "It's not like we won't see each other."

Ngozi felt squashed. This was sudden and heavy news. "Yeah, but it won't be the same," she said sadly.

"It will be okay," Femi tried reassuring her. "We can video each other on WhatsApp, and so on."

"That's true," Ngozi said, still sounding mournful. "Where is the hotel you'll be managing?"

"East Legon. I'll show you a pic." He reached for his iPhone and tilted his head to touch hers as he went to his photos and scrolled with a lightning thumb. "Here: this is the hotel—nice, right? The inside still needs to be finished, but my office is already done."

"Wow," Ngozi said as she saw the image. "Impressive."

"Right? And, look—here's the house I'm planning to rent."

"Oh, my goodness!" Ngozi said. "That's beautiful."

He looked up and their gazes locked.

"Come back with me to Ghana, Ngo," he whispered intensely. "Please. *Abeg.* Let's live together in East Legon."

"If only I could," she said longingly, "but I'll be in law school in September."

"Why not take a year off and then reapply to the University of Ghana Law School instead?"

Ngozi sighed dejectedly. "It's not that easy, Femi."

"Your father has a lot of influence," he countered. "He could make it happen. Do you even *want* to go to law school?"

"Well, yes, I do, but . . ."

"I don't think your heart is really in it," Femi said decisively. "On the other hand, where you would be brilliant is helping me manage a new hotel."

She smiled. "It's true—I would, but imagine how my lawyer parents regard being a lawyer versus a hotel manager."

"But it should be about how *you* feel, not them," Femi objected. "You know, the climb to a successful lawyer practice in Naija is not easy. They'll work you to the bone, and it'll be some time before you're making a lot of money. What's the point of having a fancy title if you're broke? Stick with me, and the bread will be rolling in, I guarantee you."

Lost in thought, Ngozi began to dress.

"Honey," Femi said, "I need some money."

She zipped up her skintight jeans. "What for?"

"For the house in East Legon. They want six months' rent in advance, and I'm short twelve thousand *cedis.*"

Ngozi was slipping on her sandals. "Hmm, not sure if I can get that much. I might be able to if I withdraw from several different ATMs tonight and tomorrow."

"Okay, love. Let me know, okay?"

PART FOUR

CHAPTER TWENTY

ON AN EARLY MORNING at the beginning of July, Femi started up the cheap Toyota pickup he had bought off a friend and began the long journey by road back to Lagos. The funeral was over now, and Femi felt that Grandpa's life on earth had reached a peaceful end. He hadn't been in pain or distress. Surely, dying in one's sleep was the best way to depart this world.

Still, after the drawn-out funeral ceremonies, Femi's emotions had swung like a pendulum from melancholy to elation. Trying to temper the volatility of his mood, he had drunk himself into an advanced state of intoxication that erased much of what he would later remember of the event. He thought it was just as well. Femi didn't want to think about any of it right now. Instead, he was savoring the notion of skyrocketing into an infinitely bright future.

Ngozi had been back in Lagos for about two weeks and had kept faithfully in touch with him. She was crazy about him, and he loved that. She was both sexy and sexual, and often asked him to send more naked pics. He had no shortage of lewd selfies to send her, and she had been responding in kind. Femi had released the freak in her, like a wild animal escaping its cage.

At the gas station when Femi stopped to fill the tank, he texted Ngozi to let her know he was on the road. They planned to spend some time together in Lagos, but then Femi would have to make his way back to Benin City. There, he would reveal to Cliffy that after years of their association—and yes, friendship—their lives were about to diverge. In the end, Femi thought, Cliffy would be fine.

After his entry into Togo from Aflao, Femi called it a day and found a room in a guesthouse he rated half a star, if that, but it was fine for one night. If he had survived Kirikiri, he certainly could get through this.

Femi lay back on the bed's thin foam mattress and tried to reach Ngozi by voice and video call. Since she didn't respond, he assumed it was due to a lack of network coverage. He dozed off and woke an hour later to try Ngozi again. Still no answer from her. Femi felt a mixture of irritation and concern as he got out of his street clothes and got into bed. He was exhausted.

NGOZI HADN'T RESPONDED to Femi's messages because she was lying semi-conscious in the back seat of her father's car on the way to the hospital. Ijeoma cradled her daughter's bloody head in her lap as Nnamdi pushed the Benz to speeds far above the limit.

"Sweetheart?" Ijeoma, tears streaming, whispered to Ngozi. "We're almost at the hospital, okay? Hang on just a little bit longer."

Ijeoma choked back her sobs. *Dear God, let this nightmare end.*

The altercation had begun earlier that evening. Ngozi had gone up to her bedroom. In the sitting room, Ijeoma roused Nnamdi, who had fallen asleep in front of the TV the way he did every night.

"Come on, Nnamdi," she said, patting him on the cheek. "Time for bed."

"Okay," he muttered, rising with a grunt.

Ijeoma turned off all the lights in the sitting room and kitchen before following him upstairs. As she reached the second-floor landing, she heard a soft murmur emanating from Ngozi's bedroom, the sound of her talking quietly on the phone behind the locked door. Ijeoma paused, reflectively tracing her fingertips along the decorative handrail. *Should she?* Nnamdi was safely in the shower for a little while. She looked at Ngozi's door for a moment, and then an overpowering desire to know more urged her to press her left ear against Ngozi's bedroom door. For a moment, Ijeoma heard nothing and thought perhaps her daughter had finished the call, but then, Ngozi said something else, which Ijeoma couldn't make out. But she did catch one small segment: *I love you. Good night.*

As Ijeoma dressed for bed, she heard Ngozi's footsteps going down the hallway, followed by the bathroom door closing and the sound of running water as Ngozi began her shower. Ijeoma, glancing once behind her to be certain Nnamdi was fully asleep, made her way swiftly to her daughter's room, opened the door, and peeped in. *Praise Jesus.* Ngozi's iPhone was lying in the middle of her unmade bed. Without hesitation, Ijeoma snatched it up.

It hadn't yet locked itself, which enabled her to get into Ngozi's WhatsApp chats. She scanned it quickly. Girlfriends, a lot of girlfriends, some of whom Ijeoma knew by name. *Femi.* Who was that? His profile picture showed him and Ngozi together in a loving pose cheek to cheek.

Ijeoma scrolled through the texts and blenched not so much at the love and sex talk, but at the photos this Femi guy had been sending to Ngozi—mostly poses showing off his muscular shirtless torso, but then a couple of full frontals while in a state of semi-arousal. *Oh, my Lord,* she thought as a cold, thin layer of sweat broke out on her forehead. Ijeoma felt a deep revulsion, yet she couldn't help taking a surreptitious second look through all Femi's provocative images, glancing around as if someone might be watching. What bothered Ijeoma was Femi's age. In her estimation, he was somewhere between twenty-eight and thirty-one, which was much too old for Ngozi. This man could be taking advantage of her. Or . . . maybe it was the other way round? Whatever was going on, Ijeoma didn't like it. It was grossly inappropriate.

She marched to the bathroom door, flung it open, and entered.

"Who's there?" Ngozi called out from behind the shower curtain. Ijeoma pulled it aside. Ngozi jumped with shock and let out a shriek as she tried to cover herself up.

"What are you doing in here?" she screamed at her mother.

Ijeoma held up the phone so the screen was facing Ngozi. "What is this *filth*? Who is this man sending you these foul pictures?"

Ngozi lunged at the phone to snatch it away, but Ijeoma moved it deftly out of reach and crisply slapped the side of Ngozi's head with the other hand. Ngozi lost her balance and slipped, landing halfway on her side. Her head struck the inner rim of the tub with a bang.

Ijeoma dropped the phone, and it fell into the tub. "*Ngozi!*"

As blood erupted from the side of Ngozi's head, she had a brief convulsion, her body and limbs stiffening and jerking.

Ijeoma screamed. That brought the maid, Olanna, running into the bathroom from downstairs. "Madam, are you okay?" She rushed to Ijeoma's side.

"She slipped and hit her head," Ijeoma shouted, hyperventilating. "Turn off the water and help me get her out."

Olanna frantically shut off the tap and then leaned over to assist in pulling Ngozi out of the tub, but her body was slick with soapsuds.

"What are you doing?" Ijeoma cried. "*Lift* her! Grab her legs, I'll get her arms."

Grunting with the effort, they succeeded in moving Ngozi onto the floor, lying her stretched out on the bathmat. To Ijeoma, blood seemed to be everywhere. She began to sob. "What is happening? *Ngozi!*"

Ijeoma was paralyzed with fright, but Olanna had more presence of mind. She covered Ngozi's body with a towel for modesty and used another to apply pressure to the head wound.

Nnamdi, roused from sleep by the commotion, rushed in and gasped. "Oh, my God! What happened?"

"I don't know," Ijeoma stammered, the lie beginning to take shape as she spoke. "I . . . I was passing by in the hallway when I heard a bang, so I ran in and found her lying bleeding in the tub. She must have slipped and hit her head."

Nnamdi knelt down by his daughter. "Ngozi? Ngozi, sweetheart?" He looked at Ijeoma. "Is she responding to you?"

"Yes, yes," Ijeoma said, "but she's dazed."

"Go get the car," Nnamdi directed her. "Olanna and I will wrap her in a blanket and bring her down. *Hurry up!*"

FEMI'S RINGING PHONE woke him. He started, propped himself on his elbow, and fumbled for the phone.

"Hello," he said, his voice thick with sleep.

"Femi?"

"Yeah."

"It's Rosemary—Ngozi's friend. I don't know if you remember me?"

Femi struggled to get his mind in gear. "Oh. Yeah, I do remember you. How you dey? What's up?"

"I'm calling from Lagos. I should have contacted you yesterday, but I had to hunt around for your number."

Femi sat up, frowning. "Why, what's wrong?"

"It's Ngo. She's in the hospital. She fell in the bathtub and hit her head and was knocked unconscious."

"What do you mean, 'she fell in the bathtub'?"

"Well, I'm not clear on the whole story, but she and I had planned to go shopping this morning, and so when I couldn't reach her on the phone, I went to her place and the maid told me something about Ngozi falling in the bathtub and hitting her head, and that she's in the hospital, so I went there to find her."

Femi's stomach swooped. "Is she hurt? I mean, is it something serious?"

"They had to stitch her head and I don't know what else, and they also said she had a cushion or something like that."

"Cushion?" Femi repeated with a frown. "What cushion? You mean concussion?"

"Oh, ya—you're right, that's what they were saying. What is that?"

Femi ignored the question. "But is she okay?" he pressed. "That's what I want to know."

"They said she'll be okay, but right now, she's very confused and doesn't remember what happened. The doctors say she must rest in bed for a couple of days, and they'll observe her in the hospital during that time."

"Which hospital?"

"Lagoon Hospital on Lagos Island. Are you still in Ghana?"

"I'm in Togo on the way back to Nigeria. When will you see Ngo again?"

"I'll visit her again this afternoon."

"Tell her I'm on my way, okay?"

"Yes, I will."

CHAPTER TWENTY-ONE

DESPERATE TO SEE NGOZI, Femi drove the rest of the way to Lagos as fast as the pickup would go. The remainder of the long trip through two more borders, Togo-Benin, and Benin-Nigeria, was mental torture. Femi released a deep sigh of fatigue and relief as he arrived in Lagos late in the afternoon. The ragged shore of the Lagos mainland was on his right. He merged onto the low-profile Third Mainland Bridge south to Lagos Island. Once there, he branched east to Ikoyi, a rich neighborhood that fit perfectly with his vision of a voluptuary life. He vowed he would build a six-bedroom home there one day. Unsurprisingly, this was where the Ojukwus lived. Lagoon Hospital, where Ngozi was at the moment, was the closest medical center to their home, and one of the best in the country.

Femi followed Bourdillon Road until the hospital, with its striking coral-orange roof, came into view. Femi's heart began to thump with anxiety. What had happened to Ngozi? The story was murky. Anything was possible, he supposed, but what young person slips in the bathtub and hits their head? How severe was the concussion?

Femi snagged a space in the hospital's parking lot, put on a still-required Covid mask, and checked in with the seated security guard at the door before entering the building to find Reception. After they had looked up Ngozi's room number, he ran up the five flights and burst out into the corridor. He went right, realized it was the wrong way, skidded, and swung around to hurry in the opposite direction. As he was about to enter Ngozi's private room, he caught sight of her in bed with a man and a woman at her side. *Her parents.* Femi stopped short. Why hadn't he anticipated they would be there? Should he take the plunge and introduce himself to them? He decided, *yes, now or never*, and entered Ngozi's room. His eyes first went to Ngozi propped up in bed with a heavily bandaged head. Then, to Mr. and Mrs. Ojukwu sitting on the side of the bed farther away from Femi. They turned to stare at him.

As Ngozi saw him enter, her face lit up. "Femi!" she said weakly. "You came!"

He went to her side and sought her hand at the same moment Mr. Ojukwu said, "Who are you?"

"Good evening, sir. My name is Femi Adebanjo." Although he had trained his gaze on the man, Femi saw the wife turn rigid in mien, as if he were an apparition. "Good evening, madam," he added.

Mr. Ojukwu seemed puzzled. "And your connection to my daughter?"

"He's my boyfriend, Daddy," Ngozi said softly. "We met in Ghana in April this year."

Realization flooded Mr. Ojukwu's countenance. "Oh. *You!* You must be the one who . . ."

"Has caused all the trouble we've had with Ngozi," Mrs. Ojukwu finished in an icy voice.

"Mummy, please," Ngozi began.

"No wonder she's been making a fuss about returning to Ghana," Mrs. Ojukwu went on, without taking her eyes off Femi's face. "No wonder she's been threatening not to go to law school."

"Well," Femi said, "that's quite true. How can you make her do what she doesn't want?"

"Listen, young man," Mr. Ojukwu said, leveling a forefinger at Femi, "you don't come in here telling us what to do. Who do you think you are?"

"How old are you, Mr. Adebanjo?" Mrs. Ojukwu demanded.

"Twenty-eight, madam."

"And Ngozi is eighteen." Mrs. Ojukwu turned her palm up. "*Eighteen.* That is a ten-year difference. This is wrong. It's almost sinful."

"Mummy, *stop!*" Ngozi said, her voice strengthening.

"No," Mrs. Ojukwu snapped, whipping her head around. "It's *you* who must stop. You cannot continue a relationship with this man."

Mr. Ojukwu spoke now. "Where did you school?" he demanded of Femi. "Which college or university?"

"I didn't go to college. Our family couldn't afford it and . . ."

Mrs. Ojukwu folded her arms and snickered. "I thought as much."

"But high school?" Mr. Ojukwu said hopefully. "I mean, I presume you did finish high school. *Abi?*"

"Oh, yes, yes, of course, sir," Femi replied, sensing that the lie wasn't going to place him in much better light in any case.

"He's lying, Nnamdi," Mrs. Ojukwu said smoothly. "I can tell he's a dropout."

"Ijeoma," Mr. Ojukwu said quietly, restraining her. "What do you do for a living, Mr. Adebanjo?"

"I'm a hotel manager. I will be working at a brand-new hotel in Accra."

"And maybe I'll join him," Ngozi sneered to her parents.

Mr. Ojukwu was incredulous. "What did you say, Ngozi?"

"Never mind," she said. "My head hurts."

Femi turned more directly to Ngozi now. "Babe, what happened?"

"I don't remember anything because of the concussion." She looked tired and despondent. "But Mummy knows. What happened again, Mummy?"

Ijeoma pressed her lips together, making it clear she wasn't about to comment.

Mr. Ojukwu cleared his throat. "The way I understand it, Ngo must have slipped in the shower and struck her head against the side of the tub. Fortunately, my wife was passing by the bathroom and heard Ngo fall. Isn't that right, Ijeoma?"

She nodded.

"Oh, I see," Femi said. "I guess the tub must be quite slippery, then?"

"Yes, I suppose so," Ojukwu muttered, gazing at his daughter with concern.

"And my phone, Mummy?" Ngozi asked.

"You must have had it in your hand in the shower," she said. "It fell in the tub. I put it in some rice, but with so much water damage, I don't think that will work."

Femi noted how intently Ngo was staring at her mother. What was wrong?

Femi had to get around this mess, somehow. "Please, Mr. and Mrs. Ojukwu, I know you don't approve of me because I haven't lived your kind of life, but . . ." He reached for Ngozi's hand. "But we do love each other, and I just beg of you to allow me to stay awhile. *Abeg.*"

"She needs her rest, Mr. Whatever-your-name-is," Mrs. Ojukwu snapped.

She may be rich, Femi thought, *but she's a bag of shit.*

"He's staying," Ngozi said flatly.

Her parents looked at each other.

"Okay, sir," the male Ojukwu said, "but you must not stay long. Is that clear?"

"Yes, sir," Femi said respectfully.

"Sweetheart, we'll be back tomorrow to see you," Nnamdi said, as he bent to kiss Ngozi softly on the cheek. Ijeoma followed his example and then looked up at Femi.

Nnamdi took his wife's arm. "Come on—let's give them a few minutes. Mr. Adebanjo, not too long, okay?"

"Yes, sir."

The Ojukwus left and Femi sat down on the bed as close as he could get to Ngozi. "How are you feeling now?"

"Headache," she groaned.

"Shall I tell them to bring you some medicine?"

"Don't bother," Ngozi said. "They'll just give me more Paracetamol, which never works."

Femi squeezed her hand gently. "I'm so sorry about this, Ngozi. And you still don't recall how it happened?"

"Last night, I couldn't remember, but this evening, the memory is back clear as crystal, and I know exactly what happened."

"You do?" Femi pulled back in surprise. "But didn't you say just now you had no recollection?"

"I did. Not true." Her eyes out of focus, Ngozi gazed at a spot at the foot of her bed. "What I was doing was giving my mother a final opportunity to tell the truth."

"I'm confused," Femi said.

Ngozi looked up at him. "She is the reason I'm in this hospital bed. *She* made me slip in that bathtub and smash my head open. She actually slapped me, Femi! I could have died. And now, the pathetic coward she is, she's lying about it. Is this my mother?"

"*Na wa!*" Femi exclaimed under his breath. "What're you going to do?"

"I'm going to punish her," Ngozi said decisively.

"Meaning?"

"I'll be right with you when you go back to Ghana. I'm leaving Nigeria and my parents. For good."

DURING HIS ENTIRE drive from Lagos to Benin City, Femi's heart sang. He and Ngo, who was now out of the hospital, had begun to secretly plan their escape from Nigeria in August, just two weeks before Ngo was due to start law school. Femi wasn't in the least bit worried that she might change her mind. She was clear-eyed about this.

It was one in the morning when Femi arrived at the apartment. Only half awake, Cliffy opened the door, muttered "welcome back," and staggered back to bed. Within minutes, Femi had stripped to his shorts, flopped down, and fallen fast asleep.

HE WOKE UP at almost noon. Cliffy was on the phone in the sitting room. Femi showered, came out cool and fresh, and bro-hugged his friend.

"*Oga!*" Cliffy said. "Good to see you."

"Yeah, my guy. Good to see you too."

"Come, come!" Cliffy said excitedly. "Make I show you something."

Femi followed him out of the apartment, down the steps to the ground floor and then around the building to the rear yard where the skimpy space was just barely enough for two cars.

"Look!" Cliffy announced, grinning.

"What?" Femi said.

Cliffy strolled over to a glimmering, green Mercedes-Benz and caressed the hood. Femi came closer. He could see the car had been previously owned, but the paint job was supreme and the finish intense.

"You like am?"

Femi stared at Cliffy, stunned. "E be for *you?*"

Cliffy grinned in the affirmative.

"*Na wa!*" Femi gasped.

"Go inside!" Cliffy said, opening the driver's door.

Femi took a seat on the smooth tan leather and stared in fascination at the busy dashboard. "Your dream dey come true," he said, smiling at Cliffy. "When you don buy it?"

"Thirteenth of May," Cliffy responded, his eyes full of pride. "You wan drive am?"

"You go 'llow me?" Femi asked, thrilled.

"Of course, my guy," Cliffy said, handing Femi the keys and then going around to the front passenger seat.

Femi turned the ignition and the powerful engine came smoothly to life. He listened to the motor's soft, rich hum, savoring it as he would a divine dish of Nigerian beef stew. Yet thoughts were intruding and turning ugly. Since Cliffy had bought the Benz in the first two weeks of May, wouldn't he have been already quite flush with cash in late April when Femi had begged him for some rent money? Yet, Cliffy had behaved as if Femi was *killing* him with the request for funds. Now, Femi realized something he may have chosen to ignore in the past: the trouble with Cliffy was that although he was a friend, he could also be a foe—a selfish, money-pinching foe.

IN THE AFTERNOON, they relaxed with a beer each and caught a soccer game on TV. When that was over, Femi cleared his throat. "Cliffy," he said finally, "I go move to Ghana in two months' time."

Cliffy looked startled. "I no *sabi wetin* you dey talk. You go move, why? *Wetin* dey happen?"

"I dey get new job there—hotel manager."

"*Na waa o!*" Cliffy slumped in his seat, shattered.

Femi hurried to reassure him it wasn't that bad. "Bro, no *wahala*. I go travel back and forth Ghana-Nigeria-Ghana."

"Oh, okay," Cliffy said dully. From his Mercedes high, he had tumbled to crushing lows.

Femi, seeing the glum look on his partner's face, added brightly that Janet Glover was eager to collaborate with Cliffy as her supplier.

"*No wahala*, then," Cliffy said, perking up somewhat.

Femi could see he was still struggling to absorb the impact of the news, but really, Cliffy had done fine and would likely continue to do so. *Just look at that Benz he's got.* Femi felt a hot stab of envy.

CHAPTER TWENTY-TWO

AUGUST 31 AT 2 A.M., it was time to depart. Ngozi waited in her room in the dark, checking her phone every few seconds. Femi was late. Finally, her phone buzzed with his message that he was about twenty minutes away, so she could begin her escape. She slid aside one of the pane windows. Behind that, the mosquito screen was thick and difficult to cut through with the kitchen knife she had selected for the job. She stabbed at the net, trying to slash it in an easy stroke. For a moment, the knife got stuck before it plunged down as the netting gave way and the blade sliced into the tip of her thumb. She pulled her hand away with a gasp of pain and a low moan. This was the worst possible time for a catastrophe.

Thrusting her thumb into her clenched fist to stop the bleeding, she fumbled in the top drawer of her bureau to find an old headscarf she clumsily fashioned into a bandage. Her phone buzzed again—Femi asking where she was. Already delayed, she didn't stop to reply. He'd have to wait for her the same way she had waited for him.

Her bedroom was on the second floor. Climbing through the window with her bulky backpack would have been awkward, so she leaned out first to drop it to the ground below. She clambered out carefully, stepped onto the ladder she had set up earlier on, and descended to the garden at the rear of the sprawling house.

The ladder was heavy, and moving it wasn't easy. Her lacerated thumb was throbbing and seeping blood through the scarf as she propped the ladder against the high wall encircling the entire property. She hitched herself with the backpack again and climbed to the top, where she peered over the other side to see Femi looking up as he waited for her on the pavement with his arms akimbo.

"Hurry up!" he said in a fierce whisper.

Ngozi was facing the electric wires. She had already switched off the current at the control panel in the kitchen, so now she had only to cut through. She had had the presence of mind to put the wire cutters in her pocket, and she began working on the wires, which proved to be unreasonably difficult. She was pouring with sweat as she cut the second out of a total of four wires. In her peripheral vision, Femi was pacing, agitated.

At last, Ngozi had severed all of them. She removed her back-pack and lowered it over the wall to Femi, then she climbed over and dropped to the ground, where Femi half-caught her. They ran to his car and she threw her backpack onto the rear seat.

"You good?" Femi said, grinning at her and starting up the Toyota.

"I'm good," she said.

Earlier on

CLIFFY HELPED SECURE the last of Femi's luggage in the bed of the Hilux, and finally the time had arrived for Cliffy and Femi to bid each other goodbye as their paths began their mutual divergence. Before Femi left the apartment for the final time, they embraced each other in manly mode.

"Yeah, you my guy!" Cliffy said in that Cliffy way.

"*Oga*," Femi said softly, as they separated. "*Abeg*, make you help me small for the journey expenses and so on."

"No *wahala*. I go get you some now-now."

He went into the bedroom and Femi followed him as soon as he heard the digital beep indicating Cliffy's safe door had popped open. As Cliffy removed some of the cash, Femi came up quietly behind him and startled him.

"I dey scare you?" Femi said. As Cliffy made to close the safe door, Femi's hand interrupted. "Why you dey hide dis money from me, eh, Cliffy? *Wetin* I do you?"

"Come on, bros," Cliffy said, laughing nervously.

"Wait," Femi said, "make I see." He pulled Cliffy's hand away and opened the safe door wide. "*Fock!*" Incredulous, he looked from the safe to Cliffy. "Why you dey hoard money, heh?"

Cliffy held out a wad of dollar bills, but compared to the amount of money in the safe, it was a paltry offering.

Femi laughed. "Na the small-small money be dis you dey give me?"

A sudden, mercurial rage seized hold of him. He felt it first as a consuming, white-hot fire in his head and then a dusky obscuring of his vision and a singing in his ears. He grasped Cliffy by the neck and smashed his face into the edge of the safe with immense force. Cliffy let out a gasp and clawed uselessly at Femi's steel grip. For a second time, Femi drove Cliffy's flesh and bone into the safe's unyielding surface.

Cliffy crumpled to the ground and then swayed dizzily as he attempted to prop himself up on one elbow. Blood streamed down his face and out of his mouth.

"Why you don fock up our friendship?" Femi demanded. "Now look *wetin* dey happen you."

He removed a scrunched-up garbage bag from his pocket and opened it up. He didn't so much as take out each bundle of cash as he did scoop it into the bag. All of it.

As he knotted the bag at the top, he said to Cliffy. "Make you give me the keys to the Benz."

Snot and blood pouring, Cliffy shook his head.

"*Fock* your Benz!" Femi said, looking down at him with contempt. "You think I dey care? When I get to Ghana, I go get three of them."

With a surprising amount of satisfaction, Femi left Cliffy bleeding, moaning, and gasping for breath on the floor.

FEMI AND NGOZI arrived at the Accra-Togo border town of Aflao at lunchtime, having been on the road for some ten hours. Ngozi had never traveled to Ghana by road—it had always been a painless, fifty-minute flight. Most stressful had been the border crossing from Nigeria into Benin. It had been chaotic, jammed with cars, massive commercial vehicles, and vendors selling food and cheap Chinese goods in the swirling dust.

Ngozi was glad to be with Femi. At each of the crossing points—Nigeria-Benin, Benin-Togo, and Togo-Ghana—he skillfully navigated the often-intimidating bureaucracy. He knew some of the officials by name, and both his and Ngozi's travel documents were satisfactorily up to date. They passed through all the borders with relative ease.

NGOZI DOZED OFF. When she awoke, they were on the N1 Highway at the outskirts of Accra. She sat up straight. "Where are we going now?" she asked Femi.

"To the hotel in East Legon. You'll love it."

Thirty minutes later, Femi pulled up to a black gate at 31 Senchi Street and pumped the horn. Someone peeped through an aperture in the gate, stepped back to open it, and let Femi's SUV in. The building looked even more spectacular to Ngozi than it had in Femi's phone pic. A pale cream rather than true white, it was two stories high with cappuccino trim and dark, reflecting windows. A central balcony overlooked the driveway.

"Wow," Ngozi murmured. "The White House."

Femi's eyes shone. "Yes! We were going to call it Senchi Palace, but you've just given it the perfect name." He beamed at her. "The White House . . . I love it."

"Then it's official?"

"Yeah, baby."

He parked, and the man who had opened the gate came up to them. "Mr. Femi. You are welcome."

"Thank you. How be, Salifu?"

Ngozi was staring at this Salifu guy because he might have been the biggest man she'd ever seen. Femi had told her about the powerful caretaker and all-around handyman, but he had never described the man in his full glory. He stood at six feet five, surely, with forearms as thick as a log. How did he fit through doorways with shoulders that broad?

The two men slapped hands with a deft terminal snap of each other's fingers.

Femi introduced Ngozi to Salifu, who, at his height, didn't need to look her up and down—just down. His face was flat and tight with deeply black, flawless skin, and a defiant flare of the nostrils.

"Please, we can go inside," Salifu said, taking the lead.

Femi took Ngozi's hand as they went up to the front door. She noticed the plants lining the walkway on each side needed some watering.

Salifu unlocked the door and they passed through a cool foyer into a large room with leather sofas and chairs, a wide-screen TV, and a pool table.

"What a change from when I first saw it in April with Awuni and Janet," Femi remarked, looking around. "Then it was totally empty. Wait till you see how fantastic the office is, Ngo. Salifu, is it locked?"

"I will open it for you, sir."

When he did, Ngozi saw that Femi had not exaggerated.

"My goodness," Ngozi murmured. "This is stunning."

"You like it, Ngo?"

"I love it."

"Let's go upstairs to see the rooms."

He led the way up, with Salifu trailing behind Ngozi. The staircase made a half circle, ending at a landing with guestrooms to either side of them. The floor was sensibly tiled to make cleaning easy. Femi opened one of the rooms, which, like the office downstairs, was now fully furnished.

"This is a standard single, but we have three suites at the other end of the hallway," Femi said.

As they walked to the other end, Ngozi felt unduly aware of Salifu's presence behind them. Was it his size that bothered her?

The suites, which overlooked the swimming pool, contained a sitting room, bar, bedroom with a king-size bed, and a large bathroom with rain showerheads.

"I know you helped move all the furniture in, Salifu," Femi said, smiling. "You've done a good job. What do you think, Ngo?"

"Absolutely." This seemed like a chance to thaw Salifu out some, so she gave him a quick smile.

Salifu beamed. "Thank you, sir, madam."

"Nice, nice," Femi said. He looked at Ngozi. "Let's go to the house now. Salifu, we'll see you tomorrow."

CHAPTER TWENTY-THREE

WHAT WAS TO BE Femi and Ngozi's new home was no more than two miles away from the just-christened White House. The remote-controlled gate slid aside as Femi drove in and parked in the open garage at the left end of the building. The two-story house was a deep maroon with white trim.

"Let's go in." Femi looked as happy as a kid with new toys. "I'll get the luggage later."

He showed Ngozi around the living room and kitchen. She was no chef, but she still appreciated the beauty of the stainless-steel range with its convection oven and five burners—so unlike the dated kitchen of her parents' home in Lagos.

They went upstairs, and as Ngozi admired the main bedroom, Femi came up behind her and put his arms around her waist and nuzzled her neck. "I think we should break in the new bed," he muttered.

"That bed is too neat to mess up," she said, giggling.

"Na lie!" he said. "Who dey tell you that?"

He picked her up and slung her easily over his shoulder. She shouted with laughter as he carried her to the sleek platform bed, which they proceeded to mess up.

WHEN NGOZI OPENED her eyes, she had a split second of disorientation. Where was this dazzling, airy room? Heaven? No, East Legon in a beautiful bed with a beautiful man—close enough.

Femi was fast asleep beside her, one arm flung unconsciously around her waist.

It was only six-thirty in the morning, but the sun was already bright. Femi stirred and Ngozi rolled over to snuggle against his chest. He opened one eye and smiled at her. "Hello, Sleeping Beauty. How was your night?"

"Slept like a baby," Ngozi said.

"Good. Me too."

They cuddled a while and then Ngozi went to the bathroom for a moment. When she emerged, Femi was watching CNN and smoking a joint. She sat next to him.

"Are you okay?" he asked.

"Of course. When I'm with you, everything is cool."

He muted the TV. "Ngo, I need to tell you something about the hotel."

"Okay," Ngozi said eagerly. "I'm listening."

Femi turned to face her more directly. "It's going to be very high-class, as you know, and of course we'll cater to the usual kinds of clientele, but we'll also accommodate men who would like to enjoy the company of ladies."

Ngozi frowned ever so slightly. "Meaning?"

"The way it will work is that the guys can go online or use an app to book a lady—or ladies—of their choice, and the room and service they would like. So, we will have an electronic record. The ladies will receive their fee in cash at the time of the physical transaction—"

Ngozi pulled back. "What are you talking about?"

"It's a very good business—"

"You mean . . . like a brothel?"

"No, nothing like that. This will be a high-quality operation."

"I don't think it makes a difference what you call it." Ngozi found this unexpected revelation disturbing. "How long have you been planning this?"

"In late April when I met Awuni and Janet—the couple I told you about—they told me that was the plan for the hotel. I thought about it for some time before deciding to go along with it."

"How did you come to meet these people?"

"When I was in Benin City, my friend Cliffy and I had a travel agency. He referred me to Janet."

Ngozi was still not clear. "But what was his connection to Janet?" she asked impatiently.

"Okay, well, Janet runs a hotel in Lapaz called the Alligator, which caters to gentlemen's desires. Most of the ladies are Nigerian, and at the time I joined Cliffy, he was recruiting women in

Benin City on Janet's behalf—at least the ones who weren't migrating to Europe."

"Europe?"

"You probably know about the Nigerians who migrate to Europe, especially Italy. Cliffy and I prepared the necessary papers for their journey—visa, passport, and so on."

"So, they fly from Lagos to Rome, or something like that?"

"Yes." Femi paused. "Actually, though, only a minority can afford to fly. Most of them go by ground transportation from Nigeria to Agadez, and then across the desert to Libya. From there across the Mediterranean to Italy."

Ngozi frowned. "I've seen some of those stories on YouTube. I thought most of those people were illegal?"

"We make it as legal as possible under the circumstances."

"Is it legal or not? You can't be a little bit pregnant. Either you are, or you aren't."

Femi cleared his throat. "They already know what they're getting into, that they're going to be illegal—"

"Don't some of them end up forced into sex work?"

"Yes, some," Femi conceded.

"Which is the definition of trafficking, right?"

"Whether or not they have an agent like me or Cliffy, they're going to try to get to Europe anyway, even if they know they're likely going to be prostitutes. People need money and some are willing to get it at any cost."

"And that's your justification for promoting it?" she demanded. "That's like running over someone with your car because accidents happen."

"I'm not running over the person in the street," Femi bounced back. "I'm slowing down so they can cross the road safely. No one is forcing any woman to do any of this, and there shouldn't be any coercion whatsoever. A woman should be paid her due, and so, getting back to what I wanted to say, I'm giving up the migrant stuff to concentrate on this. We will have gorgeous, sophisticated ladies and the guests will pay a fair price—which will keep low-class men away. And, Ngo, I want you to be the women's advocate. You will ensure they receive good pay and fair treatment. There's a right way to do this, and I know you can make sure of it."

He could see that assigning her the important role as an activist had softened her somewhat, but she wasn't all the way there.

"Why can't we just run a regular hotel?" she demanded.

"Sweetie, the thing is that we're going to have sex workers coming in here with clients whether we ask for them or not. You think all those five-star boutique hotels like Mövenpick, Monticello, or Kempinski don't already have their share of sex workers catering to the guests? They might *claim* they don't, but everyone knows that's a lie. What do they think businessmen from Europe, America, Dubai, Australia, Asia—wherever—do at night in their hotel rooms? Sit around reading the Bible?

"So, let's stop being hypocrites about this and, number one, capture the revenue the sex workers bring in while giving them a fair share, and number two, ensure the safety of our ladies. At other hotels, if a client violates or beats up a sex worker in his room, she has nowhere to turn to. The authorities will either shame her as an *ashawo* or just laugh at her."

Ngozi was impressed. She had never heard Femi speak so long and passionately about a topic, and she had to admit that he had sold her.

"All right," she said, "you've made your point, but please, Femi, you must be open with me and let me know everything that's going on, otherwise it means we don't have a relationship of trust."

"Understood," he said, kissing her cheek. "Am really sorry."

"You're lucky I love you," she said, half grumpily.

He laughed and hugged her, rocking her back and forth. "What kind of car do you want?"

She pulled back to look at him. "What?"

"I have a friend who can get us the best vehicles straight from the UK at cheap prices."

"How does he get them so cheap?"

"That's not our concern," Femi said quickly. "Don't worry about things you don't need to. What vehicle do you fancy?"

"You already know how much I love Range Rovers."

"Yes, I do," Femi said, grinning. "Just checking. And of course, a Benz for me."

"How are you paying?" Ngozi asked.

"I have dollars with me," Femi said confidently, "but if you could top it up with money from your Naija dollar account, we'll have more than enough. Is that cool?"

"I can do that," she said.

"I'll text my UK guy to get started."

"Ruby red," she said. "Metallic."

"Come again?"

"Ruby red," she repeated. "That's the color I want my Rover to be."

Femi smiled at her specification. "I will see what I can do."

CHAPTER TWENTY-FOUR

"COME IN," JANET SAID, welcoming Femi and Ngozi to her home in Lapaz. "So, you are the lovely lady Femi always talks about!"

Ngozi laughed as she shook hands. "Thank you so much."

Janet brought them through a vestibule done all in white with a faux marble table upon which stood a vase of fake lilies—that was at least one demerit, in Ngozi's mind. The high-ceilinged sitting room was huge and filled with simulated leather armchairs and a sofa as big as a Ga fisherman's canoe.

"Please, have a seat," Janet said, gesturing at the sofa. "Awuni should be joining us very soon."

Femi and Ngozi sat together in front of the coffee table and Janet took a seat opposite.

"When did you arrive?"

"A couple of days ago," Femi said.

"Welcome. Glad to have you."

Janet rang a small bell sitting on the side table and the "house-boy," no more a boy than Janet was a girl, dutifully appeared.

"Bring something for the guests, Amos," Janet ordered.

"Yes, madam."

Turning to Ngozi, Janet asked, "How are you finding Ghana?"

"It's great," Ngozi said. "You know, Naija people love to come to Accra for vacation. I lived here before, though, so I'm no stranger."

They made small talk as Amos brought in Bel-Aqua water and two bottles of ice-cold Blue Skies pineapple juice. Ngozi and Femi took the juice while Janet chose the Bel-Aqua.

They heard the front door close and someone moving around in the vestibule. Moments later, Awuni came in. He gave Femi a hearty handshake and then a softer and less familiar one to Ngozi.

"Nice to meet you," Awuni said. "Femi has been singing your praises to us."

"Really!" Ngozi said coyly.

"Absolutely," Awuni said, sitting next to Janet. Compared to her, he was quite diminutive. The drizzle outside had dampened his African-print shirt. "So, you will be Femi's assistant?" he said to Ngozi.

"Yes, I will," Ngozi said sweetly. She would have preferred the term *Femi's co-manager*, but she let that go for now.

"She's very good at organizing," Femi said, sending her a smile, which she returned.

"I will be handling the ladies from recruitment to bookings and so on," Ngozi said.

Janet crossed her legs at the knees. She unconsciously made circles in the air with her free foot. "Have you done something like this before?" she asked Ngozi, who thought she detected some condescension.

"Not as such, no."

Ngozi knew what Janet was thinking. *Aren't you a little too young for this?*

Femi jumped in. "That's one of the reasons we've come to you. For some tips from the master herself."

Janet laughed, clearly relishing the compliment.

Ngozi directed her attention to her. "Madam Janet, I was wondering how many girls you have under you."

"I have nineteen at the moment."

"Are they all operating at your hotel?"

"The Alligator? Yes. We have five roamers on the street and fourteen sitters who stay inside. We do it like that because some of the men don't like stopping on the street to negotiate and pick up the girls. Some of the clients have their favorite sitters."

"Please, how much do the girls pay you every month?"

"It depends," Janet said. "You know, the girls are from all around—Nigeria, Burkina, Côte d'Ivoire, and Togo. Most of them are Nigerians, though. We pay for their transportation, we pay the smugglers and drivers or the speedboat operators, and we also pay the immigration officials and policemen at the border so they'll look the other way and let the smugglers and women in without penalty. All that takes a lot of money, which the girls must pay back with interest. So, what they pay me is contingent on where they hail from, but using Nigeria as an example, whatever I spent to bring them to Accra, I charge them four hundred percent."

Ngozi tried not to show her shock. *Four hundred percent?*

Perhaps Janet sensed Ngozi's surprise, because she went on almost defensively, "I'm giving them a place to sleep and I've spent a lot of money bringing them to Accra. Their lives in Nigeria were horrible. Look at those Boko Haram terrorists running around kidnapping girls, torturing, and raping them and all that."

Ngozi took some offense at this. It wasn't as if Boko was *every-where* in her homeland. "So, I guess you treat your ladies very well," she said, with some implied doubt.

"Oh, very well," Janet reassured her.

"What about the girls who aren't able to pay you at the rate you ask them to?"

Janet smiled slightly. "Well, there are ways we remind them how important it is."

"They are grateful to be here in Ghana to work and make a better life for themselves," Awuni added.

Was that so? Possibly, but Ngozi wasn't completely swayed.

The front door slammed and footsteps approached from the vestibule.

"That must be Ben," Janet said.

A man in his mid-twenties appeared. He was a little shorter than Femi with a sullen mouth and empty eyes.

Janet's face lit up. "That's my son, Ben-Kwame."

"Good morning," he said to Femi and Ngozi with a nod and not much of a smile. His skin was fair compared to his mother's— or he could be a nephew she was calling "son," which wasn't uncommon.

"Ben helps at the hotels," Janet said, gazing at him with pride bordering on adoration. "How was the movie house?"

"Fine, Mummy. Just some few repairs and it will be okay."

Ben turned and left abruptly, which Ngozi found odd.

"We are thinking of buying a movie house," Janet explained to Femi and Ngozi. "But we're not a hundred percent certain, so I sent Ben to look at the place."

"That will be a great addition," Femi commented.

Ngozi was at sea. Suddenly they were talking about a movie business?

"So, Madam Janet," Femi said, "I think it will be good if Ngozi can accompany you to the Alligator and see how things are done there, and maybe see how the girls operate in the street."

"Good idea," Janet agreed.

"I'll call you," Femi said, rising.

Janet saw them to the door to say goodbye.

As Ngozi and Femi got into the car, she noticed his silence and set jaw. "What's wrong?" she asked.

"Nothing," he said, pushing the ignition button.

She looked out of the window.

Five minutes later, Femi spoke. "You need to calm down and not be so inquisitive with all those questions about what they pay the workers and all that."

"I was making harmless inquiries," Ngozi said, pouting.

Femi shook his head. "You can ask *me* such things—not them. We don't want any *wahala* between us and them."

"Okay, okay." She turned resentfully away from him, her head to the window. But she thought of something and turned back. "What were they saying about movie houses? Are they getting into the film business too?"

Femi chuckled, his mood lightening. "Technically, they show movies there, but that's not what guys go there for. They go to have sex."

"In other words," Ngozi said dryly, "another variety of brothel."

"Exactly."

"By the way, what did you think of Ben-Kwame?"

Femi shrugged. "He seems okay. Why do you ask?"

"No special reason," she said, but thinking about the man sent shivers down her vertebrae. "Have you visited the Alligator?"

"Not yet," Femi said. "Should we pass by and see the place?"

"Yeah," Ngozi said. "I'm curious."

From where they were, Femi took Nii Okaiman Avenue and made a left on Flower Street, following it to Tulip Link to make a right. From that point, the road was unpaved and dusty. The Alligator came up on the right, its name in block letters atop a chop bar to the right of a partially open, rusty gate. On a blue wall shielding the chop bar from the dust of the road was a not-too-bad rendering of an alligator, except that its tail looked more like a mermaid's than a reptile's.

The hotel had a three-star rating online, which, in Ngozi's estimation, was overgenerous. The color scheme was an odd, dysphoric green. She caught a glimpse of the courtyard beyond the gate, and from somewhere inside, loud trap music was blaring. It appeared rather desolate for now, but Ngozi imagined that at night, the scene was quite different.

"Looks like they have a bar upstairs," Femi said. "Want to stop for a drink?"

He cackled with laughter at the look Ngozi gave him, as if to say, "Over my dead body."

"Let's go somewhere for lunch," she said. "There's a nice Italian restaurant at the Marina Mall near the airport."

"Perfect," Femi said. "Let's do just that."

PART FIVE

CHAPTER TWENTY-FIVE

DIAMOND, ONLY SEVENTEEN, HAD come to Accra to escape a tough life in her Nigerian hometown, Benin City. Her stepfather had physically abused her for years. The last time he hit her was the day she left. Her right eye swollen shut from his blows, she sought refuge with a girlfriend, who tried to comfort her as she wept.

The following day, Diamond's girlfriend mentioned she knew a man called Mr. X who took Nigerian girls to Ghana, where employment opportunities abounded. There were cleaning jobs, hairstyling, shopkeeping, and so on.

This Mr. X said he had a contact in Ghana, a woman who helped runaway girls. Diamond, desperate, clutched at this straw. She never returned home, and two months later, she joined a van full of young women and arrived in Accra around eight-thirty at night after a taxing journey. Mr. X, riding shotgun, had negotiated the mess at the borders, bribing officials to ignore the inadequacy of many of the passengers' travel documents.

Dead tired, Diamond had no idea where she was, but her mood was one of elation that she was finally in Ghana. Young and strong, she could handle anything and looked forward to beginning work, no matter where or what it was to be. The girls traveling with Diamond dropped down at various locations in groups or in pairs until Diamond found herself alone in the van. After passing through dark, rutted streets, the driver pulled over alongside a two-story building with the name ALLIGATOR in large, faded yellow-and-blue block letters.

"E be here say we dey comot," Mr. X said to Diamond, "but first, you give me your passport for safekeeping."

Diamond raised her eyebrows. "Please, you say for . . ."

"For security," he said sharply, holding out his palm and curling and uncurling his four fingers in unison.

It seemed odd to Diamond, because she had paid a lot of money for the passport. Reluctantly, she handed it over to Mr. X, who muttered an insincere thank you and said, "Let's go."

Still unclear what in the world was going on, Diamond followed Mr. X through a door at the side of the entrance gate. They found themselves in a large yard in which a few scrawny girls were hanging out and interacting with men, some of whom were drunk or stoned. To Diamond's immediate right was a flight of steps up to the bar, where a DJ was spinning hip-hop music at top volume. Directly ahead was an above-ground pool in which a young man and equally young woman were playing around. To Diamond's left was a lonely chair and table upon which empty beer bottles were waiting to be collected.

The dim hue of yellow-tinted recessed lighting showcased the receptionist at the front desk dozing with her head on her forearms.

"Good evening," Mr. X said loudly, his voice echoing somewhat in the unadorned lobby.

The receptionist jerked awake, momentarily confused. She straightened her bad wig and tried to look alert. "Yes please?"

Mr. X approached the desk. "I've brought Diamond to Madam Janet."

"Ah," the receptionist said vaguely. "Then it's okay, please."

"What is okay?"

"You can leave her here, please. I will inform the madam."

"All right," Mr. X said. He turned and walked out as Diamond looked from him to the receptionist in bewilderment.

The receptionist took out her phone. "Please have a seat," she said to Diamond, pointing to a red plastic chair. On the phone she said, "The girl is here."

She ended the call and Diamond waited for her to say something, but nothing came. Instead, the receptionist stared at her phone and scrolled.

A plump girl in tight shorts and red high heels came in with an older man, and they disappeared into a corridor behind the lobby. Diamond idly watched the TV placed high on the wall while she waited.

Another woman appeared and walked up. She was bone thin and sickly looking.

"Are you Diamond?" she asked.

"Yes please."

"Come with me."

Diamond followed her up the stairs to an open corridor overlooking the driveway, then past several rooms from which muffled noises and conversations emanated. The thin woman opened the door to the second-to-last room and ushered Diamond inside.

Three girls were inside the marijuana-suffused room. One was making herself up in a cracked mirror propped up against a box on a small table full of lotions and makeup kits, and another, seated on a rickety chair, was having hair extensions put in by the third.

"This is Diamond," the escort said curtly, and left.

The girl in the blond wig smiled and said, "Hello. You are welcome. I'm Bridget. That's Lacey and Victoria over there."

Lacey was the one getting her hair done.

"Hi," Victoria said, taking Diamond in with an intense but brief stare.

Lacey muttered a greeting but didn't move her head lest she destroy the work of art in progress.

"Oh, please have a seat," Bridget said to Diamond, clearing junk off a chair in the corner.

"Have you done this work before?" Bridget asked. She was full-figured, her breasts squished into a tight top.

"Which kind of work, please?" Diamond asked.

Bridget frowned, and then her expression cleared as she grasped what was happening. "You no *sabi wetin* we dey do here, *abi?*" she asked Diamond, who had already figured out Bridget's origins. She was clearly a fellow Naija woman.

"I no *sabi*," Diamond said.

Bridget took a deep breath and let it out forcefully. "Look, my dear, this hotel, the Alligator, is a prostitution house. You are here to get clients—men who will fuck you or you give them a blowjob and so on. That's all. No mystery about it. No one told you why you were coming to this place, right?"

Diamond shook her head.

"I'm sure they promised you some kind of cleaning job or working in a shop." Bridget cheupsed. "They are always deceiving people. And I guess Mr. X took away your passport, right?"

Diamond nodded, dumbfounded.

"They do it to everybody," Bridget said, making a *what-can-I-say* face. "It's so you can't escape back to Nigeria. Okay, look, we are going to work very soon till the early morning. You can have that mat over there to sleep on. When a new girl comes, we lock the door—that's the rules—so if you need to piss, we have a bowl under the bed, you can use that."

The enormity of what was unfolding was only now beginning to take full effect. First, Diamond had felt disbelief, now it was horror.

"If you want to shit," Bridget said, "do it now and empty yourself, because we don't shit in the bowl."

Diamond nodded dumbly. What she was hearing made sense, but at the same time, nothing made sense.

IN THE MORNING, Diamond woke to find only Bridget in the room sleeping on one of a couple of floor mattresses. The room was dim, but when Diamond pulled one of the curtains to look outside, the sun was already bright and hot. Bridget stirred, picked up her head for a second, turned over, and went back to sleep. Diamond tried the door only to find it locked. She needed to go to the toilet badly. She fidgeted at the door as the pressure on her bladder intensified.

Someone fiddled with the lock from outside and pushed open the door. A woman entered, followed by a young man.

"You are Diamond?" she asked.

"Yes please."

"Welcome. I am Madam Janet." Her face bore neither smile nor frown. The man leaned against the wall with his arms folded. "And that is my son, Ben-Kwame."

"So, you will be working for us," Janet said. "Ben-Kwame will protect you from bad-men trouble. If you have any questions, you can ask us and the other girls can also help you. You will start work tonight. Do you have any other clothes besides what you're wearing?"

"A few, please."

"Okay—maybe Lacey can lend you something. She has a similar physique."

"Yes please."

"You will pay me five thousand *cedis* a month."

This was Diamond's second blow within twelve hours. First, that she was to be a prostitute, second, that she would be handing over a lot of money to this Madam Janet. *Why?*

Janet must have sensed Diamond's puzzlement. "It's for the cost of bringing you here all the way from Nigeria and having this place to sleep. I pay the rent."

When Diamond had paid Mr. X, she had thought that was the end of it. She should have known it was too good to be true.

"If you try to run away somewhere," Madam Janet said, "we will catch and beat you well-well, like you Nigerians say."

Ben-Kwame snorted and gave a one-sided smile that chilled Diamond to her bone marrow.

CHAPTER TWENTY-SIX

THE SEX WORKERS HUNG around the Alligator area, strolling up and down the street in front of the guesthouse, sometimes calling out to potential customers driving by. On this, her first night, Diamond was too timid to approach men in their vehicles. Instead, she stood passively and nervously at the side of the road waiting to be summoned by a client.

"Sweetheart," Bridget said firmly but kindly, "if you don't go to them, they won't call on you. The next one, I will go with you."

It wasn't long before a sleek BMW slowed down and stopped not far from where the two women were standing.

"Come, let's go," Bridget said, grabbing Diamond's arm. "First you greet him and ask him what he wants. Then we'll see what to do after that."

They went up to the car and Bridget shoved Diamond to the passenger window. She bent and peered inside. The driver was a big man, his beer belly almost touching the steering wheel.

"Good evening," Diamond stammered.

He gave her a stony stare.

"Please, what do you want?" Diamond asked, not sure how exactly to pose the question.

"You come to my house and then we discuss," the man said.

Bridget interrupted, elbowing her way into the window. "No please," she said with authority. "We decide right here." She ran down the prices for each service.

The man settled for a BJ.

"Get in!" Bridget urged Diamond in a loud whisper.

Diamond pulled open the door and got in. The car was blessedly cool compared to the stuffy night outside, and the seats smelled sweetly of new leather. The customer pulled out into the street, driving slowly, and looking around as if trying to locate something. He made a left at the junction, and then another left at Serious Street, where he bounced over a shallow ditch to a dark, deserted yard. He stopped the car and switched off the engine. Diamond looked around. It was dark and empty, with only the vague shadows of shuttered storefronts around them and in the distance.

The man reclined his seat all the way and unzipped his pants, pulling Diamond's head down to his crotch. She was sure she was supposed to get the money first, but she was too fearful to insist.

The man reached inside her blouse.

Diamond pulled away. "No."

"What no?"

"That's not allowed—"

He made a noise of disgust. "Okay, go ahead."

Her head in his lap, Diamond hadn't a clue what she was doing.

"Do it," the man said aggressively. He pressed her head down forcibly. She panicked and struggled out of his grip, pulling back as if she had just tasted quinine.

"Hey!" the man shouted. "What is wrong with you?"

He slapped Diamond hard across the face. The back of her head thudded against the passenger window. He slapped her again. "Get out! Stupid girl, wasting my time like this."

Diamond struggled with the door handle and stumbled out. The car pulled away, scattering dust in its wake.

Shaking, Diamond made her way back to the Alligator. *I can't do this*, she thought. *Why am I doing this?*

Inside of the courtyard, the Alligator was busier than Diamond had left it. Bridget spotted her as she entered.

"What happened?" Bridget asked. "You don't look good at all."

"He hurt me," Diamond said. She was sniffling, trying not to cry.

"The man you went with?"

Diamond nodded. Someone tapped her on the shoulder and she turned to see Ben-Kwame behind her. "Come with me," he said.

She followed him up the steps and to the left on the second-floor veranda. After they had gone past a couple of rooms, Ben stopped at the last door and unlocked it. He gestured to

Diamond to enter, after which he shut the door behind them. Diamond realized it was his private room split into a small office and bedroom.

"Sit down, please," Ben said, pointing to a chair behind her. She did so nervously.

"The man you went with in the BMW," he said, "do you know who he is?"

"No please."

"His name is Frank, and he's a friend—a very important man around town. This is the first time he has come here. He called me to tell me he paid you money but you fought him."

Diamond scowled, indignation rising. "*No.* He said blowjob first, but he didn't pay."

"Give me the money he paid you," Ben said, holding out his palm.

"He didn't pay me!" Diamond protested, her voice rising in pitch and intensity.

Ben came up to her almost casually, wrapping his right hand around her neck. "You are a liar. And a thief."

"No please," she said, her voice strangled and raspy.

"I don't like liars. I don't like thieves. Do you know what I do to them?"

OUTSIDE, BRIDGET CREPT up to the door of Ben's apartment and listened. At first, she only heard murmurs from inside, but then began the sickening sounds of body blows and the thuds of someone crashing against the walls. Bridget cringed and turned away. *He's doing it again.* As Diamond's terrified shrieks of pain grew louder, Bridget pressed her palms over her ears to block out the sound. Finally, she walked away crying, feeling utterly helpless. There was nothing she could do to rescue Diamond. This is what Ben-Kwame did to women.

CHAPTER TWENTY-SEVEN

FEMI WANTED ALL TYPES of girls to perform sex work at the White House, but they all had to be beautiful. He combed the internet in search of women with the right look: an air of confidence and sophistication, fair skin, tiny waists, ample breasts and buttocks, and impeccable hair and nails. Femi found an embarrassment of riches: hundreds and hundreds of women on Exotic Ghana, Fuckbook Ghana, Locanto, Passion.com, and countless others. All with direct phone numbers, they were easy to reach and, in general, swift to respond. Femi invited the best-looking of them to send in an audition video with the prospect of good, steady money at the White House. Those who made the cut went on to an interview with Femi, with or without Ngozi present.

For the most part, it was Femi who communicated with Awuni and Janet. He appeared to have a lot more respect for the couple than Ngozi did. She couldn't explain the discomfort she had felt in Janet's company, nor could Femi understand it.

"Ngozi, you don't have to like her," Femi remarked, "but we do need to maintain good relations with her. Up to now, you *still* haven't paid a visit to the Alligator. For the sake of PR, I think you should."

Ngozi groaned. "Must I?"

"Are you being a snob, or what?" Femi asked with a tad of irritation.

"Me, a snob?"

They both laughed. Ngozi had no problems with snobbishness as long as she was the perpetrator. Finally, backing down in response to Femi's pleas, Ngozi called Janet to make nice. They agreed to link up at the Alligator without setting a firm date, which resulted in the entire month of September sneaking by without

the two women getting together. The real reason for this procrasti-
nation, Ngozi reasoned, was that they simply didn't like each other.

One morning during the third week in October, Ngozi finally
made a valiant effort and arrived at the Alligator for a tour with
Madam Janet. The sun was already searing and a few men and
women were frolicking in the pool.

"As you can see," Janet said, sounding proud, "people enjoy the
pool very much."

They went into the lobby, which was dimly lit. The place was
shabby, but admittedly not as bad as Ngozi had imagined when she
and Femi had done the drive-by. From the lobby, they continued
to the second floor. A long balcony overlooking the pool ran alongside the guestrooms. Ngozi noticed an unfinished, two-story building
on the other side of the wall bordering the Alligator's rear perimeter.

"Is that a part of the hotel?" Ngozi asked, pointing.

Janet nodded. "Hopefully, it will be. The construction is
delayed because someone is disputing the original ownership of
the plot and the legality of the sale. We've been in court with this
thing for more than one year." She sighed and shook her head in
resignation. "Ghana for you. What can you do?"

"Try Nigeria," Ngozi said laconically.

Janet chuckled. "Let me show you one of our rooms."

Walking several meters down, she chose a key from a large col-
lection on a ring and unlocked the room. It was rudimentary, with
plain beige tiling, a queen-size bed, a thin cloth curtain on the
window, a small wide-screen TV with exposed wires, and a roughly
hewn, free-standing closet with a misaligned door.

"Mm-hm," Ngozi murmured neutrally. It was what you got for
the price. Rather smugly, she thought of the splendor of the White
House compared to this place.

They left that room, Janet locking the door behind them. Her
phone rang.

"Hello?" Janet frowned. "I can't hear you. Let me call you back."
She said to Ngozi, "Excuse me one minute while I go downstairs
for this call. The signal is bad up here."

"Of course. No problem."

While Janet went off, Ngozi idly watched the guests in the pool.
She heard a whisper and looked right and left to locate its origin.

"*Madam!*"

The door of one of the guest rooms down the line was slightly open and two eyes were peeping through.

"Yes?" Ngozi said.

"Please, can I talk to you?"

Uncertainly, Ngozi walked up to the stranger. "What's up?"

"I heard you talking to Madam Janet," the woman said, her voice hushed. "Help me, please. I need to run away."

"I don't understand."

"I'm from Nigeria," the woman said. "They brought me here telling me I was going to have work as a cleaner, but they are forcing me to be a prostitute. They've been beating me."

She opened the door a little wider and Ngozi drew in her breath at the sight of the woman's distended, battered face. "Oh, my God. Who did that to you?"

"Ben-Kwame—Madam Janet's son." Tears squeezed out of the woman's puffy eyes swollen to slits. "He says I'm a thief and a liar, and I have to pay him back money I stole. But I haven't stolen anything."

"What's your name?"

"Chioma, but they call me Diamond."

"I'm Ngozi."

Their names signified they were both Igbo. They warmed to each other at once and, keeping their voices low, switched to their mother tongue.

"They're going to kill me," Diamond said, her voice shaking. "*Abeg*, help me."

"I . . . I'm not sure if I can—"

Ngozi glanced furtively down the veranda. Janet could return at any moment. "Do you have a phone?"

Diamond shook her head. "I had one, but someone stole it before I left Benin City."

Ngozi was torn.

"*Please*," Diamond implored.

Ngozi started to think, *Femi can do it*, but she slowed herself down. She needed to be sensible about this. She didn't know this Diamond—who knew if her story was true? But, judging from her battered face, it must have been. Ngozi couldn't just abandon her—an Igbo sister, especially.

"Tonight, I will be at the roadside wearing a red skirt and white top," Diamond continued, "and I will stand—"

"*Shh!*" Ngozi said, as she heard footsteps coming up the stairs. She returned quickly to the balcony railing as Diamond shut the door hurriedly and retreated from view.

Janet appeared at the top of the stairs to rejoin Ngozi. "So, how do you find everything here at the Alligator?"

"It's a very nice place," Ngozi lied. "Congrats."

Janet looked proud. "Thank you very much. Where is Femi today?"

"He had some business to attend to," Ngozi said.

Janet walked her back to the street where Ngozi had parked her new, gleaming ruby-red Range Rover, courtesy of Femi's UK contact. She saw Janet's eyes take in the vehicle and devour it. *Oh, how Ghanaians love SUVs.*

NGOZI PULLED IN at the MaxMart in the strip mall on Nii Okaiman Avenue. There was always shopping to do.

Inside, Ngozi took her time browsing the shelves. She was in Household Goods when she realized that a man in her peripheral vision was staring at her from the other end of the aisle. She glanced quickly at him but returned to filling her shopping basket.

"Excuse me?" The man was approaching, squinting at Ngozi with his head tilted as if she were a curiosity item.

She looked at him. "Yes?"

"Aren't you . . . aren't you Ambassador Ojukwu's daughter? Ngozi, right?"

Her impulse was to answer in the affirmative, but an alarm rose quickly in her mind. She didn't recognize the man, but his accent was Nigerian and he very likely knew—or at some point had known—Ngozi's father.

"Sorry, no," she said tersely, walking away from him. She didn't want him to scrutinize her any further, so she surreptitiously abandoned her basket in one of the aisles and left the store in a hurry.

Back in the Rover, she made a quick stop at the roast-plantain seller before taking off again. Ngozi wasn't sure if she should be worried about the encounter with the man in the store. Assuming he knew her father and still had his contact info, would he call him? She was betting—hoping—that the man would forget about it and suppose he had been mistaken.

At that moment, Ngozi felt a twinge of nostalgia and realized that she missed her parents. That came as quite a surprise.

"WE HAVE TO help her get out of there," Ngozi said to Femi in the White House office.

Femi had listened to her story about Diamond. He tapped his fingertips on the surface of his desk. "Ngo . . ."

"Femi."

"It's not our problem," he said. "That's their mess over there."

"So, you're just going to ignore Diamond's plight? Is that what I'm hearing from you?"

"You're saying we should go to the Alligator to practically kidnap the woman, and then what? Bring her here? What am I going to say to Janet and Awuni? It will look like we're stealing property from them."

"She's not a piece of property," Ngozi said peevishly.

Femi rolled his eyes. "Come on, now. You know what I mean. We've barely started a business association with them—"

"*You* have," Ngozi amended. "When you met them in April, I wasn't there."

"Whatever, whatever," Femi said impatiently. "Point is, we're not going to instigate a squabble this early in the game."

"So, in other words, you don't give a fock."

Femi was becoming irritated. "Ngo, please, I don't have time for this. Awuni and Janet are running their place; we're going to run ours. We don't have to follow what they do, but we can't dictate to them either."

"I don't understand what the hell you see in those two," Ngozi said resentfully. "Especially the woman. I can't stand her."

"I know," Femi said, returning to his laptop. "Ngo, please. I need to finish up here."

His sharp tone surprised Ngozi. She pulled in a deep breath, breathed out, and got up to leave. "Okay," she muttered. "So be it."

THE PLAN TAKING a still-nebulous shape in Ngozi's mind was brimming with uncertainties and unknowns. Her biggest challenge was that Diamond couldn't be reached by phone.

Femi was still in the office and would likely be there beyond six that evening. Ngozi called him to say she was going to the A&C Mall for a "little" shopping. He said okay. He didn't worry about her when she went shopping, even if she tarried.

It took her an excruciating ninety traffic minutes to travel the mere eleven kilometers between East Legon and Lapaz. Not even the Rover could assuage her impatience. Notwithstanding the delay, it was just before eight o'clock when Ngozi reached the junction of Tulip and Flower, where she paused and pulled over. *What's the best way to do this?* She hesitated, turned right and slid slowly up Tulip toward the Alligator, stopping again two blocks away. Ngozi could hear the thud of dance music blasting from the hotel's bar. Could she simply drive by hoping Diamond was there, and if so, pick her up and take off with her? Ngozi almost laughed at her own inept idea. *In plain sight of Diamond's captors, you're going to rescue her in a conspicuously red Range Rover?* Which, Ngozi reminded herself, Janet had feasted her eyes upon earlier that day.

There had to be another way. Ngozi surveyed the landscape ahead. The Alligator was to her right. A block away, on the same side of the street, a fast-food kiosk was doing good business. Next to it, a teenager sitting on a wooden crate scrolled through his phone. At some distance behind the kiosk, to Ngozi's right, loomed the shadow of the dark, uncompleted hotel annex mired in litigation.

Ngozi eased forward cautiously and found what she had hoped for: a turnoff that took her to the front of the annex. The Rover bumped over rough, unpaved ground littered with empty water bottles and discarded plastic bags. Ngozi parked, alighted, and switched on her phone flashlight against the almost complete darkness. She went in the open side of the building, walking with care across the dusty concrete to the other end. Separating the premises of the main hotel from the annex was a flimsy wire fence with several gaps in it. Ngozi chose one and managed to widen the aperture.

She left the building to return to the junction of the turnoff with the main road and crossed the street. From behind a shuttered storage shed, she could observe the Alligator in secret. Having held in her mind the movie image of dozens of sex workers walking up and down the street, Ngozi was a little surprised she saw only a couple of women standing around the entrance until she recalled Janet saying that the Alligator had fewer "roaming" sex workers than "sitters."

Ngozi came to attention as she saw another worker exit the front gate. *That's Diamond—red skirt and white top.* Now, how could Ngozi get to her? She chewed on her bottom lip as she pondered the quandary until she came up with a solution. She trotted back to the Rover to find a pen and scrap of paper on which she wrote a short message in block letters. Then, she returned to the spot where the teenager was still glued to his phone.

"Good evening, boss," she greeted him.

He looked up with adolescent disinterest, but as Ngozi explained her proposal, he nodded and smiled. "No problem."

Ngozi bought a small serving of yam chips in a Styrofoam container and placed the note right on top of the chips. She handed the ensemble to the teenager along with his tip of ten *cedis*, which wasn't bad for a couple of minutes of work. He walked off to the Alligator entrance gate as Ngozi returned to the annex to wait for Diamond. In the ensuing ten minutes, Ngozi grew progressively more anxious as she got the feeling that her scheme might not be working, but at last, Diamond appeared at the fence and Ngozi pulled aside the gap to ease the passage through.

The two women embraced briefly.

"This way," Ngozi said, taking the lead back to the Rover. "Let's talk."

Diamond was breathing rapidly from exertion and excitement. "God bless you for coming—"

"Hey!"

The women turned at the shout. A man was at the fence training a flashlight beam on them. "What are you doing here?" he bellowed.

"It's Ben-Kwame," Diamond gasped.

Ngozi grabbed her wrist. "To my car—*run!*"

They began a sprint out of the building, but in the rush, Diamond caught her foot on a length of rebar projecting from the ground. She stumbled and fell. Ngozi helped her up as Ben vaulted the fence with extraordinary agility. Diamond's fall had cost precious seconds, allowing him to gain distance on the women. "*Hey!*" he yelled again.

As she circled around to the driver's side, Ngozi fumbled for her key fob to unlock the Rover, tugged the door open, and scrambled in. Diamond did the same, but Ben-Kwame, closer to her than to Ngozi, managed to grab one of Diamond's legs by the ankle. She cried out and tried to shake him off, but his grip was firm and Diamond was half inside and half outside.

Ngozi started the Rover as she thrust her seatbelt into Diamond's hands. "Hold on *tight!*"

Diamond did, and as the engine engaged and the Rover shot forward, the seatbelt mechanism locked and kept Diamond in place. Ben lost his grasp on her ankle and Diamond drew in her feet. With the vehicle's momentum, the door slammed shut. Ngozi and Diamond heard Ben screeching in apparent agony and crying out repeatedly, "*Stop!*"

His voice seemed unexpectedly close, causing Diamond to peer out the window into the dimness.

"Oh!" she exclaimed. "His fingers are stuck in the door! He's dragging on the ground."

"Shit." Ngozi stopped and unlocked the passenger side with her controls. "Release him—quick."

Diamond opened the door briefly and shut it again as Ben's hand fell away. "Okay, let's go."

Ngozi gunned the engine and they fled.

NGOZI DROVE A couple of miles, taking several left and right turns as she looked up frequently in the rearview mirror to be sure no one was following them. Finally, she pulled into a fuel station and stopped abruptly next to the convenience store. She looked at Diamond, and then put her head back and heaved a sigh, realizing how much she was trembling. Only then did she begin to take stock of what had just happened.

Overwhelmed, Diamond suddenly began to cry. Ngozi released her seatbelt and reached out to comfort her new friend. After a couple of moments, Diamond drew away, wiping her tears and pulling herself together. "So, what now please, madam?"

"My name is Ngozi, not 'madam,'" Ngozi said. "We're going home now."

"Okay, madam—I mean, Ngozi."

Almost at the same time, the two women realized they were wasting their energy on English when they could be happily speaking Igbo. There was nothing like one's mother tongue. On the way home, they began to relax and even laugh.

But Ngozi needed to tell Diamond something before they arrived home. "Listen, my boyfriend, Femi, told me not to come to your aid, but I've done it anyway. So, he's going to be angry, but I don't want you to worry about it. I'll take care of him."

"Okay," Diamond said, but she didn't sound completely at ease.

"What are your long-term plans?" Ngozi asked. "Or maybe I'm asking that question too soon."

"I . . . I don't know," Diamond said in a tiny voice.

They pulled into the driveway of the house and Ngozi carefully eased the Rover in beside Femi's royal-blue Benz, another relatively cheap buy from his wheeler-dealing UK friend. God forbid she scrape his brand-new baby.

Now that they were there, Ngozi's apprehension over how Femi might react increased tenfold. Frankly, the situation was a mess, and it was all Ngozi's doing. Should she have left well enough alone?

CHAPTER TWENTY-EIGHT

Ngozi asked Diamond to wait in the Rover for a moment. Trying to decide the best way to tell Femi about what had just happened, she entered the house through the garage side door.

He was in the sitting room watching MMA from the leather recliner as he ate plantain chips and yelled at the TV. He looked up as Ngozi came in. "Jesus, where were you? I texted you a couple of times."

"Oh, sorry," Ngozi said, sitting on the arm of his chair. She bent down to kiss him as he pursed his lips up at her. "I missed it."

Femi jumped up with a roar as the fighter he was backing crushed his opponent. "*Yes!* Now that's what I'm talking about, baby!"

Not a bad imitation of an American accent, either. "Honey," Ngozi said, "we need to talk. Can you switch that off?"

"Oh, shit," Femi said, turning off the TV. "I don't like the sound of that. What's going on? Wait, did you scratch my Benz?"

She shook her head.

"Okay, then what's up?"

Ngozi decided to go the blunt route. "You remember I told you about Diamond, the girl they were beating up at the Alligator?"

"Yeah, what about her?"

"I went there and picked her up."

Femi froze. "What?"

"Yeah."

"Hold on, hold on. You mean you went . . ."

Ngozi rushed through in a single breath. "I rendezvoused with her near the building they're constructing next to the main hotel. But then, Ben-Kwame came chasing after us. She got in the car, but Ben got hold of her leg and almost pulled her out. She managed to hold on and we escaped." She omitted the fingers-in-the-door part—not too much all at once, she reasoned.

Femi eyed her skeptically. "You're just kidding, right?"

"No. I'm serious."

Femi gasped. "Are you crazy?"

Ngozi stared at him in silence.

"Oh, God." In disbelief, Femi put both hands on his head. "Why have you done this? Where have you taken the girl?"

"I brought her here," Ngozi said sullenly. "She's waiting in the car."

"What?" Femi cried. "Ngo, Awuni and those guys will be on our doorstep any minute now accusing us of kidnapping."

"Why?" Ngozi stammered feebly. "They don't know it was me."

Femi groaned. "Come *on*, stop. They all know what you and your red Rover look like, sweetie."

"Well, yeah, true," Ngozi conceded. "Let her stay just for tonight—then we can figure something out."

"No."

"Femi, listen. Please. She could work for us as a cleaner at the hotel. She could be useful to us."

"But that's not the issue!" Femi shouted. "The problem is, what the fock do you think Awuni and Janet are going to do now? They're going to throw us out of the White House because you've just abducted one of their women. That's *money*."

"They were *abusing* her," Ngozi said, her voice beginning to rise as well. "Maybe you can sit back and shrug your shoulders because you're a man, but I can't, okay?"

"What does that have to do with anything? We're running a business here, not a charity." Palms to face, Femi moaned in physical pain. "Oh, Jesus, Ngo."

She watched as he paced like a caged panther.

"We're taking her back," he said abruptly.

Ngozi shook her head. "Absolutely not."

"You know what?" He stopped moving to glare at her. "It's time you do as I say. I'm in charge here, got it? You're the woman. I'm the man and I'm the boss, whether you like it or not."

"Spoken just like a fucking ignorant Nigerian man," Ngozi sneered. "In the end, you're all the same."

She never saw him coming. In a fraction of a second he was in front of her and striking her hard across the face. Ngozi screamed and tried to scramble over the back of the sofa to get away from him. But he grabbed her and threw her over the armrest to the floor. She rolled over and staggered up, breathing hard, with her hand pressed to her cheek.

"What are you doing?" she said in disbelief. "Femi, what are you doing?"

He stared back in shock of his own. As she began to weep, he came around the sofa and tried to take her in his arms. "Baby, I'm sorry. I didn't mean—"

She slapped his hands away. "*Don't touch me!*" she shouted.

They faced each other like two opposing armies at an impasse. Finally, Ngozi said quietly, "Diamond will sleep in the guest room, I'll sleep in our bedroom, and you can sleep wherever the hell you want—just not with me."

She returned to the garage, where Diamond had alighted from the Rover and was staring at something in the jamb of the front passenger door.

"What is it?" Ngozi said.

Diamond pointed. Stuck against the door jamb was a bloody object. Ngozi looked a little closer and then recoiled. They were looking at the tip of Ben-Kwame's amputated finger.

NGOZI GAVE DIAMOND some nightwear and an outfit for the morning. Diamond, who was looking around the interior of the home in awe, repeatedly thanked Ngozi so profusely and said "God bless you" so many times that Ngozi had to stop her.

She heard a car start up downstairs and went to the window in time to catch the sight of Femi leaving. For the very first time, the notion that he might be going to sleep with another woman entered Ngozi's head. She shook it off and said good night to Diamond.

Alone in her room, Ngozi sat at the side of her bed feeling wretched. Everything was fucked up, and she suddenly had an impulse to call her parents. But a voice inside her head warned her how disastrous that would be. *You have enough trouble as it is.* She showered and despondently dragged herself to bed, where she lay staring at the ceiling and wondering where Femi was. Her guess was he had gone to the White House to spend the night.

Her phone rang and the screen said *Janet*. Ngozi considered not responding, but she knew the other woman would keep trying, even throughout the night if it came to that. It was best to deal with her now.

"Hello?" she said softly.

"You bitch," Janet said. "You fucking bitch. You come and kidnap Diamond and you think you can get away with it? Ben-Kwame saw you. Do you know what you did to him? One of his fingers got cut off because of you. He's at the hospital right now."

"Not my problem," Ngozi said blandly.

"Where have you taken Diamond?"

Ngozi didn't respond. Instead, she found herself curling her lip in contempt.

"Answer me!" Janet cried.

"What was the question?"

"Heh! Don't play games with me, do you understand? Where is Diamond?"

"I've taken her to a safe place," Ngozi responded icily. "Your Ben-Kwame almost killed her beating her up like that."

"It's none of your business," Janet shouted.

"She asked for my help, and I gave it."

"You better bring her back here, or you'll be sorry."

"I'll never do that, so you can forget it."

"You will regret," Janet snapped and hung up.

"Idiot," Ngozi muttered. She had no respect for Janet and couldn't care less how furious the woman was or what kinds of threats she leveled.

She might call Femi, Ngozi speculated, but she was confident he would plead ignorance to avoid appearing even remotely involved in Diamond's rescue—or "kidnapping," as Janet called it.

Ngozi switched off the light and then switched it back on. She was exhausted but too tense to sleep. Her left cheek was still smarting and a trifle swollen from Femi's slap. Why, *why*, had he done it? Had Ngozi missed noticing a violent or abusive streak in him? It didn't seem to be in his character. Did he have anger smoldering so close to the surface that it was ready to explode at any instant?

Tears sprang and trailed down her face and onto the pillow. What in the world had she gotten herself into? Ngozi found the remote and began to watch replays of *Empire* to take her mind off the night's catastrophic events. After a little over an hour, she drifted into a fitful sleep.

AT THE HOTEL, Femi chose one of the suites, stripped to his boxers, and lay down to brood. *This wahala is not happening.* His phone rang and his heart leapt. *Ngozi.* He sat up and grabbed the phone. But it was Awuni calling.

"Fock," he muttered, rejecting the call. Predictably, Awuni called back in less than a minute.

"Listen, Mr. Femi," he said without a greeting. "I am basically a nice man, but if you try to cheat me, or steal from me, or in any way interfere with my business, I turn into a different person altogether."

"Sorry? What's going on?"

"You are quite aware of what your wife has done, and I know you put her up it."

"She's not my wife, but tell me what happened. Maybe I can help?"

"This evening she came to the Alligator and kidnapped Diamond, one of our ladies."

"She did *what?*" Femi said, with such conviction he almost fooled himself.

"I think you heard what I said."

"I don't know anything about it," Femi said, "but I'll call her right now to find out. I've been at the office all day and this evening. I'll get back to you."

"Okay, but whatever the case, I expect Diamond back here immediately."

Femi hung up and lay back. Of course, he had no intention of "getting back" to Awuni, but that didn't solve the fundamental problem at hand. Femi had thought Ngozi had had the plasticity he needed to form her in his image, but now he saw how wrong he had been. Ngozi was stubborn, and worse, she had a heart and a conscience, and that just didn't work in this business. Now, Femi was stuck with a do-gooder. Maybe his bringing her with him to Accra hadn't been such a great idea after all.

"Fock," he said again. "Fock, fock, *fock!*"

CHAPTER TWENTY-NINE

BY THE FOLLOWING MORNING, the previous night's texts from Femi, Awuni, and Janet—pleading, insulting, and everything in between—had not abated. Ngozi decided to block them on WhatsApp, at least temporarily. She needed to banish them from her mind for a while, clear her head, and find her reset button, wherever or whatever that was.

Diamond's presence in the house presented another dilemma: what to do with her. For now, Ngozi would move her into the servants' accommodations while they treaded water and bought some time. Furnishings in the quarters were minimal to none, so Ngozi was happy for the distraction of finding simple but essential items to equip the bedroom and bathroom. Over the next two days, the women worked together to make the place comfortable, and Ngozi found herself bonding with Diamond. She was unsophisticated, but she had a sweet, gentle spirit. By the weekend, she was in good shape as far as her living quarters were concerned.

On Saturday afternoon, leaving Diamond at home for a while, Ngozi went out to get her hair and nails done. These kinds of routines were comforting. That done, Ngozi picked up some additional household items and food to cook for the evening's dinner.

Returning home, she parked the Rover in her space and alighted to get the shopping bags out of the back seat. With both hands full, she shut the door with a deft hip, and started as she caught a shadow pass across the front of the garage. She began to turn but never completed the movement before someone got her in a chokehold.

"If you scream, I will cut your throat," he whispered, showing her a knife.

Nevertheless, as he dragged her back, she tried to resist, kicking out her legs and writhing, but she couldn't get out of his grip. She realized that the parked car to one side of the garage must have followed her in through the automatic gate, which had a sensor to prevent hitting incoming vehicles.

Her attacker had an accomplice, a short but burly man in a cap and Covid mask. Together, the two of them bound, gagged, and blindfolded Ngozi. Panic screamed in her brain, her first thought being that Awuni and Janet's henchmen were kidnapping her in retribution for Ngozi's "stealing" Diamond from the Alligator.

Are they going to torture me? Kill me?

The two men stuffed her into the trunk and slammed it shut. Only seconds later the car started up and pulled out of the yard. Hot gas fumes welled up from the vehicle, overwhelming her and rendering Ngozi faint and nauseated. She was drenched in sweat. She struggled against her restraints for a moment, but they were too tight to allow any meaningful movement. What was happening to her and where were they taking her?

The vehicle bounced and swerved several times. Whoever her two captors were, they were silent, but Ngozi could hear the muffled noise of traffic and people on a busy street. After another couple of turns, the sounds faded and they appeared to be on an unpaved road full of potholes, of which there were too many to count in Accra.

The car came to a stop. Because of the relative silence around her, Ngozi imagined they must be in a deserted area, the type where bodies could be dumped and left undiscovered for days or weeks or more. One of the vehicle's doors opened and approaching footsteps crunched on gravel. A key rattled in the lock. Ngozi squeezed her eyes tight underneath the blindfold and tensed up as if readying herself to be struck or otherwise manhandled. She felt the influx of fresh air, albeit warm and stuffy. She caught a soupçon of harsh body odor. The man gave her a poke, and when she didn't react, he slammed the trunk shut. With the return of the close quarters, she felt as though she was being smothered in a tight, enveloping blanket, and a new level of fear rose in her.

The vehicle stayed put for hours. Ngozi's sense of time was distorted, and she couldn't be certain of how long she floated in and out of a dreamlike state of confused, flitting thoughts and images.

Then the car started up again. Her heart rose briefly that the kidnapper would be taking her home now, but that hope dwindled the more the journey continued through busy streets again. She knew it must be night by now—possibly quite late—as she heard loudspeakers blaring popular tunes from all directions, probably from pavements and storefronts. Without earsplitting music, Ghanaian nightlife was incomplete.

Again, the ambient noise diminished somewhat as the vehicle slowed down, stopped, and reversed, its wheels crunching over a gravely, uneven surface. Ngozi hadn't been to church of any kind in years, but now she prayed as she never had.

The trunk opened, and four hands grasped Ngozi and heaved her out. Her side scraped painfully against the rear edge of the trunk and her feet struck against the ground. One of the men again lobbied the same threat as before. "If you struggle, I will cut your head off." His voice was raspy and chilling.

With no intention to make this easy for them, Ngozi became dead weight, but it didn't deter her captors much. To them, she was still feather-light. They lifted her clear off the ground and she realized they were descending a flight of steps. She counted them out—one, two, three, four, five. At the bottom, one of the men, perhaps the weaker of the two, was breathing hard from the effort. A set of keys jiggled in what sounded like a padlock and latch. They carried her into the room beyond, and the door slammed behind them. The place smelled of dank wood and concrete—a storage room of some kind?

They dropped Ngozi to the ground, which felt more like dirt than a finished floor. The men's footsteps receded and she heard the door open and bang shut again. She could feel her heart thumping. For several minutes, she was alone until the door opened and someone came in. Just one man now, it sounded like. As he got close, she detected the same body odor as before.

Without warning, he ripped off her blindfold, but it was pitch dark and she saw nothing until he switched on a phone flashlight and shone it into her eyes, which hurt. She shrank away, unable to see who was behind the harsh beam.

He held up a knife, which flashed a sharp glint across Ngozi's face.

"You scream or disobey me, I stab you in the throat. You hear?"
She nodded.

"Anyway, no one can hear you. We are underground. There are
no windows."

He freed her from the gag and she gasped involuntarily as she
caught her first unobstructed, extraordinarily gratifying breath in
several hours.

"Do you know who I am?" he asked.

She shook her head.

"You will soon," he said.

As he fished around in his pockets for something, he tilted the
flashlight, and its beam bounced against a wall in the room to ren-
der diffuse light, affording Ngozi a view not only of the extent of
the surrounding space, but also a brief glimpse of the man. He was
smaller than she had imagined, but he had one of those physiques
packed with muscle as dense as lead. He wore a cap, a Covid-type
mask, and a backpack.

He lit a marijuana joint and sat down cross-legged to smoke.
The sharp smell of the weed made Ngozi splutter briefly. He spent
some time smoking, and then scooted over to grope her. She
went rigid as he squeezed her breasts as though they were household sponges. He moved his hands down to paw her thighs and
buttocks. Her jeans were tight, and he didn't bother to struggle
with them. Instead, he inserted the knife blade underneath the
waistline and slashed the material away in one stroke. Her panties
were of no consequence. He ripped them off and she flinched,
reflexively clamping her thighs.

He sliced her ankle restraints and brought the knife back to her
neck. "Open your legs or I kill you right now."

She would almost prefer to die than to be raped. Would begging and pleading make him angrier or more humane? Would it
excite him further or tone him down?

"Please," she said. "I'm menstruating."

He was momentarily foiled. "What?"

"It's my time of the month," she explained. "Very heavy bleeding. Please, if you can wait two days, it will stop."

She was afraid he would try to ascertain whether she was being
truthful. In fact, she was on Depo injections and rarely had a

menstrual flow. He hesitated, considering her suggestion while regarding her with suspicion. Then he appeared to lose interest, turning to something else.

"Look," he said, holding up his right hand. "You see what you did?"

Ngozi saw his bandaged fingers and her stomach turned. *Ben-Kwame.*

"Do you know how much they pain me?" he asked.

"I'm sorry."

"You're sorry? *Kwasea.*" He slapped her face hard with his left hand. She jumped, but tried not to show any pain.

"Your so-called boyfriend, Femi," he sneered, "he's the one who told me to kidnap you so he can get money from your parents. What kind of boyfriend is that?"

For a moment, Ngozi didn't believe him, but then she thought of Femi's last set of vehement, malicious messages. Could what Ben was claiming be true?

He leaned over and dragged something into view—her purse. He had taken that as well. He tossed out miscellaneous items until he found her wallet. He took out the cash—five hundred *cedis*, or so—pocketed it, and then examined the rest.

"Where is your phone?"

She wasn't sure, but she thought it might have dropped between the seats in the car.

"I dropped it and it broke," she lied instead, not wanting Ben to go back to East Legon looking for it. "I was about to buy a new one."

He muttered a curse. "Which one is your ATM card?" he asked, sifting through them one by one.

"The Stanbic one," she said.

"Give me your PIN code."

She recited it, and after he had entered it somewhere in his phone, he stood up and thrust her wallet into the back of his jeans.

As he gagged her and bound her ankles again, he said, "I'm coming back. If the PIN is not correct, I will hurt you, okay?"

"It's correct," she said, praying that this wouldn't be one of the rare days in which a random electronic hiccup caused the ATM to reject the bank card.

Ben slouched away. As he opened the door, Ngozi strained to look behind her on the chance she might spot something helpful, but it was dark—nothing to see. The door closed and the latch rattled, followed by the padlock clicking into place.

Ngozi badly needed to change position. Her left hip was sending up sharp, shooting tentacles of pain from having been immobile for too long. She shifted slightly with a grunt, and then tried to flip over on her back with the momentum generated by her flexed legs. She made it and lay breathing heavily with the effort.

What did she know so far? Her abductor was Ben-Kwame. Why had he done this? His motives weren't clear. Was it revenge for what Ngozi had "done" to him, or was this a conventional kidnapping for ransom? That was a phenomenon all too common in Nigeria and burgeoning in Ghana. Again, the possibility rose in Ngozi's mind that Awuni or Janet were behind this, or perhaps Ben was just a depraved rapist who wanted to torture her, violate her, and kill her.

Her location seemed to be something like a building site, or a storage area for brick and lumber. She could be in any number of busy neighborhoods in Accra, but removed somewhat from the direct line of pedestrian and vehicular traffic—maybe by some fencing around the area to keep out squatters? A kind of sparsely populated oasis of calm in the middle of an overcrowded city. In all likelihood, people didn't frequent the area, or at all, perhaps, lowering her chances of being discovered.

Ngozi dozed off, then started awake to the sound of the door latch. Ben was returning, or—for a brief moment in which her spirits leapt, she thought it could be someone else coming to her rescue. But no. It was Ben. Ngozi's heart dropped.

Shining the light in her face, he looked down at her. "I got six thousand *cedis*. Is that all you have?"

"Six thousand is the daily limit."

He grunted "Then, I'll go back tomorrow again. I know you have more money in your account, so don't try to deny."

Ben threw his backpack down, sat next to it, and rummaged inside to remove a cigarette lighter and a pack of chewing gum. He unwrapped a stick and popped it into his mouth. That seemed innocuous enough, but his next moves were unfamiliar to Ngozi.

He removed a dirty-white fragment that looked like a small stone and dropped it into the middle of the gum wrapper, which he then began to heat up with the lighter's flame. The fragment melted into an inspissating puddle, which popped softly a few times, and before long, the vapor curled lazily into Ben's waiting nose. Ngozi understood now. Crack cocaine. He sniffed it deeply until it was all gone.

"Oh, yeah," he said. "Now, tramadol with energy drink . . ."

He chewed the tramadol tablet, then washed it down with Rush. He got up with his phone light still on and began to pace. His speech accelerated, and at times, Ngozi didn't catch what he was saying. She could tell his mood was more erratic now, with bursts of energy and euphoria interspersed with stillness as he appeared to be relishing his high. At a noticeably morose point, Ben went through a litany of complaints about his family, most of whom he seemed to despise.

Abruptly, he stopped and came next to her, switching off his phone.

"Yeah," he murmured, "now the tramadol is making my dick stand."

He stepped back, removed his pants, and returned to her side. "You say you're on your period, eh?"

"Yes," she said.

"'Sokay. You have more than one hole I can use."

CHAPTER THIRTY

Week Two

FRIDAY NIGHTS WERE THE busiest for Accra's ladies. That's when they make the most money, and the men come out of their hiding places like earthworms after the first rain of the season. This was Wednesday, however. Still—no excuse not to hustle.

Bridget, like Lacey and Victoria, had squeezed into tight blouses and short shorts that left little to the imagination. Bridget was trying out her new blond wig and expected a lot of clients because she knew how slay-queen fabulous she looked. It was going on nine-thirty at night, and already, Bridget had had ten clients since dawn.

Her gait wobbly in her exaggerated heels, she was high on weed and cocaine. Inside of the Alligator compound, the customers came in, disappeared into rooms, and walked out. Bridget took her clients up to the last room on the second floor, made quick work of them, and emerged ready for the next after each man had left. Down in the pool, two teenage boys frolicked with a girl of about seventeen, while Lacey, who wasn't having much luck hooking a man this evening, flirted and jostled with two of the Alligator regulars, who were both drunk. Upstairs at the bar, DJ Joseph played heavily auto-tuned hiplife on distorted speakers. The sharp odor of weed from all directions permeated the air.

Bridget wandered outside to the sidewalk, where the plastic-bag-clogged gutters emitted a dank, bitter smell. Now, she noticed something—no, *somebody* new. She was thin and striking with long legs, pink short shorts, a plunging neckline, and black braids down to her waist. From the opposite side of the dimly lit street, she was gazing at the Alligator as if trying to decide what to do.

Bridget crossed and walked over. "Hi," she said, "who are you please?"

"Please, my name is Ruby." She spoke in barely a whisper.

"From where?"

"Ashanti Region."

Bridget eyed her. "Is this your first night here?"

"Yes please."

"Who told you to come here?"

"Some woman at Kumasi said I should come and find one Madam Janet. My father is dead and my mother can't work because of her stroke. I need to make some money to help her and the family. I'm the oldest daughter."

"Oh, okay," Bridget said, softening. "I can see you are nervous. Don't worry, okay?"

Ruby looked a little relieved, but not all the anxiety had left her expression.

"You can meet Madam Janet tomorrow," Bridget said, "but you should start working tonight." Madam might give Bridget a small reward for recruiting Ruby. "Have you even fucked before?" Bridget asked, her voice betraying both amusement and skepticism.

Ruby smiled sheepishly. "Yes please."

"Okay, come this way and I'll introduce you to some of the girls. You know, we're all sisters here."

Bridget led Ruby to the building and into the courtyard.

"That's Diamond over there by the pool," she said, pointing. "She's new too, but now she's more used to it." She called out, "Diamond—come over."

Diamond walked toward them with a gait as wavy as cooked spaghetti. Bridget introduced her to Ruby.

"Ruby is new," Bridget explained to Diamond.

Diamond smiled, her eyes glazed.

Bridget beckoned to Ruby. "Come this way." They walked back outside to the sidewalk. "Stand around here for a little while and let's see if someone comes by to pick you. Look, swing your hips a little bit, eh? You are too stiff."

A dull gray Daewoo Matiz sidled up, and Bridget walked over to it and bent down into the passenger window. "Hey, baby! How are you? Oh, such a cute face! What are you looking for this beautiful night? I do everything for you, even anal. You can have this ass all night if you like." She turned to the side and twerked her bouncy rump. It was an amazing ass. Then, something happened. Bridget stepped back and turned to Ruby, looking surprised. "He says he wants you."

"Me?" Ruby said, pointing at herself.

"Yes. First night! You are lucky o!"

Ruby walked up tentatively. The man really did have a cute baby face. They negotiated, and Ruby got in.

IN THE MATIZ, Emma pulled her wig off and scratched her scalp frantically.

"Itchy?" Jojo asked her.

"You don't even know," Emma said.

"Maybe it's because it's so cheap. Wait, let me find a place to park and we'll talk."

He pulled into a fuel station, parking in a quiet, shadowed corner. "So, what's happened so far?"

"I've achieved at least some of our goal to make contact with Diamond," Emma said, "but she's high on something, and I can't rely on her to think clearly."

"Could be marijuana, cocaine, alcohol, or all of the above," Jojo said with some distaste. "The more drugs they give them, the riskier the sex the girls agree to."

"Yes, I noticed quite a few of them walking around with dazed expressions," Emma said, unable to keep the incredulity out of her voice. She wasn't naive, but this stuff was still bizarre to her. "I wonder if they've drugged Diamond to keep her from talking."

"How do you mean?"

"Okay, let's imagine this scenario: Ngozi rescues Diamond and takes her to the house in East Legon, and a few days later, Awuni, Ben-Kwame, and Salifu abduct them both. You with me?"

"Sure."

"Even if Salifu tried to disguise himself, he would stand out because of his height and physique, so either Diamond or Ngozi would have figured out it was him. What I'm suggesting is that the two girls were at first together, but they became separated in such a way that Diamond has returned to work, but Ngozi has mysteriously disappeared. So, *what happened?* What if Diamond saw or heard something or some*one* they don't want her to talk about, but at the same time, they want her to continue to work as if nothing happened. How do they achieve that?"

"Drug her," Jojo answered at once. "Heavily. But while I understand why the gang took Diamond—because they need to get their investment back, so to speak, to start making money for them again—what about Ngozi? How do they benefit? So far, there's been no ransom demand, and they've had more than enough time to make one."

"That's the most worrisome part," Emma agreed somberly. "I pray the motive wasn't just revenge and that Ngozi isn't lying dead or hurt somewhere. This is why I need to talk to Diamond in private as soon as the drugs wear off."

"So, what now?" Jojo asked.

"I have to go back there," Emma said. "It may be my last chance to get information out of Diamond."

"Okay," Jojo said, "but I'll be around shadowing you, so if you get into trouble, send an SOS."

WHEN EMMA RETURNED to the Alligator just before midnight, she found it relatively deserted. She hovered around the pool for a moment looking around. The last door on the second floor opened and a young man came out, followed minutes later by Bridget, who called out, "Ruby!"

Emma looked up and waved.

"Wait, I'm coming," Bridget said, walking along the landing to the stairs. She descended and joined Emma, who asked her where everyone had disappeared to.

"To Bigot," Bridget replied.

"Where?"

"Bigot. Everyone goes there after midnight. I was about to go there too, so you can come with me."

They walked from the relative quiet of Tulip Link to the noise and crowds on animated Flower Street. The density of sex workers looking for clients seemed to increase with each passing block. They hung around corners and posed on the sidewalk, but some seemed lost and forlorn, as if overwhelmed by the music blaring around them.

"This area is what we call Bigot," Bridget explained to Emma as they turned onto Nii Okaiman West Main Road. Approaching George W. Bush Highway, it began to resemble a wild marketplace, because in essence, it was. If the area around the Alligator was mud in a pothole, Bigot was a cesspool. It was dustier, filthier, ten times as dense, and far smellier. Slay queens, most in hot pants, milled around, some appearing to Emma full of wistful melancholy in their drugged-out state.

Above them, a few meters away, was an overpass for pedestrians. The lurking taxis were on duty to provide ready transport to and from nearby hotels, of which there were many.

A man had come up to Bridget to negotiate prices. Emma melted away into the crowd even as a prospective client eyed her. Searching for Diamond, Emma evaded his gaze. *Fine sex worker I make*, she thought.

She spotted Diamond ahead leaning seductively against a vacant Vodafone kiosk. She was alone for the moment, so Emma hurried to her before a predator pounced.

"Diamond!" she called.

Diamond turned and her face lit up. She appeared more alert.

"Ruby, how be?" she said to Emma, speaking loudly over the clamor.

"I'm good, o! How's business?"

Diamond shrugged.

"I need to talk to you in private," Emma said in her ear.

As she grasped Diamond's arm, a man materialized and snapped, "Where are you going?"

This must be Ben-Kwame, Emma thought, judging by his bandaged right hand.

"Oh, this is Ruby," Diamond said sweetly. "Ruby, meet Ben-Kwame. She's new with us. She needs to go pee."

He looked Emma up and down. "Are you working for Madam Janet?"

His glassy-eyed, unfocused gaze was a look with which Emma was now becoming all too familiar. "Please, I hope to start tomorrow," she responded.

"Before you begin, you go through me, you understand?"

"Oh, okay," Emma said meekly.

"So, I will test you tonight." His voice slurred, and his gaze flickered all over her body like a strobe light. "Go and pee, then you and Diamond will take a taxi with me to the Alligator to spend some time."

"Yes please."

"But I'm watching you," Ben-Kwame said. "Don't try any stupid thing. Go."

Emma and Diamond walked off together more deeply into the crowd toward wooden kiosks shuttered at night but open for business during the day. Emma glanced back briefly to see Ben on his phone following at a distance.

"What's happening now?" she asked Diamond under her breath.

"I'm sure he's calling Madam Janet to tell her about you. When we go to the Alligator, he will take us to his private room and fuck you first and then me. He likes the threesomes. Come this way."

Diamond made a quick right and snaked around two kiosks. For a little while at least, they would be out of Ben's sight.

"He picks his favorites," Diamond said. "If he wants you in his room, it means he likes you. He uses the room to fuck a lot of the ladies any time he likes."

"What about the beatings?"

Diamond grunted. "Those are for everyone, whether he likes you or not."

"What if you want to escape from him?"

"I've tried," Diamond said, quickly poking her head around the kiosk to make sure Ben wasn't close.

Emma dropped her voice as well. "What happened?"

"Two weeks ago now, a certain Madam Ngozi helped me to run away from the Alligator. As we were about to leave, Ben-Kwame came chasing after us. He tried to hold me back as we were getting into Madam's car, but he couldn't. When the door closed, his fingers got stuck in the car door and one of them got cut off."

"Was anyone else with you and Ngozi when all this was happening?"

"No please. When Madam drove me to her house, her boyfriend was there."

This doesn't agree with Awuni and Janet's version of the story, Emma thought. She leaned toward believing Diamond's instead.

"After that night," Emma said, "what was going on?"

"Madam allowed me to stay in the boy's quarters at her place, so I was there Thursday and Friday. Saturday afternoon, she went out to town and I never saw her again." Diamond's voice cracked.

"How did it come about that you returned to the Alligator?" Emma asked.

"That same Saturday, early in the evening, I was resting when someone knocked on the door. I thought it was Madam Ngozi, but it was Awuni and Janet, and she had brought a cane with her. She lashed me several times all over my body while Awuni stood by and watched."

Emma clenched her teeth. *Abject cruelty, and all for what?*

"What could have happened to Madam?" Diamond asked plaintively. "She was a good person—why should anyone harm her?"

"That's what we must find out," Emma said with urgency. "I need your help. Look, my name is Emma, not Ruby, and I'm not a prostitute. I'm really an investigator looking into Ngozi's disappearance."

Diamond drew in her breath sharply. "I *knew* something was different—you seem too good for this place."

Emma didn't have time to ponder what that meant, exactly. "Diamond, we can get you out of this situation, but you'll need to help me and I'll need to trust you."

"I'm with you all the way," Diamond said.

"Did you ever overhear Janet or Awuni discussing Ngozi?"

"No please."

"And you say Ben-Kwame has a private room at the Alligator—have you been in there of late?"

Diamond looked away briefly. "Yesterday night, for drugs and sex."

"He forces you all the time, doesn't he?" Emma said, her voice wavering and her eyes moistening. She knew all about sexual assault. It enraged her every time the ugly menace arose in a case, but she tried to keep her emotions out of the investigations, and never, ever, would she reveal to Sowah or any of her coworkers what had happened to her not so long ago.

The most important task for Emma now was to get into

Ben-Kwame's room to search it. What would she be looking for? Anything connecting Ben to Ngozi—maybe he had snatched an item of jewelry or clothing from her, something Ngozi's parents would recognize if shown a photo of it.

"Look," Emma said to Diamond in a low voice. "We're going to return . . ."

Before she could finish sharing her plan, Ben-Kwame appeared from around the corner, his gait off-kilter. "What are you doing there?" he yelled.

"Sorry, sorry," Diamond said hastily. "We're coming now."

"Follow me," Ben said. "The taxi is waiting."

CHAPTER THIRTY-ONE

WITH MOST OF THE action having relocated to Bigot, the Alligator was quiet, with only one drunk customer snoring with his head slumped forward on a table in the yard by the pool.

Ben ordered the two women to follow him up the stairs to his suite. When he opened the door, he grabbed Emma with his left hand and pulled her in. He was stronger than he looked. Diamond followed. They were in an office containing a desk and a sofa. Next door was the bedroom.

"Go inside there and sit on the bed," Ben said.

When they had done that, he took a seat opposite them on a plastic chair and lit a joint. After a few deep inhalations, he said, "Take off your clothes."

Instead, Diamond rose and turned around to show off her rear end. "Ben, come and rub my ass before we take off our clothes."

He grinned and coughed, rising to stand behind her. He made a grab at Emma, but Diamond intervened quickly, blocking his hand.

He glared at her indignantly. "Fuck you!"

"She wants to watch first, okay, Ben? Please, she's new, so let her learn first."

He cursed under his breath, beginning to grope Diamond.

Diamond switched position to face him, putting her arms around his neck and shoulders. "I want you to try something for me."

"What?" Ben said, his voice thick.

"It will make you come three times in a row and you will still be hard."

"What is that?" Ben was intensely curious now.

"A pill. If you take it now, it works in about five minutes. And you can take it again in one hour." Diamond looked at Emma with an almost undetectable wink. "Ruby, go and get the pills. They're on the table in our room. Take the key."

Emma grabbed it, left, and trotted down the veranda to the girls' room, where she looked for the pills, fumbling through creams, potions, powders, concealers, eye shadow, and false eyelashes on the table. She found an aluminum foil blister pack with a single morning-after pill. She pressed it out and returned to Ben's suite, where he was sitting up in bed naked and smoking a brand-new marijuana cigarette with his left hand, occasionally putting it down to probe, squeeze, and finger Diamond. His bandaged right hand appeared to be out of action, still.

Emma handed Diamond the magic pill.

Ben opened his eyes and fixed them on Emma. "There you are. Come and lie next to me."

"No, no, my love," Diamond said. "You take the pill first and then Ruby will come to join us. We can fuck all night." She lapsed into Pidgin for a moment. "Make you stick out your tongue and take dis pill, na? I go give you water wey you wash it down." She cast around and spotted a bottle of gin on the other side of the bed.

Emma melted away into the office next door. The first target was the desk. Nothing in the center drawer. Top right, papers, nothing interesting; second drawer, a screwdriver, hammer, and miscellaneous nails and screws. Emma's heart was sinking. *Must find something.* She felt she was close to the truth, but she needed to know which path would take her there.

In the third drawer, she found a late-model Samsung phone. She pressed one of the side buttons and it came to life. The wallpaper was a picture of Femi and Ngozi together. Whose phone was this, though? Did it belong to Ngozi, or to Femi?

"Where are you?" Ben bellowed before staggering into the room. "What are you doing?"

Diamond was following him, attempting to hold him back. "Come on, baby, let's go to the bed."

Ben stumbled toward Emma. "Are you trying to steal from me? Come here." He collided with the desk as she moved aside. "I said come here, bitch, let me beat you."

As he came closer, Emma felt a mixture of fear and fury—fear for what he might do, and fury for all he had already done to Diamond. As he grasped Emma's arm with his left hand, she went for his right, whacking it sharply on his fingertips. He jumped back with a shriek and doubled over in pain.

"Get your clothes," Emma cried out to Diamond. "Hurry!"

Ben moved toward Emma in fury, cursing and spitting. She picked up a king-size can of Oro mosquito repellent from his desk and hit him hard across his skull as if wielding an ax. Already off balance, he crashed against the desk and spun onto the floor.

"Come on, let's go," Emma said to Diamond as she emerged clutching her clothes to her chest.

The two fled, Diamond pulling on clothes as they ran down the stairs. In the courtyard, Emma glanced back, but no one was following. As she and Diamond reached the gate, Bridget walked in. "Where are you two going?"

"We did a threesome with one client," Diamond said coolly. "We're going for more."

Bridget looked impressed. "Wow, you are doing well o!"

"Thank you, sister," Emma said.

Outside, as they turned left and walked quickly, she called Jojo. "We're coming up the street. Meet us there."

After not more than three minutes, Jojo's car came bouncing along the road. The two women got in, Emma in the front passenger seat. "That's Diamond," she said to Jojo. "Diamond, Jojo, one of my fellow investigators."

"Nice to meet you," she said to Jojo as he made a swift U-turn.

"Look what I found," Emma said to him, holding up the phone.

"Whose?" Jojo asked

"Either Ngozi's or Femi's," Emma said.

"Gideon will find out for us," Jojo said confidently. "By the way, good job, Emma."

"No," she said, "we owe it to Diamond. And this time, she's not going back to the Alligator."

CHAPTER THIRTY-TWO

NGOZI HAD LOST ALL sense of time. At first, on the assumption that Ben raided her ATM account once daily, she attempted to tie the frequency of his sorties to the number of days, but as he never told her where he was going, that quickly became an unreliable method. He was away for varying durations—some short, others much longer.

Moving Ngozi a few feet away from her original location, Ben tied her to a pillar facing away from the door in a seated position. Now she couldn't see outside at all when Ben left. He had bound her ankles together, and when he left her, he tied her hands behind her back, and that's how she remained as long as he was out. At irregular intervals, he brought her something to eat on his return—*waakye*, fried yam chips, *kelewele*, and so on. At first, she refused the food or spat it out but realized before long that these acts of rebellion only led to Ben's striking her in anger, and that she was jeopardizing herself if she didn't take in nourishment.

As he was leaving, Ben often told her he would be back for some fun, and then she knew she would have to suffer his advances and his invasion of her body. At the same time Ngozi felt terror and fury over this, she experienced an inconsonant relief when she heard his footsteps outside the door, because he could be returning with some food and water, and the extraordinary bliss of having her hands free for a while would follow.

If she needed to go to the bathroom, he escorted her around a stack of bricks and turned away until she was done.

"Better?" he asked.

"Yes. Thank you, Ben."

"Welcome."

As he tied her back up, she asked, "Please, Ben, how long will you keep me here?"

"You'll be the first to know," he said.

"How many days have we been here?"

"Take a guess."

"Ten days? Or is it more?"

He laughed at her and dug into his backpack for his paraphernalia. Glancing episodically at Ngozi with a half-smile, he prepared a joint.

She stared at him. "But, why did you bring me to this place?"

"Don't you know?" he asked, cupping her chin in his left palm. "You destroyed my right hand. It will never work properly again. So now, you're paying me back, and only I will determine when the debt is paid. You get me?"

"Yes," she said.

He took a hit of marijuana. "Tomorrow I'll bring water and soap for you to wash, okay? You'll clean yourself specially for me, right? Like the last time how we did it." He squeezed her buttock and drew air sharply in through his teeth. "You know'm saying?"

"Yes," she said.

He kissed her, thrusting his tongue into her mouth for what seemed a long time. Ngozi felt a certain revulsion, but it wasn't unbearable or enough to turn her head away. She couldn't understand why, but she was too weary to ponder it.

Ben held out the joint toward her lips, but she shook her head.

"*Have some!*" he said sharply, moving around to hold her face to the joint. "Take some."

Ngozi took a puff and spluttered. She had tried marijuana three or four years ago. It had relaxed her and given her a fit of giggles. What Ben had just given her wasn't that. Her heart began to race and she felt like she was running on a path with no end. But then, she floated through a cloud of smoke and descended into dense forest. She looked left and right as the trees closed on her like a deep, narrow chasm. Ben seemed to be laughing, and Ngozi thought she might be too, but she wasn't certain. She whipped her head around to see the source of the sounds of a xylophone, and her voice, which she heard from a distance, said, "Do you see a xylophone, do you see a xylophone?"

Ben was sweeping her up. She had no sense of where her limbs were, but a searing flash of pain came up from her pelvis. She was floating with Ben, but she was horrified and wanted to get away. The noise in her ears was overwhelming, and she found herself screaming with it.

WHEN SHE AWOKE, she was lying on the ground with her jeans pulled off and her blouse pulled up over her head. Her bra was lying across her waist. Beside her, Ben snored on his side with his back to her. She leaned over and threw up. Ben didn't budge. Then it hit Ngozi. She was half-naked and bruised, but she was also completely untied.

Trying not to whimper from pain and trauma, she felt around in the dark for her jeans and found them. It took a little while to get them right-side-out in the dark, but she pulled them on slowly and listened for any change in Ben's deep breathing pattern. None came.

Hands outstretched, Ngozi navigated clear of Ben's location mostly by sound. She was careful to tread lightly to minimize the crunch of her shoes on the dirt surface. She knew quite well the direction of the door, and only once did she collide with a pile of bricks. Ngozi kept creeping, taking care not to bump into the door or a wall. She felt a flat, rough surface that must have been more bricks. She moved her hand up, down, and around, trying to find the door. She thought she was close. And then the flashlight came on, casting her crouching shadow against the wall.

"*Hey!*" Ben shouted.

Ngozi saw the door and made a dash for it. But as she reached it, Ben came around and collided with her. He opened his left palm and delivered it to her right temple. Something shuddered in her skull and the lights went out.

WHEN SHE REGAINED consciousness, she was lashed to the pillar more tightly than before, and the ankle ligatures were cutting into her skin. It took her a moment to focus in the light of Ben's phone reflecting off the ceiling. Lying on his side propped on one elbow, Ben eyed her from a few feet away. "*Kwasea!*" he spat. "You think you can get away from me? Fuck you! After all I've done for you. Like, I'll kill you just now."

Ngozi was at the end of her tether. She dropped her head and cried silently.

"What are you crying for?" Ben snapped.

"Let me go, Ben," she pleaded through tears. "I won't tell anyone."

"You think I'm stupid?" He laughed bitterly and took a few swigs of a clear liquid in an unmarked bottle, which Ngozi suspected was *akpeteshie*, the potent stuff made locally from the distillation of fermented palm wine or sugar cane. She could smell it from where she was. Along with that, he took a tramadol tablet and sat back, his eyes bulging and bloodshot. With a phlegmy cough, he expectorated, spat to the side, and gathered his paraphernalia for another hit of coke. Once he had melted down the rock, he inhaled deeply and within a few seconds let out at a "*Whoooo!* I feel so good."

For a moment, his euphoria had him laughing uproariously at nothing at all, and then he went silent and lay down on the dirt breathing shallowly. "Oh, my God," he muttered. "This is too sweet."

Ngozi panicked. Was he overdosing? "Ben, please, untie me."

"Hm?" he murmured. "Oh, fuck."

"Stay awake, okay?" Ngozi said frantically. "Ben, *Ben!*"

He didn't respond. He was lying very quietly, and his breathing pattern had changed noticeably. Now he sucked in a little air only at irregular intervals.

"Don't leave me here!" Ngozi cried out. "Ben?"

She wasn't sure at first if he had stopped breathing, but as she watched, it became clear. Something about the angular position of his limbs, the stillness of his body, and the complete loss of any muscle tone told Ngozi that Ben was dead. She began to scream. She just didn't want to die there, but if no one discovered her, she would.

CHAPTER THIRTY-THREE

THE MORNING AFTER EMMA and Diamond's dangerous encounter with Ben-Kwame, Sowah and Emma's colleagues listened to her account with rapt attention. But it was when Emma produced the plastic bag containing the Samsung phone that her audience gasped.

"My goodness," Manu said.

"Wow!" Gideon said. "Femi's phone?"

"Maybe, but the screen is locked," Emma said. "The wallpaper shows Femi and Ngozi together, but I suspect it is Femi's because the phone's pretty battered. I see Ngozi as taking better care of her stuff."

"Fantastic," Sowah said, and then hesitated. "To be honest, Emma, I wouldn't have advised you to go into that man's room. He's uncouth, violent—maybe even a killer, for all we know."

"Please, sir," Jojo said quietly, "you are right—it was dangerous, but at the same time Emma has bravely rescued Diamond."

Emma shot Jojo a silent *thank-you* for coming to her defense.

"Undeniably so," Sowah said, still appearing bothered. "Ah, well, it's done. I don't begrudge you your amazing work."

"Thank you, sir," Emma said, relieved she was off the hook. For now.

"What about Diamond?" Manu asked. "Where is she now?"

Emma cleared her throat. "Um, she's at my house."

"*Ei!*" Manu exclaimed in alarm. "Emma!"

"There really wasn't anywhere for her to go, especially at that time of night," Emma said, getting her defense in early. She stole a glance at the boss, aware that he strictly eschewed commingling agency work with home life. This was a clear breach, and he looked unhappy. Emma began to feel small. The glory of having saved Diamond was turning into something else. Had she bungled everything while thinking she was so clever?

To Emma's surprise, Sowah made no comment on what he thought of her taking Diamond home, which made Emma fear the dressing-down would come later when she met with the boss in private.

"So, Gideon?" Sowah resumed. "Can you help?"

He nodded. "Let me see the phone, please?"

Emma passed it down.

"I'm glad it's an Android," Gideon said. "They're easier to break into."

"I'd prefer you find another expression for it," Sowah said with a wince. "I think we've already had quite a bit of breaking in."

The room tittered awkwardly.

"The situation is a little sticky," Sowah continued, "but this is what I think we should do. Gideon, you work on bypassing the locked screen to find out whether the phone belongs or belonged to Ngozi or Femi. If it belonged to Femi, we'll hand it over to DI Boateng once we're done. If it's Ngozi's, we'll hold on to it until such time it's appropriate to relinquish the phone to the parents, because Ngozi is our case, Femi is Boateng's—even though we suspect they're connected."

"So, sir," Gideon said cautiously, "if the phone belonged to Femi, should I access all his data before letting DI have it?"

"I think we would be fools if we didn't," Sowah said. "Now that we've chopped down the mango tree, no point allowing the mangos to go to waste."

"Definitely," Jojo said.

"Thanks, boss," Gideon said. "I'll start working on it right now."

"Yes, please," Sowah said, "and once we've discovered whose phone this is or was, then we'll consider all the ways it could have gotten into Ben-Kwame's hands."

Emma passed the phone to Gideon, so he could get going on the new project, the kind of task he thrived on.

Sowah dragged the whiteboard from the side of the room to the front and found a marker. "While Gideon is working on that, let's diagram the case."

At the top he wrote, *Femi, dead,* and *Ngozi, missing,* circled them both, and linked them with a double-headed arrow. Below that, Janet, Awuni, Ben-Kwame, Salifu, and Diamond each got individual boxes of their own.

"For now," Sowah said, "I'm putting a positive sign between Ngozi and Femi to indicate a positive relationship. The arrow between Ngozi and Diamond is also positive, but it's a negative sign between Ngozi and Janet, Awuni, Ben-Kwame, and Salifu. The same between that gang of four and Diamond, because she was trying to flee from them and they regarded her as a fugitive from the jaws of the Alligator." He chuckled at his own metaphor. "Between Femi and Diamond, we have a question mark, because there's no indication they knew each other to any degree, plus it's unlikely Femi wanted to steal Diamond from the gang of four; that seems more like Ngozi's idea."

"One thing, though, sir," Emma said, deciding to forge on despite her earlier discomfiture, "is we don't really know the relationship between Diamond and Salifu, either. Did he even know her or meet her?"

"All right," Sowah conceded, "so it's a question mark there instead of a negative sign. Do we all agree with that?"

The room responded "yes" in unison.

"I'm inclined to concur," Sowah said, "but the picture may change when we get a look at the phone. If it belonged to Femi, the questions we need to ask are, first, who were the last people to communicate with him by voice or text, and was Ngozi one of them? What was the tone of the messages? Why was Femi at the White House so late at night? Had he been fighting with Ngozi about something and one or both of them wanted to be apart? Did Ngozi know Femi had been killed and she fled to escape the same fate? If she attempted to text Femi after his death, that's an indication she didn't know what had happened to him at the time.

"If the phone belongs to Ngozi, the questions are similar: Who was calling her or chatting with her up till the time she disappeared? Was she communicating with Femi? Did she reveal a hiding place to him, or send an SOS? How bad did her relationship get with Janet and the rest of the gang? You get the idea."

"We got it, sir," Jojo said.

"I'll be in my office," Sowah said. "Emma, I need to speak with you."

This is what she had feared. Her stomach churning, she followed Sowah down the corridor.

"Shut the door behind you and take a seat," he said, and sat on the sofa. Once Emma had situated herself, he said, "You're a plucky woman. You have twice the guts of most men I know. But when you're in the heat of a case, I need you to stop, breathe, and think about what you're doing or proposing to do before rushing headlong into it. As I said in the meeting, I have serious misgivings about your entering Ben-Kwame's room. Did you run down the dangers in your mind?"

Emma bit her bottom lip. "To be honest, sir, not consciously."

"Your partner, Jojo, was in contact with you and at the ready to help, but it seems you excluded him. Why is that? You should have asked him to come into the Alligator to at least be close for safety. This has come up before, where you seem to be running a relay race all by yourself and keeping the baton while your team member is waiting for you to pass it. You don't need to go it alone; neither do you need to prove yourself to anyone. Including your father."

That startled Emma. "Sir?"

"I know what he meant to you, but you don't owe him anything, and you have nothing to prove, either. I have an impression that sometimes you feel like he's behind you looking over your shoulder, his having been a homicide detective when he was alive. I could be wrong about this . . ."

"You could also be right, sir," Emma said, staring at the floor.

"Okay." Sowah heaved a sigh. "On a different but related topic, what are you going to do about Diamond? Your household is yours, but for the sake of all of us in the agency, I must enforce the rules to make sure that none of us should entangle ourselves personally with a witness, suspect, victim, or what have you. It may cause conflicts of interest and we never want anyone to accuse us of not being above board. Does that make sense?"

"It does, boss."

"Good. Then I leave it in your hands to resolve. I trust you."

Emma nodded. "Yes, sir. Thank you, sir."

There was a knock.

"Come in," Sowah said.

Gideon put his head in the door. "Please, just to tell you I've bypassed the locked screen on the phone, which clearly belonged to the deceased, Femi Adebanjo."

"You're a wizard!" Sowah exclaimed, clapping. "Well done! So, you, JoJo, and Emma have a lot of work to do."

She jumped up, glad to move on and get back to the investigation.

CHAPTER THIRTY-FOUR

WITH SO MUCH LEFT to probe on Femi's phone, Emma and Jojo decided to stay at work late so they would have something substantial to present to the group for the briefing in the morning, which was a Friday.

"Should we start with Adebanjo's WhatsApp?" Jojo suggested as they sat side by side at his desk.

"Yes," Emma agreed, "let's look at his chat list. Whom do we know and whom do we not?"

The familiar names were all there on the list: Ngozi, Awuni, Janet, Salifu, and Ben-Kwame. But there were others Emma and Jojo had not seen before.

"Who are Cliffy, Sade, and Effia, I wonder?" Emma asked.

"Good question," Jojo responded.

"Let's put them aside for now and go to the most important: Ngozi."

Jojo nodded and began to scroll backward through dozens of messages. "Oh!" he exclaimed. "Cover your eyes."

"*Awurade!*" Emma said. Adebanjo's nude photos, a set of four, couldn't be more graphic. "Well, he certainly wasn't shy about his body."

"He has nothing to be shy about," Jojo said dryly. "Wow." He fanned himself to figuratively cool off, sending Emma into hysterics.

"Okay," she resumed. "Let's get serious. What's the date on that pic?"

"Ninth of July. Was that before or after the Ojukwus returned to Nigeria?"

"After, I believe. Hold on, I'll check the notes." Emma reached across the table for her notebook and flipped through several pages. "I wrote it down somewhere . . . here. They went back to Naija on the fifteenth of June. I'm really confused. Was Adebanjo there as well at that time, or in Ghana? Scroll back some more to figure out when he and Ngozi met. We should be able to sketch out a timeline."

Jojo went back from September to March.

"There," Emma said. "Early April looks like the start of it all. Femi texts Ngozi to say, 'When I first saw you at the restaurant, I thought you were an angel.'"

"Smooth talker," Jojo muttered.

They went on to read the rest.

Thank you, that's sweet, only don't you say that to all the girls?

I swear I don't I'm being genuine

Okay then

Can I call you now so I can hear that lovely voice again?

If you like

"I guess he was texting her later on—after they had met," Emma said. "When do they pick up the conversation again?"

"The following day at eight-ten in the morning. Adebanjo asks her if he woke her up, and she says yes, but she's glad it was him. They go on flirting for a while . . . then, here's a part where he's asking how much longer she'll be in Ghana."

We'll be leaving sometime in June, but I don't have the exact date hbu

Not sure, I think in July, depends on some business deals in Ghana, but I can let you know

What did you say you do for a living again?

We're like a travel agency helping people get their documents together to go to Europe

Who's "we?"

Me and my partner Cliffy. The company is called Cliffemi Travels. You can google it.

I will

When will I see you again?

I can't say for certain cuz my parents have a tight leash around my neck. I hate it.

Just wanna be sure you're really 18 right?

Don't believe me? Hold on.

"And so, she sends him her Nigerian national ID," Emma said, "and yeah, she is eighteen, no lie there. So, Ngozi expected to return to Naija sometime in June, and Adebanjo wasn't certain but he thought it could be July. Keep going."

"They had a lot of secret meetings at different hotels," Jojo said, "mostly when Ngozi's parents were out."

"In May, Ngozi had a date of departure, fifteenth of June, and she's not happy about it. She wants to stay with Femi, who reassures her he'll be back in Nigeria in July to see her again. Moving forward . . . a lot of family quarrels. Ngozi seems to be furious with her mother all the time. Then . . . look at this— third of July through the . . . sixth? No, third through fifth, there's a gap in responses to Femi's texts from Emma's phone. On the fourth, he hears from one Rosemary that Ngozi's been hurt and hospitalized the night before. He repeatedly asks if Ngozi's okay and says that he's on his way back to Nigeria from Ghana."

"And on that day too," Jojo said, "Ngozi texts Femi, but using Rosemary's phone."

Femi, love, it's Ngo. I'm sorry I haven't responded. I've been in the hospital. Am using Rosemary's phone cuz mines been smashed, but I'll get a new one as soon as I can. I took a fall at home in the bathtub last night taking a shower, Mummy says she found me there unconscious, but I still don't get exactly what happened but I hit the side of the tub, got a deep wound in my head, they had to put in twenty stitches.

Am on my way back, babe. I've reached Benin, so I should be home soon. I'll go straight to Lagoon Hospital.

"What is it about, this fall in the bathtub?" Jojo said.

"I don't know," Emma said. "It's strange. Ngozi is back online with Femi on the fifth with her new phone; by then, Femi is getting closer to Lagos from the Republic of Benin, says it could have been sooner if he hadn't blown a tire, and she texts him to say, 'Mom's a liar and I'll make her pay,' and then promises to tell Femi what she means when they finally see each other. Planning vengeance against her mother? What did her mother lie about?"

Jojo gave a grunt and then reflected for a moment. "I don't

want to be overdramatic, but could they have had a fight where Mrs. Ojukwu hit Ngozi in the head?"

"While in the shower?" Emma said, cocking an eyebrow. "Jojo."

He chortled and shrugged. "At least I tried."

"Yes, you did," Emma said kindly. "I think we should get the boss to ask Mr. Ojukwu, 'Did you forget to reveal some details?'"

"I agree," Jojo said. "Let's keep going. They released Ngozi from the hospital two days after Ngozi's message to Femi on Rosemary's phone."

After that, chats between Femi and Ngozi had a wounded, indignant tone:

Did your mom confess?

Of course not, cuz she's a coward

Why not confront her? Tell her you don't have amnesia anymore and you know she's the cause of the whole accident, and anwy for what reason did she peep ur phone?

Emma looked at Jojo in surprise. "You could be right! Maybe something did happen in that bathroom, because he asks Ngozi if her mom had confessed."

Jojo clicked his tongue. "I told you."

"I'm impressed you picked that up so far in advance, bro. So, Ijeoma Ojukwu was taking an unauthorized peek at her daughter's phone, and maybe Ijeoma confronted Ngozi in the bathroom and came to blows?"

"What kind of mother picks a fight with her grown daughter in the shower?"

"One with mental problems? I don't know, but read on."

I could have been killed. She'll learn her lesson when I disappear to Ghana, and she'll regret what she did forever.

Amen! Dont worry babe, only a few weeks more

Still end of August?

For sure.

"So, she wants revenge," Emma said. "It's not just that she's devoted to Femi; it's also that she wants to punish her mother for the terrible bathroom accident."

Closer to the end of August, the text messages revolved around the planned departure day of either the thirtieth or thirty-first of

August. Eventually, they left on the thirty-first, and, going by a text Femi sent to a friend in Lagos, they arrived in Accra later that day. From that point the chats were unremarkable. That is, until the night of Wednesday, the thirteenth of October. At about 11 P.M., Femi launched a series of messages drenched in apology. After that, the exchanged texts became increasingly bizarre.

Baby, I'm so so sorry, please forgive me, I don't know what happened to me, you know I would never harm you I love you so much, abeg, forgive me. Love, please, let me come home and let's talk. I don't want to lose you

Femi continued those types of texts well into Saturday morning, but Ngozi never answered. By early afternoon, Femi's tone changed radically.

So you won't answer me? YOU BLOCKED ME? Ok, don't worry, because I don't give one shit, and yes you deserved that slap you fuckin' bitch.

"So, the truth comes out," Emma said. "He slapped her."

"And that's why she must have kicked him out of the house," Jojo said.

"Once she didn't acquiesce to him, he became furious and turned on her completely. I mean, this guy must have a serious anger problem. He's the kind to fear most. One moment they're cool, the next they're in a hot fury—aggression that lurks like a crouching tiger ready to strike."

"Wow!" Jojo looked at her laughing. "You say what—crouching tiger? *Ei*, Madam Emma! So, what do you know of crouching tigers?"

"I saw it somewhere on TV." Emma giggled and shrugged. "But you are correct, I have never personally met a tiger, crouching or otherwise. Let's continue—what are the rest of the conversations?"

"Nothing much changes," Jojo said. "Up till the time of Ngozi's kidnapping, she never answered his texts, and in fact, from what Femi says, she blocked him on WhatsApp."

"Check his phone record, though," Emma said. "Maybe she called Femi instead of texting."

"Good idea," Jojo looked through the list of outgoing and incoming calls, including the mixed ones. He shook his head. "No calls."

"So," Emma said, "according to Diamond's account, the abduction was Saturday afternoon and we know it was almost certainly after Ngozi returned from town because her vehicle had been parked and left. And later on, that Saturday night, Femi was shot dead. I'm curious about his messages with the gang of four. Madam Janet first."

"Femi's communications with her started six months back, late April," Jojo said, scrolling slowly. "Among the first was a message to Janet that she should ask for him by name when she arrived at B2B—that's Breakfast to Breakfast in Osu of Oxford Street, I'm guessing. Femi and Janet must have met there to discuss business arrangements. After that, there's not that much."

They came upon Salifu's name, and curious about what interactions they might have had, Jojo clicked on it to find a curious exchange two days before Femi's killing.

What about Saturday? Did you ask your contacts, Femi started.

Pls they say Saturday is too soon, unless Monday before they can do it, Salifu replied.

What time

Am not so sure, afternoon maybe

You don't hurt her, you hear me? And I don't want Mm J or Mr A in this at all.

Yes pls

Txt me later and let me know the time you will do it and no more delays

Yes pls no problem

Emma and Jojo locked gazes, as if searching each other's thoughts.

"What does he mean by 'her?'" Jojo said.

"Could it be . . ." The notion shattered Emma. "Could it be that Femi had asked Salifu to set up Ngozi's abduction?"

Jojo frowned. "But then, if that was the case, why did the kidnapping take place on Saturday when Salifu indicated his people—whoever they were—couldn't do it before Monday? What changed?"

Emma shook her head, suddenly feeling deflated. "I don't know."

"Ugh." With a growl of vexation, Jojo rested his forehead on the desk. "Let's take a break and get some pizza."

CHAPTER THIRTY-FIVE

EMMA AND JOJO FINISHED up around seven-thirty that evening. She took a Bolt back home agonizing over what to do about Diamond. That she couldn't stay very long with Emma was clear, especially with Akosua in the same house. If she could, Emma planned to leave work a little earlier the next day or the day after to spend some time helping Diamond get back on her feet.

As usual, the inviting aromas of dinner permeated every corner of Emma's house as she came in the door.

"Hello, Mama," Emma called out.

Akosua came out of the kitchen wiping her hands on a towel. "Hello, dear. How are you?"

"Tired," Emma said, resting her bag on the chair by the door. "Where's Diamond?"

"She went out somewhere this afternoon," Akosua said, rather casually. "She hasn't returned."

"Went out where?" Emma asked warily.

"I have no idea," Akosua said. "Will you take a shower before dinner?"

"But where did she say she was going?"

Akosua took a seat and crossed her legs with exquisite style. "Have a seat. She went to look for a job and such."

"Oh," Emma said, but didn't sit.

"Why do you look so worried?"

"She doesn't know her way around town," Emma said. "And she doesn't have any money, or a phone, or—"

"You're not her mother," Akosua said crisply. "She can take care of herself. Anyway, I gave her some money."

Emma was astonished. "You did?"

Akosua nodded. "I took pity on her."

Emma gave a little laugh. "Come on, Mama, you don't expect me to believe that. You just didn't want her here."

"Well, this is not a refugee camp, my dear," Akosua said witheringly.

That sounded cruel to Emma—dehumanizing, almost.

"She told me her whole story, by the way," Akosua continued. "Very sad."

There wasn't much feeling in her tone. She had resolved the Diamond problem with an authoritative stroke, but Emma resented how her mother had done it—undermining Emma's role and thus robbing her of the opportunity to see the matter through and finish what she had started.

"You could have discussed it with me beforehand," Emma grumbled.

"I apologize then," Akosua said. "I'll remember that next time. Anyway, that's that. Will you shower before dinner?"

Emma shook her head. "I'm not really hungry right now. Just tired. I'll take a nap and maybe eat later."

Surprisingly dejected, Emma went to her room and lay down. A few minutes later, she called Courage.

"What's the matter?" he said. "You don't sound good at all."

"I need to get out," Emma said. "Can I come over?"

"Of course, you can!"

AT FRIDAY MORNING briefing, Emma felt a growing urgency. She had no hard evidence, but her intuition told her that Ngozi was still alive, and Emma would feel that way until proven wrong. They needed to find her fast.

Except for minutes-late Manu, everyone was on time.

"Jojo, Emma," Sowah said with little ceremony, "what have you found so far from Mr. Adebanjo's phone?"

"A lot," Emma said.

She explained how, by Diamond's account, Ngozi's abduction took place Saturday afternoon, after which time, Salifu and Awuni removed her from the boy's quarters and returned her to the Alligator, keeping her in line with threats and drugs.

"But here is the most shocking thing," Emma continued,

leaning forward, "from what we found on Femi's WhatsApp, it could be that it was Femi who was making arrangements with Salifu to have Ngozi kidnapped."

"What?" Manu exclaimed.

Gideon said, "Seriously?"

"What makes you say that?" Sowah asked.

"Take a look, sir," Emma said, handing the phone to him. "Thursday fourteenth, two days before Femi's death, he's asking whether Salifu has secured the 'contacts,' he calls them—for what he was hoping to be done on Saturday, but Salifu is saying they won't be able to carry it out until the following Monday.

"But then we don't understand what happened," Jojo added, "because in the end, the kidnapping *did* take place on Saturday."

"Perhaps Salifu persuaded his henchmen to do it earlier rather than later," Gideon suggested.

"Maybe a last-minute change in plans," Sowah said.

"What kind of man has his girlfriend kidnapped?" Manu said, shaking his head in distaste.

Jojo grunted. "Exactly. Another thing, though, shouldn't the ransom demand be here by now? It's been almost two weeks now."

"This is what I think happened," Emma said, after a moment's thought. "Femi wants more money—why? Because he likes living life high and fast, but at the moment, he isn't financially where he wants to be. So, he devises a plan to get more cash by staging a kidnapping with Salifu and his macho-men friends doing the dirty work for a small price. Femi doesn't include Janet and Awuni—why should he?—but Salifu blurts the secret to them.

"Janet and Awuni confront Femi and demand a share in the ransom money because, after all, Salifu is *their* employee, not Femi's. How dare he use Salifu for his own purposes? But Femi refuses to allow them to partake of the loot, and they have a furious argument. Later on, Janet and Awuni decide to get rid of Femi so they can keep the ransom to themselves. Awuni and Salifu conspire to shoot Femi dead Saturday night before he gets a chance to send the ransom note. What do you think?"

"I think that's a good deduction," Sowah said, "and if that scenario is correct, it would tie Ngozi's kidnapping firmly to Femi's death.

"I'm very worried, now," Emma said. "What if Ngozi is also dead?"

"Let's not think that way, though," Sowah said firmly. "Keep your spirits up and let's continue the assignment at hand without flagging, okay?"

"Boss," Jojo interjected, "we also discovered some other items on the phone. Femi was communicating with a man called Professor Proph Coleman—"

"Why the double professor?" Sowah asked curiously.

"No," Jojo explained, grinning, "Proph is his first name—it could be short for Prophet."

"Hm." Sowah cocked an eyebrow. "Carry on."

"Coleman is a lecturer in Economics at the University of Ghana. I guess he's kind of famous for some kind of economic theory, and for that he was in the running for a Nobel Prize.

"From what we could figure out, he set up two university students called Sade and Effia as escorts for his friends."

"Let's suppose Coleman was making money off Sade and Effia," Sowah said, "then Femi was a threat in the same way he was to Awuni and Janet. This seems to be Femi's MO—to take advantage of other people's success by stealing whatever they have."

"How should we find out more about Coleman's involvement, if any?" Jojo asked.

"Any ideas? Ponder it." Sowah often encouraged his team members to come up with original solutions.

"I'm thinking I could pretend I'm a customer interested in hiring either Sade or Effia for her services," Jojo said, "and when I meet with her, I ask questions."

"We'll have to give her water to drink, though, sir," Gideon said, using the euphemism for a financial inducement. "She won't just sit down with you for one hour and talk for free."

"No problem," Sowah said. "Nnamdi has paid us enough to take care of miscellaneous expenses. I think we should follow Jojo's idea."

"Should we tell Diboat about finding Femi's phone?" Emma asked.

Sowah hesitated a beat. "Not yet. Let's see where this all goes. Any other leads?"

"We're wondering about some of the WhatsApp contacts Femi had archived," Jojo said.

Sowah raised his eyebrows. "What does 'archived' mean in this context?"

"If you want to keep people on your list," Gideon explained, "but you don't want them to be able to reach you, you can archive them. If at some point you want to get in touch with them, you can unarchive them. So, among the archived chats was one with a girl called Bisola and her boyfriend, Kehinde. During the July in the year before Covid, Femi was working on getting them to Europe with false documents. From what Emma and I saw on Femi's phone, Kehinde and Bisola got to Agadez, Niger, by September of the same year. Around then, Femi archived the two of them so they couldn't get in touch with him."

"So, we don't know what happened to them?" Sowah asked.

"No clue," Jojo said. "We tried contacting them using the info on WhatsApp, but the messages seemed to evaporate without ever reaching their intended destination. However, Femi's partner in this migration-trafficking thing, a Nigerian guy called Cliffy, stayed in touch with Femi by text and voice until August sometime of this year."

"And then the communications stopped?" Sowah asked.

"They did," Emma confirmed. "We don't know why, but Cliffy is still around."

"Oh?" Sowah asked with renewed interest.

"We texted him," Emma said, "and we got only one reply. After that, nothing. I'll show you." She pulled up the WhatsApp exchange and handed the phone to Sowah.

Hello, I'm Emma Djan texting you from Accra, I'm a friend of Femi's, maybe you're already aware, but I'm sorry to inform you that he was shot dead on the 16th of October.

What???

I'm sorry to be bringing you this bad news

O My God, how possible?

The police haven't found who did it and the culprit is still at large.

But where did it happen?

At the hotel where he was working. Can we do a video call pls.

"I see." Sowah looked up. "And?"

"We video-chatted," Emma continued. "Poor man—he looked so shattered. I felt sorry for him. He said Femi had been a good friend and that they had worked together for years. Cliffy said the last time he had seen Femi was when he left Nigeria for Accra in August of this year. After that, Cliffy hadn't heard from him again. Cliffy presumed Femi had lost his phone or contacts, or something. I also asked Cliffy if he knew of anyone who could have wanted Femi dead—perhaps someone in Nigeria."

"Good, *good*," Sowah said, his face lighting up with approval. "And how did he respond?"

"He knew of no one specifically, but he said it was possible Femi had made enemies along the way—after all, we know from Diboat that Femi had a criminal and prison record. I also asked Cliffy if he knew who Kehinde and Bisola were, he said they were a couple who Femi had helped get to Italy via Agadez and Tripoli. But that was more than two years ago in June, July—pre-Covid."

Sowah nodded his head slowly. "Good job. Be sure to keep in touch with this Cliffy guy. Try to prompt his memory of any enmity between Femi and someone else in Nigeria. We're looking probably for someone who has the means to go back and forth between Ghana and Nigeria."

"Yes, sir."

"Okay, anything else? You've done well, thank you. Right now, let's focus on Salifu—Emma, that's for you, and Jojo, work on the double-Prof. and the two young women he was essentially pimping."

"University professor—a pimp," Manu muttered, shaking his head in disgust. "What has happened to Ghanaians?"

"And worse," Emma added. "What about sex for grades?"

"Don't go there," Sowah said firmly. "Just get to work." He headed down the hallway.

Jojo leaned over Emma to whisper in her ear, "Wow, you're Sowah's baby girl today! He was very impressed with you."

Emma smiled at first, but then pondered the comment. She wasn't sure she liked it. Because she wasn't *anyone's* baby girl.

CHAPTER THIRTY-SIX

EMMA FELT A NEW momentum after lunch. She rang the gate bell at the White House and waited. Salifu looked out of the side door.

"Good afternoon!" Emma called out, beaming. "How are you, Salifu?"

"Am fine, Madam." He had something of a smile for her now. "And you?"

"I'm good. May I come in?"

"Of course, Madam Emma. You can come inside, please."

Emma stepped in as he opened the door wide. "Thank you, so much."

"Where is Inspector Boateng?"

"He's not working today," Emma said. "But let's sit down together under the shade of the mango tree."

"No problem."

Emma shifted her seat so she could face him fully. "I feel like people haven't been giving you the respect you deserve. They're always instructing what to do, but they never listen to *you*."

Salifu's eyes flicked up to hers and then quickly averted to his right, where they remained.

"I don't think it's fair that Femi came here from Nigeria and took your job just like that," Emma said with conviction. "And on top of that, he brought his girlfriend who started taking over everything."

Salifu released a long breath and said, "'S not easy at all," he said, an expression of regret. "It's always like that."

"Like what?" Emma pressed him gently.

"You know, I didn't complete middle school, so, I can't read or write well. So, with this"—he indicated his powerful physique, head to toe—"they think I don't get sense." He pointed at his head.

Emma understood. "*Maate.*"

"And then, they don't give respect," Salifu added, pursing his lips and stubbing a wide toenail into the dirt.

Emma backed him up. "You deserve better."

"Thank you, madam. Yesterday evening, Inspector came to see me and question me. That's why I thought maybe today he has sent you another time."

"No, not that," Emma said. "What did Inspector Boateng ask you last night?"

Salifu crossed and uncrossed his ankles. "He was trying to say that I could have killed Mr. Femi and kidnapped Ngozi."

"For what purpose?" Emma asked.

Salifu shrugged. "I don't know."

"Let me ask you something," Emma said, sensing a new approach. "I heard someone say that it was Femi, rather, who had Ngozi kidnapped."

Salifu didn't appear surprised. "It could be."

"But, why? You saw how they behaved with each other—didn't it seem he loved Ngozi?"

"In some way," Salifu said, "but she wasn't everything to him. *Money* was."

"Ahh," Emma said, in a spontaneous and bright moment of clarity, for she had never heard anyone define Femi so succinctly and with such perspicacity.

"Yes, you're right Salifu." She paused. "You know what? They have located Femi's phone."

Salifu's head snapped up. "*Where?* Who had it?"

"Ben-Kwame," Emma said. "Did you give it to him?"

"No!" Salifu pulled his head back and turned his palms outward in protest. "After they shot Femi, I called Awuni and Madam Janet to tell them. The first thing they tell me is to find Femi phone and hold it for them. It wasn't on his person, but I found it in the room where Femi had been staying and I kept it until Mr. Awuni came for it."

And then Awuni gave it to Ben-Kwame, Emma thought, understanding instantly. Because of the locked screen, the phone wasn't of any use to Awuni, and the phone wasn't in selling condition, either.

"We saw something on Mr. Femi's WhatsApp I want to talk to you about," Emma said.

"Okay," Salifu said, sounding more than willing.

"Two days before Femi was shot, he texted you to check if you were in touch with some guys to do something either the following Saturday or Monday."

Salifu's demeanor changed. "I don't understand."

On her phone, Emma pulled up the screenshot of the potentially incriminating WhatsApp chat between Femi and Salifu. "Here," she said, holding it up to him. "That's you, not so?"

"Oh. Yeah."

"What were you and Femi talking about? Was it Ngozi Femi was trying to get kidnapped? I'm not saying you did anything bad, my brother, but we need to know everything. Help us to help you, eh?"

Relenting to pressure, Salifu said, "Okay. Let me tell you the truth. The weekend before Femi got killed, he came to talk to me—right over there beside the gate." He pointed with his chin. "He told me say he need cash quick because of money he owes some guy in Nigeria."

"Did he tell you the guy's name?" Emma asked. "What was the debt for?"

"No name, and as for the debt, I don't know anything about it, but he said he want me to kidnap someone for ransom, and I ask him who, and he tell me Ngozi. I was shocked. Why should he kidnap his girlfriend? He said he knows Ngozi's father will pay anything for his daughter, no matter how much, and so it will be easy.

"He said he will pay me out of the ransom money when it will arrive. I said okay, I will check with someone who can do it. Then I had an idea that Ben-Kwame can help, because he knows a lot of macho men, but at first, I didn't tell him the reason why I was asking him. But he kept worrying me, 'Who are you trying to kidnap, who are you trying to kidnap?' And so finally, I told him, and Ben-Kwame said he has some guys who can help me but not before that following Monday. I said okay.

"Early Sunday morning, the day after Femi was killed, I went to Femi's house to look for Madam Ngozi, but she wasn't there."

"How did you get in? Wasn't the gate closed?"

"The main part, yes, but the side door where people enter was unlocked."

"What about her vehicle? Did you see it?"

Salifu nodded. "Yes—parked in the garage."

"And where was Ben-Kwame at that time? Did you communicate with him?"

"I called him and text him and he responded me Sunday afternoon. I told him Ngozi wasn't at the house."

"And?"

"He said he's sure she will be back soon, so I should watch the place and wait small-small. But she didn't return."

"Have you heard from Ben recently?"

"Not since that Sunday, please. I tried to text and call him because it was the next day we supposed to kidnap Madam Ngozi."

That's two weeks this weekend, Emma thought.

"But I think he has been ignoring me," Salifu continued, "because Mr. Awuni and Madam Janet have been seeing him or talking to him off and on until yesterday, and they say he has been acting strangely. Madam is worried about him."

Emma was worried too, because she strongly believed that Ben-Kwame had abducted Ngozi. Wherever he was, there she would be as well.

JoJo WAS STILL out when Emma returned. Gideon and Manu were chatting and laughing about something.

"Is the boss in?" she asked them.

"Yes," Gideon said.

Emma found Sowah on the phone, so she sat to wait until he finished up.

"What's up?" he asked.

"I've been talking to Salifu," Emma said. "He's more perceptive than I had thought. I feel sorry I underestimated him in the beginning."

"Tell me about it."

"I think we were all shocked by the idea that Femi would have his own girlfriend kidnapped for ransom, but Salifu pointed out something that made me think about it differently. I asked him whether he thought Femi loved Ngozi. He told me that even though she might have meant a lot to him, money mattered more to him than she did."

"I suppose that could be the case," Sowah said. "It speaks to the kind of man Femi was. I get a whiff of psychopathy with this fellow. It sounds like this Salifu opened up to you."

"He did."

As Emma began relating her encounter, Jojo materialized.

"Oh, good!" Sowah exclaimed. "You're here. Come in, come in. Emma is telling me about her visit with Salifu."

She continued where she had left off. "As far as Salifu knew, Ben-Kwame was arranging for the abduction to occur on Monday, but for whatever reason, Ben must have changed the day. Or, some other yet unknown person preempted Ben's plan by abducting Ngozi before he could get to it."

"Do you believe Salifu?" Sowah asked.

"Yes," Emma said with the smallest hesitation.

"Jojo?" Sowah asked.

"If Emma does, I do too."

"What about you, sir?" Emma said. "How do you feel?"

Sowah leaned back, his eyes unfocused as he unconsciously twirled a pen around on the desk. Then he took a deep breath. "I feel as though we could be missing something, and it's been bothering me the past couple of days. Our hypothesis is that Femi's death and Ngozi's disappearance are connected. Everything that occurs in the present is a product of the past. We know quite a bit about Ngozi through her father, but what about Femi? He had two separate but related backgrounds in Ghana and Nigeria. We've been concentrating on the Ghanaian side, but barely on the Nigerian. Why is this important? At this point, we believe Ben-Kwame might have kidnapped Ngozi, but what if behind this all is a Nigerian enemy from the past exacting revenge on Femi? Could Femi have been running away from that? Is that the *real* reason Femi had come to Ghana?"

"I see what you mean, sir," Emma said, chewing the inside of her cheek. "What do you suggest we do?"

"Good question." He looked up with an I-have-an-idea expression. "You spoke with a Nigerian gentleman who brought up the issue of Femi's possibly having enemies in Nigeria—what was his name?"

"Cliffy," Emma said. "He hasn't been responsive to my calls or texts since I first spoke with him, though. You know, some people don't open up on the phone or talk to strangers."

"You've tried video-calling?"

"Yes—same thing. For sure, he appeared visibly shaken about the news of Femi's death, but he didn't vocalize much."

"Could Cliffy himself be one of those enemies?"

"Oh," Emma said. "It didn't occur to me, but it should have."

"I think we would get a better sense of him talking with him face to face," Sowah said.

"Do you have any private investigator contacts in Nigeria?" Jojo suggested.

"I don't," Sowah said, "although I probably should."

"I'll go," Emma said brightly.

Two heads and two pairs of eyes turned to her.

"What?" Jojo said.

"Pardon?" Sowah said. "Go where?"

"Nigeria," Emma said. "We need to talk to Cliffy face to face, sir, so I'll do it."

Sowah sat back, shaking his head. "I'm not sending you to Nigeria on your own, and it's not because you're a woman. I wouldn't do that to Jojo either. It's too dangerous to go poking around on your own. You don't even know the lay of the land."

"But someone does, boss," Emma said. "What if I had a professional escort?"

"That's going to be too expensive."

"Please, what about Mr. Ojukwu?" Jojo asked. "You said his fees have covered everything so far. Maybe he'll be willing to add something?"

Emma shot Jojo a grateful look for his idea.

Sowah was clearly torn. He cleared his throat. "I will ask Nnamdi. But that doesn't mean I endorse this plan," he added quickly.

"I understand, sir," Emma said sweetly, but she was determined to badger Sowah in the event he said no.

Sowah nodded. "Jojo—anything for us?"

"I've made a connection with Sade, one of the girls connected with Prof. Coleman. I'll be texting her again tonight to meet me somewhere. That reminds me, I'll need some cash to loosen her tongue, boss."

"Yes, sure," Sowah said, pushing his executive chair back to a safe built into the wall. He punched in the digital code and the door opened with a slight whirr. Sowah took out a neat bundle of *cedi* bills and handed them to Jojo. "Here you are, and that should also cover miscellaneous transportation expenses."

"Thank you, boss."

"In the meantime, Emma," Sowah went on, "try getting hold of Cliffy to see if he will commit to speaking to someone in person about Femi and his past."

Emma hoped that someone would be her.

"And it looks like you both will be working this weekend, so you'll get overtime," Sowah added.

Emma and Jojo cheered and high-fived each other.

CHAPTER THIRTY-SEVEN

Week Three

"THIS IS NOT A problem at all," Nnamdi said. "My driver is from Benin City well. He can take us wherever we want and I'll take full responsibility for Emma."

He, Sowah, and Emma were having a mini-summit in the office just before the Monday morning briefing. Sowah smiled at Emma. "It looks like you're going to Nigeria."

"Wow," Emma said, laughing. "This is so exciting. I've never traveled outside of Ghana."

"We need to act quickly, though," Nnamdi said. "I'll find the soonest available flight and get tickets for the two of us. We'll need to find a twelve- or twenty-four-hour Covid-testing center."

Emma wasn't clear on one point. "Please, did you say *flight?*"

"Yes, why?" Nnamdi said. "Wait a minute, did you think we were going to Nigeria by road?"

"Well, I did, yes."

He was amused. "Why would we lose almost two days traveling by road across three different borders when we can fly to Lagos in one hour?"

"You're right," Emma said, a little embarrassed. "I should have realized that." Her relaxed demeanor belied her paralyzing dread of flying.

AT THE BRIEFING, Sowah announced Emma was going to Nigeria to expand the investigation. There were exclamations of awe and admiration.

"But I don't know," Manu said, once the initial reaction had died down. "You would have a hard time persuading me to go there. Too dangerous."

"Mr. Ojukwu is providing protection for us," Sowah said reassuringly.

The detectives seemed doubtful.

"Why not send Jojo?" Manu said.

Emma understood the demeaning implications of his question and felt her anger rising, but she held it down and smiled instead.

"Emma volunteered first," Jojo said quickly, "so she gets the job."

"See me afterwards, Manu," Sowah said casually enough, but Emma suspected Manu was about to get a good scolding, and she couldn't help but feel gratified.

"So, what is the plan when you reach there?" Gideon asked.

"We'll arrive in Lagos," Emma said, "and from there, Mr. Ojukwu's driver will take us to Benin City."

"Is that far?" Jojo asked.

"Everything is far in Naija," Emma quipped, to the amusement of the others. "I've contacted Cliffy and secured his promise that he'll meet with me. He says he will try locating some of the people who knew Femi so I can talk to them."

Gideon nodded with approval. "That will be good. Congrats, Emma."

Manu, staring at his phone, had no comment.

EARLY WEDNESDAY MORNING, accompanied by Nnamdi, Emma took her first plane trip ever. Every stage of the one-hour flight to Lagos was nerve-racking for her. During acceleration for takeoff, never having experienced that kind of force or noise, she shut her eyes tight and gripped her armrest. As the plane lifted, she heard a clunking sound somewhere below the floor, and she imagined something must have been shaken loose. She cast a quick glance to the world beneath them, which was becoming smaller and smaller, but that gave her no comfort, and she looked away.

Nnamdi, sitting beside her in first class, was aware of what was happening to her. "Deep breaths, Emma; deep breaths. Everything is fine. If the attendants don't look worried, we shouldn't be either."

That reassurance helped somewhat, as did the served snack,

which helped distract Emma. Not long after that, the aircraft began its descent. The bounce on touchdown caused her to jump in alarm, but she let out a long sigh of relief that they were on terra firma.

"See?" Nnamdi said to her. "Not so bad, right?"

Emma conceded that in retrospect, it hadn't been such a big deal. Once inside the Murtala Muhammed Terminal and past customs and immigration, they headed for the visa-on-demand office, since Emma had not had enough time to obtain a visa before the flight. As she waited to be called, there was a power cut and all the computers went off-line. When would the electricity return? No one knew. Until then, there was nothing to do but take a seat and wait.

"They don't have generators?" Emma whispered to Nnamdi.

"Welcome to my homeland," he said with a bitter smile. "Now you understand why Nigerians go to Ghana for vacation."

NNAMDI'S DRIVER, MADUENU, welcomed them, took their luggage, and respectfully held open the doors of a silver-bronze Nissan Pathfinder. Its climate control was a welcome contrast to the sticky heat outside, which Emma thought was more pronounced than in Accra.

Nnamdi would have liked Emma to meet his wife had there been more time, but it would have to be on another occasion. Their priority now was to get to Benin City as soon as possible. Nnamdi and Emma were aware that this expedition might turn out to be a fool's errand, but both were willing to take the gamble.

They sped west on the expressway from Lagos to Benin City, a journey of almost two hundred miles. Lush, deeply green vegetation flanked the route. Before long, they came upon their first military-operated checkpoint, where the warning to slow down took the form of large logs laid across the road. Waved over to the shoulder by the military officers, a long line of *danfos* and rickety private vehicles waited for inspections. However, the officers waved the Pathfinder through.

Ghana's police checkpoints were similar in quality but not in quantity. On this route to Benin City, Emma counted thirty-eight stops, some of which were within half a mile of each other.

"Why are there so many?" she asked Nnamdi in astonishment.

"They're supposed to be fighting kidnapping and drug smuggling," he said, sounding weary. "What most of them are really doing is collecting bribes all day long. If you're detained for some trumped-up traffic infraction, you can't leave unless you pay up, and this may happen multiple times on the way to your destination. That's how a five- or six-hour trip to Benin City ends up being ten."

As Maduenu reduced speed to expertly dodge and swerve around craters and potholes, Nnamdi added, "And then, of course, there's these roads."

"Okay," Emma said, laughing, "As for that one, we have that in common with you."

LATE AFTERNOON SAW their arrival into Benin City. Emma's immediate impression was that it was quite unlike Accra. She felt not so much that time in Benin City had stopped, but that it had slowed down to a stable, sensible pace, whereas Accra was accelerating all the time with no one at the steering wheel. Benin City's centuries-old buildings and statues of ancient kings and queens reflected its rich and ancient past as a powerful kingdom. Emma was quite certain that Ghana's capital didn't possess a fully functional church built in the sixteenth century, as Benin City did. *You'll be lucky if Ghanaians can make anything last for a decade,* she reflected, which was cynical and not very kind. Still, she felt the notion held a nugget of truth.

However ancient the city's artifacts and buildings might have been, the Protea Hotel, where Nnamdi had reserved two rooms, was anything but old. As Nnamdi did the checking in, Emma looked around the ultramodern lobby where bellboys and attendants bustled around looking suitably busy. On the other side of the lobby was the restaurant, which had just opened for dinner and was filling the air with inviting smells. Emma realized she was ravenous, a rare occurrence. *Might be the Nigerian air*, she thought.

She found her room to be lovely, not that she knew much about hotel accommodations. It all looked so crisp and clean, and the bathroom was the most brightly lit she had ever seen. Emma stretched out on the bed with relish and had a fleeting tinge of guilt over whether she deserved all this opulence.

ONCE SHE HAD showered, she joined Nnamdi for dinner before retiring exhausted. The last thing she did before climbing into bed was text Cliffy to tell him she was in town. To her relief, he replied to welcome her and ask when he would see her. Tomorrow, was her answer. They agreed on ten in the morning.

CHAPTER THIRTY-EIGHT

AT NINE-THIRTY, MADUENU PICKED Emma and Nnamdi up at the hotel and they headed into town to meet Cliffy via Ring Road, a broad boulevard that formed one of Africa's largest roundabouts, King's Square. Fittingly, monuments and statues of royalty and deities dotted the outside perimeter.

Nnamdi looked back at Emma from the front passenger seat. "If you're ever lost in this city, just ask for directions to Ring Road, and you can't go wrong. In essence, all streets lead to and from King's Square like spokes in a wheel."

From Emma's perspective, vehicles on this mammoth roundabout were traveling left, right, and zigzag—anything *but* around—aggressively cutting fellow drivers off and vociferously returning the colorful insults lobbed at them. Bottlenecks developed at the roundabout's exits as cars, trucks, and red-and-yellow *danfos* came off Ring Road to squeeze into much smaller streets. At this point, pedestrians took advantage of the impasse, weaving in and out of the tight traffic to get to the other side. Motorcycles too, had the same move, swerving between cars with barely inches to spare. And all this with a rowdy chorus of constant horn-blowing.

With little success, Emma tried to hold down her gasps every time she thought they were about to collide with someone or something. She thought she saw Maduenu, who was unfazed by the mayhem, give a little smile at her apprehension.

"I'll never again think Accra drivers are bad," Emma commented, to the hilarity of the two men.

Away from the city center, Maduenu turned southwest on Ekenwan Road, which was asphalt up until the site of an ongoing infrastructure project. After that, the road was unpaved and dug up, squeezing both traffic lanes into one. A downpour one day before Emma's arrival had turned the environment into a slippery mudscape across which pedestrians were treading carefully.

They inched forward, Nnamdi chatting with Maduenu in Pidgin, which initially surprised Emma until she remembered that Nigerian Pidgin was a legitimate lingua franca and quite distinct from *incorrect* English.

Just beyond Ugbighoko Market, Maduenu turned right onto a nameless street, glancing down at the directions Cliffy had texted him. The roadway wasn't completely unpaved as was Ekenwan Road, but it was mostly potholes, which was just as bad.

"His house should be somewhere here," Maduenu said.

"I'll text him," Emma said.

Cliffy responded, telling them to park and he would come out to meet them. As Emma and Nnamdi alighted, a lanky man emerged from behind a metal gate and approached.

"Good morning," he said. "I'm Cliffy, and you must be Emma. Welcome."

She smiled at him. "It's good to meet you."

They fist-bumped, the Covid-deemed greeting that had replaced the handshake for even West Africans, who loved shaking hands. After Emma had introduced Nnamdi, they followed Cliffy into a labyrinthine complex of compact apartments arranged around separate small compounds. A gloomy, sandy-colored dog watched them dispassionately for a moment and then trotted off.

"Here we are," Cliffy said, unlocking his front door to invite them into his cozy, air-conditioned, one-bedroom home.

Either he had cleaned and dusted in preparation for their visit or he was a painfully tidy person. Everything in the sitting room was in its place—a striped sofa facing the TV, a coffee table with a vase of flowers placed exactly in the center, two cane-backed chairs, and a small square table for two in the corner near the kitchen. Emma noticed a crucifix on the back wall.

"Please, have a seat," Cliffy said. "Would you like some water?"

Sitting on the sofa and one of the chairs respectively, Nnamdi and Emma accepted the offer. Cliffy went to the kitchen.

"Cute apartment," Nnamdi said, looking around.

Emma agreed, and as Cliffy returned, she expressed their admiration.

"Oh, thanks." He handed them a bottle of water each before taking his seat in the second chair. "I wasn't always this neat." He laughed.

Light from the window illumed Cliffy's face in relief, highlighting a defect Emma had missed: a deep, thickened scar over his left cheekbone.

"How are you enjoying Nigeria, Madam Emma?" he asked. "Your first time?"

"So far, so good. A million thanks for meeting us, Cliffy. We're hoping for any information you can give us to help find Mr. Ojukwu's daughter."

Cliffy nodded. "Of course. I'll do my best. I'm very sorry to hear this news—Femi's death and then Ngozi's disappearance."

Nnamdi sat forward, his body language laying bare how anxious he was. "We're worried she's been kidnapped."

"I hear you, sir," Cliffy responded. "This is not easy."

"Before Femi and Ngozi left for Ghana," Emma said, "did he introduce her to you?"

"Yes, Madam. He brought her around one time."

"How did she seem to get along with Femi?" Emma asked.

"I think they loved each other very much, and I could tell how well she thought of Femi by the way she looked at him."

Obviously discomfited by Cliffy's last comment, Nnamdi twitched and shifted restlessly. "But what could she see in Femi?" he asked, sounding pained and baffled.

Cliffy smiled slightly and sadly. "I mean—how to say this—it was hard for most women not to be attracted to Femi."

"You knew him for a long time, I gather," Emma said.

"Almost fifteen years, though that period was split in two by Femi going to prison for eight years. He and I were started out as petty criminals when we were teenagers. In the end, Femi got caught, but I was the lucky one."

"So, you never served time," Nnamdi said.

"No, I didn't, thanks be to the Almighty. I say that because He has rescued me from that life of crime and shown me the light. I've now given my life to God and the Catholic Church."

Hence the crucifix, Emma thought. "Congratulations," she said. "You are truly blessed. But if I may ask, what was the nature of your partnership in crime with Femi once he got out of prison?"

"While he was still at Kirikiri," Cliffy explained, "I had begun a business making travel arrangements for young women who wanted to migrate to Europe in search of a better life. I lured them with the promise that they could get good jobs in Italy or Germany, maybe even become rich. The sad thing is that most of these girls didn't even have the skills to set up a job in Nigeria, let alone Italy, and so, what they really ended up doing was working as prostitutes to pay their debt to the madam who brought them there.

"When Femi came out of prison, we had lost touch, but we managed to get back together again. That's when he too began to do the same activity as me. At the time, he was doing carpentry and painting houses, which earned him almost nothing compared to the trafficking business. I don't say it's *easy*, but you can make a lot of money if you do it right."

"And Femi did it right?" Emma asked.

"Oh, yes," Cliffy said. "He did well, if I can say that. Even through the first Covid year when business was slow, he and I were doing okay. He was an expert recruiter, so good that he got more clients in the first six months than I ever did. But the difference between him and me was while I saved money, he spent all of his—cars, clothes, shoes, jewelry, French perfume, and girls—so some of the time he would ask me for a loan, as he called it. I never expected him to pay it back, and he didn't."

"He lived beyond his means, then," Nnamdi said, his voice tinged with contempt. "I know the type—flashy and pretentious."

"Mm-hm," Cliffy agreed. "And the women he had were part of the show."

Emma stole a glance at Nnamdi. He looked sickened by the entire picture Cliffy was painting of this impostor who had enticed his daughter into a world Nnamdi wouldn't have wanted for her.

From Emma's perspective, something was still missing. "You say the women were part of the show," she said. "Do you think Ngozi was one of those, or was she more to him?"

Cliffy thought about it for a moment. "Well, I can't say for sure—only he could have answered that question, so we may never know. But what I can say is that he loved money and possessions above all else, and we all know what the apostle Timothy said: 'The love of money is the root of all evil.'"

Emma was struck by the resemblance between Cliffy's assessment of Femi and Salifu's.

"Let me ask you something," she said to Cliffy, resting her forearms on her knees. "If I told you that Femi had been plotting to use Ngozi in a fake kidnapping to extort ransom from Ambassador Ojukwu here, would you believe it, disbelieve it, or not be sure?"

Cliffy dipped his head and sucked on his teeth in regret. "I'm sorry to say, yes, I do believe you."

That was disconcerting.

"Is that what he did?" Cliffy asked.

"From what we saw on his phone, it seems so," Emma said.

Cliffy shook his head with regret. "This is sad."

Nnamdi sat back with a sigh and shook his head in despair and incredulity. "How could all this have happened?" he muttered.

"I'm very sorry, sir," Cliffy said. "I'm sure you didn't want to hear this."

Nnamdi dismissed the apology. "I prefer your telling us the truth to hiding it."

He and Cliffy slipped seamlessly into Pidgin for a while as Emma thought about what she had heard so far. In learning more about Femi, she was even more convinced that his murder and Ngozi's disappearance were directly connected, but whether Ngozi was still alive was another question altogether. Emma had an increasingly urgent sense that time was slipping away.

"Cliffy," she said, returning to the discussion, "did Femi have any enemies that you know of who might have traveled to Ghana to kill him and kidnap Ngozi?"

"I'm not positive about that." Cliffy pursed his lips as he gave it thought. "While at Kirikiri, he made friends with a guy called Ayodele, who was released at the same time and went into business with Femi for a few months in Lagos until Femi moved to Benin City to stay with me. He didn't say he had had any problems with Ayodele, but maybe Ayodele knows more."

"Do you have his contact info?" Emma asked.

"No, I'm sorry. I never had any personal dealings with the guy."

"Do the names Kehinde and Bisola mean anything to you?" she asked Cliffy. "We saw them on Femi's phone."

"Oh, yes!" Cliffy responded vigorously. "You've reminded me. Femi convinced them to try to get to Europe and we created some false documents for them—yes, that was some of what we used to do. Kehinde and Bisola were planning to get married once they settled in Italy. I had forgotten all about them until one day around February of the first Covid year when I received a surprise call from Kehinde. He had lost Femi's direct number but he had googled Clif-femi Agents and found the business number to call me. He told me Bisola had died in the desert during the crossing from Agadez to Libya. Kehinde made it, but he suffered there and almost died in a detention camp in Sabha. He came running back to Naija."

"My goodness," Emma said. "Really?"

"Yeah," Cliffy said. "And Kehinde wanted to know where he could find Femi. His voice was shaking; he sounded angry, so I didn't feel it was safe to give Kehinde the information, so I lied, telling Kehinde that Femi was in Ghana at that moment. He asked for Femi's direct number, but I told him I would have Femi call him back rather."

"Did Femi do that?" Emma asked.

"No," Cliffy said, "because he knew there would be trouble with this Kehinde."

Emma thought about the hell Kehinde must have been through on that journey; to make it even more heartrending, he had lost the woman he had apparently loved and intended to marry. He must have felt profound grief, fury, and anguish, emotions that could have compelled him to avenge the death of his cherished Bisola.

"Do you know if Kehinde might still be around?" Nnamdi asked.

Cliffy shook his head. "No, sir, but I think I still have his number." He checked his phone. "Yes, it's here. Shall I try it?"

"Yes, please," Emma said at once. "No time to lose. Thank you."

Cliffy called the number but received no response initially. But then he got a call back. "What do you want me to tell him?" he asked Emma before picking up.

"Tell him you just came across his number—"

"Hello, Kehinde? Na me, Cliffy. How you dey? Good, good. You still dey Benin City?" Cliffy nodded, giving Nnamdi and Emma a thumbs-up. "Listen, you don hear Femi die?" Emma overheard an exclamation from Kehinde. "Yeah, bros, two weeks now. Somebody shoot am. Now his girlfriend, Ngozi, too don disappear in Accra. Nobody *sabi* where she dey go . . . Me? I dey house with Ngozi father and 'im friend Emma from Ghana, dem dey try find the girl. Hold on, please."

Cliffy handed her the phone. "Hello, Mr. Kehinde, my name is Emma. How you dey?"

"I dey, o."

"First of all, my condolences for your loss. I understand you loved Bisola very much."

"Yes please. Thank you."

"Cliffy told you Femi is dead and now Ngozi has disappeared. I'm assisting Ambassador Ojukwu to look for his daughter."

"Okay, that's good, then."

"Can you help us?"

"Like how? I don't know anything about her."

"Yes, that's true, but we're hoping we can learn what might have happened through finding out about Femi. Mr. Ojukwu and I have come all the way from Lagos and will appreciate your help. We want to understand what Femi was about and why Ngozi was in love with him."

Kehinde was silent for a moment. "I don't want to speak bad of the dead," he said at length, "but Femi was a wicked person."

"We need to know more," Emma pressed relentlessly. She wasn't going to let Kehinde wriggle out of this. "Can we meet today?"

Pause. "Today?"

"Yes. Are you free now?"

"No, not at the moment. But I will be in two hours."

"So, if we meet at noon, will that be okay?"

"Yes, all right; that's fine."

"Thank you so much. Hold on for Cliffy." Emma handed the phone back. "He's willing to meet."

After a brief discussion with Kehinde about where to rendezvous, Cliffy hung up. "Like, if you hadn't talked to him," he said to Emma, "I don't think he would have agreed."

Emma beamed at him. "Thank you for helping us. We appreciate it. One thing I haven't asked you, and I hope you don't mind, how did you change from your old ways and turn to God?"

Cliffy took a deep breath and let it out. "Do you know something? It's Femi I have to thank for that."

"How so?" Nnamdi asked, sounding skeptical.

"Okay, there's something I haven't told you, something that changed my life forever. In March this year, Femi went to Ghana to visit his beloved grandfather. On the day he was supposed to leave Accra and come back to Nigeria, his grandpa died. Femi stayed in Ghana for the funeral, but he returned to Nigeria first week in July. I was very happy to see him, but as we were talking, he told me he was moving to Accra to start a new business managing a hotel called the White House—so, that meant we wouldn't be working together anymore. To be honest, I was shocked! It seemed so sudden because I hadn't seen any kind of sign that he wanted to leave our partnership to go elsewhere. But I didn't bear any ill will toward him.

"The night came for him to leave. He came to my place—I wasn't living here then—to bid me a goodbye, but then he asked me for some cash for the journey. So, I went to my safe, which was in my bedroom, and I removed some dollars to give to Femi. But he wasn't happy with my offer. He said I had a lot more that I had been hoarding.

"After that, everything happened so quickly I can't remember most of it. What I know is that Femi took my head and smashed my face against the side of the safe, not once, but twice. It broke my left cheekbone, leaving this." Cliffy turned his face to his right to show the cratered, thickened scar, which he touched gingerly as if it were still tender.

Now that Emma knew the violent cause of the defect, she flinched.

"It's little bits and pieces I remember," Cliffy said. "I know I tried to fight, but he was too strong. He beat me seriously, and then he cleared out my safe. Took everything."

"God almighty," Nnamdi muttered, clenching a fist. "And the man who did this to you is the one my daughter fell in love with."

He shook his head in sad disbelief. "I don't know how you can say you have something to thank him for, Mr. Cliffy."

"That's not the end of the story," Cliffy said. "Pretend this is the room where Femi beat me, and I'm lying on the floor in this direction." He gestured with a forefinger. "When I awoke, the room was dark. I looked up to my right and behind me and saw a cloud of dust spinning in midair, but the dust was so bright, it shone off the walls of the room. It made a sound, like a kind of rushing sound I can't really describe.

"At first, I didn't know what was happening. Was I dreaming, or what? But I wasn't. Soon, I understood God was using this incident to show me how futile and sinful my life had been up to that moment. He had chosen Femi to carry that message to me, and it had to be brutal otherwise it would have made no impact on me. Now I feel a load lifted from my shoulders just knowing what I'm going to do for the rest of my life. So yes, thanks be to God, first; thanks to Femi, second."

For a moment, neither Emma nor Nnamdi said a word. Cliffy's story was spectacular and strange.

"Does that mean you've forgiven Femi?" Emma asked.

"I have now, yes. I even tried to call him in Ghana to tell him that, but he never answered a single call, and for that, I'm sorry."

CHAPTER THIRTY-NINE

CANTONMENTS, THE HOME OF top British military brass in colonial times, was an expensive part of Accra. As immaculate and rarefied as the neighborhood was, Cantonments residents had much the same sexual fantasies as poor people; it was just that they could pay for it.

The sex workers' prices rose steeply from Oxford Street in Osu to Cantonments Circle barely a mile up the hill. In the neighborhood were the American, French, Togolese, and UAE embassies. Perhaps deliberately, the Circle had never been well lit. Shiny vehicles slid in and out of the shadows. The options were many: oral service inside the car in a discreet area, or the sex worker could ride with the client to his home or hotel room for whatever he wanted to do or have done to him for however long he wished.

The swanky hotels in the area all made money off the sex workers, directly or not. One such hotel was Mahogany Haven, where Jojo had set up a rendezvous with Sade at 7 P.M. She was punctual, texting Jojo to say she had arrived. He instructed her to come up to Room 121 where he was waiting for her. He opened the door when she tapped on it.

"Jojo?" she said, flashing a smile of dazzling white teeth.

"Hi, Sade."

She had braids to her shoulders and wore a tight, pink dress that looked like silk but probably wasn't, and pink, sparkly high heels. Jojo got a blast of her perfume—not a bad scent, just too much of it.

He held open the door and smiled in return. "Come in. How are you?"

"I'm very well, thank you, Jojo, my dear." She had the lightest of Nigerian accents. "How can I rock your world tonight?"

"Please have a seat."

Sade sat in one of a pair of chairs in the corner, while Jojo sat at the edge of the bed.

"I'm not looking for sex," Jojo said bluntly. "Better than that, I'm looking for information."

Sade stiffened visibly. "What kind of information? Who are you?"

"I do freelance work," Jojo said vaguely. It sounded less threatening than "private detective." "Just like you have clients, so do I. One of my clients is searching for his daughter, Ngozi, who was Femi's girlfriend. I believe you know—or knew—Femi."

Sade shook her head. "I don't know who that is."

Jojo had Femi's phone handy. He pulled up one of the WhatsApp exchanges with Sade and brought it close to her face. "That's you, is it not?"

Sade stood up. "This is a waste of my time."

"I'm going to pay you for this, don't worry."

Sade stopped as Jojo went into his wallet and removed six bills of one hundred *cedis* each.

"I don't think we'll even need one hour," Jojo said, "so this is for thirty minutes only." He made as if to hand the money to Sade, but he moved it out of her reach as she tried to take it. "Do you agree to answer my questions to the best of your ability?"

Tempted, Sade was looking from Jojo to the money and back.

"Six hundred *cedis* for thirty minutes—not a bad deal at all," Jojo cajoled. "That's like two hundred dollars for an hour."

Put like that, it sounded impressive. Sade sighed. "Okay."

Jojo gave her the cash and she took her seat again. "What do you want to know?"

"Thank you. First, you agree that these texts to Femi are yours?"

Sade nodded. "Yes please."

"How did he first contact you?"

"He got my WhatsApp number from one of the sex sites—Exotic Ghana, I think. I don't remember exactly."

"When was that, please?"

"End of September."

"What did he want from you?"

"He told me he was the manager of a new hotel called the

White House, in East Legon, and he was recruiting slay queens who could cater to rich clients."

Without a doubt, Sade made the grade: clean, sophisticated, and unquestionably gorgeous—not that she even remotely stirred Jojo's libido, but still, credit where credit was due.

"He was offering very good money," Sade continued. "I told him about my friend Effia, who is also a slay queen, so Femi said I should bring her along. We met, and we were happy with the arrangements Femi was proposing. It meant Effia and I could have a safe place to work from—much safer than going to people's houses. The following week, when we were supposed to start work-ing, we arrived at the White House to find out someone had killed Femi. Oh, what a shock!"

"I realize you didn't know Femi very well," Jojo said, "but do you have any idea who might have wanted him dead?"

Sade hesitated, her eyes flicking away for a second.

"What about Professor Coleman?"

Sade was visibly startled. "You know about him?"

"He didn't like Femi at all, right?"

"Yes, he didn't. Prof. Coleman accused Femi of trying to steal Effia and me from him."

"What was the arrangement between you and the professor? Was he your pimp?"

"Anyway, yes, you could say that. You see, it was Effia who first met him when she was attending university. She was failing Prof.'s class, but he offered to give her an A in exchange for sex. After that, Prof. offered to help solve her other problem: that she was completely broke. He told her she could make some cash on the side by servicing his friends. When I first met Effia, my father's restaurant in Lagos was struggling as a result of the pandemic, and it also looked like Daddy was going to move my little brother to a less expensive school. I had to help out, and I needed money quick. That's how I got into the business.

"But things have been changing fast and Prof. hasn't been keeping up with the trends. Women no longer need some man to tell them where to go and when, because, why? Because we have these." Sade held up her phone. "Clients can call us directly. We can pick and choose. We were getting much better work by placing ads online. Meanwhile Prof.'s friends were starting to get cheap, constantly arguing about what they can get for the smallest amount of money—very annoying—and Prof. too was becoming more demanding and possessive.

"Effia and I started to pull away from him and he panicked. When he found out about our contact with Femi—I didn't tell him; Effia did—he got very angry and started shouting at us. That's when I walked out and told him I wouldn't be back, and Effia did the same thing a few minutes later. That evening—I think it was the last Wednesday before the murder—Femi forwarded messages he had received from Prof. accusing him of stealing us two girls."

"Do you still have those messages?" Jojo asked.

"Yes, of course." Sade removed her iPhone from her purse. She had long, glittery fingernails that demanded considerable skill using the touchscreen. "Here you are."

Jojo studied the exchange.

Mr. Femi, my name is Professor Proph Coleman. It's come to my notice that you're trying to intrude upon the agreement I have with my ladies, Effia and Sade. I'm giving you notice that you must cease and desist immediately. What you are doing constitutes theft, and it should stop at once.

Mr. Coleman, Effia and Sade are free to do whatever they choose, and that includes working for me

But it was you who approached them and offered them an inducement, therefore I consider this a very hostile usurpation of my position

What position is that?

I'm their boss. You can't do business with them without including me. Is that clear?

I don't care who the fuck you think you are I don't answer to you or anyone else, fuck you

You Nigerians are all the same—greedy cheats and liars. You come to this country with your Yahoo boys and start your fraudulent businesses here. Be careful. Some of us will not tolerate your nonsense, so watch your back.

Jojo looked up at Sade. "This warning he gave, 'watch your back,' do you think the professor was serious?"

"Yes, he was serious."

"Do you think he could have killed Femi?"

"I don't think he has the guts," Sade said, shaking her head slowly. "Even though he does have a gun—"

Jojo nearly jumped out of his seat. "Wait a minute—Coleman has a gun?"

Sade nodded. "Yes. One day he was showing it off to Effia and me."

"A handgun?"

"Yes please."

"What is he doing with a gun?"

Sade shrugged. "He says to protect himself because he has enemies."

"Oh, interesting. Which enemies is he talking about?"

Sade tossed her head and cheupsed derisively. "This is not an enemy issue, it's a big-gun-small-dick issue."

Jojo attempted to keep a straight face, but his facade collapsed as Sade began to giggle.

He couldn't help but join in, and after that, any tension that had been in the air dissipated.

"What about Coleman hiring an assassin to do the job of killing Femi?" Jojo asked, returning to seriousness.

"Maybe," Sade replied, seeming doubtful.

Jojo was deep in thought for a moment. "Can you help me find out?"

"Like how? In what way?"

"Let's say now that Femi is dead," Jojo said, "you pay a visit to Coleman—maybe tell him you want to make peace with him and so on—and then find out where he was on the night Femi was shot, that is, sixteenth of October. Would that be possible?"

"I can try," Sade said. "But in return?"

"No worries," Jojo said. "I'll talk to the boss to send you something if you get us the information."

Sade nodded. "Okay." She smiled and laughed. "Who would have thought I would become a detective?"

CHAPTER FORTY

IN THE MORNING, SADE called Proph Coleman to make amends and apologize for deserting him. After his initial display of indignation over her "abandoning" him, he backed down and admitted he was eager to see her again—in other words, his dick was eager to see her, Sade thought. With his wife away, Proph could entertain Sade at his home on the University of Ghana campus.

Just before dusk, Sade arrived coiffed and fragrant at Coleman's house with its orange-tile roof. She wore a short skirt with a ruffled hem and a matching denim halter crop top that showed off her ample breasts. Coleman's eyes bulged with lust at the sight of her.

"My dear," he said, "how is it you are more beautiful than ever?"

She laughed as she sat beside him in the sitting room loveseat. "Thank you, my darling Proph. You always make me feel so good. What are we drinking to celebrate?"

Coleman got to his feet. "It's funny you should ask. I bought champagne for us."

"Oh, wonderful!"

They sipped the champagne and chatted while Coleman stole glances at Sade's smooth, irresistible thighs and legs, and feet with pink toenails.

He placed a hand on her knee. "So, you decided to come back to daddy?"

She smiled coyly and gave him a peck on the cheek. "You were right all along. Femi wasn't good for Effia or me."

"He was a manipulator," Coleman said heatedly. "That's why he's dead now."

"Why do you say that?"

"If you twist people around too much, eventually someone is going to hit back, and extortion will get you nowhere."

Sade raised her eyebrows. "I don't get you. What are you saying?"

"Ten days before his death he called to ask me for fifteen thousand dollars," Coleman said. "For what? I ask. He tells me, none of my business. I say, why should I give you one single *pesewa*? He told me get him the money or he was going to expose me as a pimp—that's the word he used. *Pimp*. How dare this motherfucker call me that? I told him off, but he kept threatening and threatening." Coleman took in a breath and released it. "Listen, Sade, the university has begun a probe into allegations that some university professors are running sex rings. I can't afford to be exposed with something like this. There's talk of my work in Economics possibly being recognized next year by the Nobel Prize Committee. That's an honor of a lifetime."

"So, Femi wanted to take all that away from you," Sade said with indignation. "He was threatening to ruin your work and your life. Fucking bitch. What did you do, then?"

"First, I negotiated him down to twelve thousand, and then I asked him for some time to gather the funds, and whether I could pay it in installments. He gave me two weeks." Coleman stopped and shook his head. "This just could not stand."

Sade took his hand in hers. "I'm with you, my darling. Look, if you had to shoot him, I really don't care."

Coleman's jaw dropped. "What do you mean?"

"I'm not accusing you of anything; all I'm saying is if you did it, it's all the same to me. I won't be going around saying, 'Professor Proph Coleman killed Femi Adebanjo.' No one would believe it anyway."

He still appeared dismayed at the notion. "But why should I kill the man?"

Sade shrugged, "You have the gun, and above all, you've got the balls to do it."

Coleman brightened at the new perspective. "You really think I have the balls?"

"Of course." She groped his crotch. The Viagra seemed to have taken effect.

His eyes were becoming languid with lust. "You like it?"

"You know I do. Baby, can I hold your gun again?"

He grinned lasciviously. "Which one?"

"Silly boy." Sade giggled. "You remember when you showed Effia and me the pistol you keep in the safe? I got excited when you put it in my hand."

"Really?"

"Yes. I want to look at it again. I hope it's not loaded?"

"Of course not," Coleman said, getting up and holding his hand out to her. "Safety is always a priority. Come, let's go."

Arms around each other, they went to his study via a veranda that bordered the patio overgrown with untended bougainvillea. It was a decades-old design that no one used anymore, but Sade rather liked it. Coleman retrieved a key from a desk drawer and opened the clunky, gray safe on the shelf among his Economics textbooks, a few of which he had written himself. He removed the gun, which was wrapped in an old muslin cloth, and placed it carefully on the desk. He exposed the weapon slowly, as if undressing it.

"There," he said with pride. "A Ruger GP100. What a beauty."

Sade, in reality terrified of firearms of any sort, murmured her false admiration but took an involuntary step back as Coleman checked the cylinder. "Don't be afraid," he reassured her. "It's safe."

She cradled the Ruger in her hands, finding it surprisingly heavy. "Wow."

"Like this," he said, showing her the correct way to hold it. "How does it make you feel?"

"Quite powerful," she said, truthfully, handing the revolver back to Coleman with care.

Pointing it away from them, he adopted a dramatic, two-handed stance and made the sound of a gunshot.

Sade thought this was all very silly, but she said, "One or two shots to kill Femi?"

"Only one would have been required," Coleman said with a smirk. "No matter how tough he thought he was. I'm not saying that's what happened, I just mean theoretically."

"I get you," she said. "Where are the bullets? What do they look like?"

From the safe, he removed a box labeled RUGER .357 MAGNUM

SELF-DEFENSE AMMUNITION, and took out one of the bullets for her to examine. She giggled. "It looks like a hard penis."

"Yeah," he said, croakily. "It does."

"Can I keep it as a souvenir?" she asked lightly.

"Of course." He unzipped himself. "But look, here is the real hard dick."

She bent over and kissed it.

"Let's go to the bedroom," he said thickly. "I need you."

AS WAS ALWAYS the case, Coleman collapsed after the sex. Once he was safely asleep, Sade returned to his study where he had carelessly left the weapon and ammunition on his desk. She took a picture of the Ruger and box of ammunition and was about to leave everything in place when she thought better of it and gingerly returned the items to the safe. She locked it and replaced the key in the desk.

She was getting dressed when Coleman stirred. "Leaving already?" he muttered groggily.

"Yes, my love." She kissed him on the cheek. "I have a client."

"Thanks for coming," he said. "When can I see you again?"

"Maybe soon," Sade responded accurately. Although she seriously doubted it.

CHAPTER FORTY-ONE

THE LITIGATION OVER THE land on which the Alligator annex sat had finally been settled after several years of inaction by the courts, where a massive backlog was the status quo. It was time for the builders to survey the property again and make recommendations anew after the building had lain fallow for so long.

The builders would arrive in the afternoon, so, that morning, Janet and Awuni decided to do a preliminary walk-through. They first toured the two floors of the skeletal, unfinished building and decided they should ask for some changes.

"Let's go down to the underground garage now," Awuni said. It had been his idea in the first place, and he was proud of it because underground parking wasn't common in Accra.

As they went down the stairs, Awuni could tell how worried Janet was, and it was over her son, whom they hadn't seen or heard from in over a week.

"Ben will come back," he said firmly but lovingly. "Don't you worry. I think he's just gone away to think about his life and what to do next."

"I hope that's what it is," Janet said, her brow furrowed in distress, "but I think something is wrong."

They emerged outside in the bright sun, walked to the garage, and descended six steps to the side entrance. Awuni found the key and opened the door. A revolting, putrid odor hit them immediately.

Awuni recoiled "What is that smell?"

"Oh, my God," Janet said, holding her nose. "Maybe some rats died here or something."

"I don't think so," Awuni said.

As they entered, the odor seemed to engulf them. Janet gagged, and Awuni coughed several times as he fiddled with his phone flashlight. He moved the beam slowly over the planks of wood and stacks of bricks and metal poles. He jumped as he saw a body crumpled in the fuscous dirt.

Janet gasped. "Who is that?"

Covering his nose and mouth, Awuni approached the body, which was lying on its side with one arm outstretched and the head turned away. It was bloated and Awuni saw dark fluids emanating from beneath it. He circled around to the front to find a ballooned head and a decomposing, oozing face.

Awuni backed away, stopped with his hands on his knees, and retched. Ben was unrecognizable, but his faux Gucci backpack next to him wasn't. He had proudly shown it off to Janet and Awuni the day he bought it. The distinctive backpack and drug paraphernalia scattered around him plainly told the story of death by a drug overdose.

Janet had been watching from a distance. "Awuni, who is that?" she wailed. "What's going on?"

He rushed to her side. "Come along outside with me. You mustn't see this."

"But who is it?" she cried. "He's dead?"

Awuni pulled her back. "Get out, now, Janet. Go!"

He hustled her out the door, which slammed shut behind her, leaving Awuni alone in the now-eerie underground space.

Awuni heard a groan which made him jump and whirl around with a gasp of fright.

"Who's there?" he called out, his voice trembling.

The sound came again, and this time, Awuni localized its origin. He moved cautiously around a large stack of lumber where his light beam revealed a disheveled woman tied to one of the supporting pillars. Slouched in her sitting position with her head slumped and bare feet bound, she was breathing fast and shallow.

Awuni knelt beside her. "Who are you?"

"Ngozi," she whispered.

"The one who tried to take Diamond away?"

She nodded.

Awuni hadn't met her before, but he could tell she was in

desperate shape. "What happened?" he asked her. "Ben brought you here?"

"Kidnapped me," she said feebly. "Then he OD'd on cocaine."

Awuni was shaking. The awful unfolding circumstances had adrenaline rushing through his body. "How long have you been here?" he asked in near disbelief.

She shook her head. "Don't know."

Janet was calling for him from the other side of the door, and then she started banging on it, screaming. He ignored her for now, feverishly wrestling with the coarse rope binding Ngozi's wrists behind the pillar. He awkwardly held his phone in his mouth to train the flashlight downward. The knots were ridiculously tight, and Awuni was drenched with sweat by the time he had unfastened them. Then he turned his attention to Ngozi's ankles. The ligatures there were a little easier to deal with, and he tossed them to the side when he had undone them.

"Can you stand?" he asked her. "Put your arm around my shoulder."

Awuni supported Ngozi as she attempted to get to her feet, but her knees buckled.

"Lean against me more," he said, putting his arm around her waist to steady her.

They made slow progress as Janet continued to shout from the other side of the door. At last, Awuni and Ngozi reached their destination.

"I'm going to open the door," he said, "so, please shut your eyes for a moment, because the sun is bright."

When they exited, Janet was frantically waiting. "What's going on?" she cried. "Who is this? Ngozi?" Janet was stunned as she recognized her. "*Ngozi?*"

"We need to climb the stairs," Awuni said to Ngozi. "Do you want to rest first, and I can bring you some water?"

"Yes, please," Ngozi said.

Awuni let her down slowly onto the second step, where she leaned back on her elbows to catch her breath. Only then did Awuni turn to Janet.

"She was tied up," Awuni explained. "Ben kidnapped her and he was using drugs. I'm sorry, love, he overdosed."

"What?" Janet said, incredulous. "I don't believe you. What are you saying?"

He tried to take her in his arms, but she pushed him away. "Who is that inside?" she snapped.

"I'm sorry, love. Ben is dead."

Janet let out a shriek and fell to her knees sobbing. Awuni knelt beside to console her, but abruptly, she stood up again. "I want to see him."

"No," Awuni said.

Janet yanked on the door handle and agitatedly shook it as if it would magically open. "Give me the key," she snapped, holding her hand out to Awuni. "Give it to me."

He shook his head. "I can't allow you to go in there, Janet. It's too much."

Behaving like a penned wild animal, Janet now turned on Ngozi and lurched at her. "What did you do to him?" she demanded, but Awuni held her back.

"Come on," he said firmly to Janet. "Let's go up."

He half-coaxed, half-dragged Janet up the stairs as her body became limp. At the top, a small crowd of spectators, attracted by Janet's screaming, had gathered.

"Bring me water, somebody," Awuni yelled at them, almost annoyed at their gawking.

Within less than a minute, a bottle of water materialized. Awuni grabbed it and handed Janet over to one of the Alligator receptionists with instructions to take her to the hotel to lie down.

Joseph the DJ came to Awuni's side. "Boss, anything I can do?"

"Yes, tell my driver to go directly to the Lapaz Police Station and report we have a dead body. They will dispatch a couple of detectives to return with him."

Joseph sped off and then Awuni hurried down the stairs to sit next to Ngozi, who was leaning against the staircase wall with her eyes closed.

"Ngozi," Awuni said. "Water."

She was so weak, he had to hold the bottle as she took sips through her parched lips.

"Thank you," she whispered.

It was surprising how even that small amount of water gave

Ngozi a boost of energy, enough to get her up the steps as she clutched the railing. Awuni guided her away from the crowd, which had begun to dissipate, and sat her down at the edge of the construction.

"How do you feel?" he asked her.

She nodded, but didn't verbalize.

"Stay here a moment," Awuni instructed. "I'm bringing a car over to take you to the hospital."

Dazed and frightened, Ngozi nodded mutely. Whatever negative characterizations Awuni had heard assigned to Ngozi before, he felt terribly sorry for her now.

CHAPTER FORTY-TWO

MADUENU DROVE EMMA AND Nnamdi across town toward Market Square on Sapele Road.

"I read something about an ancient moat that protected Benin City and its king," Emma said from the back seat.

"I'll show you," Nnamdi said. "Maduenu, take the next right and stop somewhere."

At length, they pulled over and parked.

"Let's get down here," Nnamdi said to Emma.

They walked from the street to a grassy area peppered with plantain trees.

"Here it is," Nnamdi said with a gesture.

Emma looked, but saw nothing of a moat. "Where?" she asked in puzzlement.

"We're standing on what was once the outer wall of the moat."

Emma gasped. The ancient engineering marvel was now a shallow depression covered with overgrown weeds and litter?

"But this is horrible!" she said. "This should be hallowed ground. There should be a fence, or something."

"You see, o," Nnamdi said, shaking his head in regret. "It's a terrible shame."

Emma came away feeling oddly sad and was silent the rest of the way to Market Square. It was medium-sized, unspectacular mall with a conventional layout. They headed to the food court, where they had agreed to meet Kehinde, and chose a table that was reasonably isolated. It wasn't difficult: an early afternoon on a weekday wasn't a peak period by any means. Only a few couples were present, and no one so far matched Kehinde's description.

Emma and Nnamdi had been chatting for a while when his phone rang. "It's Yemo," Nnamdi said. "Hello . . . *What?* Thank you, Jesus. Praise God!" To Emma, he said, jubilantly, "Ngozi's been found, and she's alive." Nnamdi listened further to Yemo, silent except for a few punctuating exclamations. "But is she responding to her treatment at the hospital?" he asked anxiously. "All right. Please let her know Emma, my wife, and I will be back in Ghana as soon as we can get a flight. And give Ngozi our love as well."

He hung up, his eyes clouding. "I'm so grateful she's alive . . . What did they do to my little girl?"

He pressed his palms against his eyes. "Excuse me, please," he said in a choked voice. Head bowed, he disappeared around the corner to release his emotions in private. As he did, Emma received a text from Jojo, who gave her a short summary of what had unfolded over the last several hours. *Well, at least I was right about something,* Emma thought. *Find Ben-Kwame, and you'll find Ngozi.*

And what did it matter who had discovered Ngozi as long as she was now safe and alive? But it did matter in a certain way. Emma was bothered by the randomness of Ngozi's rescue. It had been a fluke that Mr. Awuni had chosen to inspect the underground structure that day. Had it been even forty-eight hours later, Ngozi might have died from dehydration.

Emma felt like the investigation had lost its focus. If she had been sure Ben-Kwame had carried out the kidnapping, why had she not concentrated on him instead of flying off to Nigeria? Had she, Jojo, and Sowah completely missed the mark? Instead of imagining that Ben-Kwame had taken Ngozi somewhere remote, which was Emma's at least subconscious impression, perhaps they should have stuck to nearby locations. Didn't a kidnapper need to be physically close to their captives? Maybe it should have occurred to someone to look in the underground garage. Or was hindsight simply tormenting her?

"Hi, are you Emma?"

The voice jolted her from her reverie and she looked up to see a young man with warm, earnest eyes. He was clean-shaven and smartly but not expensively dressed.

Emma stood up. "Kehinde?"

"Yes please."

"It's so nice to meet you. Thank you for coming. Let's sit down. Can I get you any refreshments?"

"I'm good, thank you. Are you alone? I thought you were coming with the father of the woman who disappeared in Ghana."

"Mr. Ojukwu," Emma said. "He's also here—he'll be back in a minute. We have very good news. Ngozi, his daughter, has been found in Accra."

Kehinde clasped his hands. "We thank God. I'm happy to hear that."

Nnamdi returned and Emma introduced the two men to each other.

"I'm happy your daughter is okay, sir," Kehinde said.

"Thank you," Nnamdi said, with a broad smile. He had recovered nicely. "I've just called my wife to inform her, and she's overjoyed."

"What a shame you've had to go through this," Kehinde said, "but at least the nightmare is over."

They discussed the ordeal for a short while. At length, Kehinde said, "So, please, what is your mission here today?"

Good question, Emma thought. Now that Ngozi had been rescued, was there a point to this meeting, or was it a futile exercise?

"Our goal for this trip, at least up till this point," Emma said, "was to find out if Femi Adebanjo's past might throw some light on his murder and Ngozi's abduction. Of course, now that Ngozi is back with us, the outlook has changed. Still, if it's not too much to ask, can you tell us something about your dealings with Femi? Do you blame him for what happened to you and Bisola?"

"Of course." Kehinde's gaze dropped. "We wanted a better life, and he took advantage of that."

"I hear you," Emma said. "Are you willing to talk about it?"

Kehinde bit his lip as if mentally preparing himself for the pain of reliving his experience. "It's not a problem," he said finally. "I'll tell you the story."

PART SIX

CHAPTER FORTY-THREE

THE FIRST PART OF Kehinde and Bisola's journey was a twenty-hour bus trip from Lagos to Kano, one of the cities closest to the border between the Nigeria and Niger. Never having been to Kano, Nigeria's northern and second-largest city, Kehinde and Bisola were impressed by the sight of each lavish, grand mosque they passed. Benin City had mosques as well, but not like this.

At approximately noon, they arrived at the Kano bus station. They had a backpack each and a suitcase between the two of them. The first order of business was to call Hasan, Femi's Kano contact who would provide them with the documents they would need at the Nigerien crossing. Having repeatedly tried the number without success, Kehinde attempted to call Femi. The automated message said that the number had been disconnected. Kehinde frowned. Had he dialed it incorrectly? He tried again with the same result.

Bisola caught his expression. "What's wrong?"

"Femi isn't picking up," Kehinde said.

"Maybe he'll call back," Bisola said. "Why not text him instead?"

"Yeah," Kehinde said, beginning his text, but his doubts, assuaged during the bus trip, were returning. *Is Femi for real?*

Kehinde's phone rang—Hasan calling back.

"Hello? Yeah, bros. How you dey?"

"I dey," he said tersely. "Where you dey na?"

"Kano bus station. When we go meet?"

"Tomorrow early morning, make we travel cross the border."

Kehinde was unclear. "I think say you go give us travel documents for the bus make we take am to Niger."

There was a short silence. "*Which kain* travel documents you dey talk, now?"

"Document to take enter Niger on the bus," Kehinde said.

"Bus? *Which kain* bus? We go enter by smuggler route on *okada*."

"*Okada!*" Kehinde interjected. "How? Na me and my girlfriend, o! We dey get backpack and suitcase too. How we go fit take *okada*?"

"Heh?" Hasan bellowed. "You and your girlfriend! Femi never tell me say you go bring girlfriend. This na big *wahala* for me. I no go fit take two of you at my back."

Kehinde felt a rush of panic. "Oh, *abeg*, Hasan," he said, instantly changing his tone. "Make you try for us."

"E go cost you o. I charge for extra person, twenty thousand naira."

That was steep. Kehinde didn't have a whole lot of money to spare. "*Abeg*, come down small."

They bargained back and forth for a while until they came to a mutually agreed fee.

"You go put everything inside one backpack," Hasan instructed. "I go call you tomorrow to meet."

AT EIGHT IN the morning, the Kano sun was already bearing down fiercely. Hasan, a painfully thin man in his mid-twenties with silky, deep-black skin, showed up at the meeting place near the bus station on a dusty red-and-black Haojue Xpress motorcycle. With one flinty-eyed glance at the backpack Kehinde was holding, Hasann snapped, "Dis one dey too heavy! Make you comot everything, leave only water and some few clothes."

Bisola looked distraught as she helped Kehinde remove items. "What are we going to do with all this?" she said to him. "We're just going to leave it here?"

"What can we do?" he replied, exasperated.

HASAN DIDN'T TAKE the normal route to the Niger border via route RN11 through Mutum. Instead, he turned to the east off the beaten path, adding easily another four to six hours to the journey. Hardy desert shrubs became sparser as the temperature rose to 40 degrees Celsius. For her safety, Bisola was sandwiched between Hasan in the front and Kehinde in the rear. They couldn't risk her falling off the back.

The two desert neophytes now understood the utility of Hasan's sunglasses and the long cotton wrap around his head, forehead, and mouth. It protected against the hot, dry wind laden with whipping particles of sand, and now they both wished they had the same protection. They were from Lagos. What did they know about the desert?

Hasan rode like a fiend, sometimes avoiding rocky areas while dodging sections that were so sandy the motorcycle could have become stuck.

Bisola turned her head to one side and said something to Kehinde.

"What?" he shouted above the wind.

"I need to *pee*," she yelled.

Kehinde tapped Hasan on the shoulder and he nodded, apparently having heard Bisola. He slowed down to a stop and they all got off. Bisola found a low shrub that was at a discreet distance from the men, who, on the other hand, effectively stood where they were and urinated. *Men have it easy*, Bisola thought with some envy.

Kehinde and Bisola shared a bottle of now-warm water, initially sucking it down until Hasan warned them to restrain themselves. In the desert, water was to be sipped, not gulped. Using tiny amounts of the same precious fluid, they rinsed off their sandy faces. Kehinde tried to assess Bisola's state of mind, but her expression was inscrutable, or perhaps just numb. Already, the trip was turning out to be nothing like they had imagined it and certainly not the way Femi had presented it to them.

Hasan, who was sitting on his haunches for a moment of rest, sprang to his feet and called out in a harsh whisper, "*Security! Run!*"

"What?" Bisola said. Startled, she quickly scanned the desert.

Hasan pointed as he sprang onto his motorcycle and started it up. Now, Kehinde and Bisola saw the fast-approaching silhouette of a pickup on the horizon heading in their direction in the midst of a billowing cloud of kicked-up sand.

Confused, Kehinde grabbed Bisola's arm and ran toward Hasan.

"*No!*" he screamed. And he sped off alone, fleeing the pickup.

Still loaded down with the backpack, Kehinde shouted to Bisola, "This way!"

He took off, Bisola close behind him. "*Run!*" he shouted. But his ill-fitting shoes were slipping in the rocky sand. For years as a kid, he had walked barefoot, and the soles of his feet were thick and tough. In a strange but deft move, he disposed of his shoes as he ran, and once they were off, he picked up speed. For a moment, Bisola was flagging behind him, but he turned to whip her on. With a burst of energy she conjured up from somewhere deep within herself, she developed a spurt of *vitesse*, as if God had given her a helpful shove from behind, and slightly overtook Kehinde. His backpack was becoming too heavy, and now he tucked his hands underneath the shoulder straps and flung the burden off his back into the sand.

The security officers were in a Toyota Hilux, the ubiquitous and most-favored pickup for desert transportation. It was gaining fast on the two runaways, and the men were cracking off gunshots in the air. Kehinde wasn't sure that either he or Bisola could maintain their pace much longer. Bisola's breathing was becoming labored, and she was falling behind again.

"I can't," she said, and stumbled. She fell and rolled over into a heap.

Kehinde stopped and ran back to her. "Okay?"

"I can't," she said, gasping. She would have cried if she had any breath or tears left, but she had neither. "Let them . . ."

Kehinde looked up. The three security men had stopped where Kehinde's backpack lay. After searching it, they piled the items on the hood of the Toyota—clothes, bottles of water, and not much else. Apparently looking for falsified documents, they tossed the backpack away, piled into the Hilux, and started up again in Kehinde and Bisola's direction. But a new, higher-pitched sound became evident above the roar of the pickup, and out of the swirling dust, Hasan on his Haojue materialized like an apparition and buzzed the Hilux as a crow might harass an eagle. The security guys fired, but Hasan had been swallowed up in the dust cloud. The Hilux abruptly changed direction to pursue Hasan.

"They'll kill him," Kehinde muttered, his voice heavy with resignation. At this point, he wasn't sure he cared.

THE SHRUB KEHINDE and Bisola chose for shelter from the sun gave them little shade, but now, even minimal relief was a blessing. They lay together with her head resting on his chest. They didn't utter the question they both had on their minds—*What are we going to do now?*—because they didn't want to face the answer. They had no water, and they were hundreds of miles from an oasis or refuge of any kind. They were going to die. As simple as that.

They sat up in alarm as they heard the drone of an engine in the distance and saw the telltale plume of dust in the distance. Were the security guys returning? But soon, Kehinde and Bisola could see that this was a smaller vehicle. As it got closer, they recognized Hasan on his Haojue, his head garment flapping in the wind. He came up at top speed and skidded to a halt, baptizing them with sand they didn't need.

"How you dey?" he said, as if not much had happened.

Kehinde staggered to his feet in anger. "Why you don leave us like that?"

Hasan contemplated him for a moment. "Like, if we sit all for moto, dem go catch us. That's why I don tell you to run. You no see I don come back to worry them and lead them away from you?"

Kehinde conceded that the technique seemed to have worked, and he gave Hasan the credit. "Thank you."

"Make we go now," Hasan said. "We go look for oasis. And fuel."

CHAPTER FORTY-FOUR

AGADEZ, THE STAGING GROUND for the next major stage on the journey to Europe, was crackling hot, arid, and the same color as the desert. With little exception, each building was made from the rocks, gravel, and sand that it stood upon. Hailing from Benin City where color was exuberant and explosive, Bisola and Kehinde found the landscape strangely monochromatic.

They learned they were to live in a "ghetto," a large compound with a cluster of buildings around it. There, Bisola and Kehinde joined other migrants awaiting their turn to be called for their shot at the Sahara crossing to Tripoli, Libya.

Kehinde shared a small room in the ghetto with five other migrants from Nigeria and a Gambian Kehinde nicknamed "Gambi." They slept on floor mats. At night, the walls turned into a radiator, prolonging the heat well into the early morning hours.

The migration agents, sometimes called connection men, supervised all aspects of the great migration to Europe, many of them having made or at least attempted to make the journey across the fearsome Ténéré Desert, the south-central portion of the Sahara within Niger. They had established themselves in the managerial class by dint of their tough, sometimes brutal experience. They had once given up their hard-earned money to men who had held their futures in their hands. Now, in turn, they *took* money, and at the top of the heap was "Mohamed the Boss," a Tuareg chief who dictated all the terms and conditions, including the fees each migrant must pay to move on to Libya.

Kehinde could see Bisola every day, but only at a distance from the other side of a flimsy fence that separated the men's and women's enclosures. Whenever Kehinde saw Bisola, he held back tears as he felt a stab to the heart. She was suffering, and it was all his fault because he should have stuck to his guns and pulled her away from that man Femi. The hatred Kehinde had for him was violent and debilitating.

And now, one month in, Kehinde and Bisola needed more money. The Sahara crossing had become more expensive. Gone were the days when migrants freely piled into Hilux pickups every Monday morning and proceeded without hindrance. Because of a new Nigerien law, if you were caught transporting a migrant across the desert, you earned yourself a prison sentence of at least five years. That had acted as a strong deterrent and hampered business. At the same time, in fine West African fashion, officials on the take conveniently looked the other way, helping to sustain the phenomenon of migration and ensure it would continue without end.

Kehinde and Bisola had badgered their parents for another five hundred dollars each. Bisola's mother had cleared out her savings and scraped together the rest from the extended family. Kehinde's dad, who was a vegetable farmer, had managed to borrow some funds from a cooperative, but the total had fallen short. It was possible he could get some more in the next couple of months by selling off some land, but that wasn't certain.

"*Abeg*," Kehinde pleaded with his Nigerian agent, Obi, "make you take three hundred and eighty, then when I reach Tripoli, I go *mo-mo* you the rest."

Obi, who had already collected Bisola's fee of five hundred dollars, said, "If you pay now, you go leave in one month time with your girlfriend. If no, that means you go wait three months again."

The notion of staying in Agadez for so much longer was agonizing. Kehinde thought of begging a fellow Nigerian migrant for some cash, but everyone was in the same boat with no money to spare.

At the end of Kehinde's sixth week in Agadez, he received another fifty-two dollars from home. That put him over the four-hundred-dollar threshold, and he hoped that would satisfy Obi. It didn't. "You short sixty-eight," he said.

Kehinde pleaded with him. "*Abeg, abeg.* Have mercy on me, my countryman."

The agent clenched his jaw. "Okay." But he wasn't happy.

TWO WEEKS PASSED before Bisola, Kehinde, and thirty other migrants finally rose to the top of the "paid-up" list. On a Thursday evening, a day before the exodus from Agadez, Kehinde, Gambi, and the other scheduled migrants filled large cans of drinking water for the journey.

The next morning, a massive 6x6, high-profile Mercedes-Benz truck, one of the most indestructible desert vehicles in existence, stood waiting. The migrants secured the water cans so that they dangled off the walls of the truck bed. That the Benz would be the transporting vehicle came as a relief to Kehinde, because unlike the comparatively small Hilux pickups often used to cross the Sahara, this monster was unlikely to break down or suffer a blown tire.

Packing the migrants' belongings in the truck's cargo bed took an hour or so, after which the migrants formed a line to board. Mohamed the Boss, dressed in a flowing indigo robe, the hallmark garment of the Tuareg, walked down the line to give something of a pep talk to the young people about to embark on a perilous journey.

Chewing on her bottom lip, Bisola was anxious that she, Kehinde, and Gambi might not get on the truck because they were at the very back of the line of travelers, but when they got to the front, the chief connection man, a Nigerian, beckoned them forward. Bisola's heart jumped for joy. At last, they were on their way. The Benz was already tightly packed, and she couldn't honestly see how she and Kehinde were going to fit, but at this point, everybody was determined to make this work, no matter the discomfort.

Although some of the taller and more nimble migrants were scrambling up the sidewalls of the Benz without assistance, most were using the built-in side ladder located behind the cab.

"Let your girl go first," one of the attendants said to Kehinde. He held her waist to steady her on the first rung. At the top, she maneuvered herself into a suffocating crush of people as she looked around nervously for Kehinde. Just then, Bisola heard a couple of Nigerien agents having a loud, rapid-fire exchange in Arabic. Two large men stepped forward quickly to the side of the Benz. The driver started up, grinding the gears as Kehinde came into view at the top of the ladder.

"*Wait!*" Bisola cried, but the clatter of the engine drowned out her voice. "Driver, stop!"

Then, as quickly as Kehinde had appeared, he fell back, vanishing from her view.

Bisola struggled to stand up. "*Kehinde!*"

A Senegalese man pulled her down roughly. "What are you doing?" he shouted at her in French.

"They left Kehinde!" she screamed.

He hadn't a clue what Bisola was saying. He looked away with a shake of his head.

The truck surged forward and the sun and the whipping sand vaporized Bisola's tears.

IN BLIND FURY, Kehinde turned and roared at the two thugs who had dragged him away from the truck. He ran at one of them, his arms flailing. The other one came up behind Kehinde, lifted him high off the ground, and slammed him to the ground. Kehinde, the wind knocked out of him, tried to get up, but one of the thugs laid into him and punched his face to a pulp.

Kehinde lost consciousness. For how long, he didn't know. When he came around, three of his fellow Nigerian migrants were trying to clean the blood from his mouth, nose, and face using a dirty rag dipped into a small amount of water in a rusty metal bowl. Kehinde's ribs stabbed his left side as he tried to move. Racked with pain, he looked up at the sunshade and begged God to wake him from this nightmare. How he wished for his boring job back in Benin City, for the soft hand of the love of his life, even the clamor and frustration of Nigerian traffic *go-slows*, his stupid *paddies* and their dumb jokes that were so bad they weren't even funny, the smell of *egusi* stew . . . He dozed off, but woke quickly to grab his phone. He tried to reach Bisola

CHAPTER FORTY-FIVE

AFTER KEHINDE'S BRUTAL SEPARATION from Bisola, his mood changed. Repeatedly, he tried to reach her on the phone to no avail. He tried to keep his spirits up with the help of his friends, but nothing could curtail his depression and brooding. His nights were mostly sleepless, and whatever limited slumber he did get was plagued with nightmares involving Bisola.

Kehinde was profoundly bitter. The connection man had double-crossed him. Now, he claimed the Benz truck had been too weighed down and someone had to be left out, which was a lie, and a stupid one at that. Kehinde believed Gambi's assertion that Mohamed the Boss must have vetoed Kehinde's trip on the grounds that the entire fee had not been paid. Now Kehinde would have to wait. He was on the phone with his family every day to appeal for more funding, even though he knew his father was close to the breaking point.

Life began to settle into something of a routine. During the day, Kehinde went around Agadez searching for a job, but with little success. Once, he found a short-lived, part-time job for two or three hours a day at a carwash on Avenue Tegama. Kehinde found the carwash ironic, since there weren't that many cars around. Scooters and motorcycles were the default mode of transportation, even when carrying bulky, awkward items. There were also donkeys placidly and obediently hauling carts overloaded with merchandise while on top of the pile sat a blasé human rhythmically tapping the donkey's rump to remind it to keep going. For someone from Lagos, this was an unfamiliar sight that Kehinde considered quite primitive.

As in Nigeria, taxis were tiny, yellow, three-wheeled vehicles that could go only so fast. Agadez had no traffic jams, unlike Kehinde's populous homeland; the pace of life was unhurried, with most people taking the time to greet even strangers with *assalamu alaikum*, "peace unto you."

But Kehinde could never be at peace while Bisola was on his mind every moment of the day and large portions of the night. He still attempted to reach her on WhatsApp. She might have lost her phone and been unable to procure a replacement. Kehinde was still hopeful that one morning he would open WhatsApp and find a waiting message from her.

In the late afternoons, the migrants often held a soccer match organized by Mohamed to keep spirits up. Sometimes it was Mali against Senegal, or the Gambia against Nigeria or Ghana. Undoubtedly, the matches temporarily relieved Kehinde of his distress.

Kehinde heard from his father, Peju, who was selling a legacy gold statue from three antecedent generations. With that, he was confident he would be able to remit the funds his son needed with a little left over.

"Please, Daddy," Kehinde said timidly, "I need some extra . . ."

"Extra what?"

"Please, I learned that for the journey into Libya and up to Tripoli, I will need more dollars."

Peju was incredulous. "*What?* You dey craze?" His voice went up an octave, as it did when he was agitated. "How much?"

"Five hundred, please,"

His father spluttered, releasing a torrent of Yoruba swear words. "And what again am I going to sell, Omokehinde?" he shouted, using his son's full name.

"*Abeg*, Daddy," Kehinde pleaded. "You won't regret. It will come back to you a thousand times that."

His father, breathing heavily, was silent for a while. "Okay, but I can't promise. I'll call you." He ended the call without saying goodbye.

Kehinde knew that whatever amount he would receive, it would take quite some time, and so, again, he played the waiting game, distracting himself in any way he could. In classic African innovative style, one of the migrants had hooked up an old-fashioned TV in his room. At night, his comrades came over to watch soccer or whatever movie was available with the least horrible picture.

At last, just before the end of the year, nearly two months after his separation from Bisola, Kehinde received his rescue funds. He thanked his father first, and then knelt to thank God.

As Kehinde's date of departure approached, it was vital he build his strength. He knew now that, contrary to the sanguine picture Femi had painted, the trip across the desert was no joke. Kehinde made it a point to eat as much as he could get his hands on, whether Nigerien staples like rice, millet, and sorghum, or small amounts of beef or mutton if he could afford it. He would have preferred fish, but in this arid, landlocked country, no one ate fish.

The day before Kehinde was scheduled to leave, he received his official boarding ticket, which was the new system designed to eliminate errors. Uppermost in his mind was the internal pledge he had made to find Bisola once he got to Libya. He was certain she would wait and not proceed to Europe without him, but he was deeply troubled that he still hadn't heard from her.

Kehinde was disappointed when he saw that their assigned vehicle for the trip was a Hilux, considerably smaller than the mammoth truck Bisola had left in. But the arrangement of packed bodies was essentially the same. To save space, migrants at the periphery of the bed rode with their legs dangling off the side of the truck. One unexpected swerve could send any of them flying out, so they held on to stout, upright wooden poles secured to the sidewalls. They had been warned: *If you fall out, we will not stop for you.*

Kehinde's truck was the first in a four-truck convoy. It was safer to travel in groups because of the ever-present menace of the Malian and Tuareg bandits who roamed the Saharan landscape.

Kehinde was seated somewhere in the center of the roughly three dozen migrants, which included six women. They were squeezed into the bed without an inch of extra space. Kehinde had been afraid of being one of the "edge riders," but now he realized that where he was, his legs would have to remain bent at the hips and knees for hours, and he wouldn't be able to move. Standing up was not only practically impossible, it was dangerous.

Like most of the other passengers, Kehinde had wrapped a length of cloth around his face, mouth, and nose to protect against the billowing sand picked up by the trucks. To prepare for their trip, the driver had let some air out from all four tires; otherwise, they would have spun around and failed to get traction in the fine, treacherous sand.

As they pulled off, Kehinde thanked God, and made a mental sign of the cross. Another thing he missed dearly was attending church every Sunday in Benin City. It had been a way to heal and prepare for the week ahead. Now he was lucky if he remembered what day it was.

The driver of Kehinde's Hilux sped through the desert like a madman, sometimes swerving wildly and endangering the edge riders as they held on to their sidewall sticks for dear life. For hours, the sand whipped the migrants and the sun roasted their skins blacker than they already were. Then the first mishap struck: a flat tire. The migrants piled out. A jack was of no utility, because it would sink into the sand. Instead, using sheer human power, Kehinde joined a group of the migrants in lifting the affected side of the Hilux as a second group of men worked to change the tire.

But the lifters couldn't support the vehicle for long enough. The driver and assistant, who had been watching while sipping from their bottles of water, began to bark instructions in French and broken English. After a while, their lunatic idea became clear. They pointed to two of the strongest men—a Guinean and a Burkinabe—and instructed them to crouch down with the weight of the Hilux on their backs once the other men had lifted it up—human jacks, as it were.

A confused discussion began with various people shouting, and out of it came the refusal of the two men to do any such thing.

"Venez ici," the driver's assistant said to them, then translating into English, "Come here."

The two men approached hesitantly. The assistant told them to face the bed of the Hilux with their hands grasping the sidewalls. Warily, they did so, which is when the driver brought out a surprise from the pickup's cab: a bullwhip. His victims had no time to react before the whip cracked against the skin of their backs. They cried out and jumped away. The driver advanced toward them to inflict a second strike, but they put up their hands in submission.

"We will do it! We will do it!" one of them said.

Bracing themselves against the pickup once more, seven men lifted the side with the flat tire, and the two strongmen crouched and reversed into the space so that the edge of the vehicle rested on their spines. They gritted their teeth in pain, eyes bulging with the effort. The other migrants sought to help them by partially supporting the Hilux's weight as well while another couple of men tried to change the tire as quickly as they could. The driver began to yell something in Arabic, ending with the swear word, "*Wallahi!*"

At last, it was done. They had a new tire. "Come out, come out from under!" the migrants urged the strongmen. The Guinean did. The Burkinabe did not. He didn't stir. His expression was fixed in a grimace and his eyes had turned glassy and still. Bloody saliva was dripping from his mouth.

Chaos erupted as the men tried to extract him from underneath the vehicle. He came out limp and when they laid him out on the desert sand, it was plain to see he was dead. The driver shrugged. The migrants partially covered the Burkinabe's body with sand, then before the driver could use his bullwhip on anyone again, they scrambled into the pickup.

IN THE NEXT few hours, Kehinde felt he was somewhere between numbness and death. The killing of the Burkinabe should have outraged him, but he felt nothing and he was too tired to care that all feeling had deserted him.

He noticed one of the edge riders acting strangely. He would tilt forward and then jerk upright, and Kehinde realized he was falling asleep, the pickup's movement notwithstanding. The edge rider's direct neighbor tried to restrain him, but finally, the guy tilted forward one more time and this time he went too far to reverse the doze, and he fell out. As the truck kept going, Kehinde and his fellow migrants raised a ruckus, shouting to the driver to stop. He didn't, and the figure of the man receded in the distance. He seemed to be staggering around in disoriented circles. Kehinde choked up and bowed his head. The man would perish there in the wicked sun and infernal sand.

KEHINDE'S ENERGY WAS at rock bottom. He saw some of the guys looking and pointing at something. He couldn't tell how far away it was, because all distances in the desert were deceptive, but he saw it clearly enough. A pickup truck just like theirs had become stranded—engine failure perhaps—and strewn around it were bodies in the sand. Death by dehydration. Kehinde felt a frisson of horror.

He had been needing to urinate for hours now, and he could no longer hold it, so he just let it go. With his body conserving fluid, it wasn't much anyway. The other urge he had from the solid material could wait. He shut down both his bowels and his mind. He felt the truck slow down and everyone started craning their necks to see what was ahead. He heard someone say, "Wassis," and realized they were finally arriving at an oasis, where there was a well. The atmosphere turned jubilant because their water supply was all but exhausted.

Kehinde leapt from the pickup with his fellow migrants, and they ran toward the well. They crowded around it, looking eagerly into the void. Quickly, they realized that, even if there was water at the bottom of the well, there was no rope or bucket to get it.

Kehinde turned away in despair and disgust, tears of frustration brimming. With a couple of minutes available to relieve himself of the stuff sitting in his colon like cement, he hastened to a small thicket of desert scrub. But just as he was about to pull down his pants, he saw two feet sticking out from the other side of the bush. Another dead body. Kehinde approached warily. The feet were feminine. He circled around to look at the rest of the corpse, which had become mummified in the desiccating heat. Kehinde recognized her in one way, but saw her as a stranger in another, because she looked the same, but different. He identified her by dusting off the sand from her feet. Each still-perfect toenail was painted the color Bisola loved the most. Scarlet.

CHAPTER FORTY-SIX

ULTIMATELY, THE WAY KEHINDE consoled himself over the death of his beloved Bisola was by reasoning that she had never had to suffer the hell of Libya. Traveling from Agadez to the Niger-Libyan border, he had survived the inferno of the Ténéré Desert only to be plunged into another kind of abyss.

Launching from Libya across the Mediterranean was one way to get to Europe, but there were other routes through Tunisia, Algeria, and Morocco. Some migrants swore by the Moroccan path, claiming that Moroccan detention centers were less inhumane than the Libyan. But once they had committed to the Agadez-Libyan route, there was no changing mid-journey for Kehinde and his fellow migrants.

At the border, they negotiated prices with the motorcycle smugglers known as "Mafia taxis." They were effectively the only means of crossing illegally into Libya.

AFTER HE MADE it across the Niger-Libya border, Kehinde faced an arduous trek to Tripoli in three parts: from there to Qatrun via the Murzuq Desert, Qatrun to the oasis town of Sabha, and finally, Sabha to Tripoli. Each segment would be handled by a separate smuggler. Kehinde paid the five hundred dollars his father had scraped together to the first one, who was to share that equally with the other two. To reassure a wary and skeptical Kehinde, the smuggler got on speaker phone with his two partners, who confirmed the arrangement in real time.

In his veil and headdress, Kehinde was beginning to look like a real desert nomad.

As they crossed the Murzuq Desert, another small part of the almighty Sahara, Kehinde gazed with awe and some trepidation at the infinite sea of barchans—golden, crescentic dunes with the convex side facing the wind. They formed spectacular patterns of curves and shadows.

At the outskirts of Sabha, the second smuggler slowed to a stop to set up the final step in the journey to Tripoli. Kehinde, stiff from long hours on the motorbike, dismounted to stretch his legs. At two in the afternoon, the sun was punishing, but Kehinde realized that he was almost to the point that he could just shrug it off.

He could see Sabha proper in the distance, but where they were was desolate with a few sand-colored structures. A group of men languished in the shade of one building, and two veiled women walked side by side carrying containers of water on their heads.

After some thirty minutes, a short Libyan with plethoric facial features appeared in a white, flowing robe and matching head-dress. The smuggler took off, leaving Kehinde with the Libyan, who beckoned him to follow. After a ten-minute walk, they arrived at what looked like a walled compound with a black metal gate. Kehinde became wary. *What is this?* He had no desire to stay for months in another ghetto.

The short Libyan was on the phone. When he'd finished, he silently folded his arms as he eyed Kehinde with a mixture of suspicion and hostility. A couple of Libyan louts hung around looking dispassionately at their phones. The black gate opened and a massive West African came out, looked Kehinde up and down, and spoke to him in Nigerian Pidgin. "You go pay two thousand dollar now-now."

"*Wetin* dey happen na?" Kehinde cried in consternation. "Two thousand dollar? You dey craze?"

"From here to Tripoli na fifteen hundred, and five from Niger border to Sabha here," the Nigerian said.

"But I don pay five hundred already to the first smuggler," Kehinde protested furiously, looking from the Nigerian to the Libyan and back. "He tell me say he go share am among himself and the other two."

The Nigerian was deadpan. "He tell me say you no 'gree pay am."

Kehinde was irate. "*I don pay am!*" he screamed.

"You go pay two thousand now, *abi?*" the Nigerian said.

"I no get!" Kehinde cried, his voice cracking. He was stretched to his limit. Why were they doing this to him?

The Libyan gave him a look of pity and said something in Arabic. The two louts got up and stepped behind Kehinde, while the Nigerian and Libyan moved forward. Kehinde turned to bolt, but the four men had him without too much effort. Kehinde shrieked and fought as they dragged him toward the gate. It whined and groaned as it opened. Confronting Kehinde was the sight of a couple hundred emaciated Africans of all shapes, colors, and sizes. Some appeared to hail from the coastal countries like Ghana, Nigeria, and Côte d'Ivoire, while others might have been from Sudan or Chad. It was a detention center—a prison, really—worse, much worse, than a ghetto.

They took Kehinde around the back of the building, where three other Libyans were waiting, making six in all now, including the short one in the white robes. They stripped Kehinde and took away his backpack, rifling through it to find only a few dollars.

"You dey hide some cash somewhere?" the Nigerian asked.

"*Abeg*, boss," Kehinde said desperately, becoming more and more frightened. "I don spend am finish."

The short Libyan said something in Arabic to his countrymen, and then addressed the Nigerian with a name that sounded like "Goree." Later, Kehinde learned the word was *gorille*, French for gorilla, because of the Nigerian's size.

Goree translated what the Arab had just said. "You go call your family for the rest," he instructed Kehinde.

"*Abeg*," Kehinde pleaded. "My family don give me all they have."

"Make you call them now," Goree said, handing Kehinde a phone. "Tell them say you dey need two thousand dollar."

Kehinde dialed several times before getting through to his father. Barely able to keep from breaking down, Kehinde told him he needed more money. After a brief silence, Peju launched into a harsh tirade that ended with a cruel declaration that he wished Kehinde had died along with this twin brother. There *was* no money left. The entire family, nuclear and extended, was in financial ruin because of Kehinde and his thoughtlessness.

"You won't get a single naira out of us again," Peju said, and hung up.

Kehinde, his eyes brimming with tears, shook his head and gave the phone back. "He no go fit help me," he said to Goree.

"Okay, tomorrow you go try again."

"*Abeg*, o! You be my countryman, Goree. *Abeg*."

Goree looked at the short Libyan and shrugged. The Libyan sighed and nodded at the other five. Kehinde moved back as the men advanced menacingly, but there was only so far he could go before they trapped him against the wall and began to take turns slapping him across the face.

KEHINDE WAS SWOLLEN and tender by the time the gang of six Libyans were satisfied they had assaulted their new detainee enough for the day. They released him to the courtyard where hundreds of migrants hung around listlessly in the same predicament as Kehinde—the inability to pay the grossly inflated fee to Tripoli.

What was Kehinde to do now? He hadn't a clue. He was in shock and his mind was numb. He had braved and survived life-threatening desert crossings to come to *this*?

The sun was going down fast and light was fading, but Kehinde could see how different these migrants were from the Agadez group. Many of them were skeleton thin, their eyes empty and bereft of hope. They were *broken*.

Kehinde leaned against the wall, his empty stomach bedeviling him for lack of food. He looked left to his name being called.

"Kehinde, my brother!"

The boy coming up to him was gaunt, much like the others. He seemed familiar, but at first, Kehinde couldn't place him. The boy hugged him. "I'm so happy to see you."

Then it clicked for Kehinde. "*Gambi*? Is that you?

"It's me!" he said, laughing. "Yeah, I know—I've lost weight."

That was an understatement. Kehinde gaped. "Oh, my God,"

he said, not even attempting to hide his alarm. "What are you doing here? What happened to you?"

"I was on the same truck as Bisola, remember?" Gambi said.

"Yes, yes, I do. You never made it to Tripoli, then?"

Gambi shook his head sadly. "Not at all, brother. Same situation as you, now."

They slapped palms heartily, continuing to hold hands for a short while.

"Listen," Gambi said, "I must tell you something about Bisola—"

"I already found her," Kehinde said, his voice catching. "At the oasis. She was lying dead under some bushes."

"I'm sorry, brother—so, so, sorry."

"Did you see what happened?" Kehinde asked. "I need to know."

"Agh," Gambi said, clearly torn. "I don't know if I should even tell you."

"*Tell me.*"

"We stopped at the oasis," Gambi began, his tone becoming somber. "I saw her go to those bushes, you know, to wee-wee. Then, the driver and his mate followed her . . ."

"They followed her," Kehinde repeated, his voice trembling. "And then?"

"Please brother," Gambi said, wringing his hands, "I wasn't sure what to do, but finally, I walked toward the bushes. I heard some struggling . . ." He swallowed hard. "Before I could reach, one of the Nigerian guys ran after me and held me back. He said, 'Don't go there, bro, or they will kill you. You can't save her.' He told me he had tried to get to Libya before, and he had seen girls raped often. The driver came out from the bushes first, and then the mate went. We didn't see Bisola again."

They raped and killed her. Kehinde's face crumpled immediately with the impact of this news. He bellowed with uncontrollable rage, swung around, and punched the wall.

"No, my brother," Gambi said, wrapping his arms around Kehinde from behind and pulling him away. People in the courtyard were watching with interest. A Libyan guard materialized and began to yell at the two. Gambi pacified him in bad

French and led a weeping Kehinde away to another spot which offered more privacy, if only barely. Kehinde sobbed until he was spent, and then sat down cross-legged to stare in silence at the ground.

After a while, Gambi said, "We have to go inside for the night, brother."

CHAPTER FORTY-SEVEN

FROM DESCRIPTIONS KEHINDE HAD heard from migrant return-ees, he had formed a mental image of what the inside of a Libyan detention center was like. But the reality was worse by far. The large, dungeon-like room felt like an oven, and Kehinde was rattled by the sight of a mass of young African men packed together like sardines in a can. He looked up with horror at the small, barred windows high up on the walls. Most of the lights dangling from the ceiling were out, rendering the room only dimly lit.

"Gambi," Kehinde whispered, "we have to escape from here."

"Just stay with me, brother," Gambi said, leading the way. They wedged into a group clustered underneath one of the windows in the vain hope they might experience a through draft, but not a single molecule of air was circulating.

"Sit here," Gambi said, after he had created a small space beside him for Kehinde to squeeze into.

The room reeked of some two hundred unwashed men. In Benin City, Kehinde had experienced *danfo* rides in which his olfactory senses had been offended by body odor, but this was an all-out assault. Gambi must have caught the look on Kehinde's face. "They allow us to bathe only once a week," he said.

Appalled, Kehinde gasped. "Seriously?"

"Yes, brother." Gambi grunted. "Now you will know the real hell. Not the one you go to after you die. This is the one you go *before* you die."

"But why do these Arab or Libyan guys—whatever they are—hate us so much?"

Gambi shrugged. "I don't know, brother. Some people say it's because they hate Black Africans, and others say they hate migrants. In the end, it makes no difference what the reason is.

Mind you, they may hate our black skin, but they like the way we work."

"How do you mean?"

"If they have a choice between Arab and African workers, they always choose the Africans. That's why they sell some of us to Libyan farmers—they know how hard we will work to plant and harvest their crops."

"What do you mean, 'sell us'?"

"That's what they do," Gambi said. "Sometimes, you'll see them take out some of the guys from here for the farmers to bid on them to work as slaves."

Kehinde shuddered and closed his eyes for a moment. His head was hammering and he felt faint with hunger. "Will they give us something to eat?" he asked Gambi.

"Not tonight. Tomorrow, around noon."

Noon tomorrow? Kehinde was stunned.

A buzz of conversation filled the room, sometimes louder, sometimes softer, with an occasional guffaw or bout of yelling for one obscure reason or another. And there were waves of coughing. Gambi, too, was going through hacking fits that left him weak and breathless.

Kehinde was feeling the urgent call of nature. "Where are the toilets?" he asked Gambi, who pointed to the far end of the room.

Kehinde picked his way through the crowd. He knew he was getting closer by the intensifying stench, and a long line of guys waiting for the facilities with the same exigency as his. Taller than many, Kehinde could see over the tops of his fellow detainees' heads that the so-called toilets were two buckets overflowing with shit and urine.

He felt a flash of anger. "But why can't they clean this up?" he muttered.

The boy in front of him, who looked to be in his mid-teens, overheard him and turned. "For two days, we've been asking for water and brooms to wash down the place," he said in a Nigerian accent, "but they don't even mind us."

Gagging, Kehinde considered getting out of the line and forfeiting his turn until later, but by then, the conditions might be even worse. He had no choice. He set his jaw and steeled himself. *It won't kill you,* he told himself. *Remember, you endured the desert.*

Kehinde did survive the toilets, returning to Gambi with both revulsion and physical relief. Gambi had dozed off, but started awake to the sound of someone screaming incoherently. Trying to locate the source, Kehinde looked around to see a gesticulating shadowy figure across the room.

"What's going on?" Kehinde asked.

Gambi hugged his knees. "He's a Senegalese guy they say is going mad. I don't speak French, so I never understand what he's shouting about."

A few other detainees began to yell at the Senegalese man until he shut up and sat down again. Minutes later, a couple of burly Libyan guards came in and took him, screaming, out of the room.

"That's it," Gambi said, dully. "They're going to kill him."

"Oh, my God," Kehinde said. He had been about to ask why, but he was quickly learning that those types of questions didn't have answers.

He shifted to face Gambi more directly. "Have they been hurting you?"

"Yes, brother," he said wanly. "They whip me every day."

"Oh, sorry, Gambi." Kehinde rested his hand on his friend's bony shoulder and gave it a squeeze. His chest filled with emotion as he realized Gambi's physical strength was fast dwindling.

A loud crack reached them from outside. Kehinde jumped, but Gambi only said, "They've shot him now. He's gone."

AFTER AN ALMOST sleepless night, Kehinde woke with another six hours ahead of him before he would have anything to eat. Midmorning was time for their allotted one cup of water a day. The detainees formed two long, parallel lines in the courtyard, at the head of which a couple of armed detention officials stood, each with a bucket of water, a tin cup, and a bullwhip. When each detainee came forward to drink his serving, he was lashed across the back. *This is madness,* Kehinde thought. *If I want some water, I'll be whipped. If I don't want to be whipped, I won't get any water.*

Around noon, the food arrived. Kehinde, sitting next to a shirtless Gambi, who had curled up and fallen asleep on the ground, sensed the ripple of excitement through the detainees. One who was sitting close by, a tiny guy from Sierra Leone, got up and disappeared, returning about ten minutes later with a battered metal bowl, which he placed on the ground. It was half filled with a mixture of plain white rice and pasta.

"Five-five," he announced loudly.

For a moment, Kehinde didn't know what he meant, but then it hit. *Five detainees share one bowl.* Kehinde's ability to be shocked any longer was beginning to erode.

Someone reached out to help himself from the bowl, but the Sierra Leonean blocked him and slapped him across the face. "*Get away!* You're not in this group. Find your own. Stupid boy."

The offender skulked away to look elsewhere.

Kehinde shook Gambi gently. "Wake up, bro. Time to eat."

Gambi opened his eyes and turned his head slightly to look at Kehinde. "I'm not hungry. You can eat my share, brother."

"You have to eat," Kehinde said, sounding like a parent. He pulled Gambi closer and propped him up somewhat. The other three had begun to eat, using their fingers to take small, practically equal amounts of the meal. Kehinde took some and brought it to Gambi's mouth. "Eat."

Gambi took the morsel into his mouth and began to chew dispiritedly until he had a fit of coughing that made him spit up into his hands. He wiped them on his already-filthy pants and fell back. "It's okay," he muttered.

Kehinde observed how shallow and rapid Gambi's breathing had become, his ribs showing through his skin like window slats. Choking back tears, Kehinde ate in silence along with the others. The food had no taste whatsoever, but he didn't care. It was food. In less than five minutes, it was all gone with the bowl wiped clean of every particle. The thought that there would be nothing more for another twenty-four hours was harrowing.

The end of the day came quickly, and it was back indoors for another night. Kehinde was losing sense of time, however. Had he arrived yesterday or the day before? *Yesterday,* he thought. It must be. He and Gambi settled in much the same spot as the night before. Gambi was resting with his head on his forearms, which in turn lay on his bent knees. Rubbing Gambi's back gently up and down, Kehinde wondered how many fraudsters like Femi had conned the detainees in this room and sent them off to this lion's den. In Kehinde's view, charlatans like Femi should be tortured and then shot, just like the Libyans had done to the Senegalese man. God willing, if Kehinde ever got out, he would start that process with Femi.

Gambi raised his head slowly and gave Kehinde a weak smile.

"What's up, my brother?" Kehinde asked. "How do you feel?"

Gambi shook his head. "Tomorrow, they're going kill me."

"No, no," Kehinde said. "Don't talk like that, Gambi."

"Yes," he whispered, "because they know I will never be able to pay, and I'm too weak to be a slave. So, I'm no use to them. Kehinde, either you find the way to get the money, or you escape. You're still strong, and you can run. Please. *Run.*"

CHAPTER FORTY-EIGHT

IN THE MORNING, THE Arabs came to take Gambi and Kehinde to the torture yard behind the building. Goree was there holding a frayed bullwhip as four Libyan men sat around the perimeter of the space in a relaxed pose. Goree told Kehinde to sit in a corner. Gambi, his matchstick legs quivering as they undressed him, was so weak, he could barely stand. Goree reached for a bucket of water and doused Gambi. That way, the whip would sting better. Goree's first strike sent Gambi to the ground.

"No!" Kehinde cried. "*Stop!* What has he done to you?"

Before any members of the torture brigade could stop Kehinde, he leapt up and attacked Goree with arms swinging. Goree batted him away like a fly buzzing around his head, and Kehinde flew backward and fell.

Goree struck Gambi again, opening deep wounds in his back. One of the Libyans stood up to film the beating. He had a knife in his belt and a plainly visible erection in his fatigues.

Kehinde began to blubber as he begged Goree for mercy.

But Goree, bearing a serene look of satisfaction, paid no attention. By the time he was done, Gambi was almost dead. Two of the Libyan men dragged Gambi outside, and the video man followed them. Then Kehinde heard sounds of a struggle, and then screaming.

Kehinde fainted for a moment, but in the next, he looked up to see one of the Arabs holding Gambi's detached head streaming with blood. Kehinde screamed and scrambled away, but they grabbed him and began to strip him just as they had done with Gambi.

Kehinde appealed to Goree. "Massa, *abeg, abeg!*"

Goree was unmoved. As the shower of water poured over

Kehinde, he tried to get away, but he slipped on the slick concrete and fell.

"So now," Goree said calmly, "we go make video send your papa so he go see what we go do you every day you don't pay. You go beg am to pay, okay? Every time I lash you, you go say, 'Pay the money.' Turn on your belly."

The first strike came, and Kehinde bellowed and contorted, rolling onto his back.

"Tell them to pay the money," Goree said.

"Pay the money, pay the money!" Kehinde shouted, his hands up in defensive posture. "Goree, *abeg*."

"Put your hands down," Goree said. "I said, *put them down*."

The whip cracked again, opening a gash across Kehinde's thighs. He spun on his belly again, receiving a rapidly delivered series of lashes across the buttocks. The video man circled around hungrily to get the best angles. With the next set of strikes, Kehinde lost consciousness.

LATE AT NIGHT, Kehinde was delirious, floating in and out of consciousness with visions of detached, floating heads. In the dream, an Arab was pulling him to his feet, but he woke up and realized it was real: a Libyan guard was removing him from the room to take him outside. Kehinde, limping from the deep cut he had sustained over his thighs, knew it was his turn to die, and at the same time he was fearful, he wasn't certain he cared.

Shoving him ahead roughly, the Libyan took him not to the torture yard, but outside the front gate. Kehinde was confused. Were they letting him go or taking him to another place to murder him? A full moon was out in the dark sky, and Kehinde felt an invigorating rush of fresh air. The guard marched him by the neck down a gravel path to a clump of bushes, where another Libyan met them. Briefly, he switched on his phone flashlight and Kehinde recognized the video guy. He still had the knife in his belt.

The two men forced Kehinde to the ground on his stomach. The first Libyan departed, leaving the video man behind. He pulled Kehinde's shorts down to expose his buttocks and then lay upon him. Attempting penetration, he grunted and gasped as he ejaculated prematurely. Frustrated, he turned Kehinde on his back with legs up and back. As the Libyan positioned himself, Kehinde found the knife handle. He pulled it from its sheath just as the Libyan began his second attempt.

Kehinde's first stab struck one of the man's lower ribs and didn't penetrate fully. The Libyan jerked back in surprise, and now Kehinde had better leverage. He plunged the knife in again and this time it went deep to the hilt in soft tissue. The Libyan rolled away, writhing and hissing like a speared monitor lizard. Kehinde scrambled up. The Libyan groaned, attempting to get on all fours. Kehinde kicked him in the face onto his side. By moonlight, Kehinde saw the shadow of a large rock close by. He picked it up, raised it behind his head and brought it down on the Libyan's skull with all the force he could muster. Then, he turned to run, not knowing or caring where he was going as long as it was as far from the detention center as possible.

KEHINDE SPRINTED ALONG a dirt road by moonlight, which illuminated his path but caused confusing shadows. Sometimes he stepped in a pothole and fell, but he staggered up again and continued to run, his breaths coming in whimpering gasps. All along, he heard Gambi's voice saying, "You're still strong, and you can run." Sometimes, when he imagined dark shapes moving in the bushes alongside the road, he accelerated.

Headlights and the sound of a vehicle reached him from behind. In terror, he veered off the road into the bush, falling in the deep undergrowth almost immediately. He tried to get up, but exhaustion got the better of him.

The vehicle, a jeep, skidded in a cloud of dust and stopped at an angle so that the lights caught Kehinde like a performer on a dark stage. He squinted in the high beam. As two military men came out with rifles at the ready, he began to stammer, "Don't kill me, don't kill me," over and again.

The men reached him and crouched beside him. "Who are you?" one of them shouted in a heavy Arab accent.

"Don't kill me, don't kill me," Kehinde repeated.

"*Hey!*" the soldier yelled. "Shut up!"

Kehinde stopped talking and started crying.

"My brother," the soldier said more softly, placing a hand on Kehinde's shoulder, "where you run from, eh?"

"The detainment, where they detain people," Kehinde stammered.

"Detention center?"

"Yes, yes sir."

Scanning Kehinde's thighs with his flashlight, the second soldier let out an exclamation of alarm at the deep, crisscrossed wounds he saw. The two men moved around to Kehinde's back, one of them clicking his tongue and shaking his head at the rawness of Kehinde's flesh.

"My brother, come," the soldier said, and they helped Kehinde up, supporting him on each side to their vehicle. "We go hospital now, they make you better, inshallah."

"No!" Kehinde cried out. "Please, they kill me there, please, sir!"

"My brother, 'sokay. No kill you, eh? You see doctor. Good people."

They settled Kehinde into the back of their jeep, where he sat shivering with shock.

As the soldiers started up the vehicle, the English-speaking one said to him, "Which country? Nigeria?"

"Yes, sir."

A discussion between the two soldiers followed, then the soldier in the front passenger seat turned to Kehinde and said, "Why you Nigerian peoples, you like come to Libya all the time? Libya not good for you, my brother. We take you hospital, make you well, inshallah, then you go home Nigeria."

THE SOLDIERS WERE right: no one at Sabha Medical Center tried to kill Kehinde. True, they were understaffed with various supply shortages, but they were assiduous in treating Kehinde's wounds, one of which had become infected.

Six days into his stay at the hospital, a Libyan woman arrived at Kehinde's bedside from the Sabha branch of the IOM, International Organization of Migration, which helped to repatriate refugees and migrant returnees. She took down Kehinde's particulars and registered him officially with a warning that he shouldn't expect too much too soon. The return to Nigeria could take several months, up to a year or more.

Every night, Kehinde suffered through flashbacks and nightmares. He felt beaten down but triumphant. At first, he'd considered mortally wounding the Libyan video guy to be a matter of survival, but now Kehinde saw it another way: he had taken revenge for Gambi's death. If he had been able, he would have killed Goree and all the others at the torture camp. Now, Kehinde had only Bisola's murder left to avenge.

CHAPTER FORTY-NINE

As Kehinde completed his tale, Nnamdi and Emma were listening with rapt attention. She shuddered.

"I had no idea it was that bad," Nnamdi said. "I know one Nigerian who went to work in Libya with an oil company, and he told me he was treated well, so this comes as a surprise."

"But that's a completely different thing from being a migrant," Kehinde said. "Look, I realize not all Libyans are bad, of course. What I've told you are my experiences alone."

"How long did it take you to return to Naija?" Emma asked.

"Almost two months," Kehinde replied. "I got back just before the borders were closed because of Covid. The IOM returned me to Agadez first, and from there they said they would process me." Kehinde pulled a face. "I waited and waited, but nothing happened. They said I should stay in one of their Agadez camps, but I heard bad things about the IOM, so I preferred not to do that."

"What kind of bad things?" Emma asked.

"I heard they engage in beating returnees the same way the detention centers do."

"Really?" Nnamdi said, looking skeptical. "But the IOM is a legitimate international organization."

Kehinde grunted. "The IOM itself is not the problem, it's the local staff of the camps who can be wicked. Sure, when the VIP officials show up from abroad to make inspections, everything is clean and nice and they tell the officials what they want to hear, but everything goes back to the same conditions once they've left. That's why at the Agadez IOM, they don't like to see journalists or visitors coming around."

Emma exchanged a glance with Nnamdi. "That's disturbing,"

she reflected. "So, if the IOM didn't help you, how did you get back?"

"I met one American lady staying at the Auberge d'Azel hotel in Agadez," Kehinde said, with a slight deflection of gaze. "She helped me with funds to get home."

Emma didn't need the details, so she left it at that. "Was it tough to find work once you returned to Naija?" she asked.

"Yeah, but now, I'm working with my cousin who has a souvenir shop," Kehinde said. "For some time, he was the only family member who would speak to me."

"Why is that?" Emma asked.

Kehinde's expression became pained and bitter. "I failed. I borrowed so much money from my family and now I have nothing to show but a dead girlfriend."

"You didn't want that to happen," Nnamdi said. "You were tricked by that crook, Femi."

"But I could have resisted," Kehinde said, sounding both regretful and frustrated.

"I think I can understand," Emma said, "and we can see how painful this is for you. Be kinder to yourself, though."

He smiled at her. "Thank you."

"Let me ask you something," Emma said, leaning forward slightly on her forearms. "You said you wanted to kill Femi in the aftermath of your terrible experiences and Bisola's death. So, did you?"

Kehinde was startled. "No," he said at once.

"I would have killed him myself if I had had the chance," Emma said, gently urging him on. "What he put you and Mr. Ojukwu through."

Nnamdi nodded slowly. "To be honest, I'm glad he's dead."

Kehinde's chin and bottom lip were trembling and his eyes had become red and moist. He was struggling with something.

"Kehinde," Emma said. "What happened?"

He pressed his palms to his eyes as if trying to hold back the tears.

"Did you go to Ghana?"

"Yes." Kehinde choked up and dropped his head. "I rode my motorbike all the way to Accra. I arrived on the twelfth of October. I found out where Femi's office was, and I hung around until I knew his movements. So, on the night of the sixteenth, I waited and watched the place from an empty lot. I thought Femi was going to leave for home, but the hour was getting late, so I decided to go to the office instead to kill him. Then . . ." Kehinde stopped.

"So, you went there with the plan to shoot him," Emma prompted. "Where did you get the gun?"

"What gun?" Kehinde frowned and shook his head. "I had a machete."

"Sorry, but I'm confused. Didn't you kill Femi?"

"No, I didn't. I was going to, but someone got to him before me."

"What?" Emma was baffled. "You need to explain that."

CHAPTER FIFTY

KEHINDE HAD BEEN IN business with his cousin for eighteen months when he purchased the motorbike he would use for his mission. When Kehinde arrived in Accra, he found a rat-infested hotel room in a Nima neighborhood. He had done all his homework, and had found the information he needed on LinkedIn.

> Femi Adebanjo
> Manager, White House Hotel, East Legon, Accra, Ghana
> CEO & Owner, Cliffemi Travels, East Legon, Accra, Ghana
> 31 Senchi Street, East Legon, Accra, Ghana

And there Femi's photo was right beside the entry, the picture of a liar, a thief, a murderer.

AROUND SIX-FIFTEEN IN the evening, as darkness fell, Kehinde buzzed by the White House a couple of times, and on the third pass, he rang the bell at the gate. The side door opened and a tall, powerfully built man looked out.

"Yes?" he asked, scrutinizing Kehinde.

"Please, I'm looking for a hospital around here called Yeboah Hospital."

"Okay," the man said, stepping out to give directions. That gave Kehinde a brief but unobstructed view of a blue Mercedes parked in the White House's front yard. Kehinde wagered the car belonged to Femi.

Thanking the big man, Kehinde sped off, but he slowed down as he spotted an overgrown plot of land for sale less than a quarter of a mile from the White House. Notwithstanding the many mansions and high-end businesses East Legon had, there were still parcels of land available for development. Wild vegetation and a four-foot-high brick wall demarcated this one. Kehinde turned onto the adjacent unpaved road and hopped off his motorcycle. Deserted and quiet, the setting was perfect. He dragged the bike behind a clump of bushes and then vaulted the wall. From this lookout, he had a satisfactory view of the White House, and the street lamps would illuminate Femi's car when he drove out. At that point, Kehinde would follow him. Even if Femi didn't go home immediately, he would eventually, and that's where Kehinde would kill him.

He was prepared to wait, but he grew restless as the hour approached ten-thirty without his spotting Femi. Could there have been an alternative exit on the other side of the building? It was possible, but not likely. Perhaps Femi wasn't there at all even if the Benz was his. Rich guys often had a sedan like a Mercedes or Jaguar, an SUV, and a pickup truck for weekend outings to their home villages.

As midnight neared, Kehinde saw the watchman step outside the gate for a stretch, and then a pee. At that moment, a dark car, too far away for Kehinde to see clearly, pulled up to the White House entrance. The shadowy figure of the vehicle's driver appeared. He exchanged a few words with the guard, and then, quite unexpectedly, a brief struggle ensued in which the man knocked out the guard and pulled him inside.

Kehinde gasped. He was witnessing a robbery or burglary in progress. After six to seven minutes, a sharp crack rang out in the air, and in seconds, the man emerged from the gate at a run. He got in the car and took off, tires squealing slightly. As the car approached the corner and began a right-hand turn, Kehinde shrank back from the headlight beams.

My God. Did he shoot someone? Femi?

Kehinde's impulse was to run to the White House to find out what had taken place, but he restrained himself. It was a good ten minutes before the watchman, bound at the wrists and ankles, rabbit-hopped out the gate and began shouting for help. As quiet as the neighborhood was, it didn't stay that way. In good Ghanaian fashion, people appeared magically out of nowhere and began streaming into the White House property.

Now it was safe. Kehinde retrieved his bike and in seconds was at the White House where spectators were walking in and out in avid discussion. No one paid particular attention to Kehinde as he went in.

The Benz was where he'd last seen it, but at one of the building's side doors, chaos was unfolding. Seven or eight people were trampling in a pool of blood inside of the door as they milled around a body crumpled on the floor. Some were attempting to revive the victim without success. Others were arguing over what to do: leave the body for the East Legon police to handle, or take the man to the hospital.

"He made a sound!" a man swore in Twi. "He's not dead, o! He's alive!"

That settled the matter. A guy raced away to get his pickup truck.

Kehinde came closer to stare at the man on the ground. He didn't want to believe his eyes, but it could be no one else but Femi. *Someone beat me to it.*

The pickup arrived, and the men lifted Femi into the bed. He was completely limp, and it was clear to Kehinde that whoever thought Femi might have been alive was terribly mistaken.

Kehinde walked away, hands thrust in his pockets. Instead of relief, or maybe even joy over the death of this murderer, Kehinde was distraught and angry. He felt like someone had just cheated him out of a gold medal.

CHAPTER FIFTY-ONE

THE FOLLOWING MORNING, IN the hotel's business center, Emma and Nnamdi used his laptop to Zoom with Jojo and Sowah. Emma related Kehinde's extraordinary story, including his claim that another man got to Femi and killed him before Kehinde got the chance.

"Do you believe him, sir?" Emma asked the boss.

"It seems almost too convenient," Sowah said. "What do you say, Nnamdi?"

"Why would he tell this long, drawn-out tale if it weren't true?" Nnamdi asked. "How would that benefit him?"

"It's a fair point," Sowah said. "Jojo?"

"I think he started to confess the murder to Emma," Jojo said, "but he changed his mind at the last moment, but by then he was too far into the truth to turn around. So, on the spot, he made up this lie about a strange man in a strange car going to Femi's place to kill him."

Emma nodded. "To shift blame. I feel like Kehinde's terrible experience in Libya and the death of his longtime sweetheart are the most powerful motives in this case. Sure, maybe Awuni and Janet felt that Femi was a threat, but the hatred Kehinde felt for Femi was intense."

"I invited DI Boateng to the discussion," Sowah said. "I hope he can make it. Nnamdi, have you spoken to Ngozi?"

"Yes, several times, now. She's in the hospital for another couple of days. My wife flew into Accra immediately. I expect she's already there with Ngozi."

"We pray for your daughter's speedy recovery, sir," Jojo said to Nnamdi.

"Thank you very much. And Yemo—very likely, Emma and I

will get a flight from Benin City to Accra via Lagos, tomorrow or the following day. Ijeoma and I will return to Nigeria with Ngozi as soon as she's medically stable."

"Of course," Sowah said. "We look forward to your return. Aha, here's DI Boateng. Good morning, sah! I think you're still on mute . . . it's at the bottom. That's better."

Boateng looked as if he had just surfaced from bed. "Good morning, everybody. I understand you have some news for me."

"Yes, Inspector," Sowah said. "You recall I told you about Kehinde, who went to Niger with his girlfriend, Bisola, and she perished in the desert trying to reach Libya. Emma has an interesting tale."

She patiently retold Kehinde's story to Boateng, including Kehinde's claim that he went to Accra to hunt Femi down, but someone got there first and shot Femi dead.

Boateng grunted and shook his head.

"Not credible to you?" Sowah asked.

"I'm skeptical," Boateng said.

It was Jojo's turn to relate what he had.

"We have an informant called Sade," Jojo told the inspector, "a student who is, or was, romantically involved with an economics lecturer at UG called Professor Coleman. Coleman hooked up some of his friends with Sade and another student. When Femi came on the scene, he started to woo the two young women, promising them much more money at the White House, and Coleman found out about it.

"In response, Coleman sent Femi a threatening text, and what did Femi do in return? He turned right around and tried to blackmail Coleman for fifteen thousand dollars. He threatened to expose Coleman as 'Professor Pimp.' As a Nobel Prize contender, Coleman's reputation would be ruined forever. If you were Professor Coleman, wouldn't you want to get rid of Femi? I would. You talk of Awuni and Janet feeling Femi was a threat, but I think he could have been an even greater menace to Coleman. So, when Sade informed me that Coleman has a gun, to my mind, that makes him a prime suspect."

That commanded Boateng's attention. "Which kind of gun?"

"I'll show you." Jojo held up his phone to the screen. "Sade sent this pic to me. That's the pistol, and next to it is the box of bullets he uses. Could your ballistics guys at the Forensic Science Lab tell us whether the bullet found in Femi's brain at autopsy could or could *not* have come from Prof. Coleman's box?"

"Maybe," Boateng said. "It depends on how intact the recovered bullet is. I think it would be easier if we had found spent casings at the scene, but we didn't. Anyway, who told you we have ballistics experts at the FSL?"

Jojo's eyes widened in dismay. "You don't? What happened?"

"The lady we had was on loan from South Africa. She went back home a few months ago."

"Oh," Jojo said, deflated. "What about if we send the bullets to South Africa and ask her to take a look?"

Boateng wrinkled his nose, clearly not much in favor of that idea. "That's costly, you know. Jojo, why so sad?"

"I'm okay," he said valiantly, still crestfallen.

"He worked hard on this," Emma said supportively. "So, it's disappointing that it will come to nothing."

"I understand," Boateng said. He pondered over it for a moment. "You know what? On second thought, let's do this. I will confront Prof. Coleman with this evidence. If he shot Femi, I promise you, I will get him to break down and confess. But if he denies it consistently, *then* I'll try to persuade Commissioner Ohene to let us send the bullet and cartridge in."

"I think that's fair," Sowah said, nodding.

"I agree," Jojo said. "We'll send the cartridge over to you by courier. Thanks, Diboat."

"Diboat?" Boateng muttered in bewilderment. The nickname was out of the bag. "Mr. Ojukwu, sir," he continued. "I wanted to ask how your daughter is doing in Accra. Have you been able to speak with her?"

"Several times, now, thank you," Nnamdi said. "She's getting along well—just a day or two more in the hospital."

"We pray for her continued success, sir," Boateng said. "I have to go now, but I wanted to update Emma and the rest of you on the CCTV footage from the home opposite the White House the night of the murder."

"Oh, *yes!*" Emma exclaimed. She had forgotten. "Did you find anything?"

"The homeowner returned from her travels and was happy to

let us take a look. The time stamps were all wrong, so it took us some time to find the segment we wanted.

"And?" Sowah said eagerly.

"Mixed picture," Boateng said. "The video did show a car coming up to the gate of the White House around the time of the murder and someone getting out of the vehicle but unfortunately the image is not clear at all."

"No chance of spotting the license plate?" Emma asked.

Boateng looked doubtful. "I doubt it."

"Let our Gideon take a look at it, Inspector," Sowah suggested. "If anyone can clear up the image, it's him."

NNAMDI FOUND A flight with two seats left, leaving Benin City at 9:25 in the morning and arriving in Accra at 1:40 P.M. after an approximately two-hour layover in Lagos. On the way to Benin City's airport at six in the morning, Nnamdi looked back to the rear seat where Emma was gazing out of the window at the passing scenery of a city beginning to stir.

"You're very quiet this morning, I notice," Nnamdi commented. "Just checking in with you to be sure you're doing okay." He hesitated. "I could easily see you as Ngozi's older sister."

Emma's face and neck grew warm. She was touched, but self-conscious. "Thank you, sir. But I feel as if we—the agency and me—owe you an apology."

"In what way?" Nnamdi asked, shifting his position a little more toward her.

"I feel like, once I suspected Ben-Kwame in Ngozi's kidnapping, I should have considered the possibility his hideout was close to the Alligator, where he would have quick and easy access to her. That way, we might have rescued her sooner."

Nnamdi considered her misgivings for a moment. "I see what you mean. All the same, I think you're unfairly using hindsight to criticize yourself and your colleagues."

"Thanks for that," Emma said. "I hope you weren't dissatisfied with us."

He shook his head vigorously. "Absolutely not. Yemo and you with Jojo have done an excellent job, regardless of how everything turned out."

Her worries somewhat assuaged, Emma felt much better by the time she and Nnamdi were ready to board their flight.

FROM ACCRA'S AIRPORT, Nnamdi and Emma went straight to Nyaho Medical Centre, a private institution affordable only to those with means and money.

Confirming this, Ngozi had a private suite. As Emma entered the room, she did her best not to gawk at the luxury—a combination of hospital and five-star hotel. It would be the first time Emma was to meet Ngozi. Two women were in the room sharing the nicely upholstered sofa. The younger of the two looked up. "*Daddy!*"

"Ngozi, don't get up!" said the older one, who Emma presumed from the strong resemblance was Ngozi's mother.

It was too late. Ngozi half ran, half staggered into her father's arms. He bear-hugged her, lifting her off the ground and smothering her face with kisses. "My love," he said, his voice cracking, "I'm so glad, I'm so glad."

Ngozi was crying quietly, gulping down her sobs. "I'm sorry, Daddy."

"No, no, sweetie, *we* are sorry. Come along, let's get you back to the sofa. I don't think you're supposed to be up walking around, are you?"

"She's not," Mrs. Ojukwu said sternly, helping Nnamdi to guide Ngozi back to her seat.

"Oh, my love," Nnamdi said, distressed. "You've lost so much weight."

"Don't worry," Ijeoma said, "we'll be fattening her up."

Emma had hung back, feeling awkward in the presence of the family reunion, but Mrs. Ojukwu took notice and approached with an outstretched hand. She was beautifully turned out in a chic, canary yellow and black outfit.

"You must be the Emma I've heard so much about. I'm Ijeoma, Nnamdi's wife. Welcome. It's my great pleasure to meet you."

"Thank you. You as well."

"I apologize," Nnamdi said sheepishly to his wife. "In my excitement, I forgot to introduce our guest."

"It's okay, dear," Ijeoma said sweetly. "We managed our way

through, didn't we, Emma? And now, only one person remains for you to meet."

Ngozi didn't rise as Emma approached, but she leaned forward attentively as Nnamdi said, "Ngozi, this assiduous young lady put in a lot of hours searching for you."

"I owe you a debt of gratitude," Ngozi said. "Thank you, a thousand times over."

"Not at all," Emma said. "You're back with your family. That's all that matters."

When they were all seated, they engaged in conversation about everything but Ngozi's fresh and terrifying experience, which at first felt odd to Emma, but on second thought, Ngozi may not have reached the point at which she was willing to share. That would come with time.

Nnamdi and Ijeoma had a brief, quiet conversation with each other and Nnamdi turned to Emma. "We need to run out for about an hour or so. Can you stay awhile with Ngo?"

Emma had been hoping for the opportunity to talk. "Sure, I'd love to."

Once Ijeoma and Nnamdi had departed, Ngozi said, "I think I'd like to get back into bed. I was just putting on a show of strength so they wouldn't fuss over me."

Emma chuckled. "You don't like being fussed over?"

"Depends who's doing the fussing," Ngozi retorted. "Here, just give me a hand up and I can do the rest. Thank you."

Back in bed, Ngozi seemed less drawn and more relaxed. She patted a spot near the foot of the bed. "Sit here, Emma. That's better. I don't have the heart to tell my parents that they don't need to be here all the time."

"Maybe they have an unconscious fear of losing you again," Emma suggested. "But how are *you* doing, is my question."

Ngozi lay back against the raised back of the bed. "I feel strange, like I'm floating somewhere between reality and dreams. And I've had nightmares the last two nights."

"You've gone through a bad trauma."

Ngozi's eyes moistened at that, and she reached for a tissue to dab her eyes. Emma briefly squeezed her hand.

"My parents aren't aware," Ngozi said, "so please don't say

anything to them. Ben-Kwame raped me. Twice, I think, but it
could have been more. There were occasions I was unconscious."

"Oh, Ngozi." Emma, understanding the utter desolation
wrought by rape, moved closer and took Ngozi's hand. "I'm sorry."

Ngozi cried briefly into her tissue and then blew her nose.

Emma wasn't sure how to phrase the next question. "Did you
have them check for . . . I mean, you know."

Ngozi rescued her. "STIs? None so far, thank God. And since
I'm on Depo injections, I'm not pregnant."

Emma reflected a moment. "Ngozi, you must get professional
mental health care. This is no small thing."

"I hear you. When I return to Nigeria, I'll make sure of that."

"And your parents? How are they dealing with all that's happened?"

"They are not," Ngozi said flatly. "What you need to know
about my mom and dad, Emma, is that neither one is comfortable
having a deep, heart-to-heart conversation with me about *anything*.
My father thinks that's a job for my mother, and Mummy's emotional range is limited. She thinks parenting means constantly
lecturing me on what I should or shouldn't be doing. They're the
only father and mother I've got, and I do love them, but they've
also shown me how I shouldn't behave when *I* become a parent."

"Did you feel they were pushing you away?" Emma asked. "Is
that why you decided to leave?"

"Not so much that," Ngozi said, pouring herself a cup of water
on the bedside table. "Would you like some?"

"I'm fine, thank you."

"It's not so much that I was being pushed away," Ngozi resumed
after a sip. "I felt it was rather like prison. Instead of taking care of
the inmates, the prison officials are pushing them around, telling
them what to do or not do every minute of the day. Oppressive,
I think is the word. I felt oppressed. Femi offered me an escape,
and an exciting one, too. But I didn't know who Femi really was."

"How do you feel about him now?" Emma asked. "Did you love
him?"

"Looking back, I don't think I knew. I was shocked the night he
slapped me, but now I understand where his mind really was. We
were mismatched as a couple. Greed motivated him above all else

whereas I didn't have greed. I'm not saying I'm a saint—far from it—but the way I was fortunate to grow up, greed wasn't a necessary accoutrement.

"But putting myself in my own mind back then, I realize how alluring Femi and the lifestyle he seemed to be offering were. He was a handsome guy with swag; I thought I was looking at a bright future in Ghana as the co-manager of a hotel with a brand-new home, and above all, I was free of my parents.

"Femi had sent me photos of the hotel, and it looked great, but when I saw the real thing in person, I thought it was one of the loveliest buildings I'd ever seen. They were thinking of calling it Senchi Palace—how dull can you be, right? There are too many lodges and hotels with 'Palace' in their names. No, when the front gate opened and we came into the yard, I immediately thought, there's only one name for this: the White House. And that's how it came to be."

"Nice story," Emma said. "And yes, Senchi Palace is a horrible name."

The two women had a good laugh.

"Are you looking forward to returning to Nigeria?" Emma asked.

"Insofar as I'll be starting a new chapter of my life, yes."

"Have you decided to go to law school?"

"Yes, I have," Ngozi said. "I see things from a new perspective now. And once I've settled in, I'll officially invite you to visit me. It will be fun."

"Aw, that's so very kind of you! Thank you so much."

"What's next for you?" Ngozi asked. "Will you be investigating Femi's murder?"

"No," Emma said with the regret she felt. "The homicide division of the Ghana Police will handle that. My boss is strict about sticking to the job assigned, so, now that you've been found safe, that's the end of the mission as far as the agency is concerned."

"Oh," Ngozi said, her disappointment plain. "I wish you were, because I want to know who killed Femi and why. It would bring some finality to it all. Do you think the Ghana Police is up to the task?"

"I think Detective Inspector Boateng is, but it takes more than one man; he will need support and resources, and I'm not sure how much of that he'll get. We'll see how the new CID commander responds."

"I pray they'll be successful."

"Me too," Emma said. "Since we're on the topic, who do *you* think killed Femi?"

"I don't see how there could be any doubt that Janet and Awuni plotted and executed the murder," Ngozi said. "Femi had a way of luring people in and then turning on them. He began to get aggressive with them after the first few weeks, and when I got Diamond away from the Alligator, of course they couldn't imagine I did it on my own accord—"

"Of course not," Emma said dryly. "Because how could a woman do anything independent of a man?"

"I know, right? Awuni and Janet were certain Femi conceived of the idea and that established him as a direct threat to them."

"I agree with all that, but do you know of a Professor Coleman?"

"At the University of Ghana? I heard a little bit about him from Femi but don't know more than that. Why?"

"Femi was attempting to blackmail him."

Ngozi raised her eyebrows. "Really!" She shook her head. "I suppose I shouldn't be surprised. Anything for money with that man."

"You talked about how greed was driving him," Emma said, "but was there something else? Why all these desperate attempts to extract money from people?"

"For one thing, I know he owed money to the friend who supplied Femi our two brand-new vehicles. There could have been others he never told me about. He was a poseur."

"Got it."

"Why did you say, 'these desperate attempts,' plural?" Ngozi asked pointedly.

Emma hesitated, but what purpose would it serve to hide anything? "Ngozi, when we went through Femi's phone, we found a message to Salifu suggesting possibly—*possibly*—that Femi was planning to stage kidnapping you for ransom money from your parents."

Ngozi was dumbfounded. "Oh. My God."

"I'm sorry to burden you even more."

Ngozi shook her head. "No, this is the way it should be. I need to know everything now and not find out later. If you have anything else, just dump it all on me now."

MR. AND MRS. Ojukwu returned long after the hour they had indicated. It occurred to Emma that they might have orchestrated leaving the two young women by themselves to talk. Perhaps that had been a smart move. Nnamdi had made clear his positive regard for Emma, his daughter's putative "older sister."

Emma thought it was time to make her move. "I must be going now," she said, rising.

"You can't stay a little more?" Ngozi asked, looking profoundly disappointed.

"I would love to, but I need to get back to my mother, who is staying with me. She's been texting to find out when I'm getting home."

"Let me drop you somewhere?" Nnamdi suggested.

"Thank you, Mr. Ojukwu, but I'll be okay."

The Ojukwus were full of thanks to Emma, for which she felt gratified, but still lurking in her mind was a bothersome feeling, justified or not, that she could have done more to rescue Ngozi earlier—maybe before Ben raped her. Emma shuddered at the thought. It was deeply disturbing.

As she left the Nyaho Medical Centre, she didn't realize that, if only she had been listening more carefully, she could have solved the murder of Femi Adebanjo then and there in Ngozi's hospital suite.

PART SEVEN

CHAPTER FIFTY-TWO

AFTER FEMI HAD ASSAULTED him, Cliffy stumbled out of his apartment with a towel pressed to the left side of his face, which was gushing blood through the towel and dripping onto his shirt. Outside, at the front of his building, a young woman talking on her phone spotted him and realized how much distress Cliffy was in.

"What happened?" she said, rushing up to him. A short, wide woman with a kind face, she was wearing a uniform with the Shop-Rite logo and the name Victoria on her nameplate.

"I fell against my cabinet," Cliffy lied.

Victoria looked horrified. "Oh, my goodness! It's bleeding heavily. You have to get to a hospital."

"Do you have a car?"

"No, but we can get you a taxi."

The first one they flagged down took one look at Cliffy's bloody state and drove on.

A man came out of the apartment building and Victoria appealed to him. He shook his head. "I can't help you, but why don't you go to Kayode's Clinic? It's not far from here and it's open until midnight."

"I've never heard of it," Victoria said.

"Do you know St. Agatha Catholic Church?"

"Yes."

"The clinic is at the back."

Victoria thanked the man. "Let's go," she said to Cliffy.

The man had been correct about the clinic, which occupied a forlorn little building. A handful of people were waiting for treatment on the veranda outside. Cliffy and Victoria rushed in and she yelled for assistance.

A tall, slender nurse dropped what she was doing to attend to them. "What happened?" she asked from behind a surgical mask.

"He fell," Victoria said.

"Follow me," the nurse said.

Cliffy sat on a battered exam table. The nurse took a look at his face. "Wow." She shook her head. "This is serious. We can't handle this here. The doctor has left already. We'll bandage it and then you can go to City of Hope Hospital."

FATHER KAYODE HAD come out of Kirikiri with a single goal from which he had never wavered in the two years he had been falsely imprisoned: to become a Catholic priest. He went through the required four years of schooling at Saints Peter and Paul Major Seminary in Ibadan. But it was at Holy Spirit Catholic Church in Benin City where he ultimately came to practice the priesthood.

Kayode had been working late in his office that Monday night when he decided to call it a day. He exited from one of the church side doors and walked the few meters to his brainchild, the Kayode Clinic. He wanted to change the old, stuffy canons surrounding the priesthood. Kayode thought that if your head was in the clouds, at least you should have your feet on the ground. Sure, your spiritual health is important to God, but so is your physical. *Mens sana in corpore sano.* A healthy mind in a healthy body. Many in Benin City lacked basic healthcare and screening. With a Dutch NGO, Kayode had developed the clinic entirely on donations. It seemed like they were always one step from shutting down, but somehow, they kept going.

Kayode put his head in to say good night and thank the staff who made this possible every single day. He walked to the parking lot and toward his car, a Toyota Corolla. He refused to buy a Benz or late-model SUV the way his colleagues did. Jesus was humble, and so Kayode should be as well.

He heard footsteps behind him and turned to find a man following him. His head and face were smothered in bandages with practically only his lips and eyes showing, but he was clearly young, and his entire form was lissome and quite beautiful.

"Can I help you?" Kayode asked.

"Please, I want to exit to the street."

"It's on the other side of the clinic."

"Thank you."

"What happened to you?"

"I fell," the man stammered.

"But you're bleeding through the bandages—did the nurses attend to you?"

"They say they can't do anything for me here and I have to go to City of Hope."

"Wait here, I'm coming."

Kayode trotted inside the clinic, grabbed a pack of gauze, and came back out to the man.

"Use these to press against the bleeding. What's your name?"

"Cliffy, sir."

"Cliffy, I'm Father Kayode. I can take you to City of Hope."

"Thank you very much, Father. God bless you."

"Thank you. He has, and a thousand times over."

KAYODE HAD GIVEN Cliffy his business card, but hadn't especially expected a response. Hence, only a few days after the two men had met, Kayode was surprised—no, *thrilled*, to receive a call from Cliffy, who again expressed his gratitude for what the priest had done for him that night.

"It was my honor," Kayode said. "The Bible says, 'Be kind, compassionate, and forgiving to each other.'"

"Please, Father, may I talk to you about something? I have no one."

"Of course. I'm available to you to unburden yourself. Do you wish to do so on the phone, or in person?"

"Father, if you don't mind, in person, please."

Kayode had time in his schedule late that afternoon. Cliffy arrived at five-thirty in a midnight-blue polka-dot shirt and black slacks. He looked much different from how Kayode remembered him the night they had met. His face was no longer bandaged, although he had a square of gauze covering his left cheek. And, Kayode took note, the litheness and the grace of his body was still there.

Kayode showed him around the church sanctuary, which was large but not among the largest in Benin City, by any means.

Behind the sanctuary was the vestry, and Kayode's office was in a small, semidetached building connected by a short corridor. It was sparse and Kayode could do with a bigger desk, although he wasn't sure that would solve his problem of untidiness and a tendency to scribble notes on miscellaneous bits of paper.

"Please," Kayode said, pulling up a chair for Cliffy. "Have a seat."

He sat opposite Cliffy instead of behind the desk, as he'd seen many priests do.

"How are you?" Kayode asked. "The cheek—is it okay?"

"Yes please. They stitched my wound and told me I had fractures of my cheekbone. They said I have to let it heal by itself."

"Does it still pain you sometimes?"

"Yes, Father. Sometimes at night."

"You took a severe fall, then."

Cliffy dropped his eyes, and for the first time Kayode noticed how long and curled his lashes were.

"Father, forgive me," Cliffy said. "When I saw you outside the clinic that night, I wasn't truthful. I didn't fall. I was beaten. You see, I had a roommate. He was moving to Ghana and he needed money. He wasn't happy with how much I gave him, so he beat me and banged my head against the edge of my safe. After that, he robbed me of all the money I had."

"I'm very sorry, Cliffy. Were you and your roommate close?"

"I've known him since we were teenagers. In fact, sometimes I liked to call him my brother. I still do."

"It must have hurt your feelings badly."

Cliffy nodded. "Very painful. But you know, Father, I think all that happened that night was a sign from God."

Kayode was even more engaged now. "How so?"

"Me and my brother—his name is Femi—we were doing something very wrong, Father. We were engaged in human trafficking to Libya and Europe. I had been doing it longer than Femi. He joined me after his release from prison two years ago."

Kayode went rigid for an instant, and then relaxed. Femi was a common male name in Nigeria, which was a massive, populous country. As such, the Femi of whom Cliffy had spoken might not have been the same person Kayode had met at Kirikiri. On the other hand, it might.

"Go on," Kayode said.

"After you dropped me at City of Hope that night, while I was waiting there for hours, I kept thinking maybe you had been an angel."

"An angel," Kayode repeated slowly. He felt a thrill in his chest.

"Yes, Father. I think God was telling me to give up my old life, and then He sent you to save me."

Kayode's heart pounded. "God has a plan for all of us. I firmly believe that."

"And so, I've ceased my former deeds. I'm Catholic, but up until now, I've never paid serious attention to religion. Father, I ask if you will allow me to be a member of your church."

"But of course! Cliffy, all are welcome here. We don't turn people away. Jesus would never have done that, and so, why should we?"

"Thank you, Father. Will you pray for me?"

"Come. Let us kneel and pray."

They knelt on the floor facing each other. Kayode lay his right hand on Cliffy's bowed head. His haircut was fresh, and he smelled clean. Heat began to creep up Kayode's neck to his face as he experienced a powerful, disturbing impulse to hold Cliffy in his arms. The desire Kayode thought he had conquered through prayer had in fact gone nowhere. It had only hidden in the shadows.

"Amen," he said at the end of the prayer.

"Amen," Cliffy repeated. "Thank you, Father."

"You're welcome."

They stood up.

"You said you were robbed," Kayode said. "How are you surviving?"

"Well, I've managed to find a small part-time job, but . . ."

Kayode dug into his pocket. "Let me give you something small to help you on your way."

"Thank you, Father," Cliffy said, accepting the naira bills. "God bless you."

"You're very welcome. And I hope to see you in church this Sunday."

"I will be there, Father."

WHEN CLIFFY HAD left, Kayode sat disconsolately at his desk, suddenly emptied of strength by an ambush of intrusive, unwanted thoughts. *Desires.*

"Please, Father in Heaven," he murmured, "take these demons away."

He left his office quickly to go home. He pushed Cliffy from his mind and turned it to other things. But in bed that night, Cliffy returned to Kayode's imagination—the blackness and sheen of his beautiful, slender body, the silken rustle of his voice.

And, after a few minutes, Kayode became turgid, and stroked himself while acknowledging the sinfulness of it. He erupted and completed his shameful self-defilement. When he had cleaned up, he sat in a chair and wondered what to do. Prayer was the only answer. He knelt and prayed for an hour.

CHAPTER FIFTY-THREE

DURING THE MONTH OF September, Cliffy attended both church and Father Kayode's Bible study during the week. Whenever he appeared, Kayode felt both joy and anguish. His world seemed to be spinning out of control. He had been thinking of Cliffy constantly, and it was as confusing as it was distracting. If God was supposed to rescue Kayode from the predicament in which he found himself, it hadn't happened yet.

After Tuesday's evening Bible study, Kayode asked Cliffy to stay over to help put the chairs, Bibles, and other items away. When all was clean and in order, Cliffy asked, "Is it okay, Father?"

"It's good, thank you."

"Then, good night, Father."

"Oh, wait," Kayode said. "I want to look at how you're healing up."

He examined Cliffy's left cheek under a bright light in his office. The healing was uneven, with both deep depressions and thickening where the bone had been smashed.

Their bodies were almost touching and Kayode's breathing was uneven. His neck and head were fiery hot with unendurable desire.

"Does it still hurt?" he whispered.

"Sometimes," Cliffy said softly. "But it feels better when you touch it, Father."

He turned his head a little and their lips brushed. His world spinning, Kayode kissed Cliffy briefly and then jumped away with a gasp. "I'm sorry, I'm sorry."

But Cliffy moved in close and in a moment of overpowering lust, they kissed hard and deep.

Kayode broke away. "What's happening to me?" he said feverishly, backing against the wall.

"We're in love," Cliffy said. "We've been in love from the first night we met. You know it, I know it."

Kayode groaned. "No, no. I can't do this."

"You can. Come to my house and be with me."

Kayode turned his head away and covered his face with his hands. He shook his head. "It's a sin."

"To love someone? When love comes knocking like this, you can only let him in." Cliffy pulled Kayode's hands away. "Look at me."

Kayode did for a moment and then slumped onto Cliffy's chest and began to weep. It was the release he needed.

THEY WERE TOGETHER that night and several after that. Kayode always came to him, never the reverse. For the sake of the Father's reputation, they couldn't risk people spotting Cliffy leaving Kayode's home. They both knew how difficult it was to keep secrets in any Nigerian neighborhood. Before long, the rumors would fly. On leaving Cliffy's building, Kayode disguised himself with a Covid mask and a cap pulled low over his eyes. He was a public figure. The smallest misstep could ruin him, but as the days went by and September neared its end, they maintained this furtive arrangement despite Kayode's constant fear that someone would discover and expose him.

CLIFFY WAS RESTING his head on Kayode's chest as they watched TV in Cliffy's bedroom.

"Do you get tired of hiding, creeping around, Father?" Cliffy asked him. He still called Kayode by his title.

"It's just the way things are," Kayode said. "Maybe things will change in five or six generations, but not in our lifetime."

"And are you okay with God now?"

"The question is, is God okay with me?"

"He loves us all equally." Cliffy raised his head. "But what am I telling you this for? You're the priest!"

Kayode chuckled. "I know, right? Where's the remote? Turn off the TV—I want to talk to you about something."

They both turned on their sides so their breaths intermingled and their heads almost touched.

"You remember you talked about the guy Femi who beat you up?"

"Yes. What about him?"

"Was his surname Adebanjo?"

"That's right. Why?"

"Do you have a pic?"

"Yeah. Wait, I'm coming." Cliffy scrolled through the images on his phone. "Here."

He showed it to Kayode.

"He was imprisoned at Kirikiri for burglary or something like that, correct?" Kayode asked.

"Yes. How do you know?"

"Truth-telling time. I was at Kirikiri too."

Cliffy propped himself up on his elbow. "What?"

"Someone framed me for a crime. After two years in prison, they released me and dropped all charges. While I was there, I met Femi."

"How did he behave toward you?"

"He sometimes made fun of me for reading the Bible all the time, but I don't think he meant it in a bad way. But once when an inmate was teasing me, Femi defended me. We became friends."

"Continue to be truthful," Cliffy said. "I know the answer anyway. You liked him?"

"I did." Kayode's eyes clouded over. "But I made a terrible, terrible mistake." He took a breath and was silent for a moment. "You know, our prisons are badly overcrowded. At night, we slept packed together tight. One night, Femi was sleeping beside me, and I touched him in a way I shouldn't have. He woke up and started to yell at me and insult me. I was so ashamed. The next day, I heard him loudly saying, 'Dis boy na fockin' homo.' But it turned back on him in a way he wasn't expecting. Some of the inmates started to tease Femi by asking him why he had been sleeping next to me in the first place. So . . ."

"He beat you, right?" Cliffy said.

"No—worse. He set four guys upon me behind one of the buildings, and they battered me bloody and left me lying there. What hurt the most was that as they started to hit me, I saw Femi watch for a moment and then turn away."

Cliffy sat up and Kayode could see his jaw alternately contracting and relaxing. Kayode knew that meant he was full of inexpressible anger.

"Come, my love," Kayode said. "It's all in the past. Everything is fine now. Come on, lie down with me."

Cliffy did so in silence.

"Are you okay?" Kayode said softly.

Cliffy nodded. "I'm good."

"Anyway, let's talk about other things," Kayode said. "Before I forget, I'll be going to a Catholic conference and retreat in Ibadan from the tenth to seventeenth of October."

"What kind of conference is it?"

"This year they are calling it 'God's Call to Action.'"

"Oh. I wish I could go with you."

"Alas, it's not open to the public."

"I see," Cliffy said, sounding resigned. "I will miss you."

"I'll miss you too."

They lay quietly for a while, then Kayode said, "I have to be going, my Cliffy boy. Long day tomorrow."

"Why can't you stay the night?"

"Because," Kayode said, planting a kiss on his lips, "I find it impossible to get out of bed when you're beside me."

PART EIGHT

CHAPTER FIFTY-FOUR

SIX WEEKS HAD PASSED since Ngozi had been rescued. The Ojukwus had returned to Lagos, and Emma had heard from Ngozi often—about her healing process both mentally and physically; the insights she was gaining from therapy; and the navigation through her feelings about her parents, particularly her mother, who had finally confessed her perpetration of the bathroom confrontation leading to Ngozi's head injury. The family was going through what they had termed a "truth and reconciliation" process.

With nothing new since Ngozi's case, Emma had a lighter work-load and could often leave work a little early. The good news was that she could spend more time with Mama, but that was the bad news as well. It was mid-December now, and she intended to stay until the new year before returning to Kumasi, after which Emma would get her freedom back. She looked forward to it, although, she admitted to herself, she and her mother had equilibrized their relationship, such that, like a balance toy, they returned to normal even with a potentially destabilizing event. Mama was now more accepting of the career path Emma had chosen, and that had a lot to do with it.

Four-thirty Friday afternoon, Emma was contemplating her Christmas gift list and wishing she had begun shopping earlier. She didn't have a lot of money to throw around, but she was deter-mined to get quality gifts, the price of which tended to shoot up in the holiday season. Christmas in Ghana was serious business, driven by as much commercialism as anywhere else.

"I'm off," Emma announced to the others, after putting her files away and shutting down the computer.

"Have a nice weekend," Gideon said. "Don't forget all the things you're buying me for Christmas."

"Ha!" Emma said with a snort. "You're funny."

"Let me walk you out," Jojo said, getting up to join Emma.

"Wow," she said, smiling. "To what do I owe the pleasure?"

Jojo laughed, but when they got outside, he became serious and he said, "I've been meaning to apologize to you."

"For what?" Emma said in surprise.

"For the comment I made the other time about you being favored by the boss. It was uncalled for and not even accurate. So, I'm sorry."

Honestly, Emma had forgotten about it. "It's okay, Jojo," she said. "Really, it is."

"Thanks. You're a great colleague, you know. I'm so happy to be working with you."

"Aw," Emma said. "I feel the same way about you."

"Hug time?"

"Of course."

They embraced, laughing.

"Silly boy," Emma said affectionately. "Hey, are you done for the day?"

"Just about, why?"

"I just had an inkling to visit Salifu at the White House."

"Is he still there, and why do you want to visit him?"

"He's still there—I texted him earlier. Why the visit?" Emma shrugged. "No special reason."

Jojo regarded her with suspicion. "Emma, what are you up to?"

"Nothing," Emma said innocently.

"I know you better than you think. What's bothering you is that we still don't know who killed Femi, isn't it?"

"Okay, yes, I confess. You have to admit it's frustrating, Jojo. The case has gone cold; Diboat has run out of ideas; Coleman has no alibi for that night but continues to deny any involvement, and even though Diboat managed to send off the bullets to South Africa, it will probably be months before we get the ballistics report, if we ever do.

"The CCTV footage from the night Femi was shot is still blurry, even after Gideon worked on it at Diboat's request, and so we can't make out the car that pulled up to the White House front gate, nor the person who got out of the vehicle. Awuni and Janet support each other's alibis, and even though Diboat thinks they're protecting each other, he can't get either one to budge. Ben-Kwame is dead, so we'll probably never know if he murdered Femi . . . It's all so vexing."

"I know what you mean," Jojo said, nodding his head slowly while rubbing his chin in contemplation. "I feel like that footage could be our ticket to a breakthrough. Let's talk to Gideon again about it."

They returned to the office and planted themselves on either side of Gideon, who smiled knowingly. "What do you want?"

"It's about the CCTV footage Diboat gave you to work on," Jojo said.

"Yeah, what about it?"

"Can you try again to make the car and the license plate visible?"

Gideon leaned back, shaking his head slowly. "The problem is the optical range of the camera is insufficient to capture something on the street, especially in low light. The cam is designed to detect events within the premises of the house."

"So, no chance?" Emma said, making a sad face. "No chance at all? Even for someone as brilliant as you?"

Gideon smiled. "Thanks. Well . . . I mean, there's a chance, but it's very small . . . Let me try one more thing. I'll take it to my friend who owns an electronics shop—he has much more video editing software than I do."

"*Thank* you!" Emma said. "You're the best."

"One thing, though," Gideon said, holding up a warning finger. "The plates will *not* show clearly enough to read them, even if we can sharpen the car—I can guarantee you that. This isn't the movies where you can zoom in on a license plate and see the letters and numbers clearly. In fact, it's the opposite."

"Understood," Jojo said, rising and clapping Gideon's back. "Whatever you can do, we're grateful."

"So, you want to talk to Salifu—why?" Jojo asked Emma when they were outside again.

"I still believe he's keeping something from us," she responded. "I need to visit him again and break him down. You want to come with me?"

"Sure, why not? And after that, we need to get something to eat."

"Yes," Emma agreed. "Your tapeworm needs food."

THE CHANGES TO the White House since Emma had last visited were immediately obvious. Planters with flowers bursting with color now lined the entrance. The gate was more elaborate with decorative lattice work. Emma rang the bell and Salifu opened the side gate almost immediately. He grinned. "*Ei*, Madam Emma! How are you?"

"I'm well, Mr. Salifu, and you?"

"Fine, fine. Come in."

"This is my very good friend, Jojo," Emma said as they entered.

Inside the courtyard, she saw more modifications: clearly marked parking spaces, newly planted shrubbery, and a gazebo on a bright green lawn. "Wow! What's going on here?"

"How do you like it?" Salifu said, beaming at her. "Some Italians bought the place from Awuni and Janet, but the new owners said I can stay on, and they're giving me more responsibility and better pay."

"I'm very happy for you," Emma said.

"The place is beautiful," Jojo commented, looking around.

"Oh, you can have a seat over there," Salifu said, pointing at the gazebo. "Do you want some water?"

"That would be nice," Emma said.

Salifu went off to the hotel while Emma and Jojo walked to the gazebo.

"Holy shit," Jojo muttered. "The man is magnificent."

"He is," Emma agreed. "Are you in love?"

Jojo giggled, but left the question unanswered.

The gazebo sheltered them from the sun. With the harmattan on its way, the weather was turning dry as the Sahara itself. At the height of the season, the tiny particles of sand suspended in the air could partially block the sun.

"Interesting that someone has bought the place," Emma said.

"Why do you say that?"

"I think that may be what Femi wanted to do—buy Awuni and Janet out. That's why he was trying to extort money from Coleman and why he was planning a fake kidnapping for ransom."

"It could be so," Jojo said. "Or just plain greed. There are people like that, you know."

Salifu returned to the gazebo with bottled water for each of them and took a seat.

"How is your friend, Inspector Boateng?" he asked.

"He's fine, thank you," Emma replied. "But he hasn't found out who killed Femi yet."

Salifu grunted. "As for that one, I think we will never know."

"Why do you say that?" Emma asked.

"Because Ben-Kwame is dead and I'm sure he's the one who killed Femi."

"Okay," Emma said. "You could be right. But Mr. Salifu, now that Awuni and Janet no longer employ you, can you tell us more about what was going on? I got the feeling you didn't tell me everything because you were afraid of the possible repercussions."

"Oh, no," Salifu said, laughing gently with some embarrassment. "No be so, Madam Emma. I haven't been hiding anything at all."

"So, nothing more to add?" Emma said, disappointed.

"No," Salifu said. "Wait, one thing . . ."

"Yes?"

"The only thing I can remember was that one time when Awuni was talking to me, he said he hated swindlers like Femi. So, I don't know if maybe that was something."

"But Awuni never said he was going to kill Femi or asked you to do it for him?"

"Yes please; he never did."

"Okay, thank you for that," Emma said, although she wasn't sure how much this added. She gazed at the White House. "What's missing?" she said.

"The name," Salifu said. "The new owners took it down, and they want some kind of Italian name instead. They were saying, 'Why should it be White House? Is this America?'"

"Ah, but it's not Italy either," Jojo pointed out.

Salifu and Emma joined Jojo in laughter at his nimble jibe. The plain truth was sometimes funny.

"Well, I think they should have kept it," Emma said. She liked the name that had come to Ngozi so spontaneously. It had a certain majesty.

Their water bottles drained, Emma and Jojo thanked Salifu and left. The short visit hadn't yielded much.

"It's the happiest I've seen Salifu," Emma said as they walked along Senchi Street, where the buildings in the posh neighborhood were spectacular. "I'm glad for him. You know, he's turned out a lot better than I had given him credit for."

"We need food," Jojo said, looking at his phone for restaurants in the area. "Why are these places so expensive?"

"Because it's East Legon. The same reason the White House was built here." Emma stopped walking. "Wait a minute."

"What?" Jojo asked, still examining the impossible restaurant options.

"Hold on. Don't talk." Emma shut her eyes with her hand on her forehead as if that would enable clearer thinking. "Oh, my God. How could I have missed it?"

"What?"

"Staring me in the face," Emma muttered. "This is my fault."

"What are you talking about?"

"I know who killed Femi Adebanjo."

CHAPTER FIFTY-FIVE

WHEN KAYODE RETURNED FROM the Catholic retreat on the evening of the seventeenth of October, his first action was to text Cliffy.

Can I see you tonight?

It was a while before the reply came back, a little unusual for Cliffy, who was one of the speediest text responders Kayode had ever met.

Tonight, I can't, unless tomorrow

Ok, are you alright?

Sure, just a little busy at my cousin shop that's all

The tenseness of Cliffy's tone came through even in the form of a text. Was everything okay? Maybe he had found a new boyfriend. Or he just didn't want to continue the relationship. Kayode caught himself thinking jealous thoughts and sent up a silent prayer that God take his mind elsewhere. He buried himself in work.

THE FOLLOWING DAY, Cliffy called him. "Can I come to your office?" he asked.

"Yes, but only after hours," Kayode said. "Why, you don't want me to come to your place? What's happening?"

"You know I love to have you over, Father. But this time, I must see you on church grounds."

"No problem. I can't wait to hold you in my arms again."

WHEN CLIFFY WALKED into Kayode's office, it was clear something was wrong.

"What's the matter?" Kayode said, standing up. "Has something happened?"

"Father, I need to confess."

"Have a seat," Kayode said, worried. "What's going on?"

It took some time for Cliffy to begin speaking. "Father, I returned from Accra late yesterday. That was the real reason I couldn't see you last night."

"I'm confused," Kayode said. "*Accra?* What for?"

Cliffy was trembling. "Bless me, Father. I've sinned greatly."

"Unburden yourself, then, Cliffy. Let your heart be light."

"For months, I've had anger that has been eating my soul," Cliffy said. "Of all the things that have hurt me, what Femi did to me is the worst of them all. I loved him like a brother." His voice cracked and dropped to a whisper. "But look at what he did to me, Father. Look at my face. It will remain like this forever. Whenever I wake up in the morning and see myself in the mirror, sometimes I even want to cry."

"Cliffy, to me, you are beautiful the way you are—just know that. But I understand how this anger must have been festering. Is this what has been troubling you?"

"When I found you, Father, everything seemed to be new and smooth, as if I had pulled onto a fine highway from a bumpy village road. My anger with Femi faded into the background and all was well. Until you told me what Femi had done to you at Kirikiri. Why did he betray people so? Yes, I was living a sinful life, trafficking humans, but I was always loyal to Femi in every way. Then he beats me brutally and steals all the money I've saved up all those years. And you—he took your friendship at Kirikiri and turned it into violence against you. This is sheer wickedness.

"Look at your case. You spent time in prison, but after your release, see the blessed person you've become, caring for your community like no other priest I've seen. But Femi came out even worse than when he went in. We need to spread good in the world, not evil. Father, I set off to Accra to look for Femi. I didn't have a passport, so I crossed the border by one of the illegal routes and I arrived on the twelfth while you were away on your retreat."

Kayode wasn't sure where any of this was going. Sure, unlawfully crossing the border was a transgression, but in the catalog of sins, it was of minimal import and Kayode wouldn't have placed it at the top of the list unless drugs were involved. The more pressing question on Kayode's mind was why Cliffy had gone looking for Femi.

"It wasn't difficult to find him," Cliffy continued. "I learned he was a manager of a hotel called the White House. After I had located the place, I bought an illegal gun in Accra."

Kayode was startled. *A gun?* Cliffy's narrative was beginning to veer off in another direction.

"On the sixteenth of October, a Saturday," Cliffy went on, "I waited for Femi to leave the office and go home. I waited and I waited, but Femi never left. So, I went to him. I had to knock out the watchman and tie him up, and I'm sorry for that. Then I went to Femi's door and called him on a new SIM card to come outside to the side door, that his old friend Cliffy was there to see him. Yes, he knew what he had done to me, but the way I was speaking to him sounded so friendly, and so he came to the door. 'Cliffy?' he said. 'Is that you?' He didn't recognize me at first because of my deformity.

"I said, 'Yes, it's me. I look different because of what you did to my face.' He was shocked, and he started to apologize, but you see, an apology from Femi means nothing at all. He has no real feelings for others. I told him, 'I'm here on my own behalf and that of the man I love most in the world, Father Kayode, whom you met at Kirikiri and whose friendship you betrayed by having your *paddi* prison gangsters beat almost to death.' You know what Femi told me right there standing on his doorstep? He said, 'I don't know what you mean.' What a shameless liar."

Kayode's heart was beating so hard, he felt as if his entire body was being rocked back and forth. "Cliffy," he whispered, "Cliffy, you didn't do it, did you? Please tell me you didn't."

Tears streamed down Kayode's cheeks as he rose, knelt before Cliffy, and tried to put his arms around him. Cliffy pushed him gently away. "Now, we are in God's house, Father," he said. "You must listen to me as a priest, not as my lover."

"I can't," Kayode said, crying. "I just can't."

"One bullet to Femi's forehead," Cliffy said, pulling Kayode back to him and cradling his head in his lap. "I didn't use a knife or machete to kill him as I would have liked, but the man is—was—so strong he could easily have turned the knife back on me and killed me instead, and what a fool I would have been. Travel all the way to Accra to be killed? I don't think so. When I shot him, he fell backward in the doorway. I felt like a burden had been lifted off me; I had a great feeling of satisfaction. Finally, this wicked man was gone. He would never hurt anyone again."

So surreal was this moment, Kayode felt detached from his own body in a space between nightmare and reality. And then he was filled with the deepest sadness. "Cliffy," he murmured. "Oh, my God, Cliffy."

Cliffy bowed his head, resting it against Kayode's. "Pray for me."

Through tears, they recited the Lord's Prayer together, and then Kayode, choking on his words, said, "My Lord God, look upon Cliffy your child, and bless him. Forgive him his iniquity, and guide him to the light, for he knows what he has done.

"Blessed Father, I have a covenant with those who confess to me that I will keep all that is said confidential, for the sacramental seal is inviolable, but Lord God, show Clifford the path to justice, and make him know that when the law stretches its long arm out to him, he must go with them quietly." Kayode wept, but he pushed on. "Lord, let Cliffy understand he must not break another of your Commandments by lying to the police, or any other agent or person or intermediary who might come to him in search of the truth, Lord. All this we humbly ask in Jesus's name, amen."

"Amen," Cliffy said.

And then, silent and motionless, they remained with each other for a very long time.

CHAPTER FIFTY-SIX

"PLEASE," EMMA SAID TO Boateng and the Nigerian detective who was Ghana's CID contact, "just at the beginning, let me go in by myself. He may not talk if he feels threatened."

The two cops exchanged skeptical glances.

"Look," Emma said fiercely, "don't try that nonsense that I'm a woman who needs male protection."

"Yes, boss," Boateng said grinning, probably because that was exactly what he had been about to say. "We'll be close by, but out of sight. In case something goes wrong, scream for us at once."

Emma could guarantee that would not happen, but she withheld the comment. They climbed the three flights of stairs together, but then the two men hung back in the stairway.

Emma had texted Cliffy to let him know she was back in Benin City and would like to see him. She sent another text with the single word here, and just as she got to his door, Cliffy opened it. "Emma, Merry Christmas!"

"To you as well. How are you? You're looking good!"

"So are you, my dear. Please, come in."

Cliffy's air-conditioned home was a welcome refuge from the Nigerian heat.

"It feels so good in here," she said.

"Thanks. Can I get you anything?"

"Water would be great, thank you."

He got her a bottle, and she drank half of it in almost a single swallow.

"So, what brings you here this time of the year?" Cliffy asked, taking a seat.

It was the twenty-fourth, and Emma typically spent the season with her mother in Kumasi. This year was different.

"Are you spending Christmas in Nigeria?" Cliffy asked.

Emma chuckled. "In a way, but the real purpose of my visit is to talk something over with you."

"Wow," Cliffy said. "Then it must be important! What's up?"

"You remember when I called you after Femi's death?"

"Yes," Cliffy said cautiously. "Why do you ask, Madam Emma?"

"You looked shocked and devastated," she said. "I remember clearly how struck I was by your expression, and how sorry I felt for you."

Cliffy stared at her mutely.

"But it was all an act, wasn't it?" Emma continued. "Because all along you knew who had killed Femi. And all the time we went around together during my first visit to Benin City, you were pretending, leading us on, *lying*."

Cliffy pulled his head back. "Emma, what are you talking about?"

"You remember you spoke of how Femi returned from Ghana to tell you he was going to be leaving Naija—and you—for a job as a manager of a hotel in Accra?"

"Right. Some place called East—"

"Legon," Emma finished. "You remember the date that Femi told you this?"

"Not the exact date, but definitely in July sometime."

"And what did Femi tell you about the hotel?"

"Not so much," Cliffy replied, still puzzled. "He said it was called the White House. Am I wrong?"

"No; you are correct. Now, after Femi left, you were feeling hurt, and rightfully so. You wanted to speak to him, I'm sure, to get an understanding of what happened. Why had he treated you like that? *Why?* A beloved brother beating you and smashing your head? He could have killed you. And then, after that, he cut you off completely, correct? He never picked up your calls, and he never called you back."

"Not even once," Cliffy said sadly. "I'm sure he archived me or blocked me on WhatsApp. But what does this have to do with what you said? That I killed Femi?"

"Wait, I'm coming," Emma said. "It was the height of betrayal what he did to you after your long years of partnership. What a coward Femi was to turn his back on you."

"Yes," Cliffy said, stiffly.

"Since you never heard again from Femi after he left for Accra, how did you know the name of the hotel was the White House? Did you google it?"

Cliffy, appearing baffled, said, "Why did I need to google it when Femi had already told me?"

Emma nodded. "But he didn't. He could not have. Because, at the time—July—the hotel hadn't yet been named."

"I don't understand you." Cliffy's voice had turned cold.

"Ngozi named the hotel the White House after she arrived in Accra with Femi in *August*."

Cliffy was breathing heavily. "You're confused."

"How so?"

Cliffy shrugged. "I don't know. You're just confused."

"Not at all," Emma said, unflustered. "When Nnamdi and I met you early November, you slipped up when you told your story. The only reason you knew the hotel had been called the White House was because you went to East Legon in *October* and saw the name on the side of the building, not because Femi had told you. He could not have. It's impossible."

Cliffy's mien stiffened. "I've never been to Ghana in my life," he said in a tight monotone.

"Cliffy," a quiet voice said.

Emma turned to see a man in the bedroom doorway. He was older than Cliffy, but trim in jeans and a linen-white polo shirt. He entered the room.

"This is Father Kayode," Cliffy said. "He's a Catholic priest."

Emma stood to bump fists with him. "A pleasure to meet you, Father."

"I *used* to be a priest," Kayode told her as he took a seat next to Cliffy—very close, Emma noted, "until the Catholic church recently defrocked me."

"Oh," Emma said. "I'm sorry. Was that because . . . I'm sorry, I don't mean to intrude."

"It's okay," Cliffy said, taking his lover's hand. "Yes, that was the only reason. They spied on Father and uncovered that we were together. So, they turned on him viciously with the usual hypocritical nonsense, and yet he's one of the few priests I know who cares more about other people than himself or his material possessions. Why are people so evil to each other?"

"It's a shame," Emma said despondently. "The church leaves the bad ones in place and sacks the good. Well, gentlemen, we must now proceed with the item of business."

Father Kayode turned to Cliffy and spoke in a low voice. "Cliffy, we talked about this. You made a promise first to God, and second to me. Right?"

Cliffy dropped his head for a moment. "Yes." He looked up at Emma. "Father knew you, or someone like you, would come for me one day."

Emma smiled. "I'm not surprised. I can tell what a wise man he is. Cliffy and Father Kayode, two detectives are waiting outside. I asked them not to come in at first out of respect for you. I don't want them to be rough with you."

Cliffy didn't answer. Father Kayode pulled him closer and spoke softly. "Recall our study of the book of Isaiah. 'Do not fear, for I am with you; do not be dismayed, for I am your God. I will strengthen you and help you; I will uphold you with my righteous right hand.' You remember?"

"Yes," Cliffy whispered.

"So, now, are you ready?"

Cliffy nodded, and with just a slight flick of the head, Father Kayode indicated to Emma that they could proceed. When she opened the front door, the two detectives were there waiting.

"Please, come in," she said.

Emma knew that Boateng would have liked to have made this journey to Nigeria several days ago and not right up against Christmas day, but he had had no choice. Communications between the Ghanaian and Nigerian police authorities had been bogged down and hadn't gone as efficiently as he would have liked. Another factor? Almost every high-ranking officer that could have made things move more expeditiously was out of town for the holidays.

Emma made the introductions, noting with interest that, cognizant of where prejudices might lie, Cliffy and the Father had now moved far apart on the sofa to erase any signs of a romantic relationship.

Cliffy's guests sat down facing him and Kayode. "How are you, Mr. Cliffy?" Boateng said, almost casually.

"I'm very well, thank you. And you?"

"I'm good, thanks. Merry Christmas to you, by the way."

Cliffy smiled, but he was still obviously wary. "And the same to you, Inspector," he responded.

"We're here concerning the death of Femi Adebanjo, whom I understand you knew very well."

"Yes please."

"To start, my primary interest is to find out what you were doing in Ghana during the month of October."

"Like I told Madam Emma, I've never been there in my life."

He'll deny it for a while, Emma thought. Oddly, she thought she might do the same were she in his shoes.

"You own a green old-style Benz, not so?" Boateng asked Cliffy.

"Yes please," he said, with a slight hesitation.

"Your vehicle looks like this, right?" Boateng held his phone to Cliffy's face, which reflected his acute shock as he saw the image. "A CC camera on a building on the other side of the street picked up your car in front of the White House on the night of October sixteenth."

"Please, I don't think you can say that it's my car," Cliffy challenged, politely but assertively. "There are other Benzes in the world like that. Mine isn't the only one."

"Okay," Boateng said, returning to the phone. "Then, please explain this."

Cliffy barely glanced at the screen image the detective was showing him. "I don't know what that is," he said, looking away.

"Then, let Emma explain it to us." Boateng passed his phone to her.

She hadn't seen the image before, but it was clear within seconds what it was about.

"Cliffy," Emma said, looking up, "the record from the immigration authorities shows that you crossed the border from Togo into Ghana on the tenth of October. There's also a notation of a green-colored Mercedes and its plate number, which is the same as your Benz parked outside."

"Cliffy," Kayode said gently. "It's all over. Time to confess."

"Let's get it over with, my friend," Boateng said. "Did you shoot Femi Adebanjo dead?"

A long silence ensued, at the end of which Cliffy whispered, "Yes, sir."

"Do you have the weapon you used?"

Cliffy shook his head slowly. "No, but . . ."

"But?"

"I can show you the secret spot I threw it away in Accra. It's deep in a well."

Boateng looked at his partner. "I don't have the authority."

The Nigerian detective nodded and stood up to place his hand on Cliffy's shoulder. "This is to advise you that you are under arrest for the murder of Femi Adebanjo and the assault of his watchman with a deadly weapon."

EMMA RODE IN the same battered police vehicle that transported Cliffy to the station. She and Boateng stood to the side watching the procedural rigmarole of booking Cliffy in, and the controlled to-and-fro chaos of arrestees, complainants, witnesses, and miscellaneous stragglers.

"I was surprised when you showed Cliffy an image of his car outside the White House," Emma said, turning to Boateng. "Did Gideon get it enhanced enough to make out the Benz?"

"He did!" Boateng said, munching on tiger nuts out of a plastic bag. "In fact, he got it to me just in time while we were waiting outside Cliffy's door. I'm grateful to him."

"He's truly a gem," Emma said. "What will happen to Cliffy?"

"Ghana will ask for his extradition," Boateng replied, "but the process may take months or even years. Whatever the case, Cliffy will stay behind bars for a very long time."

CHAPTER FIFTY-SEVEN

THE SATURDAY MORNING AFTER Cliffy's arrest, Emma relished the feeling of once again being able to have Courage stay at her apartment overnight. Akosua had returned to Kumasi.

Courage was lightly snoring behind her, his arms tight around her waist. She fumbled for her phone and when she saw the time, she drew in a panicked breath and turned to shake Courage. "Wake up!"

He groaned and barely opened his eyes. "What's wrong?"

"Aren't you working today? It's almost seven-thirty."

"No," he muttered. "I switched with someone else so I could be with you all weekend."

Emma let out a breath. "Oh, thank God. I thought you were late. The commander would kill you. Aw, such a sweetie pie—wanting to stay with me all weekend."

Courage chuckled and turned on his back, drawing Emma closer. He dozed off for a short while and then opened his eyes. "Emma."

"Courage."

"Do you think I'm getting fat?"

"Getting?"

He was silent a moment. "I'm going to get you back for that comment. Just you wait and see. The moment you least expect it, I'll get you."

"Like a crouching tiger."

"Huh?"

"Never mind." She pinched Courage's cheek. "I was just teasing. Honey-bunch, you're fine." She patted his tummy. "You know I like some extra padding. You're so cushiony and cuddly, and I love you like that. Look at me—skin and bones."

"Cushiony. Is that a real word?"

"It is now."

He chuckled. "How are you feeling about the Femi and Ngozi case? Are you satisfied with the results?"

Emma hesitated. "Yes, but with reservations."

"Such as?"

"On the Ngozi side, I feel we could have gotten to her earlier. And on the Cliffy side, I should have spotted the lie much earlier than I did. Not acceptable."

"Did anyone else figure it out?"

"No, but—"

"But nothing. Baby, the world you imagine where everything occurs in perfect sequence just doesn't exist. Especially here in West Africa. So, give yourself some credit, and by the way, you're perfect for me."

"Thanks. That means a lot." She ruminated a while. "But back to Cliffy and Father Kayode, I think it's one of the saddest things I've seen. They were so devoted to each other, but now they may never be together again."

"I don't quite agree," Courage said. "Kayode's spirit will always be at Cliffy's side."

"I never thought of it that way," Emma murmured. "You could be right. Cliffy said something interesting. He asked why people are so evil to one other, but for a short while, he was blessed with the deep love of Father Kayode."

"Yeah, I'll show you what deep love is," Courage said, tossing off his covers. "It's right down here waiting."

"Oh, no," Emma said, scrambling out of bed. "Not again. Don't you ever get tired?"

"Such a spoilsport," Courage grumbled, turning over to sleep some more. "But you do make a good detective. I'll give you that much."

When Emma emerged from her shower, Courage had left the bed. From the sitting room, he put his head around the door. "Someone here to see you, love."

"Oh? Who is it?"

"Come out and see for yourself. It's a surprise."

"Okay. Coming."

After throwing on a T-shirt and shorts, Emma went to the sitting room. There, on the sofa looking lovely in a white silk blouse and rose-colored skirt was someone who was at once familiar but transformed from the way Emma remembered her.

"Diamond!" she gasped.

Diamond smiled shyly and stood up. "I made a promise to myself I would be back to see you to give you thanks for all you did for me, but it took me a while to get a little more settled."

Emma laughed as they embraced. "That's okay. It's wonderful to see you. You look so beautiful! Sparkling like a diamond."

Now, they both laughed.

"Please, have a seat," Emma invited.

"Thank you."

They sat on the sofa together.

"I hope my mother wasn't unkind to you when you left?" Emma asked.

"Not at all," Diamond said. "She helped me start to get back on my feet. Is she still with you?"

"No, she went back to Kumasi."

"Oh, then please greet her for me. She's a special lady."

Emma nodded and after a beat, she said, "You know something? I agree. She *is* a special lady."

GENERAL GLOSSARY

Akpeteshie (*Ak-peh-teh-shee*): strong alcohol made locally from the distillation of fermented palm wine or sugar cane

Ashawo (*ah-shah-WHO*): prostitute, sex worker

Banku (*bang-KOO*): fermented corn dough stirred with boiling water

Boko Haram (*boh-koh-hah-RAM*): terrorist organization based in northeastern Nigeria

Boreadaso (*bo-ree-ah-DA-so*): traditional, indigenous herbal preparation used for diarrhea

Bros (*bross*): bro (combination of *bro* and *boss*)

Burkinabe (*bur-kih-NAH-bay*): a person from the country of Burkina Faso

Chinchinga (*chih-cheeng-GAH*): Ghanaian shish kebab

Danfo (*DAN-foh*): minivan used to transport fifteen to twenty passengers

ECOWAS: Economic Community of West African States

Egusi (*eh-goo-see*): soup thickened with melon seeds, cooked with palm oil, leafy vegetables, meat, fish, or shellfish

Fufu (*foo-FOO*): soft, glutinous staple made from pounding cooked cassava, plantain, or yam (or combination)

Ga (*Gah* [nasalized]): language and people indigenous to the Greater Accra region and several coastal areas

Harmattan (*HAH-mah-tan*): season from December to February characterized by a very dry, northeasterly wind from the Sahara Desert to the West African coast

Igbo (alt. *Ibo*) (*IG-bo*): language and people indigenous to south-central and southeastern Nigeria

Kelewele (*kay-lay-way-lay*): ripe plantain cubes fried crispy with ginger, red pepper, and other spices

Kwasea (*kwas-YAH*): idiot, fool

Maakye (*mah-CHIH*): good morning (Twi)

Maate (*mah-tih*): I've heard you, I understand

Mo-mo (*moh-moh*): mobile money, also verb, e.g. I'll mo-mo you

Na (*nah*): is, or this is

Naija (*ny-JAH*): Nigeria, Nigerian

Okada (*oh-KA-da*): motorcycle

Okro (*oh-kroh*): okra

Oyibo (*oh-YEE-boh*): foreigner, white person

Paddi (*pah-DEE*): friend, buddy

Paracetamol (*pah-rah-set-amol*): acetaminophen, brand name

Pesewa (*PEH-swah*): Ghanaian monetary unit (coin); 100 *pesewas* equals 1 *cedi*

Sabi (*sah-BEE*): know, understand

Swallow (*SWAH-loh*): food balls made of wheat, corn, or cassava, served with soup (termed "swallow" because not chewed)

Tiger nuts: small tubers, crunchy in texture, and having stripes on the exterior.

Tuareg (*TWAH-reg*): large ethnic group principally occupying the Sahara Desert

Twi (*chwee*): Akan language spoken widely throughout Ghana

Vitesse (*vee-TESS*): speed (French)

Yahoo boy: young man engaged in internet fraud

Yoruba (*yor-ru-bah*): language and people indigenous to southwestern Nigeria

Waakye (*wah-chih*): a dish with rice and red beans (or black-eyed peas) cooked with an infusion of millet leaves, which gives the rice a pink to red tinge

Wahala (*wah-HAH-lah*): trouble, fuss, issue

Wallahi (*wah-lah-hee*): I swear to God (Arabic)

Zongo (*ZONG-go*): urban neighborhood with large Muslim populations

NIGERIAN PIDGIN GLOSSARY

Abeg (*ah-BEG*): please (from "I beg you")

Abi? (ah-BEE): Is that the case? Or?

At all-at all (at-awl, at-awl): not in the least

Comot (*com-AWT*): take/get out, exit, leave

E don tey (*wey I see you*): It's a long time since I saw you

Fall one's hand: to disappoint someone

Gats (gats): need to/have to

How far na?: How's it going?

How you dey?: How are you?

I dey: I'm well

Kain (*kine*): kind

Kishi (*kee-shee*): money

Mo-mo (*moh-moh*): mobile money, also send money via mobile phone

Moto: motorcycle

Na lie: That's a lie

Na so: That's it

Na so?: Is that right?

Na wa/waa: Wow!

No wahala: No worries

You dey craze?: Are you nuts?

You don fock up: You['ve] fucked up

Talk true: for real

Well-well (well well): very well, thoroughly

Wetin? (*way-tin*): What? e.g., *Wetin dey happen?*

ACKNOWLEDGMENTS

I OWE A DEBT of gratitude to several people who helped me in the three separate countries in which this novel is set.

In *Nigeria*: Huge thanks to Confidence and Evans Aguiyi, superb tour guides and owners of ucomeafrik.com, who modified their standard tour to suit my research needs and provided contact with migrant organizations and migrant returnees from Libya and Agadez.

Also to Rex, Deborah, Mariam, Success, and Salomi, migrant returnees from Libya who related to me their arduous journeys from Benin City, Nigeria, across the Sahara Desert to Tripoli, Libya, and their harrowing experiences both en route and at their destinations.

Confidence Aguiyi and Nnamdi Oguike have my many thanks for assistance with Nigerian Pidgin English terminology and conversation.

In *Niger*: Thank you to Abba Djitteye of tourhq.com in Niamey, and local guide Ibrahim Alhassane in Agadez, who showed me the ins and outs of the city and provided a unique experience in the Sahara Desert.

In *Ghana*: Solomon Mensah, PI and Yahya Azure, PI, who facilitated my investigation into the lives of sex workers and the rapidly evolving and complex sex-work infrastructure in Accra.

"*Medaase*" most of all to my editor Rachel Kowal for her marvelous patience and sharp-eyed guidance, and the indispensable work of the proofreaders and copy editors, and all those dedicated to the complete elimination of the dangling modifier.

To the entire *famille* Soho—organizers extraordinaire Rudy Martinez and Steven Tran, the astonishingly encyclopedic Paul Oliver, artistic genius Janine Agro, luminous star Alexa Wejko, fantastic publicist Erica Loberg, and author-editor-wife-mother *fabulosa*, Juliet Grames, all under the leadership of the always elegant and erudite Bronwen Hruska.

Finally, I'm extremely grateful to fellow writers Leye Adenle and Kalisha Buckhanon for taking the time to preview the novel and provide their generous blurbs.